WAR OF THE
REALMS

READ ALL THE BOOKS
BY KATE O'HEARN

THE PEGASUS SERIES:
The Flame of Olympus
Olympus at War
The New Olympians
Origins of Olympus
Rise of the Titans
The End of Olympus

THE VALKYRIE SERIES:
Valkyrie
The Runaway
War of the Realms

WAR OF THE REALMS

A VALKYRIE NOVEL

BY KATE O'HEARN

ALADDIN

New York   London   Toronto   Sydney   New Delhi

ALADDIN

An imprint of Simon & Schuster Children's Publishing Division
1230 Avenue of the Americas, New York, New York 10020
This Aladdin hardcover edition January 2018
Text copyright © 2016 by Kate O'Hearn
Published by arrangement with Hodder & Stoughton, Ltd
Originally published in 2016 in Great Britain by Hodder Children's Books
Jacket illustration copyright © 2018 by Anna Steinbauer
Jacket damask pattern by Thinkstock
All rights reserved, including the right of reproduction
in whole or in part in any form.
ALADDIN and related logo are registered trademarks of Simon & Schuster, Inc.
For information about special discounts for bulk purchases, please contact
Simon & Schuster Special Sales at 1-866-506-1949 or business@simonandschuster.com.
The Simon & Schuster Speakers Bureau can bring authors to your live event.
For more information or to book an event, contact the Simon & Schuster Speakers Bureau
at 1-866-248-3049 or visit our website at www.simonspeakers.com.
Jacket designed by Karin Paprocki
Interior designed by Mike Rosamilia
The text of this book was set in Goudy Old Style.
Manufactured in the United States of America 1217 FFG
2 4 6 8 10 9 7 5 3 1
Library of Congress Cataloging-in-Publication Data
Names: O'Hearn, Kate, author.
Title: War of the realms : a Valkyrie novel / by Kate O'Hearn.
Description: First Aladdin hardcover edition. | New York : Aladdin, [2018] |
Series: Valkyrie ; 3 | Summary: With the rainbow bridge closed, Freya and the Valkyries must find another
way to try to stop the war that threatens not just Asgard, but the human world, as well.
Identifiers: LCCN 2017007097 (print) | LCCN 2017033772 (eBook) |
ISBN 9781481447454 (eBook) | ISBN 9781481447430 (hc)
Subjects: | CYAC: Valkyries (Norse mythology)—Fiction. | Mythology, Norse—Fiction. | War—Fiction.
Classification: LCC PZ7.O4137 (eBook) | LCC PZ7.O4137 War 2018 (print) | DDC [Fic]—dc23
LC record available at https://lccn.loc.gov/2017007097

DEDICATION

For my brother John Patrick O'Hearn
March 17, 1955–December 14, 2014
We miss you.
(You met Azrael before me, JP.
Say hi to him from me. . . .)

RAGNARÖK

THROUGHOUT TIME THERE HAS ALWAYS BEEN HOSTILITY within the Nine Realms. Most often it was between the different giant species. Sometimes the frost giants would leave their homes within the walls of Utgard on Jotunheim and attack the Great City in the fire giants' domain on Muspelheim. Occasionally mountain giants would join in the conflict. But, being equally matched, there was never a strong victor and the fight always ended long before they involved the other realms.

At other times there would be tension between the Light and Dark Elves, which would sometimes draw in the dwarfs and turn into short outbreaks of violence. But none of these battles ever resembled anything like the War of Legend—also known as the War to End All Wars—or, in Norse, *Ragnarök*.

So dreadful, so terrifying was Ragnarök, that its name is rarely spoken aloud. Occasionally there would be whispers, uttered late at night by the warriors of Valhalla, telling how this one final war would involve all the realms and eventually consume Yggdrasil, the Cosmic World Tree that was home to all the realms—thus causing the end of everything.

It was fear of Ragnarök that made Odin, leader of Asgard, continue to bring the fallen warriors from Earth's battlefields to Valhalla, to train and prepare for this ultimate conflict. Though they trained and were always prepared, no one, in all the realms, ever thought the legend could truly become real.

Until now . . .

1

"THIS IS IT," FREYA WHISPERED TO HERSELF. "WAR IN THE realms." It was too terrible to consider, but there was no avoiding it.

The young Valkyrie stood outside the closed barn doors at Valhalla Valley, the home of her Earth family. She and Archie had been thrown out by Thor, who was furious with her and held her personally responsible for the start of the war.

Thor was partly right, but she hadn't intended anything like this to happen. All she had set out to do was free her twin brother, Kai, from the Keep of the Dark Searchers before he took his final vow and drank the potion that would destroy his voice forever. She couldn't let him become one of the feared Dark Searchers without offering him the choice of another life. How could she have known that going to Utgard would cause so much trouble?

After a few minutes, the barn door swung open and a large Dark Searcher shoved Kai and their young cousin Mims outside, to join Freya and her best friend, Archie.

"I am no child!" Kai protested loudly as he tried to push his way back inside. "You cannot throw me out while the 'adults' talk. I am a Searcher; my place is in there with you!"

The imposing Dark Searcher said nothing, but held up a warning finger to Kai. After a moment, he closed the door and they heard it lock behind him.

"Thor is really mad." Mims turned to Freya. "He's blaming you for everything."

"Seems like they all are," Archie added. "But if the Searchers in there hadn't followed us from Utgard, Dirian would have killed them, too. They should be thanking us, not treating us like criminals."

Freya nodded and pressed her ear to the door. The discussions inside the barn were heating up as Asgardians, Angels of Death, and humans clashed. Thor was raging, and blaming Loki as much as he blamed Freya.

"Thor is accusing Loki now," Freya reported. "He's saying that Loki and I went to Utgard to cause trouble."

"That's a lie!" Archie said.

A fist slammed against the other side of the door, knocking it into Freya's cheek. "Ouch!" she cried. She rubbed her bruised cheek and punched the door back.

A moment later it opened, and the same Dark Searcher who had evicted Kai and Mims poked his head out. He wasn't wearing his helmet, and his dark blue eyes blazed in threat as he snarled, "You have caused enough trouble, Valkyrie. Leave here, now!"

"Come," Kai said to everyone. "If we are not welcome, we'll go."

They moved away from the barn and headed back to the farmhouse. They climbed the three steps up to the porch and stood there, glaring at the barn.

"We should be in there," Freya said.

Kai nodded. "They only see us as children. But we are warriors, and we are prepared for this war."

"How bad do you think it'll get?" Archie asked. "I mean, you don't think this could actually be the start of Rag—"

"Don't say it! Don't even think it!" Freya said quickly.

Archie was being trained in Valhalla to fight and wield a sword, alongside the soldiers the Valkyries reaped from Earth's battlefields. He was lucky enough to be personally tutored by one of Valhalla's best warriors, Crixus, the ancient gladiator. So it was no real surprise that Archie had the Great War on his mind.

Mims looked at Archie and frowned. "What are you talking about? What is Rag?"

Freya realized that her cousin—the daughter of a wingless

Dark Searcher and a human mother—had never been told any of the Norse myths. She knew nothing of her origin or the stories of her Asgard people.

"It's actually called Ragnarök," Freya corrected. She hated to have to be the one to tell her about the legendary war, but Mims needed to know how bad things could become. As Freya filled her in, all the color drained from her cousin's face. "Ragnarök means the end of everything—all the realms, including Midgard," Kai added.

"But isn't Earth called Midgard?" Mims asked.

Kai nodded. He was taller than Freya, with eyes the color of ice. His long hair was jet black, contrasting with the brilliant white feathers of his wings. He was the only Dark Searcher with white wings, so they had caused him lots of trouble over the years, just as Freya's black wings had done for her, among the white-winged Valkyries.

"I'm sure it won't go that far." Freya tried to sound reassuring.

"But it could," Kai said.

"What a little bundle of joy you are," Archie said. "Look, if everyone in the realms knows about Ragnarök, they'd be insane to start a war that big."

Kai tilted his head to the side. "Are you serious? Weren't you just in Utgard? Didn't you see the frost giants up close? Do you really think they care, or even plan beyond their next meal?"

Freya shuddered as she thought back to their experience in Utgard, the land of the frost giants. She recalled how she and Archie had nearly been squeezed to death in the hand of a giant. Kai was right. Frost giants wouldn't think twice about starting a war that big.

She'd never encountered the fire giants outside of the Ten Realms Challenge, but rumor had it that they were even worse. To all of them, the future was abstract. War, peace—it was all the same. Dark Elves were just as bad. Granted, they were more intelligent, but it was well known that they were as short tempered as the giants. It wouldn't take much to set them off.

"We've got to stop it," Archie said.

"Isn't that what they're discussing in there?" Mims asked.

"Yes," Freya said as she jumped down from the front porch. "And we should be in there. If only they would trust us, I'm sure we could help."

"Gee, where are you going?" Archie called, using his nickname for Freya.

"Back to the barn. I have to hear what they're saying."

"But that roadblock of a Searcher is guarding the door," Archie called after her. "You'll never get in."

"I'm not going to the door. Look—there's a large window into the hayloft. We can fly up there and hear what's going on."

"*Freya, are you determined to have Thor cut off your wings?*" Orus cawed from her shoulder.

"They're talking about the War of the Realms, and that involves all of us. We have a right to know what's going on." She turned to Kai. "I'll carry Archie up if you take Mims."

Freya and Kai flew through the open hayloft window and landed on the upper level of the barn. Creeping forward over the bales of hay, they peered down upon the large gathering.

Thor's voice boomed as he pointed an accusing finger at Azrael, the Angel of Death. "You should have warned us this was coming. Why didn't you say something? You could have told Odin at the Ten Realms Challenge!"

"For one thing, we couldn't be certain," Azrael said calmly. "Yes, we knew something was brewing, but we had no idea who the traitor was or when they would strike. Two, Odin already knew something was in the air. Like us, he wasn't sure who the instigator was, so he remained silent until he had more information. Had he revealed his suspicions too soon, he would have given Dirian the opportunity to plan his attack more carefully. But now, because Freya intervened at Utgard, Dirian has exposed himself before he was ready and has had to move his plans forward, which may cost him dearly."

"It has already cost us dearly, Angel," Kris, Freya's uncle, rasped, his face red with rage. His blue eyes flashed as he pushed through the line of Dark Searchers. Even without their helmets on, they were an imposing sight and an intimidating force. "Dirian has slaughtered our brothers and destroyed our keep with his betrayal. We, the few who remain, can never return there."

"You didn't belong there anyway," Eir, Freya's mother, said. "You are our kin. You should have lived with us in Asgard and not been exiled to Utgard."

Loki waved his hand dramatically. "Not that this family reunion isn't touching, but all this talk is getting us nowhere. Bifröst is closed, and soon the frost and fire giants will march on Asgard."

"They cannot get there with Bifröst closed," Thor said. "Just as we are trapped here until father has Heimdall open the bridge again."

Loki's eyes opened wide in disbelief. He gasped and then started to cough with explosive laughter. "This . . . this is what I've always loved about you, Thor," he gasped. "You're all brawn and no brains!"

Thor's face contorted with rage. "Stop laughing at me!"

The more Thor protested, the harder Loki laughed. "Stop . . . please . . . you're killing me!"

"Thor said stop laughing." Kris caught Loki by the neck and hoisted him off the ground. "Now is not the time for your games," he growled.

Loki clutched at the Searcher's gloves and kicked out his feet.

"Kris, enough!" Freya's younger uncle, Vonni, intervened. "All this bickering is getting us nowhere. You've banished the kids from being a part of this discussion, but you're behaving worse than them!" He caught his older brother's arm and pulled it away from Loki's throat.

Freya studied her two uncles closely. Vonni had been raised on Earth. His wings had been removed by Azrael when he was born and, like Mims, he had never been told his true nature. All he knew was that he, like his mother, was immortal. Vonni was a gentle and loving husband and devoted father, but he also had great strength and all the powers of the Searchers.

Then there was his older brother, Kris. A full-winged Dark Searcher who had been raised in Utgard at the Keep of the Dark Searchers. Trained to be vicious and obedient, he was a powerful fighter. As much as they looked alike, they couldn't have been more different.

"Kris, please," Vonni repeated. "Let him speak. If there is another way to travel beyond Bifröst, we should know about it."

The huge Dark Searcher looked at Thor for direction. When the son of Odin nodded, Kris released Loki.

Loki collapsed to the floor, gasping and rubbing his neck. "You could have killed me, you great big oaf!"

"And you would have deserved it," Thor said. "Now talk. How will the frost and fire giants reach Asgard? Surely Bifröst is the only way—everyone knows that."

"Everyone is wrong," Loki said, rubbing his neck. "There is another way, and you should be thanking me for knowing it."

"There is no other way," Kris rasped.

"Oh no?" Loki teased. "And just how do you think I've been getting in and out of Asgard without Odin's permission when Heimdall is always at his post?"

"You used drugs," Eir said. "Just like you did when you helped Freya cross Bifröst without permission the first time. You used a potion to render Heimdall unconscious."

Loki nodded. "True, because getting Freya killed in the tunnels wouldn't have done me any good."

"Tunnels?" Eir demanded. "Those are an old myth."

Loki turned on her. "Ragnarök is a myth too, but suddenly everyone here is talking about it. And you're right to do so. Now that Bifröst is closed, those hidden tunnels connecting the realms through the roots of Yggdrasil are the only way to reach Asgard from the lower realms. And I hate to say it, but most of them pass right through here in Midgard."

"What are you saying?" Vonni demanded.

"I'm saying that before long, Earth will be crawling with every kind of frost, fire, and mountain giant there is. They'll be coming out of one tunnel and finding their way to another leading up to Asgard. Not to mention the Dark Elves and dwarfs—and anyone else who has sided with Dirian."

Up in the hayloft, Freya inhaled and looked at Archie and Kai. She leaned closer to her brother and whispered, "Did you know about these tunnels?"

Kai shook his head. "I knew about the ones in Utgard

that ran under the keep and the other one that ran under the outer wall. But I've never heard of the roots of Yggdrasil."

Freya flashed back to her visit to the keep in Utgard. To the dark tunnels, cut into the ground with the roots hanging down, smelling of mold and earth. They had barely been wide enough for her to spread her wings. But they were there.

Down below, Thor exploded. "You're lying!"

"Are you willing to risk it?" Loki challenged. "You know I have been deceptive about many things in my life. And perhaps I do enjoy a bit of mischief—now and then. But this is too serious for games."

"This is just another trick," Thor spat.

"I'm not lying," Loki insisted. "There are tunnels that cut through all the realms. I know of at least five entrances scattered across Earth from the lower realms. And if I remember correctly, there are seven leading out of Midgard to the upper realms. If the frost giants want to go up, they need to pass through here first."

"Surely we would have known," Balder said.

Azrael cleared his throat. "Though I am loath to admit it, Loki is correct. There are many tunnels that pass between the realms. I have no doubt that if the giants know about them— and I suspect they do—Earth is in a lot of danger. . . ."

Freya and her friends remained in the hayloft unnoticed for half the night, eavesdropping on the arguing below. They all knew the problem, but there seemed to be no solution. Finally Freya shook her head. "I've heard enough. All they're doing down there is shouting. I need some fresh air."

"Me too," Archie agreed. "Those guys couldn't agree on the color of the sky, let alone how to stop the war."

They flew out the barn window and touched down on the ground outside. The night was cold, but the air was fresh and clear. Stars blazed in the black sky above them and the moon was dipping on the horizon. Freya looked at all the peaceful beauty around her—the trees, the snow-capped mountains, and the lake in the distance. All of it could soon be lost.

"All this is going to be destroyed, and it's my fault," Freya said.

"Gee, stop it," Archie said. "It's Dirian's fault, not yours."

She knew what he was trying to do, but it wasn't working. "It was me, and we both know it. I'm too impulsive— always jumping in without thinking of the consequences. We shouldn't have gone to Utgard."

Freya looked up at the raven on her shoulder. "Orus, you were right. You tried to warn me, but I wouldn't listen. Now look at the mess I've made."

Orus ruffled his feathers. *"Freya, feeling sorry for yourself isn't helping. If we hadn't gone to Utgard, you wouldn't have found your brother."*

Kai nodded. "And I'd be dead now, because I would never

join Dirian. So would all the other Searchers and maybe even Thor and Balder. Is that what you'd prefer?"

"No, of course not. But . . ."

"No buts," Orus continued. *"If what Loki says is true, Dirian has found a way to keep those he kills dead forever. We might have been the trigger that started the war, but it was going to happen anyway."*

"Only now there are still a few Dark Searchers left to defend Asgard," Kai finished.

Archie nodded. "Gee, this isn't the time to doubt ourselves. Odin needs us now more than ever."

"So does Earth," Mims added. "If it's true that giants are going to come here, what will happen?"

"From the little I've seen and heard of your world, it won't be good," Kai said. "Midgard isn't prepared for this—they don't even know giants exist. It will be down to us to stop them."

"What can we do?" Freya said, still sounding defeated. "There aren't enough of us. A few Valkyries, a dozen or so Dark Searchers, Thor and Balder. I don't know about the Angels of Death and whether they could join us or not. But even if they do, what can we achieve from here?"

"A lot!" Archie insisted. "And before you discount us humans completely, Earth does have its own defenses. We have armies and big weapons. We've even got nuclear warheads. We could do just fine against them, and maybe even stop the giants before they reached Asgard."

"What?" Mims cried. "Fight the war here on Earth?"

"Why not," Archie said, "if the giants are coming here anyway?"

"It won't work," Freya said. "I've been to plenty of Earth's battlefields and seen what your military can do. One frost giant can do more damage than a whole country's army. If they come to Earth, the best thing to do would be to stay out of their way."

"Surrender?" Archie cried. "Are you serious?"

"Very," Freya said.

"She's right," Kai agreed. His blue eyes grew intense. "Do you have any idea how powerful one frost or fire giant is? Even a small one? By their size alone, they could destroy this home with one kick. An army of them will decimate Midgard in days. Even Asgard, with all of Odin's strength, won't be able to stand against the united giants for long."

"You're saying we've already lost," Mims commented.

Kai shook his head. "No. I'm saying that this war won't be won with open engagement. If we were to rely on strength alone, the war is over long before it starts—especially against the giants. We need another plan."

"Well, who do the giants hate?" Mims asked.

"*Us*," Orus said. "*And everyone who sides with Odin.*"

"I liked it better when giants just hated each other." Freya sighed.

"Exactly!" Kai said. "United, they are a danger to all the realms. They will be unstoppable."

They began walking toward the lake in silence, each lost in his or her own thoughts. They occasionally heard the sound of raised voices coming from the barn, Thor's ringing loudest as they argued and debated a way to save the realms.

They stood by the lake, looking at the dark beauty around them. In the distance, the howl of wolves shattered the silence. Their lonely calls, echoing off the mountains, only added to the deep sense of desperation.

"I've been thinking." Kai stretched and flapped his large white wings. He rubbed his shoulder to massage away an ache. "Not all the giants will join the war or fight against Odin. I had a few giant friends in Utgard. And there are others who make Asgard their home. I wouldn't be surprised if they join Odin's forces to fight against Dirian."

"So there are some giants on Odin's side?" Mims asked.

Kai nodded. "Not all giants hate Odin. Right now Dirian's united the giant kings against him, but I doubt it would take much to set them on each other again. . . ."

The moment Kai finished, there seemed to be a collective understanding among them—a simultaneous idea that offered the faintest glimmer of hope.

"So, if we could find a way to set the giants against each other again . . . ," Freya started carefully.

"*It could stop the war!*" Orus finished. "*That's it! That's how we defeat them. We don't—we let them defeat each other!*"

2

FREYA LED THEM BACK UP INTO THE HAYLOFT. THEN THEY jumped down to the floor of the barn completely unseen. Everyone was too busy arguing—it seemed no progress had been made since they had left the barn.

Loki was still facing off against Kris and several Dark Searchers. Thor and Balder were looking even more thunderous, while Freya's sisters stood back, arguing with their mother and Brundi.

"I don't know about you guys," Archie said, "but I'm not going to interrupt them. We're likely to have our heads chopped off or feel the force of Thor's hammer long before we tell them our idea."

"*Coward,*" Orus teased. "*Besides, you're already dead! They can't hurt you.*"

"Maybe not here," Archie agreed. "But you've seen how Thor can hold a grudge. What about when we make it back to Asgard?"

"If we don't find a way to stop the war, there won't *be* an Asgard." Freya caught Archie's arm. "C'mon. We have to find a way to get them to listen to us. We don't have a moment to waste."

In the center of the barn, Balder was holding Thor back to stop him from hitting Loki. Even in this most dangerous of times, it appeared that Loki was causing trouble. He just couldn't help himself.

They saw Azrael standing with his angels, and Freya knew he was the only one who would listen to them. "Azrael." Freya crept up to him, careful to avoid being seen. "We've had an idea, but we need your help to get the others to listen."

"I doubt anyone could do that. What's your plan?"

They filled him in as fast as they could. "We're just not sure how to do it," Freya added. "We don't really know a lot about the giant kings or what it would take to turn them against each other."

Archie added, "Or how to get Thor to listen to us."

Azrael rubbed his chin thoughtfully and started to nod. "You know, it's so simple, it just might work." He caught Freya by the hand. "Come with me. It's your idea. It's only fair you should take the credit."

"No, Azrael, I can't!" Freya begged as she tried to pull

away. "I'm in enough trouble already. There's no telling what Thor will do if he sees us back in here."

"He will listen; that's what he'll do," Azrael said. "This is the perfect opportunity for you to redeem yourselves. You must tell him."

Azrael's grasp was too strong for Freya to break away from him. He led them to the front of the barn, where the loudest fighting was going on.

"Excuse me!" Azrael shouted. His voice rang out louder than Freya had imagined possible. Everyone in the barn stopped and looked at the Angel of Death. Azrael smiled. "Now that I have your attention, Freya and Kai have something to say."

Thor's blazing eyes shot from Azrael to Freya and then Kai. She could actually feel the weight of his anger toward her. "What are they doing back in here? I told them to go!"

Azrael shook his head. "Thor, you should be thanking them for exposing Dirian's betrayal before he had the chance to kill all the Searchers in the keep."

"That remains to be seen," Thor said. "But even so, they are hardly experienced fighters. There is nothing they can say that will help with the war."

"That's the problem," Azrael said. "You're thinking like warriors. But you can't possibly win against the combined strength of the giants."

"Of course we can; I have Mjölnir." Thor lifted up his

hammer proudly. "And the Searchers and Valkyries have their fighting skills, powers, and weapons."

"Granted, your hammer is great," Azrael said. "But it, like you, can't be in more than one place at a time. The giants aren't going to line up for you while you strike them down one by one. They will come at us from every direction."

"So what are you suggesting?" Thor challenged.

"Not me," Azrael said. "Them." He drew Freya and Kai closer. "Tell them what you just told me."

Freya felt everyone's eyes resting heavily on her. She stepped closer to her brother.

"Well?" Thor demanded. "You have our attention. Tell us, what is this monumental idea of yours that will stop the giants?"

The rage in his blue eyes held Freya's tongue. Kai too was left speechless under the intensity of Odin's son's gaze. But then Vonni came over and put his hand on her shoulder. "Go on; just tell us your plan," he encouraged.

"It—it was really Kai's idea," Freya said. "We were talking about the giants and how they always hated each other until Dirian united them."

"We already know that," Thor said, irritated. "What is your idea?"

Freya inhaled deeply. "Well, we know we can never beat them in a fight. They're just too big and strong. But what if we broke their truce? If Dirian could unite the giants, maybe we can turn them against each other again. Then the frost and fire giants would be too busy fighting each other to attack Asgard."

Thor's face was unreadable. His eyes bored into Kai. "You thought of this?"

Kai straightened his back and tried to look like the brave Dark Searcher that he was. But Freya could feel his nerves as he faced Thor. "It wasn't just me," Kai said.

"You know, Brother, this could work." Balder took a step forward. He was known in Asgard as the most gentle and reasonable of Odin's children. The two brothers couldn't have been more different. Because of this, they were very close. If anyone could calm Thor's fiery temper, it was Balder. "I'm sure if a demented Searcher like Dirian could get the giants together, someone could drive a wedge between them just as easily."

"Could it really be that simple?" Vonni asked.

Thor was scratching his long red beard. His bushy eyebrows knitted together in deep thought. He slowly nodded. "It really could." His eyes settled on Freya. "That idea, little Valkyrie, may have just saved your life."

Dawn arrived unnoticed as the fighters in the barn discussed the best way forward. The plan itself seemed simple enough. Working out how to achieve it wasn't.

As morning became afternoon, large picnic tables were set up for food to be served in the barn. The size of the new, winged visitors to the farm meant dining in the house was impossible.

Freya stood with Archie and Azrael, watching the banquet. Her uncle Vonni was dishing out potato salad onto Mims's plate as she sat between her parents. When he finished, he nudged her playfully before passing the dish along. Freya felt a pang of sadness as she watched that simple action. Mims had a father who adored her. He was a powerful Dark Searcher, but his love was obvious.

For most of her life, Freya had wished she knew who her own father was. All her mother would say was that he was a warrior at Valhalla. She yearned to know more, but knew it was forbidden. Valkyries were never told who their fathers were.

"I still can't believe what I'm seeing," Archie complained. "Dark Searchers and Valkyries are sitting with the farmhands like nothing is wrong."

"I know," Freya agreed, pulled from her reverie. "We're wasting precious time. We have a war to stop, but look—everyone is just sitting there eating and laughing like it's a celebration. Don't they realize what we're facing?"

"They know," Azrael said seriously. "That's why they're enjoying themselves. Everyone in this barn realizes this may be the last opportunity for a normal gathering. Some, maybe even most, may not survive what is to come."

Freya looked back at the table, seeing things differently. Azrael was right. Yes, Maya was flirting with a handsome young Dark Searcher, and yes, her mother was smiling as she cradled Vonni's new baby son and spoke with his wife, Sarah. But she sensed beneath their smiles and felt the collective dread.

"I'm sorry," she said softly to Azrael. "I spoke too soon. They know what we're facing."

"There's no need to apologize. We're all frightened for the future," responded the Angel of Death. "Now, if you will excuse us, my angels and I must return to our realm."

"Aren't you going to help us stop the war?" Archie asked.

Azrael nodded. "Of course we are. But we must return to Heofon to tell of what we've learned and to make our own plans. When this war reaches Earth, we must all be prepared to fight for humanity."

Freya felt something heavy settle in her chest at their parting. "I *will* see you again, won't I?" she asked nervously.

Azrael smiled, but it held traces of sadness. "Of course you will. You're my favorite Valkyrie in all the realms. Just call my name and I will come to you, always." He gave Orus a long stroke down his sleek black feathers. "Keep a good eye on this one, Orus."

The raven bowed his head. "*I will.*"

After saying his farewells to Archie and the others, Azrael and his angels opened their wings and took off into the clear blue sky.

When he was gone, Freya said nothing for several minutes. She couldn't shake the awful feeling that she might never see him again.

3

BY LATE AFTERNOON, THE FIRST EMBERS OF A PLAN WERE
being stoked. Maps were laid out and Loki indicated the tunnel entrances the giants would use to enter Earth and then head through up to the upper realms to reach Asgard.

"There could be more tunnels that I don't know about," Loki admitted. "But these are the ones I've used." He pointed down at the world map. "There's a good one here in the Florida Everglades—that's my favorite. It's big and wide. I'm sure it's going to be the tunnel of choice for the giants. Then there's one in France, one over here in Russia, and then another in China. The fifth tunnel is down here in South Africa."

Thor followed Loki's finger on the map. "What about the exits out of Midgard going up toward Asgard?"

Loki nodded. "The closest one in North America is here, in northern Quebec." He then pointed to multiple places on the map, revealing the giants' routes to the upper realms.

"There are so many," Eir, Freya's mother, said.

"I'm sure there are more that I don't know about," Loki acknowledged.

"And all scattered too far around the world for us to cover," Vonni said. He stared at the map and shook his head. "If they do come, and if they use this entrance through the Everglades, they'll tear a path right up the East Coast of the United States to make their way to Canada. It'll be a disaster."

"They will come," Thor said. "Have no doubt about that. We can wait at the various entrances and fight them there, stopping them from getting any farther into Midgard. Or maybe I could close the entrance with Mjölnir."

Loki glared at Thor and shook his head. "Can't you get it through your thick skull? These are entrances to the Yggdrasil root system. If you destroy these entrances, you'll disrupt the flow of energy that feeds the tree. If the tree dies, we die with it! Your hammer could do more damage than the giants."

"Who are you calling thick skulled?" Thor challenged.

"You, if you can't see the lunacy of your plan!"

"All I see is your finger in this. I'm still not convinced you didn't start this mess with the giants."

"What?" Loki cried. "You're still accusing me of starting the war?"

Thor loomed over him. "That's exactly what I'm saying. Why should we trust you now? You've done nothing to earn it!"

Archie shook his head in disbelief. "I can't believe they're still at each other's throats."

"I'm getting out of here before Thor turns on us again." Freya walked out of the barn.

"Where're you going?" Archie called after her.

Freya sighed. "I don't know, just away from them and their constant bickering."

"It's Loki who always starts it!" Orus said. *"I'm with Thor. I still don't trust him, and I think he might be behind everything."*

"That's just it—he could be," Freya admitted. "But we don't know."

Too restless to stay in one spot, Freya turned to Archie. "Do you want to go flying with me?"

"Now?" Archie said. "Gee, it's still light out. You could be seen!"

"At this point, I don't care. Frost giants could be here any minute; being seen by a few people is the least of our problems. Besides, if I stay here much longer, I'm going to go insane. We won't go far, just up to the mountain where Azrael took us. The view is breathtaking and the air feels clearer up there."

Freya put her arm around Archie and opened her wings.

She sprang up into the air and started to fly. The day was cool and the fresh air felt wonderful on her face. Rising higher over the lake and to the mountains behind it, she felt calmed by the beauty around them.

They touched down at the top of the mountain and gazed over the valley. "Archie, this is real . . . ," Freya started.

"Of course it is."

"No, I mean *really* real. Asgard is at war. Earth is in danger, and I'm terrified that this could be Ragnarök."

Archie hesitated before he responded. "Gee, when I first started to train with Crixus, he told me about Ragnarök. He believes if we all pull together, it doesn't have to be the end of everything."

Freya frowned. "He said that?"

Archie nodded. "That's why he trains me and the other warriors so hard, so that we are prepared to do our part and make sacrifices. He said Ragnarök will bring dark times, but if we hold true to ourselves, from it the light will rise."

"Crixus, the gladiator, told you that?"

"He's not the savage that you think he is. He's really cool."

Freya had only spoken to Crixus once or twice. He had seemed awkward and uncomfortable in her presence, and she was sure she had once caught him looking at her strangely when she and her sisters sang in Valhalla. She never imagined that a gladiator could think so philosophically.

"Do the other warriors feel that way?"

Archie nodded. "Most do. That's why they train so hard."

"All that training will be lost if we don't find a way to turn the giants against each other," Orus cawed.

"And that's the problem," Freya said. "How do we do it?"

She took a seat on the boulder that Azrael had hidden her coat beneath. That seemed such a long time ago, but it was only a matter of months. Archie sat beside her. Saying nothing, he held her hand as they looked out over the mountains.

As the sun slowly crossed the sky and started to descend in the west, they were still no closer to a solution.

"Okay, let's think. . . . What do we know about frost giants?" Archie asked.

Freya shook her head. "Not a lot. Loki is part frost giant. Maybe he knows what can turn them against each other."

"But can we trust him?" Orus asked.

"That's the trouble," Freya said, considering all her encounters with him. "We can't."

"So we're stuck." Archie stood at the edge, peering over the valley. "Earth is about to be invaded and we can't stop it."

As they stood together, Freya heard a sound that was all too familiar—a sound that chilled her blood. It was the heavy thumping sound of large, powerful rotors.

"Do you hear that?" Orus cawed.

Archie frowned and looked around. "That sounds just like . . . Over there, look, just coming over the mountains! Army helicopters."

A large squadron of military helicopters was flying over the mountain range. They crested the highest peak and started to descend down into the valley—their destination clear.

Terror clutched Freya's heart. "They're heading to the farm!"

Freya grabbed Archie and leaped off the side of the mountain. Flapping her wings with all her might, she drove toward the valley. Even before she got close, the sound of gunfire echoed in the mountains.

"It sounds like a war down there!" Archie cried. "Faster, Gee. Fly faster!"

When they cleared the trees and flew over the lake, Freya saw a long line of military trucks tearing down the dirt road toward the farm. As they flew closer, they saw even more were already at the farm. Soldiers were pouring out with their weapons raised. Some were firing into the barn. Helicopters landed in the paddocks as more soldiers arrived.

They could hear Thor shouting and the sound of his hammer smashing the ground. The sides of the barn rattled and soldiers were knocked off their feet.

Freya touched down on the closest shore, and she and

Archie raced into the trees. But before they made it into the clearing of the farm, something attacked Freya from behind and tackled her to the ground.

A hand slammed against her mouth. The grip of her attacker was terrifyingly strong as she squealed and struggled in the viselike arms. No matter how hard she fought, or how much she flapped her wings to cast him off, she could not break free.

"Freya, stop fighting me!" Loki hushed. "Soldiers are everywhere. Stay quiet or they'll hear you."

"Let her go!" Archie cried.

"Not until she promises to stay quiet and not go charging in there."

Freya squealed again and tried to break free of Loki's grip, but he was much stronger than she ever imagined.

"I told you to keep quiet!" he ordered. "I'll release my hand if you do. Will you stay quiet?"

Defeated, Freya nodded reluctantly. When Loki removed his hand, she looked up into his blazing eyes. "Get off me. They're taking my family!"

"That's my family in there too!" Loki challenged, still holding her fast. "Brundi, Vonni, Sarah, and the kids may not be my blood, but they're family just the same. But if you go charging in there, they'll capture you, too."

"Not if you change into a dragon or even a full frost giant and we attack them."

"Then what?" Loki demanded. "More will come. This is not the time to engage the Midgard military. We have a plan and this is all part of it!"

"What plan?" Archie demanded.

"If you promise not to go flying in there, I'll tell you," Loki said. "Do we have an agreement?"

Freya stared into Loki's eyes and couldn't decide if he was telling the truth. Finally she relaxed in his grip. "All right, I'll listen. But if you're lying to me . . ."

"I'm not." Loki let her go and rose to his feet. He offered her his hand.

Freya swatted it away. "I can do it myself."

When she was on her feet, Loki scanned the area, checking that they were still alone. "Follow me. We'll get closer so you can see what's happening. But if you try anything, I'll stop you—and we both know I can."

Loki led them through the trees. Keeping low and hidden, they moved toward the farm. Freya gasped when the large red barn came into view. It was surrounded by rows of armed soldiers.

"Look how many are here!" Archie cried.

Ahead of them, the soldiers pressed forward. They shouted orders into the barn, threatening to open fire and demanding that everyone surrender.

"Thor will never surrender," Freya said softly.

"He'll die before he does," Orus added.

"Just watch," Loki said. "I told you, it's all part of the plan."

No sooner were the words out of his mouth than they heard Thor's booming voice. "Hold your fire—there are innocent humans in here. We are coming out!"

Thor and Balder appeared at the entrance. Both had their hands in the air—though Thor still clutched his hammer. Directly behind him were the Dark Searchers. They were back in their full armor and helmets, though their swords were stowed away in their sheaths. With their hands up and large black wings open, they surrendered.

Freya sought out her brother among them and saw him advancing with the others, though he kept his white wings closed.

Behind them were the Valkyries. Freya's mother and sisters were also in their battle armor, but without their helmets, their wings open and arms raised in surrender.

"Why are they allowing themselves to be seen?" Freya asked. "If they wore their helmets, they'd be invisible and safe."

"Keep watching," Loki whispered.

Soldiers rushed forward and tried to put restraints on the Dark Searchers. Even though they lowered their hands, they refused to allow themselves to be chained.

When a soldier approached Freya's mother, she pulled her hands away. "We're Valkyries. If you touch us, you'll die.

We will do as you ask and go with you, but no one must ever lay a hand on us."

"*Eir, don't do it*," Orus cawed.

Freya watched helplessly as her family, Thor, Balder, and the Dark Searchers were captured by army soldiers and loaded into the military trucks.

"Now do you understand?" Loki asked. "You know they could easily fight off the soldiers, but they've let themselves be captured. It's the only way."

"Why?" Freya asked.

"We know we can't fight the giants here on Earth alone," Loki whispered. "We need help. But simply asking the military would not work. They have to feel they are in command. After all the sightings of you on Earth, and with the noisy arrival of Thor, Balder, and the Dark Searchers last night, they had to know about us and track us here. So Vonni had a plan. It took some doing to convince the others to go along with it, but they finally agreed to let themselves be captured. Then they'll tell the military command what's coming."

"You don't actually think they'll believe them?" Archie cried.

"They will the moment the first frost or fire giant steps foot on Earth."

"*Then what?*" Orus demanded.

"Then, hopefully, they will work with us to stop the invasion."

"And if they don't?" Archie asked.

"If they don't, Thor and the others will simply break free and go after the giants themselves."

Archie stepped away from them and walked closer to the trees. "I don't like it, and I don't trust you! Why are you here and not there with the others?"

"You don't have to trust me, ghost!" Loki spat. "And I'm not here for you. My job is to stop Freya from doing something stupid like getting herself captured along with the others. . . ."

"Why?" Freya demanded.

Loki sighed and combed his fingers through his long dark hair. "Because we have our own mission."

"What mission? What are you talking about?" Orus cawed.

Loki grinned. "We're going to cause the trouble between the giant kings and stop this war!"

"What?" Freya cried.

Loki slammed his hand across her mouth and shoved Freya up against a tree. "Shut up! Are you trying to get caught with the others?"

"I'm warning you, let her go!" Archie charged at him.

"Or what?" Loki challenged. His eyes burned red with fury as he turned on Archie. "What will you do, ghost?"

The tension between Archie and Loki was quickly getting out of hand. Freya reached up and pulled Loki's hand away from her mouth. "Stop it, both of you!" she said. "All right, I'm listening."

Loki glared at Archie a moment longer. He stepped away from Freya and reached for a package hidden behind a tree. "Not here. Let's go somewhere we can talk without fear of you doing something stupid!"

Freya looked back toward the barn to see her mother and sisters climbing up into the back of a large truck. Mims was among them, looking frightened. The worst thing, though, was seeing Vonni, Sarah, and the baby being separated from the rest. They were taken to a car and put in the backseat. Even before the trucks moved, the car pulled away from the farm, taking her uncle, aunt, and infant cousin to an uncertain future.

Every nerve in her body screamed for her to do something. Anything. That was her family being taken away. Even though it was part of a greater plan, it was still tearing at her heart to watch.

"All right," she finally said. "It's almost dark out. I know where we can go." She faced Loki. "But if you're lying to me, I swear I'll kill you."

4

BY THE TIME NIGHT FELL, FREYA, ARCHIE, AND LOKI WERE back at the top of the mountain.

"So this is where you hang out," Loki said, putting his large bundle down.

"I don't hang out," Freya countered. "But we do come here to think." She turned on the troublemaker. "All right, you wanted to talk—so talk."

Loki paused, and then something strange happened. His air of self-confidence slipped away. His shoulders slumped and his expression became unreadable. He wouldn't look up to meet her eyes. "I know what you and everyone else thinks of me," he started. "I've known all my life and usually I don't care. But I do now."

Freya knew him too well to be completely fooled. But

still, there was something in his expression that seemed genuine. "What changed?"

"This—the war."

"You mean because everyone thinks you're behind it?" Archie said.

Loki's eyes darkened for a fraction of a second, but then he nodded. "I'm not. But I can't convince the others."

"Everyone is suspicious of you because of your behavior," Freya said. "You constantly cause trouble, and Ragnarök would be your ultimate trick."

"Ragnarök is the end of everything! What would I stand to gain? Thor, Odin, and everyone else, *including me*, would die! There's no point in causing trouble if, ultimately, I'm not around to enjoy the fruits of my labor."

In a strange kind of way, it made a lot of sense. There would be nothing for him if war destroyed everything. "But why cause trouble at all?" Freya asked.

Loki sighed, and it made Freya uncomfortable. She was used to his arrogance, his bravado. Not this new, almost defeated, Loki. "Because it's fun," he finally said. "And because it keeps people sharp. Look at what I did for you."

"Are you serious?" Archie cried. He started to count off on his fingers. "You nearly got her de-winged, blinded, and banished! She was almost killed by Dark Searchers, and then nearly died being squashed by frost giants—"

"No, no, no! Those were side effects," Loki said. "Because

of me you are braver and more independent. Odin knows you now; so do Thor and the other senior Asgardians. They know your name, who you are, and what you are capable of, and they respect you for it. You can claim the head Angel of Death as a personal friend! Tell me, what other Valkyrie has ever achieved that—and at such a young age?"

Freya hated to admit it, but part of what he said was true. Because of Loki, she had accomplished things she never dreamed possible, including having Archie, her brother, and Azrael in her life.

"Did you tell this to the others?" Freya asked.

"They don't trust me. Nothing I say will ever change their minds. They think I'm behind all this trouble and won't consider anything else."

"If they think that, why did Thor send you on this secret mission?"

Loki turned his back and walked up to the cliff edge.

"Loki?" Freya asked.

"*He didn't!*" Orus cawed. "*There is no mission—you ran away from the barn so you wouldn't be captured by the soldiers!*"

"What a liar!" Archie cried. "You're here to save your own skin!"

"All right, it's true. I lied!" Loki admitted. "There isn't a mission for us. But there should be. I have an idea that I know will work, but they wouldn't listen to me. They thought I was just trying to escape capture. But not this time—this time

I'm fighting for all of us. I'm fighting to stop Ragnarök."

"So my mother and Thor don't know you're with me?" Freya asked.

Loki shook his head. "No. They think I fled in fear. But they must be relieved that you haven't been captured with them."

"Gee, if we leave now, maybe we can follow the convoy. We can get them out of wherever they are taken!"

"You stupid ghost," Loki cried. "They can break free anytime they want. No human prison could ever hold them—especially Thor! It's all part of the plan to engage the human military. But that strategy will only slow down the giants. It won't stop them. My plan will!"

"What plan?" Freya asked. "You keep talking about a plan. What is it?"

"It is a plan that will only succeed with your help."

"You're stalling," Orus cawed.

"Just tell us," Freya demanded.

Loki looked at her. "How good is your memory?"

That surprised her. "It's all right. Why?"

"Think back to your early history lessons. Do you remember the stories about the Aesir-Vanir War?"

Freya frowned, trying to remember. "We of Asgard were the Aesir, and the people of the lower realm, Vanaheim, were the Vanir. I don't remember why they were fighting, but the war went on so long, they finally called a truce. We sent two hostages to their realm and they sent two to Asgard. There's been peace ever since."

"So? What is your point?" Archie asked. "We don't have all night, you know."

Loki shot him a withering look, but continued. "The Aesir-Vanir War started because Odin and his people were jealous of the magic of the Vanir. They wanted that power to help rule the realms, but the Vanir didn't see it that way and rebelled. The war ended only because each side grew tired of fighting. The Aesir used brute force, swords, and steel, whereas the Vanir used magic as their weapon. If I'm honest, the realms would be completely different—and maybe better off—if the Vanir had won."

"They didn't and we're all peaceful now," Orus said.

"But we aren't, are we?" Loki said. "Obviously there has been some resentment of Odin for some time. Otherwise Dirian couldn't have compelled the other Dark Searchers to join him—and he wouldn't have been able to convince the giant kings, who are notorious for hating each other, to work together against Asgard."

"What does this have to do with the Vanir?" Freya asked.

"Everything!" Loki said. "Don't you see? The moment the giants start moving through the realms to reach Asgard, the Vanir will be drawn in. We can't be sure whose side they'll take. They've been a silent mystery for millennia, never leaving their realm, even to join in the Ten Realms Challenge. As far as I know, no one from Asgard has ventured to Vanaheim in many generations. We don't know how strong their magic has become, or what their feelings are toward Odin or Asgard. But I believe it's there that we will find the solution to the war."

"You want us to go to Vanaheim?" Freya cried. "Are you crazy? We can't—it's forbidden for anyone to go there!"

"When has that ever stopped you?" Loki said. "You went to Utgard knowing full well that the Valkyries weren't allowed there. You even entered the Keep of the Dark Searchers. Suddenly you care about rules?"

"Utgard is one thing, and I was looking for my brother. Vanaheim is another! It's wild and savage. Magic rules there, not logic—"

"Exactly!" Loki said. "And it's going to take a lot of Vanir magic to get the giants to stop." Loki bent closer and his intense eyes bored into her. "Freya, we are fighting for all the realms. If we fail, those who survive will wish they'd died. Giants will overrun the Earth, maybe even destroy it. They will capture Asgard and enslave those they don't kill. You've experienced them up close. Would you want to see that happen?"

Freya looked down into the dark forest beneath them. Her Valkyrie vision let her see everything—the beauty and wonder of the world around her. The thought of frost or fire giants here was too terrible to consider.

"What's in it for you, Loki?" Archie asked. "You don't do anything without a reason."

Loki's hand flashed out to strike Archie across the face, but since Archie had no substance on Earth, Loki's hand passed right through him.

"You missed!"

"Archie, stop, please," Freya said. "This is too serious for you two to keep bickering."

"That's the point—it's deadly serious!" Loki turned on Archie. "Nothing's in it for me! Nothing but the protection of my family and those I care about." He focused his whole attention back on Freya. "I have burned a lot of bridges in my life. I know it. No one trusts me, especially you. But I am not lying—not about this. The Vanir can help end this war before it goes too far."

"Why do you need our help?"

Once again Loki's shoulders slumped. "Because I can't do it alone. As one of Odin's Battle-Maidens, you might be able to convince the Vanir Elders to take our side in the war. I imagine they'll trust you more than me. I'm sure the giants are expecting them to remain neutral, if they've even considered them at all. But their involvement could mean the difference between peace or Ragnarök."

"You've really thought this through, haven't you?"

"Yes!" Loki cried. "I'm not trouble all the time, you know! Occasionally I try to do something good. This is one of those times. We can't win this war without the Vanir on our side. It's as simple as that."

Freya felt conflicted. She didn't trust Loki—they'd been through a lot together, and he'd always been deceitful, always had his own agenda. But at the same time, what he said made sense. She looked up at the raven on her shoulder. "Orus, you've lived in Asgard just as long as me. You've seen everything and know the history. What do you think we should do?"

"Why are you asking me?" Orus cried.

"Because whatever I do, you have to do too. This is too big a decision for me alone. You know I trust your advice."

"You're going to listen to a bird?" Loki cried.

"Orus is more than a bird, and you know it," Freya said.

"But why now?" Orus cawed. *"After all the times I told you not to do something and you did it anyway, why would you care what I have to say now?"*

"Because this is more than us—it involves all the realms."

"Freya," Orus finally cawed. *"What does your heart tell you to do? That has never steered you wrong before."*

"He's right," Archie said. "Your instincts are good. You know I'll go anywhere with you and support whatever you decide. But this is up to you."

Freya looked at Archie and then up to Orus. This was the biggest decision of her life. Stay and fight with her family and maybe make a difference. Or go off with Loki on a crazy quest to an unknown realm that could get them killed—but if they succeeded, could save all the realms.

Finally, she turned to Loki.

"All right, let's go!"

5

LOKI STARED AT FREYA FOR SEVERAL HEARTBEATS, HIS expression unreadable. Freya wasn't sure if she saw gratitude in his eyes, or doubt. Whatever it was, it lasted for only a second, then vanished.

A moment later he said, "Good. Now, before we leave, you need to change. You can't go to Vanaheim dressed as a Midgard country bumpkin." He handed the bundle he was carrying to her. "Don't take too long. Every moment counts."

Freya looked down at the clothes she was wearing from Mims's wardrobe: a floral skirt and lacy top with slits cut in the back for her wings to fit through. He was right—it wasn't exactly standard Valkyrie attire.

Inside the bundle she found the clothes she had worn during her visit to Utgard. It was a Dark Searcher uniform, complete with black helmet. She sighed at the thought of having to wear it again. She lifted it and gasped. Hidden underneath was her golden, flaming sword—the one she'd won at the Ten Realms Challenge—along with her dagger and Valkyrie armor. "How did you get my armor? I left it in Utgard."

"I went back, remember? I collected it from where we hid it. Good thing I did, too. You may need it where we're going."

Freya frowned. "How did you know I would agree to go with you?"

"You're not stupid. I knew you'd see that this is the only way to stop the war."

Freya wasn't sure if she should be flattered by him saying she wasn't stupid. She took the bundle and went behind the boulder to get changed. She emerged wearing the Dark Searcher uniform, with her armor breastplate over it. She drew the gauntlets up her arms and then pulled the heavy black cloak around her shoulders to cover her wings. Finally, she wrapped the sword belt around her waist and stowed the helmet away for later. "All right, where do we go to find the root down to Vanaheim?"

Loki looked up into the star-filled night. "It's going to be a long flight, but there's only one exit I know of that goes down to that realm."

"Where is it?" Archie asked.

"A small island off Greenland called Kaffeklubben Island. It's the closest landmass to what the humans call the North Pole."

"We're flying to the North Pole!" Archie cried. "That's thousands of miles away from here. Gee will never make it in one night."

Loki looked Freya up and down and then glanced back to Archie. "She could if she tried, but she won't have to. I'm going to carry her . . . and you too, I guess." He stepped away from them and started to shimmer and grow. A moment later, the large black dragon was standing before them. It lowered its head to the ground and invited them up onto its back.

Freya stole one final look down into the valley—knowing this might be the last time she saw it. Finally, she nodded and climbed up onto the dragon's back.

As Dragon Loki climbed high into the sky, Freya used one hand to hold on to a tall spinal plate, while the other held tightly to Archie. Orus was tucked under her cloak. Having never ridden a dragon before, Freya had not realized how uncomfortable it would be. Loki not only had slippery, pointed spinal plates, but he also had razor-sharp scales running down his sleek dragon body. The scales caught her cloak and cut painfully into her legs. Yet despite the discomfort, with each powerful wing beat they were moving faster than she'd imagined possible.

Heading north and then east, they watched the midnight sun sitting sullenly on the polar horizon. This time of year it set only briefly, never rising high in the sky, casting the area in a kind of strange twilight.

"It's beautiful," Archie said, gazing around. "Look, it's the middle of the night and you can still see. It reminds me of Utgard."

They were flying over snow-covered ground. Freya reckoned they were soaring over northern Canada. This far north, there were no signs of human habitation, and the terrain remained wild and untouched. Well above the tree line, very little grew, with only the hardiest of animals able to survive in the harsh environment.

Hours later, they were passing over the ocean and then approaching Greenland. Continuing north, they saw a few scattered islands along the shores. Loki started to descend as they passed over water again. In the distance, the small outline of a narrow island appeared. Ice floes were floating in the water, making it difficult to distinguish between land and water.

The dragon glided smoothly over the rocky surface of the island until he approached the northern tip. Tucking in his leathery wings, Loki touched down. While the dragon shimmered and returned to human shape, Freya and Archie looked around.

"Wow," Archie said. "It's hard to believe we're still on

Earth. I never dreamed a place could look this barren. I bet it's cold, too. It's a good thing I'm a ghost and can't feel it."

"I can," Freya said. "It's not as cold as Utgard, but it's sure not warm either."

Loki stepped up to them. "Well, it's better than being in the center of New York City. At least here no one will follow us to Vanaheim. Come. Time is not our friend."

"Where?" Freya asked, turning in a circle. "There's nothing here. No fjords, caves, or mountains. It's all flat and empty. Where's the entrance to the root system?"

"It's not on the island," Loki said, charging forward. "It's under it. I'm afraid we're about to get very wet."

"*Figures,*" Orus complained, flying up to Freya's shoulder. "*Have I ever told you how much I hate water?*"

Freya patted the raven's back. "Every chance you get."

"*But still, here we are—about to go for a swim in the freezing ocean.*"

Loki stopped and turned on the bird. "If you're not happy, you can always stay here."

"*No way,*" Orus said. "*I'm not letting Freya go anywhere alone with you.*"

"Then stop complaining and shut that black beak of yours!"

Orus was about to protest when Freya grabbed his beak. "Let it go, Orus. I'm not looking forward to getting wet either, but I don't think we have much choice."

"No, we don't," Loki snapped.

At the shoreline there was more frozen slush than free-running water. It became solid ice just a few yards out. "In a couple of weeks, it'll all be frozen over," Loki said. "At least now we can still reach the entrance. Any later in the year and we'd need to burn our way in. Come. It's this way."

Showing no reaction to the cold, Loki entered the water and waded out to chest level. He turned. "Well, are you coming or not?"

Freya caught hold of Orus and tucked him into her breastplate. Then she reached for Archie's hand. "Come on, let's get wet."

Despite living in Asgard, which was much colder than Earth, Freya inhaled sharply from the shockingly cold water.

"You should see your face." Archie laughed.

Freya shot him a withering look. "Just wait till this is over. We'll go back to Utgard and I can laugh at *your* face."

"No one is going anywhere if we don't stop this war," Loki said. "Hurry up—the water's not that cold."

"Says who?" Freya called. Her teeth were chattering and she was sure her lips were turning blue.

"It's going to be a treacherous swim," Loki said. "But I'll be there to guide you. Now, hold on tightly to Archie and Orus. If you let go, you won't have enough breath left to go back for them." He gave Archie a dark look. "And don't expect me to come back for you, because I won't."

"Don't worry about me," Archie said. "But if this is a trick—"

"How deep are we going?" Freya cut in.

Loki glared at Archie a moment more. "Deep enough that I'll have to transform into a whale to get you there. When I change, I want you to put your hand in my mouth and keep it there. I'm going to bite down on you, hard. But it's so I don't lose you."

"You're going to bite her?" Archie cried.

Loki narrowed his eyes. "Consider yourself lucky that I can't bite you!" He turned to Freya. "Now, do you under-stand? Don't pull your hand free of my mouth."

"I won't."

Loki closed his eyes and started to shimmer. A moment later, a beautiful white beluga whale floated in the water beside her. It let out a high, squeaky whistle and opened its mouth.

Freya caught hold of Archie's hand and looked down at Orus, hidden in her breastplate. "I hope you can hold your breath long enough," she said to the raven.

"*Me too,*" Orus agreed. "*But if I drown, don't worry. I'll come back to you.*"

"Promise?"

"*I promise. Just don't let Loki eat or bury me.*"

"I won't."

The beluga whale whistled impatiently and spat a mouth-ful of water at Freya.

"I'm coming!" She looked at Archie. "You ready?" When he nodded, Freya placed her left hand in the whale's mouth. Loki closed it on her hand, and his sharp teeth cut into her skin.

"Ouch!" Freya cried. "Loki, not so tight!"

The beluga whale whistled again but didn't lighten his grip. Instead, he took a deep breath through his blowhole and dived down into the icy waves.

Freya barely had time to take her own breath before she was pulled down beneath the surface. Her hand was stinging from the salt water and the ferocious bite of the whale. But as they sank deeper into the dark water, she found she was grateful for the tight grip.

Deeper and deeper they descended. Freya could feel Orus squirming and his fear rising as he ran out of breath and slowly suffocated. Every nerve in her body shouted for her to go back to the surface, to get him back to air. But Loki wouldn't let her go.

Forgive me, Orus . . . , Freya called with all her heart. Soon the raven stopped squirming and passed out.

There was little time for Freya to worry about Orus as she felt the pain coming from her own lungs. But still Loki drew her deeper into the ocean depths.

Thought soon slipped into dizziness as she started to struggle against the grip that kept her in the water. Her lungs screamed for air. Suddenly her mind was cast back to the Ten

Realms Challenge, when Dirian strangled her to death. This was just the same.

The sound of blood started rushing in her ears. The pain in her chest intensified as her body fought for breath. A strange disorientation hit, and then, finally, nothingness.

6

"GEE, WAKE UP. . . ."

"Come on, Freya, we don't have time for this!"

Freya felt warm lips pressing against her mouth and a full, painful breath of air being forced into her lungs.

"Breathe!" Loki commanded.

The lips and then warm breath again . . . This repeated several times as Freya struggled back to consciousness. Suddenly feeling very sick, she rolled over and coughed up a lungful of bitter, salty water.

"Finally!" Loki said, sitting back on his heels.

"Gee!" Archie cried. "Talk to me! Are you all right?"

Freya's head was pounding and her lungs felt like they were still filled with brine. "I—I'm fine. . . ." She coughed. "What happened?"

"You disappointed me," Loki said. "I thought you would be able to hold your breath longer than that."

"Wha—what?"

"You drowned," Archie said. "Loki had to resuscitate you. But I don't think you died."

"Almost," Loki agreed. "But not quite."

"Drowned . . ." Freya suddenly sat up and winced, as she was crushing her wings. "Orus!"

Loki handed the limp body of the raven to her. He was wet and deathly still as his head lulled to the side. "We should bury him down here and get going. We still have a long journey ahead of us."

"No!" Freya cried. Her senses told her that a small spark of life remained in Orus. She opened his beak and, as Loki had done to her, she breathed air into his tiny lungs. "He's still alive. He's going to be okay!"

Loki stood. "If you're sure . . . But if he dies, don't expect me to carry his smelly carcass around."

"I won't," Freya said as she clutched Orus to her and gave him another breath. "You promised," she whispered to the raven, breathing into him again. "Come back to me, Orus. I need you."

With each breath, Freya felt more of the raven return-ing. Soon he was breathing on his own, but he remained unconscious. Satisfied that he was going to pull through, Freya climbed painfully to her feet. They were in a spacious cavern with a high ceiling rising far above their heads. "Where are we?"

"In a big cave under the island," Archie said. "Come here—this is so cool!"

Freya followed Archie over to a massive, rough wall. Looking along the length, she couldn't see the end of it. The texture was different from what she'd expected. When she touched it, it was warm and seemed to hum and vibrate. "This isn't rock. What is it?"

"Yggdrasil," Loki said. "That's one of its smaller roots."

Freya gasped. "This is the Cosmic World Tree?"

"No," Loki said. "I told you, it's one of its roots."

Freya touched the root with great reverence. Then she pressed Orus to the wall. "Feel it, Orus. That's Yggdrasil. Feel how warm it is. It's humming to you, telling you to wake up."

"It's warm because it's alive, and those vibrations are all the lives in all the realms it supports," Loki said. "But it won't last long if we don't stop Ragnarök. Now, come, put the bird away. We've got to move before we find we have very unwelcome company in here."

"What do you mean?" Archie asked. "Will the giants come this way?"

"Not giants, but Nidhogg," Freya explained as she tucked Orus gently inside her breastplate. "Do you remember the dragon Azrael fought during the Ten Realms Challenge? That was Nidhogg. It's said that he guards the roots of Yggdrasil. That he patrols all these tunnels and will kill anyone he encounters. But I honestly thought it was just stories."

"No, it's all true," Loki confirmed. "I've met him down here more than once, and each time was unpleasant. I'm hoping that, with the giants using the other roots, he'll be too occupied with them to come after us."

"But couldn't he help us?" Archie asked.

"Not really," Loki said. "Nidhogg won't take sides. His duty is to protect Yggdrasil from everyone—he'll kill anyone he finds. But if the tunnels are filled with giants, he may be overwhelmed and defeated."

"Then we'd better hurry," Freya agreed.

As they traveled deeper into the tunnels, a kind of glowing lichen grew on the root and cast a greenish light. It was not enough to read by, but certainly enough to guide them down toward the lower realm.

Time became immeasurable; whether it was night or day, they didn't stop. The tunnel was too treacherous and winding for Freya to use her wings, so they had to keep walking, which slowed them even more.

"How much farther is it?" Archie asked.

Loki stopped and looked around. "By my estimate, we've only come a third of the way at most."

"Wow, it's a long way."

"Of course it's a long way, you idiot!" Loki snapped.

"We're traveling between realms. This isn't a short walk around the park, you know. We are going to a new world."

"Hey, there's no need to be a jerk," Archie said. "I was just asking."

"Well, don't!" Loki snapped.

Archie looked at Freya and shook his head. She was thinking the same thing. Maybe this wasn't such a good idea after all.

They continued in silence as they carefully picked their way through the seemingly endless tunnel. At one point the way ahead narrowed and they had to squeeze around a particularly tight corner. Freya felt part of the root cutting into her wings and back as she pressed forward.

"It's a good thing we're not claustrophobic," Archie commented. "Mind you, if it stays like this much longer, I'm gonna be." He pulled himself through an opening that was almost too small, and a sharp part of the root cut the back of his hand.

"Ouch!" he cried.

"Archie, you're bleeding," Freya cried.

"It really stings!"

Loki walked back to them and inspected the wound. "And you wonder why I call you an idiot!" He shook his head and walked away.

"What?" Archie said. "What is it? Tell me."

Loki paused. "You really are that stupid, aren't you? You're hurt because you've regained your physical form. We've left the influence of Midgard, where you were just a ghost, and we're now within the power of Vanaheim. Meaning you have a body again. A body that can be hurt and killed."

Of course! It made complete sense. Freya felt like the idiot for not realizing it sooner. She could even feel Archie's presence with her again. She focused in on her Valkyrie senses and picked up on other things that she never felt on Earth. There were people ahead, but definitely not human. And she sensed a density of life that she'd never experienced before, even in the thickest of Earth's jungles.

Knowing they were drawing closer to their destination, they put on more speed through the narrow passage until Freya was sure she could see a faint light shining in the distance.

"I think I see something."

Archie frowned and leaned forward. "All I see is the green glow. I don't know if I'll ever see normally again!"

"Stop complaining," Loki snapped. He looked past Archie to Freya. "Put your helmet on and keep walking. I'm going ahead to see where we're going to come out of the tunnel."

Before she could say anything, Loki shimmered and turned into a colorful hummingbird. His tiny wings were flapping so fast, she could no longer see them. A moment later Loki darted away.

"I really don't like him," Archie said.

"I don't think he cares much for you either," Freya said.

"Or me, for that matter. But he needs us and—I hate to say it—we need him if we hope to stop this war."

"And that's what really bugs me," Archie agreed.

Freya and Archie kept walking toward the pinprick of light. Finally, she felt movement against her chest.

"Orus!" Freya reached inside her breastplate and freed the large raven.

"Did you get the name of the giant that hit me?" Orus moaned. *"My head is pounding!"*

Freya hugged the bird tightly. "You really scared me," she said. "I thought you'd drowned."

"Me, drown? Never," Orus said. *"I was just taking a long nap."*

"Well, the dive almost killed Gee," Archie said. "But Loki gave her mouth-to-mouth and she came back much faster."

The raven's eyes went wide. *"Loki kissed you?"*

"Oh, gross!" Freya cried. "No, he didn't. He gave me mouth-to-mouth resuscitation so I could come back faster. But that's not kissing."

"It's miles away from kissing," Archie agreed. "It was first aid."

As Orus recovered, he rolled over onto his legs, but he remained cradled in Freya's hands. *"Maybe, but he didn't offer to give me first aid, did he?"*

"No, I did that," Freya said. "Would you have preferred Loki?"

"Are you kidding? No, thank you." The raven looked around. *"So, where are we?"*

"We're nearing the entrance to Vanaheim. Loki's gone ahead to see where we are. That little light, way ahead, is the exit."

"Way up there?" Orus cawed. *"Good. I'm tired and I'm going to take another nap. Wake me when we get there."*

Freya leaned forward and kissed the back of his feathered head. "I will. Just rest and recover."

She tucked Orus safely behind her breastplate and carefully picked her way through the tight passage. Eventually it opened and the light shining from the entrance grew brighter. They paused long enough for Freya to put on her helmet.

Around them the walls of the Yggdrasil root grew wider and more cavernous. The air started to smell different too. Gone was the stale "green" aroma of the lichen and a tunnel that had never known wind or fresh air, replaced by the beautiful, sweet fragrance of flowers, rich earth, and growth.

Archie paused and inhaled deeply. "That's much better," he said. "I thought I was going to puke from the smell in there."

"You're lucky," Freya said. "You haven't been solid for most of the journey. I've had to endure it the whole way. I'm sure we're going to stink of it for a while."

Thick layers of vines grew down from above and obscured the exit. Freya realized that unless you knew what the tunnel actually was, you'd never know it was the hidden route to another realm.

"I wonder where Loki is," Freya mused.

Archie shrugged. "I don't think he'll go far. He seems a bit freaked by everything that's happening."

Freya nodded. "He's not the only one."

Pushing back the vines, Freya and Archie stepped into the blazing daylight and discovered they were high on a lush, green mountain. The ground dropped away just ahead of them into a sharp cliff. Across a great divide, they saw a stunning waterfall that started from the top of the neighboring mountain. As they walked up to the edge of the cliff, their eyes followed the waterfall down into a large, crystal-clear lake, hundreds of yards below.

Behind them, and all around, they were surrounded by thick, dense jungle. Trees taller than they'd ever seen before rose high in the air, with leaves almost as big as Archie. The air was humid, sweet, and filled with birdsong. The sunlight beating down on them was warm and came from a sun much larger than that of Asgard or Earth.

"Wow," Archie breathed, turning a full circle. "Vanaheim is awesome!"

"It sure is," Freya agreed. She could feel the area around them teeming with life—too much for her to comprehend. It was like nothing she'd felt before, and she was overwhelmed.

"There's too much life here," she said. "I can't take it all in; it's making me dizzy."

"Don't try," Archie said. "Turn off your senses."

"Really? That's your solution—to turn off my senses? Can you stop your nose from smelling all these flowers, or turn off your hearing from the birdsong?"

"Well, no, that's silly," Archie said. "I can't turn them off. They're part of me."

"And my senses aren't part of me?"

"I just meant that maybe you can turn them off."

"Unfortunately, I can't. I can focus them if I need to, but they're always with me and always picking up things."

Suddenly the jungle behind them exploded with sound and movement. Voices shouted in an unfamiliar language, and Freya and Archie were scooped up into the air.

Freya tried to open her wings but couldn't. Her feathers caught painfully on something invisible that wouldn't give. She reached back to free her wings and touched the braided edges of what felt like a net.

"Hey!" Freya cried. "Let us go!"

Freya wriggled and fought in the confines of the net. As Archie struggled alongside her, his elbow smacked her in the helmet.

"Archie, move," Freya cried. "Your elbow's killing me!"

"Me?" Archie cried. "What about you? Your knee is

digging into the middle of my back! And I won't tell you where the hilt of your sword is pressing!"

They squirmed and struggled in the tight net, but couldn't break free. Still unable to see their attackers or the net imprisoning them, they were carried higher in the air. Soon they were gliding over the treetops.

Archie grunted as he tried to move. "What was that you were saying about not being able to shut off your senses, and how you're feeling everything?"

"Not funny, Archie!"

With Archie's arm pressing her helmet up against the ropes of the invisible net, Freya peered around, searching for signs of their captors. But like some of the Asgardians, she couldn't feel anyone around her. It was as though they were simply floating in the sky.

"*Hey, what's happening?*" Orus awoke. "*Let me outta here!*"

Freya tried her best to pull the cloak away from the raven as he crawled out of her breastplate. She whispered to him, "Orus, quiet. We've been captured."

"*By whom?*"

"I'm not sure."

Orus crawled up to her shoulder. Finding the edge of the invisible net, he pecked at it a few times and then poked his head out. "*Hey, let us out of here!*"

"We've already tried that," Freya said. "They won't answer."

Freya thought she heard fluttering wings very close to her. But when she turned her head to follow the sound, she couldn't see anything. They floated over the waterfall and followed along the path of a winding river that fed it. In the distance, she spied a small clearing. Smoke rings curled in the air from small cooking fires.

As they drifted closer, Freya had her first glimpse of the people gathered in the clearing. From afar they looked just as normal as Asgardians. But when they got closer, she realized they looked like nothing she'd ever seen before.

"Cool!" Archie cried. "Hey, Gee, can you see them? They're butterfly people!"

"They're the Vanir," Freya said. "And I think they know we're coming."

The net carried them down toward the group of tall figures with colorful butterfly wings on their backs. They carried no weapons, but they didn't need to. The Vanir were a race that used magic, not steel.

"Look at that girl," Archie breathed. He squirmed in the net to get a better look. "She's gorgeous. Her wings look like a swallowtail!"

A girl of about Freya's age stood with the other butterfly people. Her hair was long and as black as Freya's feathers. Her large wings were open—also solid black, but down at the bottom, near where the extra bits of wing swooped out gracefully, there was a large dot of the deepest sapphire blue.

The girl moved into position with the other Vanir people, making up a large receiving circle. Freya was reminded of the ring of angels circling Dirian in Chicago. Only this time they were the prisoners, and not the Dark Searcher.

Just before they touched down, they stopped. As they hovered no more than a few feet aboveground, the invisible net came away and they landed unceremoniously on the leaf-covered earth.

Freya rolled away from Archie and climbed to her feet. Suddenly, her invisible captors and the large net they carried became visible. They were a mix of butterfly people and those with four see-though insectile wings that reminded Freya of the dragonflies that lived in Asgard. She reached for her sword, but the moment her hand touched the hilt, she found she couldn't remove it from its sheath.

"That's enough, Searcher," a deep voice called. "You will not draw your weapon here."

A middle-aged butterfly man moved forward. He had black, white, and orange hair and wings.

"He looks like a monarch butterfly," Archie commented softly.

"But tell me, what is this?" he said, stepping closer. "A Dark Searcher that isn't a Searcher at all, but a Valkyrie." He waved his hand, and Freya's helmet slipped off her head.

There was a short intake of breath from the circle around them as Freya was exposed.

"I am Freya, daughter of Eir, the head Valkyrie of Asgard. We come in the service of Odin. It is urgent that I speak with the Elders of Vanaheim."

"I am Kreel, leader of this community. If you are in the service of Odin, why have you come here in disguise as one of his Searchers?"

"Because we didn't know what to expect."

"So you thought to come as a dreaded Dark Searcher, bearing a weapon?"

"We intended no harm," Freya said. "But it has been an age since an Asgardian has come here."

"True," Kreel said. "And why has Odin not come himself?"

"Bifröst is closed and he's unable to leave Asgard."

"This we already know," Kreel said. "Tell me, with Bifröst closed, how is it that a Valkyrie and her servant have arrived in our realm?"

"Hey, I'm not her servant," Archie said.

"You are a dead human traveling with a Valkyrie. You bear her mark on your hand. That makes you her servant."

"Yes, Gee gave me her mark, but we're friends. I'm not her servant or slave."

"Archie, that's enough," Freya warned. "It's true. Archie is my friend and not a servant. Orus here is my raven advisor. It is imperative that we speak with the Elders."

"Why?" Kreel demanded. "Could it be that foolish squabble the giants have started?"

Freya gasped. "You know about the war?"

"It's not a war, just the giants moving on Asgard again. What happens there won't affect us here."

"You're wrong. All the giants are working together. They'll take Asgard and then come here. If we don't stop it now, it will draw in all the realms, and Yggdrasil could be destroyed."

Kreel shook his colorful head. "Ragnarök? I hardly think so. No, I think you are here to start your own trouble with the Vanir, Freya of Asgard. You, the boy, and Loki have come to Vanaheim without permission."

Freya was shocked to hear Kreel mention Loki. Once again her doubts about Loki rose to the surface. Had he set them up?

"Yes, Valkyrie, we know about Loki as well. His presence and yours is a pollution of our world that we won't tolerate. You have broken our laws and will be punished." Kreel looked at his guards.

"Take them away and lock them in a cage, where they belong!"

7

"PLEASE LET FREYA BE OKAY," MAYA WHISPERED TO
herself over and over again. Since arriving in the military
installation deep beneath a Utah mountain, she had heard
nothing of her missing sister. Had Freya been captured and
taken somewhere else? Was she all right?

So far the Asgardians had been treated well, although
they'd been subjected to countless medical tests and exami-
nations. Blood and other tissue samples had been taken, and
they were constantly being questioned.

The doctors had taken special care with Maya. She was
put through a machine called a CT scanner, which gave
them a full look inside her body and at the injuries she'd sus-
tained during the attack from the hunters at the farm. After
that her shattered wings were treated more effectively than

the farm's veterinarian had been able to do. The moment they were properly set, Maya felt the healing process begin.

Maya's raven, Grul, was also in the final stages of healing. At first the soldiers had tried to take him away from her, but Maya had turned on her charm and talked them into letting her keep him close. As the minutes passed, Grul was getting better.

After her final treatment, Maya was returned to the holding cell she shared with her Valkyrie family. Peering through the thick iron bars, she looked into the opposite cell. The Dark Searchers stood at the bars, looking ready to do battle with anyone who challenged them.

Her brother, Kai, stood among them—a bit smaller, but just as imposing. He was still a mystery to her. But it was clear that Freya was already devoted to him. If there was one thing Maya knew, it was to trust her youngest sister's instincts. She just needed time to get to know her "new" brother for herself.

The Dark Searchers remained in their full armor and helmets. It was only Vonni's strong negotiating skills that convinced them to surrender their weapons peacefully. Looking at them—powerful and intimidating—she didn't think they needed them. They were a ferocious sight—even when they were simply standing still.

Thor and Balder had been locked in the cell beside the Searchers. But earlier in the day they had been escorted out of the cell block. If the situation weren't so serious, watching the soldiers trying to get Thor to surrender his hammer would have been funny. When they threatened him, Thor slammed the hammer down on the ground so hard, it caused the whole mountain to shake and cracked open the floor of the holding facility.

Thor was allowed to keep his hammer after that. The soldiers led Thor and Balder away, and the brothers hadn't returned since.

"You don't think they'll hurt my little brother, do you?" Mims asked, wringing her hands beside Maya. "They wouldn't let me see him or Mom. What if they're dissecting him?"

Maya took her cousin's hand. "Don't think like that. They wouldn't dare hurt him. They may study him, but these are not stupid people. They know what we'd do if they damaged even one feather on his tiny wings."

"But—"

Maya shook her head. "No buts—little Michael is going to be fine. You know, despite his noise and bad temper, Thor loves children. If they dared to hurt the baby, nothing could stop him from using his hammer to tear down this mountain."

Mims nodded and descended into silence, but Maya could still sense her cousin's fear. They were all in a situation they'd never experienced before. Would the military side with them? Or were they facing a battle with the humans as well as the giants?

They'd been held in their mountain prison for two days, and the military wouldn't believe them despite their warning of the impending giant invasion. Instead, they pursued their continuous questioning and examination.

As the hours of the day ticked away, they heard the heavy door at the end of the corridor open and Thor's booming voice echo down the passageway. "Foolish humans, what will it take to convince you? This realm is in grave danger."

"Thor, calm down," Balder said.

Soldiers streamed into the prison block and lined the walls of the corridor as Thor and Balder were escorted to their cell.

"You're more stupid than trolls," Thor called out as they streamed past the Valkyries' cell. Everyone knew the bars would not hold against the strength of the Dark Searchers if they tried to break out. There was little chance they would hold against the Valkyries either. The human soldiers knew it too, yet they continued with this charade.

The Searchers stood to attention as Odin's sons passed by.

"Stand down," Thor ordered. At his word, the Dark Searchers relaxed—but refused to sit.

"What news?" Brundi called to Thor.

"These fools refuse to believe us," Thor answered. "I almost wish the giants would arrive. Remaining here is wasting precious time. There's no telling what's happening in Asgard!"

"Perhaps now is the time to leave," Kris called with his broken voice. "Vonni's plan has failed. If they will not believe us, we must go."

"Give Vonni a little more time," Brundi called to her oldest son. "He will convince them. I know he will. He may not have trained in the Keep of the Dark Searchers like you, but he has served in the human military many times. He knows how they work and how to speak their language."

"One day more," Thor said darkly. "We will give him one more day to convince these fools. After that we will make our own way back to Asgard and leave Midgard to the mercy of the giants!"

8

FREYA COULDN'T TAKE HER EYES OFF THE VANIR AS THEY marched her and Archie away from the small village and into the dense jungle. They were the most unique beings she'd ever encountered: a parade of color with delicate, insectoid wings. She was mesmerized by their enchanting appearance, but she knew there was more to them than met the eye. Freya could feel that they were capable of great power and ferociousness.

"You don't understand. We must speak with your Elders. It is a war, and it will destroy Vanaheim as well as Asgard and the other realms!"

"Silence!" ordered one of the dragonfly guards.

Freya looked around at the guards. Most were middle-aged or older, but one looked to be around Archie's age. He had intense gray eyes and four clear, narrow wings, folded tightly down on his back. He was barefoot and wore roughly woven shorts and a tight top that blended in with the lush green jungle environment. He wore a flat cap of leaves over his long brown hair. His eyes found and held Freya's for a moment before he turned and looked away.

"What do we do now?" Archie whispered.

"I'm not sure," Freya answered. "Maybe we can break away."

"Drowning must have addled your mind worse than mine," Orus cawed from Freya's shoulder. *"This is Vanaheim, where magic reigns. You won't get anywhere."*

The dragonfly boy stepped closer and shoved Freya in the wings. "Do you not realize that we can hear you?"

She shot an angry look back at him. "Well, you wouldn't listen to us about the war—so I figured you weren't paying attention now."

"You're talking nonsense." The boy snorted. "There isn't going to be a war."

Archie turned on him. "Listen, Peter Pan, how stupid can you be! Of course it's a war. And before long, I bet this Neverland of yours will be crawling with frost and fire giants."

"You're lying," the boy said. "All who come from Asgard lie."

"I'm not from Asgard," Archie said. "I'm from Earth."

"Where?"

"Midgard," Freya corrected. "And whether you believe us or not, it won't matter when the giants get here."

"Enough chatter," the leader of the guards said. "Quinnarious, get away from them before they poison you with their words." The leader pointed at Freya. "And you, Valkyrie, stop talking before I am forced to do something unpleasant to stop you."

The boy nodded to his commander and stepped back into the ranks while Freya shut her mouth and turned forward. They continued in silence.

They were led through an area of dense trees and bushes. Vines grew along the ground and tangled around their feet while exotic, monkey-like animals and birds pressed in all around them, unbothered by their presence. Everything they had seen of Vanaheim was wild and untamed. Including its citizens.

The leader of the guard stopped. He waved his hand in the air, and two large cages appeared. They looked to be made of bamboo and were held together with thin string.

Loki was locked in one of the cages. He walked up to the bars and nodded at Freya but said nothing.

"Inside," the leader of the guards commanded as the door to the empty cage swung open on its own.

When Freya hesitated, the leader raised his hand. She and Archie were shoved inside by an invisible force. Then the door slammed shut and string secured it tightly—all without anyone laying a single finger on them or the cage.

"You will remain here until we figure out what to do with you," the leader said.

"Wait," Freya cried. "You must believe us—Vanaheim is in danger! Once the giants conquer Asgard, they'll come here. You must realize that."

"What happens here is no concern of yours," the guard said. Just before he turned away, he raised his hand again. Freya's sword and belt came away from her body and flew between the bars of the cage and into the leader's hand.

"You won't need that again," he said. The guard turned away and opened his dragonfly wings as he and his men launched into the air.

"Wow. They're like big faeries. You can't even see their wings move," Archie said, turning his head to follow their departure.

"But they're infinitely more dangerous," Loki called.

Freya moved to the side of the cage closest to Loki. "When did they get you?"

"Moments after I left you. They caught me when I was still a bird. I'm surprised they let me return to this shape."

Freya inspected the bamboo bars and the string holding them together. It didn't look that strong. She grasped a bamboo joint and started to pull. No matter how much strength she used, the bars didn't even bend.

"You think I haven't tried that?" Loki sighed. "These cages could be made of paper, but they're still too strong for us to break. There's powerful magic binding us in here."

"How did Vanaheim not win against Asgard during that battle all those years ago?" Archie wondered. "If they had all this magic, they could have easily defeated Odin!"

"They are most powerful in this realm. When they leave Vanaheim, their powers weaken. Even so, I don't remember them being this strong."

"How do you know all this?" Archie asked.

"Foolish ghost, you still don't know who I am? I was there!"

That surprised even Freya. She knew Loki was old, but she had never imagined he was *that* old. "You saw the war?"

Loki casually inspected his fingernails. "Of course. Thor was very young and didn't have his hammer yet, and I myself was just a boy, but I saw enough to know that the Vanir have changed a great deal since then. I doubt even Odin knows how powerful they've become. If we somehow manage to stop the war with the giants, Asgard may have another unexpected problem—Vanaheim."

Freya shook her head. "Let's take it one war at a time!" She started to inspect every inch of her cage. It didn't make sense. It was made of sticks and string—how could magic be strong enough to keep them inside?

"What about you?" Freya asked. "Can't you turn into a bird or something and fly out between the bars?"

Loki slapped his hand to his head. "Why didn't I think of that?" He shook his head and snapped, "Of course I've tried that! I've also turned into a giant to break the bars. But watch . . ."

Loki shimmered and turned into a fly. Long before he could reach the bars, the cage magically shrank to meet the fly's size. Another change and Loki turned into an elephant. Once again, the cage altered to meet the size with larger, thicker bars that the elephant couldn't break free of.

He returned to normal. "Any other brilliant ideas—O wise one?"

"There's no need to be sarcastic," Freya said. "I was only trying to help."

Loki flopped down to the ground and crossed his legs. "Escape is impossible. We have to find another way, and soon. Each moment counts."

Freya didn't need Loki to tell her how urgent the situation was. But in all her life, she had never encountered circumstances like these. There was magic in Asgard, present within the Light Elves and faerie communities, but nothing like this. Not even her Valkyrie strength could break the bars.

As the day passed and the shadows of the large jungle leaves grew long, Freya was startled by the return of the guards. They didn't fly in; they just appeared out of thin air.

"Has anyone ever told you how annoying that is?" Loki snapped. He climbed to his feet and approached the bars of his cage. "Now are you ready to surrender to me?"

Archie nudged Freya. "Is he serious? That attitude isn't

helping. If he's not careful, he's going to get us all shot!"

"They don't need guns here," Freya whispered. "But I think I know what he's doing, and it's rather clever."

"What?" Archie asked.

Freya was about to answer when she became aware of Quinnarious watching her. The young guard was standing near their cage and staring right at her. The expression on his face was unreadable. Freya tried to feel what he was thinking. For an instant she could sense him. Then he seemed to realize what she was doing and forced the connection to break. He continued to stare at her and shook his head ever so slightly, as if trying to convey a message to her.

Freya nodded imperceptibly and stepped away from the bars, wondering what this was all about. She had a feeling there was more to Quinnarious than met the eye. She turned from him and focused on Loki's exchange with the commander of the guards.

"I told you, we're not spies. Can't you get it through that thick, bug head of yours? War is coming. If you don't get involved now, you'll go down with the rest of us."

"Silence," the guard commanded, waving his hand so that the door magically opened. "Come forward."

Loki crossed his arms over his chest. "Ah, no. Thanks all the same, but I think I'll stay. You bugs can fly away and find a big spider's web to play in."

"Come!" the commander ordered.

Invisible arms caught hold of Loki and dragged him out of the cage. The moment he was free, Loki turned into the large black dragon and inhaled deeply to release a stream of fire on his captors. But even before he could let it go, the guard raised his hand and the cage behind him grew and enclosed the dragon. When Loki released his flame, it was contained within the cage and bounced back at him. The dragon roared in pain and rage and returned to Loki's human form. His clothing smoldered and his hair was singed shorter. He patted out a lingering flame on his sleeve.

"Shall we try this again?" the guard said calmly. "Or should I make it really uncomfortable for you?"

Smoke and the stink of burned dragon followed Loki as he exited the cage again. "I don't like you very much."

The guard opened his dragonfly wings and prepared to fly. "I don't care." He reached for Loki's arm and lifted him lightly off the ground. In moments, the guards took to the air and carried Loki away.

"How can these morons not know what's coming?" Archie said, kicking the side of the bamboo cage. "They've gotta know what'll happen if the giants beat Odin."

"Maybe they believe their magic will protect them," Freya suggested. "It's really powerful. Perhaps it will."

"Will magic save them if Yggdrasil is destroyed?" Orus asked.

"No." Freya looked up, watching the guards carry Loki away. "I wonder what they'll do to him."

"Torture, probably," Archie said. "Get him to talk."

"But we've already told them why we're here. We're not holding anything back."

"*We're* not, but what about Loki?" Archie said. "Do you really trust him?"

Freya considered a moment and shook her head. "No, not completely. He seems sincere, but I just don't know."

"Me neither."

As the warm sun started to set, Freya and Archie inspected every inch of their cage. They tried lifting it to get under the bars. They tried untying the binding and anything else they could think of. But nothing worked.

Night arrived and, with it, other jungle sounds. There was no light, and with the full jungle canopy above them, they couldn't see if Vanaheim had a moon or stars. Large, unseen creatures moved noisily through the trees around them, but even with her Valkyrie vision, Freya couldn't see what caused the sounds.

She started to pace the confines of the cage as her thoughts went to her family. What was happening on Midgard? Were they safe? Had the giants arrived yet? Had the war started? There were so many questions, with no way of knowing the answers.

Sometime during the long night, the wild sounds of the jungle stilled. The silence was worse than the loudest noise.

"I don't think we're alone," Archie whispered as his eyes scanned the area. "Gee, what can you feel?"

Freya cast out her senses, but once again, with Vanaheim teeming with life, it was hard to focus on any one thing. "I feel everything; that's the trouble. But I agree with you. We're not alone."

She stepped up to the side of the cage. "Whoever you are, show yourself! We know you're out there!"

Freya waited, but there was no response.

"Coward!" Archie shouted.

"Silence!" a hushed voice called. Quinnarious suddenly appeared beside the cage. His eyes were wide and wild, and he was carrying a small satchel made of woven leaves.

"If you're here to cause trouble, you can just turn around and fly away, bug boy," Archie said.

Quinnarious frowned. "I am here because I need to understand."

"Understand what?"

"Everything," the dragonfly boy said. "Vanaheim is in danger. I know it. But the Elders won't tell us what's happening. They've taken your friend to the Well of Knowledge, but they've been gone ages and haven't returned."

"Loki's not our friend," Archie said. "We're just traveling with him."

"What is the Well of Knowledge?" Freya asked.

"It is where the truth is drawn out. No one can resist its

powers. After Loki, they are planning to take you both there."

"That doesn't sound good," Archie said. "What'll happen to us?"

"They will make you drink from the well and then ask questions. If you tell the truth, you are safe. But if you lie, you will die in agony."

Archie looked at Freya. "Loki wouldn't know the truth if it bit him! He's toast!"

"Why are you telling us this?" Freya said. "What does it matter to you what happens to us?"

"When we first captured Loki, I heard Kreel talking with the others. They remembered him from stories of the ancient war. They said Loki caused a lot of trouble back then and will do so again. But then you came and everything changed. There is a lot of fear and hushed talk in the villages."

"Good!" Archie said. "There should be. War in the realms is real. You won't escape it, and locking us away won't change it."

"Some of us already know there is great trouble coming. But the Elders are trying to suppress our knowledge of it. They will seek to silence Loki and you before you can warn everyone. Even if he tells the truth, I know they will kill him. You too. But it has gone too far. Killing you won't change what is coming."

Orus cawed, *"They are going to kill us!"*

Quinnarious nodded. "The Vanir hate the Aesir. They won't tolerate you here."

"But why?" Freya asked. "The war between our realms was a long time ago."

"It's because of what you represent," Quinnarious said. "You coming here could mean a change to our way of life. The Elders don't want that. They want things to remain the same."

"But it won't stay the same if the giants invade Vanaheim," Archie said. "Quinn, you've got to let us out of here now!"

"My name is Quinnarious," the boy corrected. "Not Quinn, or that other name you called me, Peter—"

"Okay, I'm sorry I called you Peter Pan," Archie snapped. "But honestly, have you looked in the mirror lately? You look just like him."

"What are you saying?" Quinnarious challenged.

"Both of you, stop it," Freya said. "Archie called you Quinn because it's easier than your full name. But it wasn't meant as an insult." Freya paused. "At least I don't think it was." She turned to Archie. "Who is Peter Pan?"

"He's from a book. He dresses just like Quinn and can fly too."

"*Hello?*" Orus cawed. "*Does that really matter right now? Didn't you hear him? The Vanir are going to kill us!*"

Freya turned back to Quinn. "Please, you must set us free. We know how to stop the war. That's the only reason we came here. Not to change your way of life or to challenge the Elders. Just to stop the war."

"How?"

"The combination of Vanir magic and Aesir strength should be enough to stop the giants."

Quinn shook his head. "Vanaheim will never join forces with Asgard. We called a truce long ago, but that doesn't mean we trust Odin or would fight beside him."

"Then it's over," Archie said. "The giants will destroy us all."

Quinn considered for a moment. "Not necessarily. Even now some of us are planning to challenge the Elders. If you promise to help me, I will release you. Then I'll show you the way out of Vanaheim."

"How can we possibly help you?" Freya asked. "It seems you have a lot more power than we do."

"Promise to help me, and I'll tell you everything."

"Why should we trust you?" Orus demanded.

"Because if you don't, Kreel and the others will come for you, question you, and then kill you—not because you spoke about the war, but because you come from Asgard. For them, that is crime enough."

Freya looked at Archie and Orus. "We don't have much choice, then." She turned back to Quinn. "You have my sworn word as a Valkyrie. If you let us out, we'll help you. Then you'll help us get out of Vanaheim."

"Agreed."

Quinn waved his hand in the air and the cage door swung open. "I really hope I can trust you. This is too serious to risk a mistake."

When Freya walked free, she nodded. "You can. Loki, I'm not so sure about. But if Archie, Orus, or I give you our word, we always keep it."

"So do I," Quinn agreed. "Come, we must move. They'll be here for you at dawn." He opened his clear, insectile wings. "It's this way—you'll have to fly."

Freya put her arm around Archie and opened her own black-feathered wings. She leaped into the air and, with Orus flying at her side, followed behind Quinn. They kept close to tree level, and Freya realized he was trying not to be seen.

All through the long night they flew. A canopy of bright stars shone above them while three sullen moons rested on the distant horizon. After a time, there was the blush of pre-dawn glow rising behind them.

"How much farther?" Freya called.

"Not far," Quinn said. He pointed ahead of them. "Just beyond that mountain range."

They had flown only a short distance farther when Freya and Archie felt powerful, invisible hands catch hold of them and start to drag them from the sky.

Freya flapped her wings hard and fought against the unyielding force, but nothing could halt their descent. Their screams echoed together as they were pulled through the canopy of trees and crashed down to the ground far below.

9

FREYA HIT THE GROUND HARD. BUT WEARING HER breastplate kept her from serious injury—though it didn't stop the pain in her shoulder when she landed on her side.

"Are you all right?" she said to Archie as she rolled over and saw him lying beside her.

"Ooof—I landed on something hard. . . ." He sat up and pulled a fist-sized rock from beneath him. "This is one time I wish I were still in ghost form."

Quinn touched down lightly beside them and reached for Freya's arm to help her up. "I'm sorry we had to do that to you, but we needed to ensure we weren't being followed and that you weren't working with others."

Freya climbed painfully to her feet. "You did that to us? You nearly broke my wings!"

Quinn looked alarmed. "I didn't mean to hurt you, but we must be careful."

Freya tried to massage the ache away from her shoulder. "This isn't the best way to get us to trust you."

"But it was the only way to ensure you weren't being followed," an elderly voice called.

Behind them, two women emerged from the trees. One looked as old as time itself, with a tattered brown cloak that dragged along the jungle floor, collecting leaves, sticks, and dead insects. Her face was almost impossible to see under all the wrinkles in her skin. The other woman was much younger and carried an air of elegance. "I am sorry, Freya and Archie, but it was necessary."

"Do you know us?"

The older woman nodded. "I have known both of you from before the time of your birth." Her ancient eyes settled on Orus at Freya's shoulder. "And you, young Orus, I watched you hatch."

"Who are you?" Freya asked.

"I am Urd," the old woman said, "and this is my sister Verdandi."

Freya's eyes flew wide. "Urd and Verdandi? You can't be serious!"

The younger woman nodded. "We're quite serious."

"But—but you don't belong in Vanaheim," Freya cried. "You are supposed to be at the base of Yggdrasil at the

Urdar Fountain. You feed the Great Cosmic Tree."

"Who are they?" Archie whispered.

The older woman took a step closer to Archie and stroked his cheek. "We are the Norns." When confusion rose on his face, she continued. "You might know us as the Fates. We have many names."

"Fates?" Archie said. "I think I've heard of you . . . from the myths."

"We are no more myth than Freya." She nodded to Freya. "Normally, we *do* reside at the base of Yggdrasil, keeping the tree fed and healthy. But something has happened to disturb our work."

Archie frowned. "Wait, aren't there always three Fates— Past, Present, and Future?"

Urd nodded. "Indeed there are. Our youngest sister has been taken from us, and we need your help to rescue her."

"Skuld is missing?" Freya cried.

The two sisters nodded. "She was taken by a Dark Searcher. He tried to abduct all three of us, but succeeded only in capturing our youngest sister."

"Was it Dirian?" Freya said.

Verdandi nodded. "He must have used some kind of enchantment to approach unnoticed. He attacked us before we could prepare a defense."

"What does he want with Skuld?" Archie asked.

Urd sighed, and it carried the weight of ages. "I do not

think you understand just who or what we are. We are the Norns. I, the eldest, know everything that has ever been. My dear sister Verdandi knows all that currently is. Skuld knows all that is yet to come. . . ."

Freya understood that this was important, but she couldn't grasp how. "And . . . ?" she said softly.

"And," Verdandi said, "now that Dirian has our sister, by controlling her, he controls the future."

"But if Skuld can see the future, why couldn't she see this coming?" Archie asked.

"We believe powerful Dark Elf magic is involved," Urd explained.

"I still don't understand," Freya said. "If Dirian took your sister, why are you here in Vanaheim? Surely you should be going after her?"

Quinn came forward. "Vanaheim has enough magic to keep these two safe. If they were to be captured and united with their sister, Dirian would possess the past, the present, and the future. He could take ultimate control of all time across all the realms."

Archie's mouth hung open. "That's intense. . . ."

It seemed inconceivable that one insane Dark Searcher could cause so much havoc and incite a war of epic pro-portions. Suddenly a terrible thought came to Freya. "Tell me, does Skuld have the power to alter or end someone's future?"

"She wouldn't do that," Urd said. "She can see it and advise on it, but she mustn't get involved."

"But could she, if she were forced?" Freya pressed.

The two Norn sisters looked at each other. They nodded.

Freya gasped. "This is too terrible. . . . That's how he's doing it!"

"I don't understand," Quinn said.

"Yeah, Gee—doing what?" Archie repeated. "What are you talking about?"

"That's how Dirian is keeping fallen immortals dead!"

Orus cawed as the realization struck him. *"It all makes sense now. It's just like Loki said when he came back to the farm—Dirian killed those who wouldn't join him, and when they died, he found a way to keep them dead. Skuld is doing it! She is ending their destiny."*

Urd cried out, "Of course! Our sister has control of everyone's fate. She could end their destiny. But she wouldn't do it."

"Not unless she was being forced," Quinn said. He turned to Freya. "This is much worse than even I feared—we must warn the Elders. With Dirian controlling Skuld, he could demand that all the realms surrender to him or he will force her to bring on Ragnarök!"

10

LOCKED IN THE MILITARY FACILITY, MAYA FELT THE
tension from her family and the other Asgardians growing.
Despite their best efforts, the humans still refused to believe
the danger facing their world.

Being so deep underground, there were no windows, but
somehow everyone knew it was late in the night. Come the
morning, Thor planned to break out and lead everyone to
the tunnel heading up to Asgard. After that, Earth was to be
left to fend for itself.

Just before dawn, the doors at the end of the cell block
burst open. Vonni charged in, followed by a large group of
soldiers.

Maya hadn't seen him since their capture, and she was
stunned when he arrived wearing an army uniform. She

had been on the battlefields long enough to recognize his rank. Vonni Angelo, a Dark Searcher born of a Valkyrie and secretly raised on Earth, was a colonel in the United States Army.

"Open them," Vonni ordered. "All of them!"

He moved down to Thor's cell. "Thor, Balder, they're here. The giants have started invading Earth. The first wave just arrived in Florida. Now they're appearing all over the world. It's just like Loki said; they're using the roots of Yggdrasil. The military are ready to listen to us now. Please, will you stay and help Earth?"

Thor looked at his brother and then nodded. "Get us out of here."

Maya stayed close to Mims as they were led away from the cell block. For the first time since their arrival, the soldiers around them kept their weapons down. She and the Asgardians were no longer perceived as the threat. She could feel that the soldiers were terrified and looking to them for hope.

They passed through the research center of the vast facility and up the stairs into the full military level, entering a large, open hangar. Hundreds of chairs had been set up, and leaders from all the military forces filed in and took a seat.

"This way," Vonni said.

All eyes rested on the Asgardians as Vonni led them up to the front. He took his place at the podium next to four higher-ranking officers. Occasionally they would turn to stare back at the Valkyries and Dark Searchers.

"Good morning, everyone," Vonni started. "My name is Colonel Giovanni Angelo. Before we get started, I must tell you that I, like those standing behind me, am immortal." Murmurs of shock rippled through the audience.

Vonni nodded. "I have served in the United States military since its beginnings in the Revolutionary War. In addition, I served in the American Civil War under General William Tecumseh Sherman, the Spanish-American War under Major General William Shafter, then on to World War One and Two."

Not a sound was heard in the hangar as the guests stared in open shock. Finally the crowd erupted in calls and questions. One of the higher-ranking officers beside Vonni raised his hands to calm the gathering and came forward and started to speak.

"Good morning, everyone. For those of you who don't know me, I'm General Wilcox. I appreciate how all of this must sound, but what Colonel Angelo says is true. We've checked our archives and found detailed records of him and his military service, covering hundreds of years. He and his people"—the general waved his arm back to include the Asgardians—"are here to help us with this giant situation."

The general stepped back and handed the microphone to Vonni. Vonni began, "Seeing what is happening around the world is difficult to believe or accept. But it is time the people of Earth knew the truth. . . ."

Maya stood back with Mims and her family and listened to Vonni explain about Asgard, Odin, the existence of Yggdrasil—and Earth's place within the Nine Realms.

"The people of Earth have lived in isolation for so long that the stories of the realms have become little more than myths and fodder for comic books and movies. But these aren't myths. The giants invading our world aren't comic book monsters. They are very real and very dangerous. It's difficult to believe that we could be part of such an amazing collective as the realms. But we are. The Valkyries have been coming to Earth—or Midgard, as they call it—unseen, since the dawn of time. Our ancient Vikings knew of the realms and told the stories of Odin, Asgard, and Valhalla." Vonni paused and stepped back to Thor. "Many of you have grown up hearing the tales of Thor and his mighty hammer, along with his brother, Balder, and their fights against the frost and fire giants. I am here to tell you now—those aren't just stories. It is my honor to introduce you to the very real Thor and Balder, sons of Odin—here on Earth, from Asgard."

There was stunned silence in the room as all eyes fell on Thor and Balder.

"And here," Vonni continued as he walked along the line of Searchers, "these are the servants of Odin. His Dark Searchers and the Valkyries—my family."

The room exploded into noise. Comments and questions were once again fired in quick succession. "How do we know the giants haven't sent them? Why are you here? Is this an alien invasion? Where is Odin? If it's all true, where are your wings, Colonel?"

The general came forward and again held up his hands. "Silence! Silence! We have a lot to get through today. I'm sure there will be time for questions later. But right now we are in crisis. I assure you, Colonel Angelo is what he claims to be. He's here to explain what we're up against."

Vonni looked at the soldier who'd asked the last question. "General, I will answer a question now, if I may." He focused on the crowd and removed his military jacket, undid his tie, and started to unbutton his white shirt. "Just like you, I was born on Earth. It's the only home I've ever known, and it is the world I love." He pulled off his shirt. "But do not doubt what I say. I was born a Dark Searcher. To keep me safe and hidden, my wings were removed when I was a baby." Vonni turned his back to the crowd to reveal the two large scars where his wings should have been. He faced the crowd and then reached for an empty chair. Vonni lifted it up and easily bent the thick metal legs like a pretzel to prove his non-human strength. "But I hide no more. Earth and all the realms are in danger and if we are to defeat the giants, we must all work together."

Maya cast out her senses over the crowd of military

personnel and felt their fear and doubt. She couldn't blame them—it was a lot to take in. But as the minutes turned to hours and the briefing finally drew to a close, she felt the emotions in the hangar change. The soldiers were moving on from shock, fear, and doubt to determination to fight for their world.

She watched them with increasing sadness. These soldiers had no concept of what they were about to go up against. All their bravado and their bravery would vanish the moment they engaged the giants.

By late afternoon, the hangar had become the Central War Room of the US military services during "Operation Giant-Stop." It was in here that Vonni and the generals coordinated battle strategy against the invaders.

Maya stayed with her family, making their own plans for confronting the giants. Their weapons had been returned, and as large maps were laid out on tables, they were shown all the locations where the giants had been spotted emerging from the tunnels.

"There are so many," Eir said, strapping her golden sword to her waist. "There must be more tunnels than Loki knew about."

"I'm sure he couldn't know all of them," Brundi said.

"It doesn't matter." Thor was stroking his beard. He pointed to the map and the Florida entrance. "This is where we'll go first. This tunnel is the largest, and has the shortest route to the next tunnel going up to Asgard. It's the most dangerous for all of us."

Long before the assignments were doled out, Vonni came rushing over with a private close behind him. His face was ashen.

"There's big trouble," he said. "Reports are in that a large group of giants are heading this way. They're moving fast—it's only a matter of minutes before they get here. We're evacuating the mountain."

"It's us," Balder said grimly. "The giants can feel us here. Capturing me and Thor would be a great prize in this war. In this mountain, there will be no escape. We must go."

"Transports are waiting to take you away, sir," the private offered.

"No," Kris growled. "We will use our own wings, not Midgard machines, to move Thor and Balder."

"Mom!" Mims cried. She dashed away from Maya's side and ran up to her mother, who had just entered the hangar. Sarah was clutching her baby.

"Von," Sarah called, joining them. "We've just heard. Giants are coming. We're being evacuated."

Vonni nodded and turned to the private. "I want you to get my family out of here." He stopped and looked at Maya. "You too. Those wings of yours aren't healed yet. You can't fly. Go with Sarah and the baby, Mims, and your gran."

Maya shook her head. "I can't fly yet, but I can fight."

"Yes, you can. And I need you and Kai to fight to protect your Earth family."

"Me?" Kai said. "I am no child minder. I will stay with my brothers, the Dark Searchers."

Kris turned to Kai. "You will do as Vonni commands. Once the infant Searcher is secure, you will join us in the fight. Until then you are ordered to escort the others away from here."

Disappointment showed on Kai's face, but as a fully trained Dark Searcher, he obeyed his orders. "As you command."

The good-byes were brief as Maya and her family were led away from the other Asgardians. Walking beside her brother, she could feel his disappointment.

"Don't worry, Kai. There will be plenty of giants to fight soon enough. Let's just get the others to safety and we can come back."

Kai stopped and looked at her. "I don't care about fighting. Freya is missing—I was hoping to slip away to look for her. I haven't felt her in too long and I'm starting to worry."

"You're worried about her too?" Maya asked. "I've been frantic. But you haven't said anything."

"Of course I'm worried," Kai said harshly. "She is my sister, my twin. We have a bond that I can neither explain nor deny. I must find her." He paused, and his eyes bored into Maya's. "And I will, with or without permission."

"I'm coming with you," Maya said sharply. She looked at

her brother with a new understanding. They hadn't known each other very long and hadn't had a chance to speak. All she knew about him was what she knew of the Dark Searchers. They were cold and distant. She was shocked to find out he cared. Then she caught on to what he said. "Wait, what do you mean you haven't felt her? When we're in Midgard, I can't ever feel her—do you mean that you can?"

Kai nodded. "I've always felt something, but I didn't understand what it was. It became clearer at the Ten Realms Challenge, when we first touched, and this bond has grown ever since. I can feel her when we're in the same realm. But now that's gone. I fear she and Archie may have left Midgard."

Maya's eyes went wide. "How? Where?"

Kai leaned closer. "Don't forget, Loki is missing too. Last time they were together, they came to Utgard to find me. I am convinced they are doing something together again."

Maya looked back at the Valkyries as they were being led away. "We should tell the others."

Kai shook his head. "No. They will try to stop us—but I won't be stopped by anyone."

Maya was struck by his strong will and determination. He was just like Freya. "All right. We'll get Sarah and the baby to safety, and then you and I can set out. Do you know where she is?"

Kai shook his head. "All I know is that she's not in Midgard."

11

DEEP IN THE VANAHEIM JUNGLE, VERDANDI WAS convincing Quinn not to take Freya and Archie to the Elders. "No, child. By the time you do, it will be too late. You must rescue our sister first. Only when Skuld is free do we stand a chance of ending the war before it goes too far."

Freya shook her head. "I'm sorry, Verdandi, but we must speak with the Elders first. We know how to stop this war and we need their help!"

Verdandi addressed her. "Getting the giant kings to turn on each other is a viable solution. But it will only succeed if Skuld is free and there is no chance of Dirian replacing the giant kings with those who will do his bidding."

"How do you know our plan?" Archie demanded.

"We are the Norns," Urd said. "We know all. I have seen everything you have been through. . . ."

Verdandi nodded. "And I know all that is current. I know you came here to engage the Vanir in this struggle, but it will take more than your word and certainly more time than you have to get them on your side. Their distrust of the Aesir runs too deep."

"So what do we do?" Archie said.

"We put aside our old resentments and work together to free Skuld. It's the only way." Quinn turned to Verdandi. "Where are they holding your sister?"

"She is being held in a keep in the desert in Muspelheim," the younger woman said.

Freya gasped and Orus cawed.

"What?" Archie said. "Where's Muspelheim?"

"It's the realm of the fire giants."

"The fire giants?" Archie choked. "The same guys we saw at the Ten Realms Challenge? The ones always on fire?"

"That's them," Freya said.

"*Muspelheim is the most dangerous of all the realms,*" Orus cawed. "*We'll be killed!*"

"It is," Urd agreed. "Your journey will be fraught with danger, and you will be risking your lives. If Skuld is doing Dirian's bidding, should you be killed, I fear you will not rise again."

Freya nodded. "I'm sure Dirian would love to kill me for good if he got the chance."

"Me too," Archie said. "Remember, I nearly cut his hand off."

"He will kill all of us if he learns of our intention to free Skuld," Quinn said.

"We should free Loki," Freya suggested. "He could help us."

"No way!" Archie cried. "Gee, how do we know he's not working for Dirian? That bringing us here wasn't just a distraction to get us out of the way?"

Urd shook her head. "Your suspicion of Loki is justified. He has done many bad things in the past. But I can assure you, this time his intentions are genuine. He is on the side of peace and was not leading you to harm in bringing you here."

Verdandi nodded. "Unfortunately, the Vanir do not trust him any more than you do. He is now suffering at their hands."

"If he's innocent, we must save him," Freya said.

Verdandi shook her head. "No, child. You must go to free Skuld. Whether Loki survives his ordeal or not will make little difference if Dirian gains control of all the realms. Urd and I will present ourselves to the Vanir Elders and explain what has happened. We will plead for Loki's life. But your quest is set. You must leave here now."

* * *

Freya had no reason not to trust the Norns. They were renowned for never taking sides—they were observers of all, but never became personally involved. Since Dirian had taken their youngest sister, they had been drawn into the fight. Freya just hoped it wasn't too late.

They sat in the small clearing as Quinn pulled out several maps, drawn up on a roughly woven fabric. The first and largest map was a detailed picture of Yggdrasil, the Cosmic World Tree. There were circles drawn on the tree to show each of the Nine Realms and their placement within the branches of the Great Tree. At the top was Asgard and Valhalla. Midgard appeared beneath it. Below and to the left of Midgard was Vanaheim, and then along the bottom from left to right was Jotunheim, realm of the frost giants; Helheim, realm of the ancient dead; Nidavellir, the realm of the dwarfs; and then Svartalfheim, realm of the Dark Elves. Finally, on the far right, was Muspelheim—realm of the fire giants.

Quinn pointed to Muspelheim. "This is where we must go. We can travel through all the lower realms to get there."

Freya looked at the map and shook her head. "It will be too dangerous for us to journey through all those realms, especially while we're at war. Look, the best way is for us to go back through the tunnel we took to get here, and return to Midgard. Then we can find the secret tunnel that will take us directly to Muspelheim. It will cut out all those other realms."

"What are these tunnels?" Quinn said.

"The roots of Yggdrasil," Freya said. "That's how we got here."

Quinn looked at the two Norns. "Is this true? Do the roots of Yggdrasil connect all the realms?"

Urd nodded. "They have existed since the beginning of time. But very few know of them. Most believe them to be a myth."

"It's no myth," Archie said. "We used one to get here. Loki thinks the giants will use them to get to Earth and then take other tunnels leading up to Asgard. It's kind of like a weird game of snakes and ladders. You arrive through one tunnel and head up through another."

"Loki is correct. The giants have already started using them," Verdandi said. "They are in Midgard now, making their way up."

"What?" Archie cried. "No, they can't be. It's too soon!"

"I do not lie, child," Verdandi said. "I tell only what I see. It is happening right now. Frost and fire giants are entering Midgard as we speak. They are bringing their allies—the Dark Elves, dwarfs, and trolls—with them." Verdandi closed her eyes and lifted her head, as though she were focusing on something very distant. When she opened them, her face revealed great sadness. "Midgard forces are trying to fight them, but they stand no chance."

"What about Thor?" Freya cried. "He's in Midgard right now. So are the Dark Searchers who are standing against Dirian. What about my mother and sisters? Can you see them?"

Verdandi shook her head. "Fear for our sister is distracting me. I cannot see them."

A stone settled in Freya's stomach. Had the giants killed her family and those fighting for Asgard?

"We have to go back!" she cried, getting to her feet.

"Wait," Quinn said. He searched in his pouch and pulled out a blank, woven parchment and quill and handed them to the Norns. "If you know of these tunnels, please, show us where they are. Freya says she can lead us back to Midgard. When we get there, how do we find the passage to Muspelheim?"

Verdandi hesitated for a moment. "These are sacred tunnels, meant to be kept secret."

Urd nodded. "Show them. The secret is out."

Verdandi started to draw on the parchment. Freya immediately recognized the continents of Earth. The Norn put a small dot on the map. "This is the only root that will take you to Muspelheim. And when you have our sister, you must go back to Midgard and take this tunnel to get you straight up to Asgard. This is an especially secret root that only we, the Norns, use. No others know of it. But it is the fastest way to Asgard and Odin's protection of our sister."

Freya looked at the map and frowned. "What about a root from Muspelheim directly to Asgard? Surely that would be faster."

Urd nodded. "Indeed it would. But that tunnel will be filled with Dirian's servants. You must keep Skuld safe and away from them."

Verdandi nodded. "Once Skuld is free, Dirian will lose his power to keep his enemies dead. Then, when you set the giants against each other, the war will end."

"So we know our plan," Quinn said. He rose to his feet and tucked the precious map in his bag. "Let's get going. We don't have a moment to waste."

12

BY THE TIME THEY LEFT, THE SUN WAS HIGH AND HOT IN the brilliant blue sky. Freya hated leaving the two Norns in the jungle, looking so vulnerable and alone, but Urd insisted they go. She said rescuing Skuld must be their only priority.

Freya, Archie, and Quinn took off, heading in the direction of the tunnel where the security team had first captured them. As before, they remained close to the canopy of leaves to help hide their presence.

Despite the teeming life around them, Freya's senses were in overdrive as she reached out to feel for any Vanir fighters in the area. When they were just over halfway back to the mountain, she felt the presence of others.

"Quinn, they're coming!" she cried. "Get down!"

Freya heard Quinn call something back, but with little time to waste, she tucked in her wings and dived headfirst down into the dense carpet of trees. She clenched her eyes as thick branches and vines bit into her skin and the wings on her back. Archie cried out as the same branches scratched his face and arms.

When they pulled free of the trees and reached the ground, they heard Quinn calling. A moment later he landed beside them without a scratch. "Are you deaf? I told you to wait. . . ."

Moments later, three young winged warriors landed. Two had the same dragonfly wings as Quinn, while the other was the butterfly girl she had noticed earlier, with the black wings and big blue dots. Freya searched for a weapon. But even before she reached for a thick branch, invisible hands wrapped around her and held her tight.

"Freya, stop!" Quinn said. "They're with me!"

"*Freya, help me!*" Orus cawed. The raven was high in the trees overhead and trapped in a tangle of vines.

The young girl with the butterfly wings floated up and freed the raven from the tangle. "You're all right," she cooed softly, stroking his feathers. "We're not going to harm you."

She released him, and Orus flew to Freya's shoulder.

"These are my friends," Quinn said, releasing his grip on Freya. "That's Parsi, Skyrian, and Switch. Everyone, this is Freya and Archie."

"*And Orus,*" the raven said.

"Yes, of course—and Orus," Quinn corrected.

The girl who had freed Orus stepped closer to Archie. "If it's easier, you can just call me Skye."

"I'm Archie," Archie stuttered awkwardly. "Everyone just calls me, er, Archie. I'm from Earth—I mean Midgard."

Skye blushed lightly and her butterfly wings fluttered. Her black eyes sparkled. "I've never met a human before. You have no wings?"

"Nope. Humans don't." Then he added, "But yours are really cool."

Switch nodded to Freya. "We know something is happening that the Elders aren't telling us."

"It's worse than we imagined," Quinn reported. He, Freya, and Archie explained what they knew. "We must free Skuld," he continued. "Nothing else matters if she remains a prisoner of Dirian."

"I never liked what I heard about the Dark Searchers," Parsi said. "They're all feathered Aesir scum!"

"Don't blame the Aesir for this!" Freya shot. "We're in more danger than you are."

"Why shouldn't I blame you? A Dark Searcher started this war," the tall dragonfly boy spat.

Freya's hands balled into fists as she advanced on the tall boy. "My brother is a Dark Searcher, and in case you hadn't noticed, I have feathers!" Freya opened her wings threateningly. "So take that back, Vanir, before I make you!"

"What are you going to do, Valkyrie, reap me? Turn me into a slave, like this dead human?"

"Hey, I'm no slave!" Archie cried. He stood beside Freya and faced down the troublemaker. "It's called friendship and loyalty. Something I'm sure you know nothing about!"

"Enough!" Quinn cried.

Freya wouldn't back down. She poked her finger into Parsi's chest. "Listen, bug boy, it's not our fault that Dirian's insane. He's working against all of us."

Parsi looked at his friends. "That's so typical of the Aesir, ready to use violence first."

"You wanna see violence?" Archie said as he raised his fist. "Keep going after Gee like that and I'll show you what humans can do!"

Skye stepped between them. "Everyone calm down! Fighting among ourselves isn't helping." She looked back at Quinn. "We know what the problem is, so how do we solve it?"

"First, we stop accusing each other. Then we free Skuld. After that, Freya has a plan that the Norns said would work. We're going to turn the giant kings against each other."

"We?" Archie said. "After your guys just blamed us for everything? You still expect us to work together?"

"We must," Quinn said. "This war will involve all the realms. The Vanir can't avoid it, no matter what the Elders say. Only together will we stand a chance of stopping Ragnarök."

Freya nodded. "Quinn's right. Unless we put our old resentments aside, we don't stand a chance." She turned to Parsi. "I'm willing to try if you are."

Parsi nodded reluctantly. "I'm in." He paused, and a slight smile came to his lips. "As long as you don't call me 'bug boy' again."

"Fine, just as long as you stop insulting my feathers," Freya said.

"Agreed," Quinn said. "Here's our plan." He pointed to his two dragonfly-winged friends. "You two will go to the Norns and make sure they get safely to the village. You must make the Elders release Loki and convince them what will happen if we don't side with Asgard."

"What about me?" Skye asked.

"You're coming with us to Muspelheim."

"Are you sure about that?" Archie asked. "It's going to be very dangerous."

"Yes, and . . . ?" Skye prodded. "Don't you think I'm a warrior or brave enough?"

Archie blushed. "Of course you're brave enough, but, um . . . I mean, that's not what I mean. Look at you. You— you're so—so delicate. Your wings look like they can be damaged very easily."

Skye smiled, and Freya could see it had a devastating effect on Archie. "Don't worry about me, Archie. I am quite capable of taking care of myself."

Quinn nodded. "She is. In fact, Skye's got more magic than the rest of us."

"I—I'm sorry. I didn't mean to hurt your feelings . . . ," Archie stuttered.

Freya watched her friend and smiled. In all their time together, she'd never seen Archie this flustered.

"I can't believe what I'm seeing," Orus whispered in her ear. *"Look at him! Archie is tongue-tied around her."*

"I'm sure she'll do fine," Freya said. "Archie, we're going to face dangers we never imagined before. I for one am happy to have Skye with us. We're going to need all the help and magic we can get if we hope to save the realms."

"It is agreed, then," Quinn said. "Let's get moving."

"Wait. I have something for Freya." Skye reached back between her two large butterfly wings and pulled out Freya's sword and belt. "I think you might need this."

"My sword!" Freya cried. "How did you get it?"

"Kreel is my father," Skye explained. "He had it in our home. He says weapons like this are crude, ugly, unnecessary things. But since we're not staying in Vanaheim, I thought you might want it back."

"Thank you." Freya accepted the sword. "But won't your father be angry when he finds out what you've done?"

Skye nodded. "But saving the realms is more important. He'll understand when we get back."

"If we get back," Orus cawed.

Grateful to have her golden sword back, Freya fastened the belt around her waist and felt instantly better. The Vanir might use magic to defend themselves, but she was still a Valkyrie, raised on the battlefield and trained to use weapons.

"Now, does everyone know what they're doing?" Quinn asked.

Parsi nodded. "We'll get the Norns to the Elders and convince them to side with Asgard. Good luck freeing Skuld."

Quinn raised his hand and used magic to lift them all back up through the dense trees and into the open sky.

"For Vanaheim," he cried, as the two groups parted on their missions.

"For all the realms!" Freya echoed as she opened her wings and led her team toward the cave.

13

MAYA AND HER FAMILY WERE EVACUATED TO A SAFE house on the beach along the California coast. Just north of Los Angeles, it was far from where the giants were entering the country.

Standing on the balcony that ran the length of the house, several yards above the sand, Maya gazed out over the Pacific Ocean. The water before them was calm and the beach was empty. But it was an illusion. The world was anything but calm.

Kai stood at her side lost in thought—though his emotions were running wild with concern for Freya.

Hours earlier they had received a call from Vonni to say he and the others had made it safely out of the mountain facility moments before the giants arrived. They were now on the East Coast, near Boston, preparing to engage the enemy. Vonni said there was a steady stream of frost and fire giants coming up from the south.

"Have you felt anything at all from Freya?" Maya asked, breaking the painful silence.

Kai shook his head. "Nothing." He turned to her, and his ice-blue eyes were filled with worry. "But I'm sure she's all right."

Maya nodded, knowing he was trying to convince himself more than her. "Of course she is. Freya is resourceful. It's the rest of us I'm worried about."

The television in the lounge behind them droned on— filled with news reports from all over the world, talking about the invasion. Giants, Dark Elves, and a terrifying assortment of other creatures were appearing on every continent.

"There's Thor!" Mims cried.

Maya and Kai ran back into the house. The large television screen on the wall showed Thor taking on four frost giants at once. Hammer in hand, he was dodging their attempts to kill him while he attacked them with lethal hammer blows.

"I've never seen him use Mjölnir like that before," Maya said. "He's only ever fought with swords at Valhalla. He's unstoppable."

"He's never had to," Brundi said. She was sitting on the sofa between Mims and Sarah, who was holding the baby. "Thor is an army unto himself."

"Thank heavens he's on our side," said one of the soldiers

assigned to them. "Look at him. He's minuscule compared to them, but he's bringing them down."

"Look, there they are!" Kai cried, pointing at the television. "It's the Searchers—and there's Mother!" The camera changed angles and was showing the Dark Searchers and Valkyries fully engaged with the giants. Their blades moved so fast, they couldn't be followed by the cameras. Though the giants were massive in comparison, by working together, the winged Asgardians were able to bring down two fire giants and were taking on a third.

The report cut away to other battles around the world, and the news wasn't as encouraging. London was under attack as giants arrived from a tunnel in the Scottish Highlands and left a path of destruction through Edinburgh and all the way down to the south coast. The giants then entered the English Channel to cross to France. From there they stormed through to Germany, where Maya and Kai knew a hidden tunnel led up to Asgard.

Tanks and jet fighters from the world's united military forces took on the giants but couldn't stop their advance. Despite humanity's best efforts, their weapons had little effect on the large invaders—though they were having success against the trolls, Dark Elves, and dwarfs.

With each passing moment, Maya felt despair coming from the three soldiers in the room. "We can't win against them, can we?" the corporal asked her.

Maya shook her head. "Not even Asgard will stand long against the united giants."

"I should be there," Kai said as his white wings fluttered, and he punched the back of the sofa. "I'm doing nothing here but watching my brothers fight!"

One of the soldiers nodded. "So should we."

"You are where you must be," Brundi said. "I am sure Vonni will send for you when you are needed."

Maya stayed to watch a little longer. But with each new report showing the path of devastation left by the invaders, she felt despair crush her. Finally she walked back out to the balcony to be alone.

"*I know what you're thinking,*" Grul said. The raven was finally recovered and back on her shoulder. "*You want to join your mother and sisters in the battle and be there too.*"

Maya nodded. "Midgard is overwhelmed, and I feel help-less here." She walked up to the railing and grasped it tightly as she slowly opened her wings. They were stiff and sore but healing quickly now that they'd been properly set. She winced as she flapped them lightly.

"*It won't be long,*" Grul said.

Maya massaged her right wing and nodded. "They're feeling much stronger. I'm ready to try to fly tomorrow—just a short flight at first."

"*Then what?*" the raven asked. "*Please don't say you're going to join the fight. You're not ready for that.*"

Kai arrived back on the balcony. "That's exactly what we're going to do. The moment Maya can fly again, we're leaving."

"But what about Brundi and Mims? What about the baby? They need your protection."

"They have the human soldiers. Grul, we can't stay here doing nothing while the world falls," Maya said.

"Then it's decided," Kai said. "Tomorrow, if you can fly, we'll go."

They remained glued to the television, watching the reports of the invasion until late into the night. Of the combined forces of Asgardians and humans, the only ones with any success against the giants were the Asgardians, finally winning them acceptance as allies.

When Maya retired to bed and lay down in the room she shared with Mims, she was unable to sleep. She was more conflicted than she had ever been in her life. Part of her wanted to join her family in battle, but another part was called to find Freya. Neither option held any hope of success. Finally, she decided what she would do. She would join her family against the giants, but she had no illusions. They were fighting a losing battle.

Maya turned onto her stomach and flexed her wings open and closed. She could feel them getting stronger with each passing moment. By morning, she was confident they would be healed enough to carry her to the East Coast.

When she had finished her exercises, she rolled onto her side and tried to sleep. She needed all the rest she could get. But just as she started to doze off, she felt a blaring alarm going off in her head.

Maya jumped up and went to the window. The moment she and Grul looked out to the dark ocean, her jaw dropped. Two frost giants were emerging from the water.

"Mims, get up!" She ran for the door and out of the bedroom. "Everyone up!" she shouted. "It's the frost giants—they're here!"

Kai was first to appear in the hall. "From where?"

"The ocean! There must be a tunnel entrance we didn't know about just offshore—"

Any further comment was cut off as the timber beams of the house creaked and the ground beneath them shook. Suddenly a frost giant's voice boomed like thunder. "Kill the Valkyries!"

"They're tracking us!" Brundi entered the hall, pulling on her robe.

There was no time to react or move as the ceiling suddenly exploded. Timber flew in all directions and debris rained down. The last thing Maya saw before darkness overwhelmed her was the horrifying sight of a massive frost giant fist smashing down through the house.

14

"SO THIS IS THE ROOT OF YGGDRASIL?" ASKED SKYE, staring at the rough walls covered with glowing green lichen. Freya had led the group into the cave leading to Earth.

Freya nodded. "If you touch it, you can feel it vibrating with life."

The two young Vanir stopped and touched the living wall. "I can hear her singing!" Skye cried.

"Who?" Archie asked, pressing his ear to the root. "I don't hear anything."

"It's Yggdrasil. If you know how to listen, you can hear her. She's beautiful."

Archie shook his head. "I still don't hear anything."

"Me neither," Freya agreed as she touched the dark brown root. "But I can feel it humming with life."

Quinn closed his eyes and listened to the song of the Great Cosmic Tree. "Let us never forget, this is what we are fighting for."

When they reached the halfway point, Archie became a ghost again. "I hate this!" he complained. "One moment I'm solid, and the next I'm not. I just wish the realms would make up their mind. Am I alive or dead?"

"You're both," Freya said.

Archie gave her a black look. "That doesn't help."

"You're alive to me," Skye offered.

Color rose on Archie's face.

"Who'd have thought a ghost could blush?" Orus teased.

Freya smiled at her friend but said nothing as she took the lead, guiding the Vanir through the tunnel. Soon the passage began to incline up toward an opening. Spread out before them was the underground lake that would take them to the surface of Midgard.

"All right," Freya said, standing on the shore. "I should warn you. To get to Midgard, we have to swim. The water is freezing cold, and you're going to need to hold your breath for a long time. Can you do that?"

Quinn nodded. "We swim a lot back home."

"But this water is freezing—will you be able to cope with it?" Freya asked. "I heard it never gets cold in Vanaheim."

Skye shook her head. "It doesn't, but that doesn't really

matter here—we won't get wet. Take our hands and we'll show you how."

Freya tucked Orus into her breastplate and took Quinn's outstretched hand. Then she caught hold of Skye.

"And you, Archie." Skye offered her free hand to him. "Join us."

The moment their hands were all linked, Freya felt a strange sensation, as if an electric current were flowing through them. Her hair started to stand on end. Beside her, Quinn's hair also started to rise.

"Show us the way," Skye said to Archie.

They entered the water together, and it was as if they were traveling in a big bubble of air. The freezing water never touched them as Archie gave instructions to Skye on the route that Loki had taken.

Safe within the protection of the bubble, they looked around in wonder at the Arctic Ocean. Soon they burst through the surface of the water. To Freya and Archie, it seemed they had only just left. But here the ocean water was almost solid ice, and Kaffeklubben Island was covered in snow.

When they touched the shore, Skye let go of Freya's hand and the bubble vanished.

"That was awesome!" Archie said. He slapped Freya playfully on the arm. "Why can't you do cool stuff like that?"

"Sorry to disappoint you," Freya said, "but I'm just a

poor Aesir, remember? We use crude weapons and brute force, not magic."

Quinn looked at Freya and grinned mischievously. "Just so long as you remember that."

They walked around the small arctic island. The sun was sitting sluggishly on the horizon, giving no clue as to whether it was day or night. There were no signs of life anywhere. "Well, at least the giants haven't been here yet," Quinn said.

His comment brought home the danger. Urd and Verdandi had said that the giants were already on Earth. What damage had they done? "We're too far north," Freya explained. "The tunnel to Asgard is much farther south. That's where we'll see the real damage."

Orus cawed, *"I hate to imagine what they've done."*

"Well, we won't know until we get there." Freya looked at the two Vanir. "How are you two for endurance flying? It's a long way south."

Quinn grinned. "We'll keep up with you, Aesir. Don't worry about us."

Freya grinned back at him. "Really, Vanir? My feathers against your insectoid wings—the first person who needs to land loses!"

"Deal!" Quinn cried as he flapped his four dragonfly wings and launched into the arctic sky.

"Go get 'em, Gee," Archie cried.

Freya caught hold of Archie, flapped her larger, feathered wings, and took off behind Quinn and Skye.

The journey south was much longer than the journey up had been. Then they'd ridden a large black dragon. This time they were using their own wing power and could fly only as fast as Skye's butterfly wings could manage.

Freya could sense Quinn and Skye growing fatigued. For all their bragging, they obviously weren't used to long-distance flying.

The sun had set hours ago, and with thick storm clouds above them, they were traveling in total darkness.

"There is no shame in stopping for a rest," Freya called as she maneuvered closer to the two Vanir. "I'm used to this. You're not."

"We're fine," Quinn panted.

"Don't be a jerk!" Archie called. "Skye's really struggling. Her wings aren't built like yours or Gee's—it's harder for her to keep up with us."

Quinn looked back at his companion and saw Skye battling to match their speed. But with her light wings, she fluttered in the windswept sky, unable to fly in a straight line. She nodded to the others but was too tired to speak.

"All right," Quinn said. "Let's take a short break."

Freya slowed down and glided over the snow-capped mountains of northern Canada. They touched down at the top of one of the mountains.

Quinn waved his hand in the air, and suddenly a large, warm campfire appeared in the thick snow. He pulled out a small cloth and wiped a film of sweat off his brow. "I don't think I've ever flown that far before."

"Me neither," Skye gasped as she fluttered down to the ground and gulped air. Her butterfly wings drooped and her shoulders sagged. "I hate to admit it, but I'm exhausted. It's true, feathers are better for long distances."

Freya wanted to say "I told you so," but she didn't have the heart. After all, she was the best flyer in Asgard. Mentioning it would only sound like bragging. "But I can't use magic," she said instead.

"True," Quinn said. Then he grinned at Freya. "Which means we can do this and you can't!" He waved his hand again, and a banquet of food appeared on a leafy blanket beside the roaring fire. From breads to exotic fruit Freya had never seen before, it all looked delicious. "I'm starving. Let's eat."

As Freya took a seat on the leaf cover, Archie harrumphed. "It's just not fair. It all looks delicious, but I can't eat!"

Orus emerged from Freya's breastplate and cawed, *"But I can—I'll enjoy it for you!"*

While they ate, Quinn and Skye stared around them. "We've never been to Midgard before," Skye said. "Does it all look like this?"

Freya shook her head. "No. This realm is really special.

It seems to have a bit of all the realms in it. There are even a few jungles that look just like Vanaheim."

"Really?" Skye asked. When Freya nodded, she continued. "When this is over, I want to come back here and see more."

"I'll be glad to show you around," Archie offered.

Quinn watched the exchange between Skye and Archie. He frowned. "Archie, aren't you and Freya . . . you know, together?"

"Me and Gee?" Archie choked. "Are you serious? No way. We're just friends."

Freya couldn't resist kicking his foot. "Thanks, Archie, but you didn't have to make it sound like the idea was a fate worse than death!"

Archie blushed. "I didn't mean it like that! I just wanted Skye to know that we were just friends."

"She knows now; that's for sure," Freya teased. She looked at Quinn, who was looking down and smiling to himself, as if pleased to hear this new piece of information. Freya flushed and cleared her throat, changing the subject. "So, after all these years without contact between our realms, what do the Vanir think of the Aesir?"

Quinn shrugged. "Not a lot, really. But we're always preparing for war."

"With Asgard?" Archie asked.

Skye nodded. "We're raised to be ready for any kind of

attack. From the moment we can fly, we're required to train for battle and use our magic skills to fight."

"So you're all in the army?" Archie cried.

"He means you're all warriors," Freya corrected.

Quinn nodded. "Whether we want to be or not."

"What *do* you want?" Freya pressed the Vanir. "You seem like a leader to me."

A slight blush of pink rose in Quinn's cheeks. "I always dreamed of exploring the other realms and cataloging the wildlife. There's so much to see. But we're forbidden to do anything like that. We can't leave Vanaheim."

"What'll happen if you're caught here with us?" Archie asked.

"We'll be executed," Skye said softly. "And because my father is the leader of our village, he'll be executed too."

"What?" Archie cried. "You never said that would happen. You shouldn't have come here!"

"We had to," Skye said. "If this war escalates to Ragnarök, nothing will survive. We must try to stop the giants, even if it means punishment for breaking our laws."

Freya looked at her new Vanir friends. She hadn't realized the risk they were taking coming with them. Vanir punishments were much harsher than Odin's.

Silence fell as they gazed into the fire.

"Speaking of giants," Archie finally said, "Gee, can you feel them? Are they really here?"

Freya had dreaded that question from the moment they arrived. But Archie knew how acute her senses were. When he asked again, she nodded reluctantly. "Yes, they're here. So are the Dark Elves, dwarfs, and others."

Quinn raised his eyebrows. "Can you really feel them? I can't. Where are they?"

"Everywhere—all around us." Freya pointed south. "But most are down that way. There are a few behind us, but not on this continent. They'll be using the other tunnels."

A renewed silence fell over the group. The War of the Realms had started, and the giants were moving on to Asgard—via Earth.

"I wonder what the military is doing about it?" Archie asked. "The people here don't even believe in the other realms. How can we possibly fight them?"

"You can't," Freya said. "The safest thing for everyone would be for the military to stay out of their way and let the giants go for the other tunnels."

"You know they won't do that, right?" Archie said.

Freya nodded but said nothing. She stood up. "I can't eat any more. If you're all up to it, we should get moving."

"And about time, too!"

Freya turned and saw Loki striding up to them.

"Loki!" Before Freya realized what she was doing, she ran forward and threw her arms around him.

"Puh—lease!" Loki said as he pulled free of her embrace. "A little decorum, if you don't mind."

Freya looked him up and down. He was dressed in the leather armor she hadn't seen him wear since her First Day Ceremony. He carried his staff in his right hand. It was taller than him and had a large jewel at the top.

"How did you get away from the Vanir? Verdandi said they were torturing you."

"It was just a minor, but rather unpleasant, misunderstanding. When the Norns came and explained the situation, they released me. To make up for their actions, they re-created my armor and staff. Urd told me about the plan to rescue Skuld, and I had to catch up with you. Of course you'll need my help."

Freya smiled at his bravado. "Yes, I guess we do."

"Do the Elders know that Skye and Quinn have left Vanaheim to come with us?" Archie asked.

"They do now," Loki answered. He looked at the two Vanir. "I wouldn't want to be in your shoes when you get home."

"I don't care what the Elders say or do," Quinn said bravely. "If we fail, Vanaheim will fall just like Asgard. Then breaking the law will mean nothing."

"What about the Elders? Will they side with Asgard?" Freya asked.

"I believe so," Loki said. "The Vanir will be drawn in whether they want to be or not. I can't see them joining the giants." Loki reached down for a piece of bread. "Now, if you've finished your little picnic, we should get going."

"Loki," Freya started, "Skye and Quinn aren't used to this much flying. Do you think . . . ?"

Loki held up his hand. "Don't say it. You want to hitch a ride."

"Not for me," Freya said. "I'm fine. It's for the others."

Loki made a point of sighing dramatically. "All right, all right. You don't have to cry about it."

Freya frowned. "I wasn't."

"Sure you were—just like you were worried about me and frightened the Vanir might hurt me. Admit it—you actually like me, and it's so gosh darn sweet!"

Within seconds of his arrival, Loki had managed to irritate her again. "If you're just here to cause trouble, you can turn around and go back to Vanaheim!"

"Loosen up, Freya. You're too uptight." Loki laughed. He rubbed his hands together eagerly. "Now, where are we going?"

"Muspelheim," Archie said.

"I know that, ghost! I meant via which root of Yggdrasil. I don't know of any direct tunnel to Muspelheim from here. Urd said she told you where it is."

Quinn pulled out the Midgard map and lay it down on

the ground. He pointed to the spot Urd had indicated.

Loki studied it for a moment and nodded. "Machu Picchu—that makes a lot of sense. The Incas knew all about the realms. Some of them must have found the tunnel and tried to reach Muspelheim. Maybe they even saw a fire giant or two. They would have viewed them as sun gods."

Archie frowned at the map. "Is that Brazil?"

Loki looked at him and snorted. "No wonder you're an idiot! Is that what they're teaching in school these days?"

"Hey," Archie cried.

Freya quickly stepped in. "No, Archie. It's in the Andes of Peru. By the time I was old enough to go on the reapings, Machu Picchu was already abandoned. But Mother says it was once a wondrous place."

Quinn picked up the map and stowed it away. "And that's where we're going."

15

FLYING ON THE BACK OF THE BLACK DRAGON, THEY reached the first of the northern settlements just before sunrise.

As they passed over the homes, Freya immediately felt powerful emotions rising from the people below. The closer they got to cities, the more intense the feelings became.

"I can feel the people from here," Freya said. "Everyone is terrified."

"Of course they are," Archie said. "Earth is being invaded by monsters—it's like a disaster movie!"

By midmorning they approached a large city and witnessed the source of everyone's fear. "Look!" Quinn shouted. "Are those frost giants?"

"That's them," Freya said.

Ahead of them was a long line of frost giants standing taller than the highest buildings and moving steadily north. Military jet fighters flew at them from all directions, launching their rockets. But the weapons did little more than irritate the giants. When the jets flew closer to use their guns, the giants simply swatted them away like flies.

"They look so much bigger here than they did in Asgard. Earth doesn't stand a chance," Archie moaned.

Suddenly Loki veered sharply in the sky, nearly tossing Freya and the others off his back. Seconds later a rocket shot past the dragon's side.

"Hey, they're shooting at us!" Archie cried.

"They can't tell us apart from the invaders!" Freya leaned forward on the dragon's back. "Loki, take us higher—away from the fighting!"

Instead of following Freya's advice, Loki glided lower in the sky and used his large, powerful wings to maneuver expertly between the giants and the military fighters.

They glided up to a tall building and landed on the roof. Even before everyone had climbed off his back, he was returning to his normal form. They ran up to the edge of the roof and witnessed the sickening sight of a world in trouble. Frost giants were storming through the city, kicking buildings out of their way and challenging anything that came at them. Perched on most of the frost giants' shoulders were masked Dark Elves. Their hands were moving too fast to follow. But with each movement, a jet fighter was knocked magically out of the sky.

Beyond the long line of frost giants was an even more terrifying sight. Fire giants—looming taller than the frost giants, their skin and hair flaming red and glowing, while their clothing was engulfed in living flame. All they had to do was touch a building and it became a raging inferno.

"Where are we?" Archie asked, gazing all around.

"Montreal, Quebec," Loki answered. "Or rather, what's left of it."

"I've never seen a fire giant before," Skye said in a whisper. "They're even more frightening than the frost giants."

"They're meaner, too," Loki said.

As the long line of giants swept past them on their journey north to the Asgard tunnel, several stopped and turned in their direction.

"Uh-oh," Archie said. "I think they can feel us. Get ready to fly, everyone."

"Not yet," Loki said. "But stand back. I want to see just how much power the Vanir gave me to work with."

"They couldn't give you power," Quinn said.

Loki looked back at him. "Wanna bet?"

He turned forward again and raised his staff. The jewel at the end glowed brilliant green. When the closest giant was no more than two steps away, Loki called, "Alpeera."

The jewel exploded in a blazing flash of green lightning

that struck the giant and knocked him backward into the others. The ground shook as three giants lost their balance and fell, landing on a multistory parking garage and collapsing it to the ground. The giant who took the blast lay still as his chest smoldered.

"Wow!" Archie cried. "It worked."

As the other giants saw their companions go down, they roared in fury. The stomping of their feet charging toward the building rattled the ground like an earthquake.

"Uh, Loki . . . ," Freya cried as she drew her flaming sword. "Would you please use that thing again and stop those giants before they get here and squish us!"

Loki raised his staff. "Alpeera!"

Once again, the green jewel sent a blast of lightning at the frost giants. It knocked them to the ground with explosive impact.

Everyone on the roof cheered as the giants went down. But their joy was short-lived as fire giants charged in their direction.

"Loki!" a fire giant roared. "I know it's you! You're dead!"

For a third time, Loki used the staff, but even though the blazing green lightning struck the approaching fire giant in the chest, it had little effect on him.

"Well, isn't this disappointing," Loki said, casually inspecting his staff. "It doesn't seem to work on fire giants. I think we might be in trouble. . . ."

Freya looked back to Quinn and Skye. "I've got my sword, but it won't do much against them. What can you do?"

"More than that," Quinn cried. "Skye, you're with me. Freya, do what you can to slow them down—we need time to prepare a spell!"

Freya looked up at Orus on her shoulder. "Get into the air and stay back. They're too big for you."

"*They're too big for all of us!*" Orus cawed, and he launched off Freya's shoulder and took flight.

"Archie, stay here," Freya ordered as she flapped her wings and took off. She circled around him once and called, "Remember, you're a ghost. They can't hurt you. Even if this building goes down around you, you'll be okay! Stay here and I'll be back for you."

"Be careful!" Archie cried.

Freya nodded and focused on the first fire giant. Quinn and Skye were beside her. "Do what you can to keep him focused on you," Quinn ordered. "We're going for his legs."

Freya nodded and let out a loud Valkyrie howl, calling the giant's attention to her. The closest fire giant saw her in the air and shouted, "I hate Valkyries!"

He swatted at her, and Freya felt the blast of searing-hot air. But she was fast enough to dart out of the way of the giant's fiery hand.

"Come on, you can do better than that!" Freya teased. "Here I am—come and get me, Fire-Face!" She raised her sword and dived forward toward the giant's burning ear. The heat from his flaming head singed her skin, but in a quick maneuver, she was able to pierce her sword right through his earlobe. "Now you can wear an earring!"

The giant screamed and slapped his hand up to his ear, missing her by a breath. Distracted by the pain in his ear, he failed to see Quinn and Skye at his knees. As Freya moved in for a second attack, she stole a look down and saw that the two Vanir had joined hands and were casting a spell.

Moments later the fire giant roared as he tried to move and found that his two legs were magically fused together.

"Freya, knock him over!" Quinn shouted.

Freya dived at the giant again. But she didn't need to touch him. The fire giant behind him swatted at her but missed. His hand struck the trapped fire giant with a blow so hard, it knocked the restrained giant off his feet and into a large, round building. The impact was enough to tip the building over, taking the flaming fire giant down with it.

There was little time to celebrate. No sooner had one fire giant gone down than there were two more to take its place. Working as a team, Freya, Quinn, and Skye managed to bring down four more giants. But they weren't down for long, as Dark Elves arrived quickly and used their magic to release the spell restraining their legs.

"It's the Dark Elves," Quinn cursed. "There are too many here. Their combined powers are greater than ours."

"Just do what you can!" Freya called as she flew at another giant.

Fighting the giants was like trying to push back the ocean with a spoon. They couldn't possibly win, even with the Vanir's powers and her skill with a sword.

Above them, jet fighters saw Freya and the Vanir fighting against the giants and joined in the attack. But even working together, they were badly outmatched.

Behind Freya, frost giants roared Loki's name. When she circled back, she was stunned to see the Loki she knew was gone. He had changed and grown into one of the largest, most ferocious-looking frost giants she'd ever seen.

Everyone knew Loki was part frost giant. But Freya had never seen him in his true form. He was as terrifying as he was big. In fact, he towered over the other giants around him. Loki still had his recognizable long dark hair, but his face had taken on frost giant features: a large bulbous nose, protruding forehead, and full lips. His eyebrows were so bushy, she could barely see his eyes. His body was heavily muscled in his large green leather armor. But there was no mistaking the fact that this was still Loki.

The magic of the staff had grown with him. Loki wielded it like an expert and knocked over any giant who dared to come near. When he fired a blast of power at the frost giants, the effect was devastating and killed every frost giant it struck.

The frost and fire giants lost interest in Freya and the Vanir and started to go after Loki.

"Loki, look out!" Freya shouted.

Loki turned toward his attackers and charged. In the middle of the dense city, the powerful giants came together in an explosive, rolling battle that completely destroyed everything around them. Buildings fell like dominoes, and roads and bridges were torn up under the strain of the fight.

From somewhere in the middle of the melee, Loki shouted her name. His voice was deep, guttural, and rolling like thunder—but his message was clear. "Freya, get everyone outta here; you know what you must do!"

Freya had grown up on the battlefields of Earth and thought she'd seen a lot. But she'd never witnessed anything like this. The violence of the fight was worse than anything she could imagine. Nothing could withstand the impact of the wrestling giants, and before long, the beautiful city of Montreal lay in ruins.

"Go!" Loki roared again.

Freya turned away, flying toward Quinn. "Where's Skye?"

"She's gone to get Archie," he called. "Loki's right; we can't stop the giants. We have to go!"

Moments later Skye fluttered back to them with Archie clutched in her arms. Freya flew closer. "I'll take him. It's easier for me to carry him."

Archie shook his head. "No, Gee, not right now. You

need to keep your sword arm free in case more giants come after us. I'm too much of a burden."

"But Quinn and Skye have their magic—it's stronger than me and my sword."

"Not now," Skye admitted. "The Elders were right. In Midgard, the Vanir lose their powers. Ours are fading fast. You must protect us until we reach Muspelheim, where they should be restored."

"They're right," Orus called. *"Let's go—we can't help Loki or Midgard now."*

Freya hesitated a moment longer and watched Loki fighting the other giants. Though he was taller and, by the looks of it, a lot stronger than the others, he was badly out-numbered.

It wasn't long before he was overwhelmed by giants. The last thing Freya saw was Loki going down and all the others moving in to tear him apart. She was sickened to realize there was nothing she could do.

Loki and Earth were lost to the giants.

16

MAYA AWOKE TO THE SOUND OF SCREAMING. OPENING
her eyes, she discovered that she was buried in thick rubble.
She started to cough as the settling dust filled her lungs. She
took stock of the situation. She was sore, but nothing new
was broken. Lying on her side, she found she was buried, but
not trapped, in the rubble.

She could feel that the giants had gone. In the ruins of
the house, Kai was buried to her left and just starting to stir.
Grul was on her right. The raven was alive, but barely. The
soldiers in the house were dead. Farther down the long corridor, Brundi was unconscious but very much alive. Mims
was conscious and starting to panic as she tore through the
remains of the house.

"Mom!" Mims cried again. "Where are you?"

"*Maya?*" Grul moaned.

"I'm here," she said urgently. "Just hold on. I'll get us free!"

Maya started to push back debris. A heavy ceiling beam was lying across her body, but the rubble beneath it kept its weight from crushing her. She'd been lucky. If it had hit her fully, she knew it would have broken her wings again, maybe even worse. With a bit more digging, she freed herself and then started to dig for Grul.

By the time she found him, Grul was in rough shape. His back was broken and a wing was bent at a terrible angle.

Maya's hands trembled as she freed him. "Is it very bad? Are you in much pain?"

"*I—I can't feel anything.*" The raven panicked. "*Maya, I can't move!*"

"Calm down, Grul. You're alive—that's all that matters to me."

Kai climbed from the debris beside her. His face and black hair were gray from building dust. "How is he?"

Maya fought to keep control. "His back is broken. He's paralyzed. But he's alive!"

"Mom!" Mims screeched as her panic intensified. "Maya! Kai! Where are you? I need your help!"

"*Go.*" Grul moaned. "*Leave me and help Sarah.*"

Maya refused to release Grul and carried him through to the back bedroom that housed Sarah and the baby. The strong sound of Michael's cries was a relief to her. At least he was alive. But as she stumbled through the remains of the doorway, she felt Sarah's life force fading.

"Maya, over here. Hurry!" Mims cried. "Please, we have to save her."

The house had been cast into darkness by the attack, but with her Valkyrie vision, Maya was able to pick her way through the bedroom. Mims had cleared most of the rubble away from her mother.

Sarah was lying on the floor beside the bed with Michael sheltered in her arms. It was obvious to see that Sarah had protected him from the collapse with her body.

"Mom, please . . . ," Mims cried.

Maya handed Grul to Kai and then lifted the baby away from Sarah. She placed Michael in Kai's other hand. "Get them both out of here and stay on the beach. If the giants come back, don't wait for us—just fly away. We'll be right out."

Mims was holding her mother's hand. "Maya, please, help her."

Kneeling beside her young cousin, Maya looked at Sarah. The damage to her human aunt was fatal. Nothing could save her now. Mims's growing Valkyrie senses already told her the truth, but she couldn't accept it.

"I'm so very sorry I can't save her. I just don't have that kind of power," Maya said.

Mims shook her head. "I can't lose her. Please . . ."

Maya sighed sadly. "You know there's only one thing I can do, and that's to end her pain."

"She's going to die?" Mims sniffed.

Maya nodded. Her aunt had been struck by the giant's fist. That she managed to save her baby was proof of her love. It tore at Maya to have to tell Mims the truth. "Her time has come. It's too soon, but I can't change that."

"Will you reap her?" Mims choked through her tears. "Please, don't let her suffer."

Maya felt her own eyes welling up. Sarah was a good woman who didn't deserve this violent end. "She named you, so you've already given her your name. We'll reap her together, you and me, so you can always be together." She took Mims's hand and spoke the words she'd said so many times before. But this time, their meaning had never meant more.

"Sarah Angelo, your time has come. Let us end your suffering."

Together they reached up and gently caressed Sarah's forehead. Maya made certain her little finger grazed along the dying woman's skin. Her throat constricted as she said, "Come, join us now. . . ."

"Mom . . ." Mims wept as her mother took her final, unsteady breath.

Soon her spirit rose and looked around in wonder. She glanced down at her body and then frowned at the gold-and-black Valkyrie symbol blazoned on the back of her hand. "Am I dead?"

Maya nodded. "I'm sorry, Sarah. It was the giants."

"What happens now?" she asked in confusion. "I don't want to leave you."

"You won't," Maya said gently. "That symbol on your hand means you belong with the Valkyrie Myriam-Elizabet. Mims reaped you, so you will stay with her."

"But the baby?" Sarah panicked.

"Michael is unharmed. You kept him safe. He's with Kai outside."

"Mom . . ." Mims threw her arms around her ghost mother and held her tight. "I'm so sorry I couldn't save you . . . ," she sobbed.

Sarah held her daughter the same way she had in life. "It's all right, sweetheart. The worst is over and they can't hurt me anymore." She looked at Maya and nodded. "Thank you. Now I can stay with my family."

"Sarah . . . ?"

Brundi climbed unsteadily into the bedroom. There was a large cut on her forehead and she was moving stiffly, but she wasn't seriously injured. When she saw Mims and Sarah, her head dropped. "I'm so sorry, child."

"Don't be," Sarah said gently. "When I was alive, I was a liability to you. Now I might have more strength to join in the fight against the giants."

Leaving the wreck of the house behind them, they walked down to the beach and joined Kai with the baby and Grul. Maya took her raven back and cradled him gently. "You'll fly again, my sweet Grul. I promise you will."

The sun was just coming up to reveal the full damage done to the house. Beyond it lay a trail of complete destruction as the two giants made their way inland. Seeing the devastation wrought by the giants, Maya was surprised that any of them had survived.

Her senses told her that they were alone. The million-dollar beach homes surrounding them had been abandoned as their inhabitants had fled the moment the giants arrived. A soft, sweet ocean breeze was coming off the calm water. At any other time, it would have been beautiful. But now it only reflected the desolation of the area and the eerie silence around them.

Maya looked back out over the ocean with an uneasy feeling. "More giants are coming—we must leave here now."

Brundi nodded. "And I want to call Vonni to tell him what's happened."

Sarah shook her head. "Please don't. It will only distract him. I'm fine. The baby and Mims are fine. He's needed where he is."

"But he should be told what happened to you."

"He'll find out soon enough," Sarah said. "Earth needs him now. We can't ask him to come back when there's nothing he can do for me."

Kai stepped forward. "She's right. Our first priority is getting away from here." He looked at Maya. "Are you strong enough to fly?"

Maya opened her wings and gave them a full workout. She nodded. "They'll work. Just as soon as I get all these bandages off them, we'll go."

With Mims to help her, Maya's wings were soon freed from the bandages. She took a quick test flight along the beach and came right back. Landing with the others, she nodded. "All set. Let's go."

17

turned away from the terrible sight of Loki going down. For all the trouble he had caused her, all his sarcastic barbs, he had become a big part of her life, and she realized she would miss him.

"Come on, Gee," Archie called from Skye's arms. "You can't help him now. None of us can. But he's given us the chance to get away. We can't waste it."

Archie was right, but it was still hard to leave Loki behind. Freya maneuvered in the sky and hung poised, ready to fly away. Now that she'd experienced fighting the giants, she was able to come up with a strategy. "Remember, the giants can't move very quickly, and they aren't agile. Keep low and fly no higher than their knees. We're too small and fast for them to hit us. Follow me!"

Freya led her small group of fighters away from the city and continued to fly south. Along the way they saw a straight, wide path of destruction. East Coast cities that had stood for hundreds of years were burning ruins as the giants followed a course leading from the Florida Everglades up to northern Canada.

In the sky above them, military fighters took on the giants, but their struggle was in vain. Rockets couldn't wound or even slow their progress, and on the ground, large military tanks lay quashed by giant feet. Humanity could do nothing to stop the invaders.

Occasionally they saw evidence of a small victory as they encountered a dead giant. It seemed that when a fire giant died, its flames were extinguished. In death they looked just like frost giants. Freya and the others knew that the immortal giants would rise again, but they didn't know how long this process would take. Hopefully, the war would end before then.

As they flew over the ruins of Boston, they spied several giant corpses whose wounds gave Freya hope. She called the others to land and flew up to the head of one of the dead giants.

"Look." She pointed at the wounds. "There is only one thing in all the realms that could do that kind of damage to a frost giant."

Archie came up beside her and peered at the wound. "Could it be?"

"What?" Quinn asked. "What killed him?"

"Thor," Freya and Archie said as one.

Archie continued. "Only his hammer could make this kind of dent in a giant's head. Thor's fighting them here on Earth. The military must've let him go."

"Or he escaped when the giants arrived," Freya said. "Either way, he's free and fighting. Maybe my family is free as well." She looked around, hoping they might still be in the area.

"I wonder where they are," Archie mused.

"I can feel Kai. He's alive, and not very far from here." She closed her eyes. "But something is wrong."

"Of course something's wrong," Archie said. "There are giants on Earth!"

Freya shook her head. "No, it's more than that. . . ."

"I am sorry, Freya, but whatever you're feeling means nothing right now," Quinn said. "We must get moving if we are to stop this war."

"I know," she reluctantly agreed. "I just wish I could let my family know what's happening."

"They could be anywhere," Orus said. *"Quinn's right; we don't have time to look."*

A furious roaring of giants sounded behind them, followed by explosions and gunfire. The battle was starting again as the next wave of giants descended upon the area.

"Hey, you kids, get out of there!"

Battle-weary soldiers ran at them but slowed when they saw the wings on Freya and the Vanir. They raised their weapons and their leader came forward.

"Who're you fighting for?" he demanded.

"We fight for you," Freya said carefully. She could feel their despair. They were fighting a losing battle. She tried to sound reassuring as she extended her wings. "We are with Thor and the Asgardians. You might know of my mother and sisters, who also have feathered wings. We all serve Odin and are on the side of peace."

The soldiers lowered their weapons. "I'm sorry, miss. I'm Sergeant John Romin," the soldier said. "These days I can't tell the good guys from the bad." He looked back at his men. "They're on our side." As an afterthought, he warned them, "But don't any of you touch them. This young lady is lethal."

"So you know my mother and sisters?" Freya asked hopefully. "Have you seen them?"

"Not personally," Sergeant Romin said. "But we've all heard of what happens to those who touch Valkyries. We've been ordered not to fire on anybody with wings until we know who they're fighting for."

"How long have the giants been here?" Archie asked.

Freya shook her head. "Archie, you're a ghost—he can't see or hear you." While Archie cursed, she repeated the question to the sergeant.

"A couple of weeks," he said. "They're appearing all over the world. Here in the United States, they're crawling out of a big hole in Florida, and we've just heard reports of more coming out of the Pacific Ocean."

"And they're heading to a tunnel in northern Canada," Freya finished.

"That's right," the sergeant agreed. "But nothing we try seems to stop them. So far the only thing that has been able to kill them is your people."

"But it's not enough." Freya called Quinn and Skye forward. "Sergeant, I need you and your men to find Thor or my mother, the head Valkyrie, and get a message to them—"

"Look, miss, I'm grateful for what your people are doing, but we've got a war to fight. We ain't a courier service."

"If you don't pass along this message, the war is over and the giants have already won. This information is crucial to the survival of Earth."

The soldier hesitated for a moment and then nodded. He pulled out his mobile phone, dialed a number, and then handed the phone to Freya, careful not to touch her. "It's the command center—give them your message."

"Hello?" a voice called over the phone.

"Hello, I'm the black-winged Valkyrie your people saw in Chicago some time ago," Freya explained. "It is imperative that this message reaches my mother, the lead

Valkyrie, and Thor, leader of the Asgard forces and his Dark Searchers."

"Hold a moment, please. . . ."

A couple of minutes later, another voice started to speak. "I am General Pickers, central commander of the International Coalition of Defense Forces for the United States. Who am I speaking with?"

"I'm Greta, the black-winged Valkyrie that caused a lot of trouble in Chicago," Freya said.

"I remember reading the reports about you," the general said. "And I've seen more than a few photos of you in action. You caused quite a stir back then."

"But that's nothing compared to what the frost and fire giants are doing to Earth right now."

"True," the general agreed. "What can I do for you?"

"It is critical that you get a message to Thor and his people. This information could change the outcome of the war in the realms."

Not being face-to face with the man meant Freya couldn't read him fully. But her senses were acute enough to hear his breathing change. "You know what I'm talking about, don't you?" she asked.

"Ragnarök," the general breathed.

"Yes," Freya agreed. "Now, please, listen to me. Thor and my mother must hear this. It's desperately important information."

The tone of his voice changed again. "Greta, I'm recording this conversation right now. Tell me what you want them to hear. . . ."

"Mother, Thor, it's me, Greta," Freya started. "I'm sorry I disappeared from the farm, but I've been with Loki. He was on our side all along—though I just watched him fall in battle in Montreal." Freya's voice caught for a moment as she recalled the sight of Loki being overwhelmed by the giants. "Loki took us to Vanaheim to ask the Vanir to help us defeat the giants. While we were there, we found out Dirian and his men attacked the Norns at the base of Yggdrasil. Urd and Verdandi escaped, but he's taken Skuld to Muspelheim and is using her to end the destinies of those who oppose him.

"There is only one thing we can do to stop this war. We're going to Muspelheim to try to free Skuld. Once she is safe, we hope the fallen immortals will rise. Or, at least, we hope that those who fall after she is free will be able to rise. Then we will go to the giant kings. I'm with two Vanir warriors. They'll use their magic to get the giants to turn on each other again."

Freya paused, knowing the reaction that this news would bring to her family. "Mother, we know the danger we're facing, and it's likely we'll die and perhaps stay dead in the attempt. But it's the only way to save the realms. Urd and Verdandi agree with us. Skuld is the key to ending the war. If we fail and are killed, you must follow us to Muspelheim and free her. As long as Skuld is a prisoner of

Dirian, none of us are safe and all the realms will fall.

"We're leaving now, and must travel down to the Andes. There's a hidden, direct tunnel to Muspelheim. It's in the ancient city of Machu Picchu. When we find the entrance, I'll mark it with my crest, so you'll be able to follow us.

"Thor, please forgive us for doing this without you. But you are so desperately needed here on Earth. We've seen the damage the giants are doing. Midgard needs you, just like Skuld needs us."

Freya took a deep breath and looked at her companions. "Have I forgotten anything?"

Quinn shook his head. "No. That's everything."

Freya focused on the phone again. "That's all. Thank you, General. Please ensure that the message reaches Thor and my family as soon as possible."

Just as she was about to hand back the phone to the sergeant, she heard the general call, "Greta, wait."

"Yes?"

"I will ensure your family hears this message. You have my word," he said. "And I want to thank you on behalf of the people of Earth for your efforts. But please, let us help. There's nothing our Earth forces can do to stop the giants; we know that. Nuclear weapons have been discussed, but we've been told by Colonel Giovanni Angelo and Thor himself about Yggdrasil and that the tunnels are the roots of the Great Tree and that to kill the roots is to kill the tree and end all of us.

"It's still so hard for us to accept, but considering what we've seen, I must believe in the existence of the Cosmic World Tree and the damage nuclear weapons pose to it. So we will do what little we can to support the Asgard fighters." He paused for a moment and then said, "And you."

"I don't understand," Freya said.

"I'm asking you to let us help you," he continued. "You are in the Boston area, and it's a very long way to Peru. Let us take you there in military transport. If you are going to fight for us, I don't want you exhausted from flying thousands of miles before you engage the enemy. I can make all the arrangements now. We can have you in the air in half an hour. Will you let us do this for you?"

Freya's initial instinct was not to trust humans. But this time was different. They were united in war. She told Archie what the general had said. "Do you think we should trust him?"

"Are you serious?" Archie cried. "Of course you should trust him! This could save us a lot of time!"

"*Do it, Freya,*" Orus cawed. "*I know it goes against everything you believe, but this time, we must trust them.*"

Freya said into the phone, "Thank you, General. We would all be grateful for the ride."

Six hours later they stood at the back of a large military transport airplane, escorted by multiple fighter jets. Freya had been on an airplane only once before and it had terrified her then. This was worse.

The aircraft was larger than the one her uncle Vonni had flown, but it was bumpier and much noisier. They were surrounded by soldiers who looked at them with a mix of fear and awe.

Little could be said on the flight as it was too loud to be heard above the noise of the plane. But as she stood holding on to cargo netting for balance, she watched her new friends' faces. Quinn was taking it all in his stride and wasn't bothered by the sights and sounds around him. Skye was more anxious but just as determined.

"How much farther?" Freya called to one of the soldiers escorting them to Peru. They had been flying all night and the sun was already up.

"Just over an hour," answered a female soldier with her dark hair tied back in a neat ponytail. Even though she looked to be only in her early twenties, Freya sensed she had seen more than her fair share of battle. "We're taking a bit longer to stay on a route that's giant-free, so we don't encounter any trouble."

The hour dragged and the tension grew. It was one thing to plan to go to Muspelheim; it was another to actually get there. What horrors lay ahead in the land of the fire giants? Yes, she had her silver breastplate and armor for protection, but Quinn and Skye were exposed. She'd heard that Muspelheim was hot. But just *how* hot was hot?

Finally they felt the tilt of the airplane, signaling their descent.

"Greta, we're approaching the jump point," the female soldier called to her.

"Thank you, Corporal . . . ?" Freya noted the corporal's name wasn't on her uniform.

"Corporal Biederon." She smiled, but her expression held the same anxiousness Freya felt. "But you can just call me Tina."

"Thanks, Tina."

They heard the large airship groan as the rear cargo doors opened and a long, wide ramp slid out into the open air. Morning sunlight blazed into the darkened hull, and all the soldiers around them rose to their feet and prepared to jump out of the airplane.

Freya had argued that she and her team should travel alone. But the general had insisted on a protective escort to see them safely to Machu Picchu. He reasoned that their mission was far too important to risk locals attacking the winged visitors.

Sergeant Romin had requested that he and his soldiers be the ones to escort Freya. Permission had been granted, and as they prepared to jump from the transport ship, the sergeant leaned closer to her. "Greta, let me and my people jump first and then you and your team can follow us. I'm sure, with your wings, you could land before us. But please don't. Stay with us and land when we do. We know this area is seeing a lot of activity from frightened people escaping the giants and coming here to pray. There may be trouble when they see you."

Freya nodded and watched the soldiers check their parachutes a final time. When they got the green light, one by one they ran down the ramp of the open cargo doors and jumped into the blazing blue sky. The sight of the parachutes opening reminded Freya of the wild mushrooms that popped up in the Asgard forests. When the last soldier had jumped, Freya nodded to her team. "Ready?"

Skye caught hold of Archie again, and Orus launched off Freya's shoulder and was the first out of the cargo exit.

"Let's go!" Freya said. She ran after Orus and, keeping her wings closed tightly, dived off the ramp and into the sky. Turning around in midair, she watched Quinn and Skye follow behind her.

When she turned to see where they were going, Freya was struck by the sight. Machu Picchu was a magnificent stone city at the top of one of the mountains. As with most ruins, the roofs were missing, but the walls and structure of the ancient homes, temples, and meeting places were still intact.

Tiers had been cut into the side of the mountain, which

held all of Machu Picchu stable and kept landslides at bay. Freya wished she'd been old enough to see it when it was still a thriving city.

Halfway down to the ground, Freya opened her wings and started to glide. High in the Andes, they were surrounded by tall mountains covered in tropical and subtropical vegetation, with two distinct peaks directly beside the ancient ruins. The sights were stunning as they dropped down into the lush green area.

Freya maneuvered closer to the parachuting soldiers and stayed with them as they headed toward their destination on the open, grass-covered Central Plaza of the old city. As she glided past the soldiers, they waved at her and gave the thumbs-up signal.

"Who'd have ever believed this?" Orus cawed as he stayed close to Freya. *"For years we've remained invisible to human soldiers. Now we're actually flying with them and they're here to protect us."*

"I guess war does change the rules," Freya admitted. When they approached the plaza, she understood what the soldiers were concerned about. There were hundreds of people gathered in the area. Their feelings of fear confirmed to Freya that they weren't tourists visiting old ruins. These were desperate people looking for any kind of protection from the invaders.

"Greta," the sergeant shouted. "Keep your team in the

air until we secure the area and make it safe for you to land."

Freya acknowledged the message and flapped her wings to climb higher in the sky. With Quinn and Skye close beside her, they heard the crowds shouting and saw their fists waving in the air at the sight of the winged visitors. These people didn't see her as a black-winged angel, as so many in the past had. To them, Freya and her friends were part of the invasion.

"This isn't good," Orus cawed. *"They'll tear us apart if they get the chance."*

"We won't give them the chance," Freya said.

When the soldiers touched down, the crowds rushed forward, and the soldiers were forced to fire their weapons in the air to drive them back. But with tensions running so high, it wouldn't take much to turn the situation into a violent riot.

"Quinn, Skye, follow me," Freya called. She descended and landed on the tallest stone structure above the flat plaza. "Keep your wings open and get ready to fly if they try to climb up after us."

Freya stood at the edge of the stone structure and looked out at the people rushing at the soldiers. She took a deep breath and released the loudest Valkyrie howl she could manage.

Civilians and soldiers alike covered their ears and tried to escape the harsh sound. But they couldn't—the howl of a

Valkyrie could be heard for miles, and it echoed through all the Andes Mountains.

"Hear me!" Freya called, using the special Valkyrie power that allowed her to be understood by anyone, no matter what language they spoke.

The gathered masses shook their heads and tried to clear their ears.

"We are here to defend Earth, not conquer it," she started. "You need only look at the soldiers with us to see the truth. We are on a special mission. If we succeed, the giants will leave Earth. I am from Asgard, and my companions are from Vanaheim. Our realms are in as much danger as yours. We, like you, are fighting the giants, and our worlds, like yours, will fall if we fail."

Freya's senses told her that the people were listening. Many still had doubts, but at least their hostility was fading. "We know a way to defeat the giants and we know that there is a special place we can go to stop them. The tunnel to that place lies here, buried deep below the ground of Machu Picchu."

Confusion rose in the crowds. An older man came forward and shouted in Spanish, "How can we trust you? It's demons like you that are destroying our world."

"We are not demons," Freya called. "And we are united with you in our struggle against the giants! Please, will you help us find the tunnel that will lead us to the realm of the fire giants? It is there that we will stop them."

"Freya," Orus cawed. "You can't promise that when it's likely we'll fail."

"If we fail, it kinda won't matter what Gee promises," Archie said. "Earth will be toast anyway."

"Look at them," Freya said. "They're terrified and helpless to stop the giants. Let me give them a little hope, if only for a while." She turned back to the crowds. "To help us is to help yourselves. It's the one thing you can do against the giants."

That struck a chord with the people. They nodded, and their posture changed.

"Greta," the sergeant called. "Where do we go? Where is the tunnel?"

"Quinn, use the map. Where's the tunnel?"

Quinn pulled out Urd's map. It showed the details of Machu Picchu, including the two peaks behind them. Using them as the starting point, he looked at the map and then toward the stone structures. "It's down there, just past the Central Plaza, in a place called the Temple of the Sun."

Freya opened her wings and jumped off the structure. She landed among the soldiers. "We need to find the Temple of the Sun."

"Temple of the Sun?" a middle-aged woman asked nervously in perfect English with a strong Spanish accent. She was small and round and dressed in a colorful poncho and full skirt that was characteristic of the area. "It is down here, not far at all. I can show you."

The woman turned to the crowds and called out in Spanish. Freya understood she was telling everyone they needed to find the Temple of the Sun.

Soon the masses of crowds parted and formed a path. The soldiers completely surrounded Freya and the two Vanir to ensure that no one came within touching distance. After a short walk, the woman stopped and pointed to a cluster of walled-off ruined structures. "It is that one," she said.

"Gee, look, it's the only place here with a round tower."

Archie was right. While the other structures were square, angular buildings, the Temple of the Sun was a perfect semicircular structure built into the surrounding rock to match the natural environment.

"How do we get into the tunnel?" the sergeant asked Freya.

Freya shrugged. "I don't know. But if the Incas knew that this was the tunnel to Muspelheim and knew what would happen to anyone who ventured there, it's likely they would have blocked it off completely."

"There is a large sacrificial stone inside," the woman said. "It is in here that the priests performed the sacrifices to the gods for a prosperous harvest and to gain insight into the future. No one was allowed inside but them."

Freya turned to the woman. "How do you know so much?"

"I am a tour guide here. Or at least I was until the giants

came. Now we all come here seeking protection from the Ancient Ones." She looked at Freya and the Vanir and bowed her head. "Ancient gods like you."

"We aren't gods," Freya said. "We just come from another realm."

"Isn't that the same thing?" she asked.

"Not to me," Freya said. "Would you please take us in and show us the stone?"

The woman bowed again and led them into the maze of structures that surrounded the entrance to the temple. "It is this way."

They entered the temple and went into a small chamber with two large windows on opposite ends.

"Wow!" Archie cried as they went toward the area of sacrifice. "That's not a stone. It's the top of the mountain! How're we going to lift it?"

The altar stone was lying on the floor and took up most of the chamber. It was at least three yards long and two yards wide. To the casual viewer, it looked as though it was a natural stone that was part of the mountaintop and that the temple had been built around it. But as Freya bent down and inspected the stone more closely, she could see it had actually been placed there. Casting out her senses, she could feel a cavern beneath it. Grasping the corner of the massive stone, she started to lift.

The stone shifted a bit, but as she continued to strain, Freya realized that she couldn't lift it.

Panting, she stood up and looked at Quinn. "It's under here. I can feel it. But I'm not strong enough to lift it on my own."

"We can all help," the sergeant said. "Hook ropes on it and pull through that window."

Freya shook her head. "It will take more than all of us together to shift it."

"Gee, you're not giving up, are you?" Archie asked.

"No, but it's going to take more than strength to move it."

"Like what?" the sergeant asked.

Quinn and Skye were doing their own inspection. "Magic will shift it," Quinn informed them. "Whoever placed this here didn't want others moving it to access the tunnel."

"Maybe it was to stop the giants from coming up," the sergeant offered. "There haven't been any sightings of them here in Peru."

Freya shook her head. "Believe me, if they wanted to come through here, that rock wouldn't stop them. No, they either don't know about it or, more likely, they can't fit through the tunnel and had to take another route."

"But we'll fit through it," Quinn said. He looked at the sergeant. "Would you take your people out of here and move the crowds back? We don't want anyone hurt."

The sergeant nodded and ordered most of his soldiers out of the temple. A few minutes later, one called through the window, "All clear out here, sir!"

"All right," he said. "It's up to you now."

Freya stepped up to Quinn and Skye. "Please tell me you have enough power left to do this."

"I hope so," Quinn said. He took Skye's hand and then looked at Freya. "Give me your hand as well. Let's see if that Aesir blood of yours holds any power."

Freya took Quinn's hand and stood facing the ancient stone. As the two Vanir started to cast a spell, she felt a strange tickling sensation go through her.

Her mind burst with wild, vivid colors, and she could feel a power older than time itself. It was a natural power that came from all around them—from the earth below their feet, the blue sky above them, from the trees in the mountains surrounding them, from the animals and all the people anxiously waiting outside the temple. Finally she felt the presence of the Great Cosmic Tree itself.

As the moments ticked by, the Vanir's spell grew louder and more intense. Because it was spoken in an ancient tongue, Freya couldn't understand the words, but she could see the result. The stone that had lain undisturbed for millennia started to tremble. Dust rose from the dry ground, and a rumbling arose from deep inside the earth. Soon the massive stone started to lift.

Freya stole a look at Quinn and saw his eyes were closed in deep concentration. Skye's were the same. The stone was moving slowly, as though it were on a hinge. The back edge was staying put, but the front was lifting like a trapdoor. Higher and higher it climbed until the bottom of the stone finally lifted out of the pit, revealing the narrow tunnel beneath it.

A whoosh of stale, hot air blasted Freya's and the Vanir's hair back. It smelled of sulfur and earth.

When the stone was secured, standing on its long edge, Quinn and Skye opened their eyes. Their faces were covered in a thin film of sweat from the effort.

"Awesome . . . !" Archie breathed.

The soldiers beside them were speechless. They stared at the massive stone and then back to the two Vanir who had moved it with only the power of thought. The sergeant came forward and touched the edge of the stone to ensure it was secure. It wouldn't move.

He looked back at Freya and the Vanir. "Remind me never to annoy you kids."

"It wasn't me," Freya said. "It was them."

"It was all of us," Skye said. "We can manipulate the energy of life. Without it, we have no magic." She turned to Freya. "I never knew Valkyries had so much power in them."

"Me? Really?" Freya said. "All I have are strong senses."

Quinn shook his head. "No. You have much more than that. But it's wild and untrained. With a little practice you could be as powerful as the Vanir."

"Cool!" Archie cried. "Gee, you gotta learn to do that!"

"*We've got to survive this war first,*" Orus cawed.

"And to do that, we have to go down there." Freya pointed into the dark tunnel.

The sergeant nodded. "I'll gather my soldiers together. We'll leave as soon as you're ready."

"Wait," Freya said. "You're not coming with us."

"Yes, we are," the sergeant said. "We're your escort. We've signed on to support your mission, and we're going to follow that through."

Freya shook her head. "You can't. Earth is the only realm that can support human life. I assure you, you'll die if you try to follow us."

The soldier looked doubtful. "We have our orders. We'll take you as far as we can, and then if we see signs of trouble, we'll stop."

Freya could tell there would be no arguing with him. He was a dedicated soldier, trained to follow orders. "I won't stop you from following us, but this is foolish."

"Let me be the judge of that," the sergeant said.

While the sergeant pulled his team together, Freya walked out of the stone temple and drew her flame sword. Having been crafted by the power of the dwarfs, nothing could hurt or dull the enchanted gold blade. She used the tip to carve her ornate Valkyrie mark on the wall. If her mother or the others tried to follow, they would know where to start.

When it was time to enter the tunnel, Freya led the way,

with Archie, Quinn, and Skye close behind. The eight soldiers followed at the rear. As they descended deeper, the soldiers turned on their flashlights.

Tina gasped as she touched the wall. "Sir, feel this—it's warm."

The sergeant touched the wall with his bare hand. "It feels organic, not like rock."

Freya looked back at them. "It is. We told you, we are following one of the roots of Yggdrasil. That wall is a living root."

"That tree you keep talking about is actually real?" the sergeant asked.

Freya nodded. "Of course it's real. Yggdrasil connects all the realms. Without it, we'll all die. So it must be protected."

Awe rose from all the soldiers as they each took turns touching the root of Yggdrasil.

Archie burst into laughter. "Look at their faces—that's priceless! Maybe we should tell them that Santa Claus is real too. I bet they'd believe us!"

Freya grinned and whispered to him, "Be nice. Remember, your expression was exactly the same the first time you saw me."

Orus was on Freya's shoulder, watching the soldiers with concern. *"I don't know if it's a good thing that humans learn that the realms and Yggdrasil are real. It could make things difficult for us."*

"How?" Freya asked. "They can't live outside Midgard, so visiting or even making war on the other realms is impossible."

"*I've seen human determination,*" Orus said. "*They'll find a way eventually.*"

"And we'll be ready for them if they do," Freya finished.

After two days and nights in the dark, narrow tunnel, the temperature increased and the soldiers started to suffer the first signs of realm-change difficulties. Progress slowed, and Freya was feeling the pressure to keep moving without them. But at the same time, she knew she couldn't leave them behind.

As they stopped for a break, Sergeant Romin couldn't catch his breath. He was in his fifties and feeling the pressure more than the younger soldiers. Freya sensed his heart was beating too fast, struggling to pump his thickening blood around his body. It would soon become dangerous for him.

"Now do you believe us?" she asked the panting sergeant. "By tomorrow we'll be out of the influence of Midgard completely and heading toward Muspelheim. You must believe me when I say it will kill you. Look at your people. You're all sick. If you go much farther, I promise you you'll die."

The sergeant lifted his head and frowned, not at Freya but at Archie, standing beside her. He squinted and then jumped. "There's someone beside you!"

Freya nodded. "This is my friend Archie. He's been with us all along."

"I don't understand," the sergeant said. "How? I haven't seen him."

"That's because, technically speaking, I'm dead," Archie explained. "On Earth, I'm a ghost, which is why you couldn't see me. But as I pass into the other realms, I regain my physical presence. Now that we're in an area of transition between realms, I'm becoming solid just as you're getting weaker."

"You're—you're really a ghost?" the sergeant asked.

Freya nodded. "I reaped Archie when he was critically wounded in Chicago. This is what I've been trying to tell you. Midgard is unique. Only in death can humans visit the other realms—otherwise, the journey to the realms kills them."

"So you've gotta go back," Archie insisted. "Look at you. It'll only get worse if you stay."

"But our orders . . ." The sergeant panted.

"Your orders weren't to die," Freya insisted. "Your commanders wouldn't expect you to go to the bottom of the ocean without proper protection. This is the same thing. Living humans can't survive this environment."

The sergeant struggled to his feet. Like all the other soldiers, he was ghostly pale and could barely breathe. His lips and fingertips were turning blue. "So," he gasped, "if you touched me, you would reap me, and I could continue this mission."

Freya nodded. "Theoretically, yes, but I wouldn't touch you because it would kill you. So you must all go back."

Before Freya could stop him, the sergeant grasped her bare hand. She shouted in protest, but it was too late. In an instant, and completely against her will, Freya's Valkyrie powers reaped him.

"No!" she cried as she watched his body fall to the ground, dead.

18

"WE NEED TO GET TO SAFETY!" MAYA CALLED TO KAI AS they headed east in the sky. Between them they were carrying Brundi, Mims, Sarah, and the baby. They followed the trail the giants had made and saw that they were moving north, heading toward the tunnel to Asgard in northern Canada.

Maya changed direction and led them south toward Colorado Springs, in the direction of the Cheyenne Mountain Air Force Station. It was one of the most secure places in the country and central command for all the defending military forces. They had originally declined its sanctuary and chosen the California safe house instead. But now Maya and Kai agreed it was the safest place for Brundi, Mims, and the baby.

They flew down toward a large circular tunnel entrance

where a carved sign read, CHEYENNE MOUNTAIN COMPLEX. They soared over the security gates and past the armed soldiers posted there. There was furious activity below as the various military forces arrived and left in response to the giants.

They touched down a few yards from the entrance and were immediately surrounded by armed guards in camouflage uniforms. A captain ordered the others to stand down and rushed forward toward Kai, but when his eyes landed on Maya, he headed straight to her as if she had some magnetic pull over him.

"I'm Captain Miller. Are you the Valkyrie I've heard of . . ."

"You can call me Mia," Maya said, being careful not to give him her real name.

The captain frowned. "I was told your wings were broken and that you were grounded."

"They've healed," she said. "We were at the safe house in California, but the giants destroyed it. I'm sorry, but the soldiers with us were killed, and my raven has been gravely wounded."

"I heard about that," he reported. "More giants have appeared on the coast, and California has fallen to them. Like all the others, these giants are moving north."

Kai stepped forward, thrusting his chest out and confronting the soldier. "Captain, we have brought our family to you. You will protect them with your life, or you will answer to me."

Maya realized Kai had no experience with talking to humans and still had a lot to learn. "Please excuse my brother's manners. What he means is that we hope you can offer sanctuary to this baby and these two wingless Valkyries. And I would be in your debt if you would have your medical people help my Grul. He is very precious to me."

"Of course," Captain Miller said. "You're all welcome here. We've been authorized to offer sanctuary to all Asgardians"— he smiled radiantly at Maya—"including their ravens."

Kai shook his head. "Mia and I aren't staying."

Brundi choked, "Of—of course you're staying! You're both too young to be going off and fighting giants."

Kai shook his head. "We're not going to fight the giants. I can feel Greta. She's back in Midgard and needs our help."

"Where is she?" Maya asked.

Kai shrugged. "I don't know Midgard well enough to tell you. Only that I will be able to track her through our link."

"Greta and her team are in Peru," the captain offered.

"What?" Maya cried. "What's she doing down there? And what team?"

Captain Miller called for a jeep to transport them into the tunnel. "We received a message from Greta explaining everything. Let's get inside and you can hear it."

They drove deep inside the busy mountain facility. Everyone they encountered, be they from the air force, army, or foreign services, all reacted in the same way to the winged visitors. They nodded in respect and, in a few cases, even saluted.

Maya acknowledged them with a nod. She could feel from them the hope the Asgardians offered. She just prayed they could live up to the expectations of humanity.

They took an elevator down two thousand feet below the surface. When they emerged, they were escorted to the command center. The room was cavernous, with an incredibly tall ceiling, and filled with large wall screens showing different locations where the giants were marching through the world. Seeing the devastation playing out on the large screens stole Maya's breath away. Cities were being decimated by the storming frost and fire giants.

Other screens revealed military jets and helicopters trying to engage the giants, but their rockets were useless against them.

"We can't stop them," the captain admitted sadly. "Nothing we've tried works. Thor and Balder have been the most effective against them, and then the Dark Searchers and Valkyries, when they fight together. All we can do is offer support."

Everyone stood in silence, watching the screens until a senior officer arrived. They were introduced to General Pickers, the central commander of the International Coalition of Defense Forces for the United States. He was the one who had spoken personally to Freya and recorded the message. He held up his phone for everyone to hear.

Maya heard her sister's voice and the desperation it held. Freya had been to Vanaheim and had engaged two of the Vanir in their mission. The greatest shock was hearing that Dirian had taken Skuld. Suddenly the war made sense. With Skuld under his control, no one stood a chance against him.

"Muspelheim!" Brundi cried when the message finished. "That's insanity! She'll be killed!"

"They all will," Maya agreed. "I swear that sister of mine is going to be the death of me. General, have you heard anything from Montreal? Is Loki really dead?"

"We don't know for sure," he admitted. "By the end it was hard to tell him apart from the others. I do know the city is in ruins and the giants are still flooding through there, so I fear it may be true that he was killed in the fight."

"Greta is too young to be going to Muspelheim on her own," Brundi insisted. "She has no idea what kind of realm she's heading to. It will be a disaster."

General Pickers nodded. "Perhaps, but she's our best and only hope against the invaders. The transport dropped them off over Machu Picchu earlier today, and they've entered the tunnel to Muspelheim. There is a team of eight soldiers with them, and others are keeping the area secure. We're just awaiting word."

"We're not going to wait," Maya said. She focused on Kai. "If Greta has gone to Muspelheim to free Skuld, then that's where we're going to help her."

The general nodded. "I'd hoped you'd say that. There's another air transport fueling up right now to take you there. Your team will be ready to leave with you shortly."

"Thank you, General," Maya said formally. She turned to Mims and gently handed over Grul. "Would you take care of him for me and see that he gets lots of special love and care?"

Mims nodded. "I will. I promise."

To her grandmother Maya said, "I've never been to Muspelheim before—what can we expect?"

Brundi was wringing her hands. "You're not just going to another realm. Child, you're going to hell."

19

DEEP IN THE TUNNEL TO MUSPELHEIM, THE SERGEANT'S spirit stood beside Freya, looking curiously down at his body. "Wow, that was intense . . . ," he muttered.

The others around him climbed to their feet. "John!" Tina cried.

Freya turned on the sergeant's ghost. "You foolish man— why did you do that? You knew what would happen if you touched me!"

Sergeant Romin looked around in wonder, and then back to her. "I did it to serve my country and my world. I've been in the military for more than twenty years and I'm an experienced soldier. I have skills you need, but I'm no good to you alive. This way we stand a chance of defending Earth against the giants."

"But it's suicide!" Archie cried. "You just killed yourself."

The sergeant shook his head. "No, not suicide. I just changed my skill set for the benefit of the mission."

"Don't you understand? You're dead!" Freya cried. "There is no going home. If we survive this mission and stop the war, there's no getting your life back. It's over! You will either ascend to heaven or stay in Asgard. But you'll never know the love of your family again."

"It's because I love my family that I did this," he insisted. He turned to the other soldiers. "I won't ask you to do the same. But if any of you want to join us, you must touch this Valkyrie."

"No!" Freya shouted as she jumped back. "No one's going to touch me, do you understand? This isn't a game. It's life and death."

"Yes," another soldier said as he stepped forward. "The life and death of Earth. I don't have any family back home, but I love my world and I'm prepared to die for it. Each of us knows the sacrifice we might be called to make. I am prepared to make it right now for this mission."

Freya was struck silent as two more soldiers approached her. "And me," they each volunteered. "You shouldn't have to face those giants alone. Not when we can help."

"This is insane," Freya cried. "You can't all want to die!"

"None of us *wants* to die," Tina said. "But if that's what it takes to defend Earth, we will."

"Greta, listen to me," the sergeant said. "We're grateful for what you're planning to do. You, Quinn, and Skye have amazing powers. But we have skills too. This is too important a mission to risk on just the three of you."

"Four," Archie added. "Don't forget me."

The sergeant nodded. "All right, four of you. Believe me, you need us—you just can't see it. You think because we're human we're weak. But we're not."

Freya shook her head. "I have never considered humans weak—ever! If you really understood what I am, you'd know that Valkyries bring only the bravest fighters of Earth's battle-fields to Asgard to serve in Odin's army. Right now it's dead human warriors who will be taking on the giants when they invade Asgard. So don't think any of us ever thought of you as weak or undeserving of a place in our realm."

"So what's the problem?" another soldier said. "You know we're brave and strong, and like it or not, we're a team. And to stay a team, you've gotta reap us."

Freya's head was spinning. In all her life she'd never encountered a group of warriors *wanting* to be reaped. It went against everything she believed about humans. She looked up at Orus on her shoulder. "What should I do?"

"What does your heart tell you?"

Freya whispered, "That I should do it. But what if I'm wrong?"

"You're not," Archie offered. "We do need their help."

Quinn and Skye both nodded in agreement. Freya looked back at the soldiers. They were standing before her, looking a little frightened by their decision but determined. If she reaped them, there would be no going back—but they could help their mission. If she didn't, they faced a dark future in a world devastated by giants.

"This goes against all the rules," she started. "But the realms have never faced such danger before. Still, it must be an individual decision. No one must feel pressured into joining us. So be warned, I have senses to read people. If you come to me to be reaped and don't really want to, I'll know and will send you away. So think hard. Those who wish to continue on this mission, step forward and I will reap you. Those who wish to serve their world by returning and report- ing what has happened, stay back."

Of the eight soldiers, five were reaped. Their bodies were neatly lined up, sitting against the wall, looking more asleep than dead. The remaining three soldiers returned to the surface.

Freya, Quinn, and Skye had to carry the new ghosts' equipment until their physical presence formed as they passed from Midgard into Muspelheim.

Soon things returned to a strange kind of normal as the soldiers took back their packs and weapons and moved on as though nothing had happened. The only big change was that Freya told them her true name.

Eventually the stink of sulfur increased and Freya's senses

started to pick up on signs of life. "We're getting close," she warned. "I can sense it just ahead."

Quinn nodded and waved his hand in the air. The tunnel filled with light, and a banquet of food appeared before them. "Our powers are back to full strength too."

Knowing this could be their last meal for some time, they stopped for a break and to make their plans. The reaped soldiers were shocked to discover that they could not only eat, but could actually enjoy all the food of the Vanir.

Quinn pulled out the map Verdandi had given to him. He laid it down on the table. "All right, here is where Verdandi said we would emerge from the tunnel." He traced his finger along the map until it passed over a large desert. "And here is where they're holding Skuld."

"How far is that?" the sergeant asked.

"A good day's flight," Quinn responded.

The sergeant looked at Freya. "Now that we're—you know, dead—can we fly?"

Freya shook her head. "No, not unless you could fly when you were alive. Though when you're in Midgard, with no substance, you can learn to fly."

"I tried it," Archie said to the soldiers. "I managed to float for a couple of seconds, but then fell back down to the ground. I wouldn't recommend it."

"*That's because you keep thinking like a living human,*" Orus cawed. "*You're hopeless at letting go.*"

"That's easy for you to say," Archie said. "You've got wings. It's harder for me."

"Flying is hard for everyone until you know how to do it," Freya said. She looked at the map again. "If we stay on the ground, it is a good distance over terrain that may be too hot to walk on. But I should be able to carry at least three of you."

"I can carry two," Quinn offered.

A light blush came to Skye's face. "I'll carry Archie again. I—I mean I don't mind, and he's not too heavy for me."

Freya stole a look at Archie and saw the color rise in his face. He was looking at Skye and smiling. Freya gave him a nudge. "Archie, focus!"

"What?" he protested. "I was."

"Yeah, right, and I'm a golden eagle!" Orus teased.

"I've never been to Muspelheim," Freya said, drawing the conversation back to the matter at hand. She pointed at the mark on the map where Skuld was being held. "I don't know what we'll encounter or where this is. It could be some kind of keep, prison, or even like Valhalla. I just don't know."

Archie nodded. "There's only one way to find out what it's like. Go there."

The soldiers checked their weapons as they prepared for the final leg of the journey. The air became hotter and the wall of the tunnel, the root of Yggdrasil, grew thick bark that would occasionally shed away as it developed newer and thicker armor against the hostile environment.

"Now I know what a Thanksgiving turkey feels like," Archie complained as the tunnel started to climb. "I'm being roasted alive!"

"We all are," Freya agreed. She was keeping her wings open because it was too hot to keep them closed and pressed against her back.

"I didn't think we'd feel the heat," the sergeant said.

Freya stopped. "Maybe I should tell you this now. Yes, you are dead, and on Earth, you'd be nothing more than insubstantial ghosts. But here in this realm, you are very much alive. You have bodies and they will feel everything as before. That means you can be hurt. The only difference is, you will heal much quicker, and if you are killed, you will rise again."

"We're immortal?" Tina asked.

Freya nodded. "You are, unless Skuld has been ordered to end your destiny. Skuld holds the power over each of our futures. Which is why this mission is so important."

"Can she kill us?" the sergeant asked.

"No," Quinn answered. "She can't. But what she can do is cut the thread of your future. So if you're killed on this mission and she's cut your lifeline, you won't rise again. If she hasn't cut the line, you will. But you must be killed for any changes she has made to take effect."

The sergeant shook his head. "I don't think any of us realized just how important this is. Stopping the giants won't mean anything if this girl, Skuld, isn't safe."

"Exactly," Freya agreed.

The heat intensified, but so did the smell of fresher air. Before long they saw light filtering down through a narrow gap in the ceiling. The group stopped beneath the gap and looked up.

"Please don't tell me that's where we've got to go," Archie said.

Freya nodded. "That's the entrance to Muspelheim." She looked up at Orus on her shoulder. "Would you fly up there and tell us what you can see?"

The raven cawed and launched from her shoulder. They followed his progress through the narrow gap at the top. After a few minutes, Orus returned.

"You won't believe it!" he cawed excitedly. *"It's not all fire and dead, burnt things. It's beautiful up there. Hotter than I've ever felt before, but it looks just like Asgard. I couldn't see any giants."*

"If everyone is ready, Skye and I will get us up there." Quinn whispered a few words, and they lifted off the ground and floated toward the tunnel exit. As they got near the top, Quinn spoke again and they moved, single file, through the narrow gap.

They touched down on the ground between blades of

grass that rose higher than their shoulders. It was more like walking between trees than grass.

Archie shook his head. "Orus, you said it looked like Asgard. . . ."

"*It does,*" the raven said. "*Yes, the grass is much taller and everything is giant-sized, but it's very similar.*"

"I don't think so," Archie said as he stood amid blades of grass. "Since when does Asgard have red grass? And look at the trees—the leaves are orange." He looked around. "There's nothing green here at all. It's all shades of red, yellow, and orange."

"*It looks the same to me,*" Orus said.

"Then you're as blind as a bat."

"Orus doesn't see color the way we do," Freya explained. "To him this looks the same. To us it's very different. Lovely, but different."

Skye came forward. "I thought everything would be burning in Muspelheim. But it's normal. Just much bigger than I'm used to."

A scream rose from behind them, and they turned to see one of the soldiers standing beneath a fruit tree, bent over at the waist and clutching his hand. "It burns!" he cried.

Freya ran up to the young soldier. "What is it? What burns?"

He lifted his hand and opened his closed fist. The skin on his palm was red and blistering. "I just picked an apple from one of these low-hanging branches. But it was like touching a burning piece of charcoal!"

"That's not an apple," Freya warned. "This is Muspelheim, a giant realm. That's a small berry bush." She looked up at the tall bush and tentatively touched the skin of a berry with the tip of her finger. "Ouch!"

Her finger was blazing with heat.

The sergeant looked at her. "What in the world possessed you to try that? You saw what it did to Jimmy."

"I needed to see if it only affected humans," Freya said, sucking on the tip of her burnt finger. "Now we know it affects Asgardians, too." She looked at Quinn. "Be careful, but try touching something. We need to know if it hurts the Vanir as well."

Quinn raised his hand toward a piece of hanging fruit, and like the others, he was burned. Then he tried a massive leaf and suffered another burn.

Skye reached down and picked up a rock from the ground. She cried in pain and dropped it. "Even the rocks burn us. Be careful not to touch anything!"

The sergeant looked at the sole of his boot. "Uh-oh."

"What is it?" Freya asked.

"We're not feeling the heat yet, but look. Whatever's in this soil, it's starting to melt my boots."

Skye didn't hesitate. She called out a magic spell and lifted everyone off the ground—careful not to brush against the stalks of grass. "It was hurting my feet," she said. She showed them the light sandals she wore. They had been woven from Vanir plants. In the short time she'd been standing there, the soles of her sandals had burned away.

Freya looked around. "This is so bad. Of all the things I was expecting, this wasn't one of them."

"What do we do?" Archie said.

"We do what we came here for," the sergeant said. He turned to the Vanir. "If you two don't mind keeping us in the air, we can continue with our mission unscathed."

Orus cawed and looked up at the sky. *"Unless it rains on us—look at those dark clouds coming this way."*

The sky above them was filled with fluffy pink clouds. But in the distance, angry red and black clouds were forming. There was no mistaking it; a storm was brewing.

"We could go back in the tunnel, but it might fill with water. I suggest we look for shelter up here," Archie said.

"He's right," Freya agreed. "We need to find a safer shelter." She opened her wings. "Skye, let me go—I'll see what's out there. Everyone, stay here. If the skies open, get down in the tunnel. It's not ideal, but it's better than staying out in the open."

Orus joined her, and within minutes of flying, Freya discovered another problem.

"Orus, do your feathers feel strange?"

"Yes. It feels like they're melting, and the air is burning my eyes."

"Me too."

It wasn't disrupting their flight yet, but at this rate Freya was worried the hostile air would eventually eat away all her feathers—leaving her grounded.

"We need to find shelter as soon as possible," she called to Orus. They searched for a cave in an area covered by giant-sized woodland and shrubs. They saw a large trail worn into the ground by giant feet, but there was nothing to offer any kind of protection.

Freya followed the trail farther until they reached the outskirts of a village. Unlike Utgard, with its mishmash of architecture and buildings built on top of buildings, looking ready to fall down in a strong wind, this village was very organized and symmetrical. Homes were built in a circular design, which gave the giants a full view all around.

Freya was surprised to find that nothing was burning. Despite the fact that the giants were always aflame, it appeared that they didn't set their wooden homes or environment on fire.

Climbing higher in the sky, they looked beyond the village and saw the outskirts of a neighboring town. Beyond it was the Great City of Muspelheim. According to Verdandi's map, Skuld was being kept prisoner well past the Great City and deep in the desert. It would be a long flight in this hostile climate.

"We're going to need Quinn and Skye's magic more than

I thought," she called to Orus. "We'll never make it to Skuld without it. . . ."

As Freya glided in the sky, she became distracted by the feeling of something very strange, yet sickeningly familiar, like a prickling on her skin. She sensed a presence she knew—a presence that terrified her. She was so occupied by the feeling that she didn't notice the fast-moving clouds above her.

"Ouch!" she cried. "Something just stung me!" Freya faltered in the sky as she tried to reach the burning spot in the center of her back, between her wings, but before she could, another burn stung her scalp.

Beside her, Orus cawed in pain.

The sky turned black above them, and Freya realized it was the first drops of rain hitting her.

"*Freya!*" Orus cawed as he was burned again. "*It's raining acid!*"

Freya swooped over to Orus and scooped him up in her arms. She pulled him close to her breastplate to shelter him from the storm before turning to head back the way they'd come.

The raindrops burned through her clothing as she flew. She had to clench her mouth shut to stop herself from howling and alerting the giants to her presence. But with each drop of rain that touched her, it was harder to keep from screaming.

"*Hurry!*" Orus cried.

The skies opened and the acidic rain poured down. Freya couldn't contain her screams any longer. Her whole body was on fire as the hostile water soaked through her clothes and reached her skin.

Finally the tunnel entrance appeared—there was no time to think, no time to make a proper landing. Freya tucked in her burning wings and dived through the entrance. She smashed down into the floor below and rolled away from the opening, protecting Orus, still in her arms, from the rain pouring in.

"Gee!" Archie cried. He and Quinn were there to drag her away from the growing puddle of acidic water.

Freya was barely aware of the others wiping her dry. She was in more pain than she'd ever experienced in her life. Dirian's blade couldn't compare to the feeling of her skin blistering and melting. There wasn't a part of her that wasn't on fire.

She started to shake all over and, despite the severe burns, shivered with cold.

"Skye, Tina, help me get her out of those clothes," Sergeant Romin called. "We've gotta dry her off."

As Skye and Tina reached for her breastplate, Freya held up her hand. "No! Stop. Skin damaged . . . It will tear away. . . . Leave me. . . ."

"But you're covered in third-degree burns. You need medical help," the sergeant insisted. "We have first-aid kits."

Freya was in too much pain to speak clearly. It was a fight just to keep from screaming and tearing at her skin. "Hu-human medicine—bad—Valkyrie . . ."

Skye understood. "She's saying human medicine won't help her because she's a Valkyrie. But I have something that will." She magically produced a cup of green liquid. "Here, Freya, drink this. It will take away your pain."

Skye pressed the cup to Freya's blistered lips, and she drank the sweet, green liquid. The effect was immediate as the pain dimmed and she felt the drawing of sleep.

Quinn reached down and lifted Freya gently in his arms and carried her away from the risk of getting wet. "Go to sleep, Freya. We'll keep you safe while you rest."

Freya tried to speak, to tell them what she'd seen and felt, but sleep was pulling at her, offering to take her away from the pain. She closed her eyes and surrendered to its embrace.

20

THE SOUNDS OF HUSHED VOICES DREW FREYA FROM sleep. As she came to the surface of consciousness, pain was the first sensation to greet her. It reminded her that she was still alive, but in Muspelheim. Her face felt hot and swollen, and her eyes were puffy and difficult to open.

"Freya!" Orus cawed. "Archie, everyone—she's awake."

Freya was lying on her side, her burnt wings fanned out behind her. She winced as she tried to move her hand to get up. The skin on the back of her hand was blistered and peeling.

"Take it easy," Quinn said, gently but firmly pushing her back down. "You're covered in burns. Just lie still for a bit longer."

"How long . . . ?" Freya coughed and tried to speak through swollen lips and a scorched throat. "How long asleep?"

"All day," Archie said. "The rain stopped, and now it's dark out."

"Too long," Freya rasped. She pushed past Quinn's hand and climbed unsteadily to her feet. She was dizzy and had to lean against the wall to keep from falling. The pressure of standing was making her skin throb, and the pain was nearly unbearable. She tried to fold in her wings, but it was agony. Not only were her wings badly burned, but her back was as well.

When Skye offered her another cup of green liquid, she shook her head. "Can't. It will make me sleep again. We don't have time. We must go."

Archie shook his head. "You can't go anywhere yet. You should see yourself, Gee. You're a big, walking red blister!"

"Believe me, I feel worse on the inside than I look on the outside," Freya rasped. "But we don't have time to waste."

"You need to heal, Freya," the sergeant insisted. "You're no good to this unit as you are."

"And the war will be lost if we don't get moving while it's still dark out. Orus and I have seen where we need to go, and it's a long way from here. There are giant settlements everywhere. We must leave now if we want to avoid being seen." She looked at Skye. "Is there something you can give me to take away the pain but leave me awake?"

Skye looked at Quinn and he nodded.

"It won't take away all the pain; only sleep can do that.

But it will be diminished," Skye said. "And you will heal faster."

"That's all I need."

After Freya drank the new brew, she watched the others pull on strange-looking shoes. Archie brought a pair to her.

"What are these?"

"Skye and Quinn made them from the discarded bark of the Yggdrasil root. Look, this bark hat has been covered in acid rain, but the water didn't hurt it."

Quinn nodded and held up a strange, wide-brimmed hat. "When the storm was at its worst, I went out and tried it. The water couldn't penetrate it, and these bark shoes will protect our feet in the same way."

Freya looked at the odd shoes and strange wooden hats the others were pulling on. "I wish you'd thought of this before I went flying. It would have helped in the rain."

"And I wish you hadn't gone flying in the first place," Quinn countered. He grinned at her and pushed her lightly. "Next time talk to me first—all right?"

Freya felt his genuine concern. She felt something else, too, but was in too much pain to consider it. She nodded and smiled. It split a blister on her lip, and she winced. "Yes, sir," she said, saluting like the soldiers.

When they were ready, the sergeant came up to her wearing a grim expression. "This isn't the time for heroics, Freya. Can you move? I want a full status report."

"That's funny coming from a soldier who heroically reaped himself for the good of his world," Freya said. "But I'll be fine. I promise. I wouldn't endanger this mission. There's too much at stake for unnecessary risks . . ." Freya stopped midsentence and inhaled sharply. She suddenly remembered what had happened right before the rain started.

"Gee, what is it?" Archie said. "You look like you've just seen a ghost!"

Freya could hardly breathe. "How could I forget?" She looked at Skye. "That drink you gave me, it made me forget. . . . We must get out of here now, before they come for us!"

"Who?" Archie said. "What are you talking about?"

Freya turned on her friend and grabbed him by the shirt. "The Dark Searchers! Archie, Dirian is here! I felt him right before the rain started. I felt him and . . ." Her eyes were wild. "He felt me, too. Dirian knows I'm here!"

21

MAYA AND KAI STOOD AT THE BACK OF THE HEAVY, LOUD airship as it approached the jump point over Machu Picchu. The soldiers traveling with them were doing their final parachute checks as they prepared to deploy.

One of the soldiers turned and smiled at Maya. She nodded, smiled back, and then leaned in to Kai. "This feels really strange. Valkyries usually stay hidden from soldiers. I never imagined I'd be working with them."

"We all have something to lose if we fail," Kai said. "We are stronger if we work together—even if it feels strange."

Maya nodded but remained silent. Her shoulder felt empty without Grul sitting on it, and she couldn't get the sight of his broken body out of her mind.

"We're here," a soldier called, giving Maya and Kai a thumbs-up.

Maya nodded and stepped up to the open ramp. "You ready?" she asked her brother.

Kai nodded and fluttered his white wings in preparation.

Maya and Kai jumped, glided down alongside the soldiers floating with their parachutes, and directed themselves to the landing point. It had been a very long time since Maya had been here, and she was saddened to see how much Machu Picchu had changed.

"This place used to be a bustling city," she called to Kai as they soared down to land. "Now it's just ruins."

Kai took in the strange, mountainous environment. "It looks beautiful to me," he called. "But then again, compared to Utgard, anywhere is beautiful."

Despite the seriousness of their situation, Maya laughed. "Wait till you see more of Asgard!"

They soon touched down in the central square of the abandoned city—though it looked far from abandoned; hundreds of people milled around. When they spotted Maya and Kai in the sky, they waved their hands frantically and called to them.

Soldiers were already on the ground and approached them as they landed.

"Mia? Kai?" a soldier greeted them. "We've been told why you're here. Come, the Temple of the Sun is this way;

it's where Greta and the others uncovered the tunnel to Muspelheim."

They followed the soldiers through the parting crowds. People continued to call and wave at them desperately.

"Is this normal?" Kai asked, wide-eyed and staring at the people as they pressed to get closer to him.

"It is now," Maya said. "They're hoping we'll defeat the giants."

"Then we'd better not disappoint them." An expression of determination appeared on Kai's face, and Maya saw traces of a mature Dark Searcher rising from within him.

When they reached the Temple of the Sun, Maya saw her sister's mark cut into the ancient wall. It confirmed what she already knew: that Freya had actually been here. Maya paused and touched the mark.

"This way," their escort said.

Once inside the temple, they found three soldiers waiting for them. They were sitting against the wall, looking weak.

The most senior of the three struggled to his feet. "Mia, I'm Corporal Hillson. I was with Greta and the others in the tunnel. I have to tell you what happened down there. . . ."

As he explained, Maya looked horrified. "She reaped them?" she shrieked.

"She didn't have much choice," the corporal said. "Sergeant Romin grabbed her hand—he died instantly. The moment he touched her, Greta went ballistic and warned everyone else to stay back. But then the others convinced her it was the only way they could complete their mission." He dropped his head. "She reaped five soldiers, but it was under protest. I'm sorry. I just couldn't do it. I have a young family that needs me. I couldn't die."

"Listen to me," Maya told them as she felt waves of shame and guilt coming from the survivors. "There's no need to apologize or feel guilty for thinking of your families first. What the others did broke our Valkyrie rules. In all likelihood Greta was grateful to you all for not asking her to break her oath further."

The corporal shook his head sadly. "But we left their bodies down there. We were just too weak to bring them back with us."

Their failed journey to Muspelheim had taken a terrible toll on the surviving soldiers. Their eyes were sunken and ringed with dark circles, and their skin was sallow. It would take some time for them to fully recover—if they ever did.

"When this nightmare is over, we will bring back their bodies for their families," Maya promised. "But for now no one is to enter this tunnel. Is that understood? It's too dangerous for you."

"But we have our orders . . . ," one of the soldiers traveling with them began to protest.

"And I am changing those orders right now." Kai seemed to grow in height as he stood over the soldier. "You will all stay here and keep this tunnel secure while Mia and I go down. Your deaths will serve no one but the giants."

As Maya drew her sword and stood next to Kai as backup, she mused that he had never looked or sounded more like a Dark Searcher than at that moment.

"Don't make us fight you over this," Kai said darkly. "Not when we are united against the giants."

The soldiers stood back, accepting their new orders. Kai looked at Maya and took the first step into the tunnel. "Let's go."

22

"WHO IS THIS DIRIAN?" SERGEANT ROMIN ASKED FREYA. "I've heard that name before, but I don't know anything about him."

Freya described the rebel Dark Searcher who had killed most of the brotherhood of Dark Searchers because they wouldn't follow him. "He's insane, and is filled with pure hatred for me. He's the one who orchestrated this war and took Skuld. But I never imagined he'd still be here. I was certain he'd be leading the attack on Asgard."

"Gee, wait. I think this is a trap . . . ," Archie said. "Think about it. Dirian stayed here, waiting for you to come after Skuld. He's using her as bait. We've got to go back to Earth."

"That's crazy," Tina said. "How could he know Freya

would come here? You make it sound as if he started the war just to get back at her."

"Exactly!" Archie cried. "You don't understand how Dark Searchers think. They're like the Terminator. They have one function: to obey Odin. When he commands them to retrieve someone or undertake a mission, the Dark Searchers don't stop until they've completed their assignment. He sent Dirian after Freya when she came to Chicago to help me. But he failed in his mission."

"He's become obsessed with me." Freya sighed. "Because of his hatred for me, he disobeyed a direct order from Odin. As punishment, Odin cut off one of his wings and banished him from Asgard. Now Dirian blames me for everything. He killed me once during a competition between the realms, and then he nearly killed me again when I tried to find my brother—if Thor hadn't intervened, he'd have chopped me to pieces. But now, with Skuld under his power, he can order her to cut my life thread so that if he kills me again, I'll stay dead."

Every part of her hurt as she walked to the tunnel exit and peered up. "He knows I'm here and he'll be coming for me." She looked back at the others. "You can't be near me when he does, or he'll get you, too."

"I have an idea," Quinn said. "Dirian being here could actually be good for us."

"How?" Archie cried. "Did you miss the part where Gee said he wants to kill her for good?"

"I know," Quinn said. "But if he's as obsessed as you say he is, Freya is all he's focusing on—which means if we split into two groups, he'll almost certainly go after Freya. So the group without Freya stands a good chance of freeing Skuld."

"That could work," the sergeant agreed. "This mission is more important than each of us individually. Freya, if you draw him out, we can move on Skuld."

"Wait," Archie said. "Are you saying Gee should sacrifice herself so Skuld can be rescued?"

Quinn nodded. "That's exactly what he's saying. And he's right."

Freya listened to the argument heating up. Archie was defending her, and she knew why. He too had fought Dirian—and lost. Apart from her, Archie and Orus were the only ones who had a clue what they were truly up against. The thought of facing the dreaded Dark Searcher again terrified her. Could she really do it? This war was bigger than her, bigger than all of them. She had to put her emotions aside.

Freya walked over to her best friend. "That's exactly what I'm going to do. Archie, we all know the danger. We're not all going to survive. But if I do this, if I can distract Dirian, maybe you guys can get Skuld away from here. Get her back to Vanaheim to her sisters or to Odin in Asgard. Then maybe you can stop this war."

"No way," Archie argued. "You're talking like you're already dead."

"Look at me," Freya said. "I'm burned everywhere, my feathers are damaged beyond repair, and I can't fly. The only reason I'm still moving is Skye's pain potion. This is the best and only solution."

Orus cawed in misery. *"No, Freya . . ."*

"You know I'm right," she told him. "I'm not giving up. I have my sword, and I will fight with all I have left. And I may get lucky and wound him. But even if I don't, while I distract Dirian, you guys can free Skuld."

"I'm staying with you," Archie insisted. "And don't try to tell me no. Dirian knows we're always together. If I'm not with you, he'll suspect something."

"Me too," Orus cawed.

Freya closed her eyes and dropped her head. "You're right; you should come with me. We've gone this far together— let's finish it together."

"Now that that's agreed," Sergeant Romin said, "let's get out of here and get moving before they come after us."

Skye used magic to lift everyone out of the tunnel. The moment the hot air touched Freya's burnt skin, she clenched her teeth and fought the pain. Her hands started to shake, and she shivered all over.

"Are you all right?" Quinn asked, moving closer.

Freya nodded. "It's just the heat. Give me a moment and I'll be fine."

KATE O'HEARN

The sergeant called his soldiers together. "All right, you all know your assignments. Quinn, Archie, and Freya will head out first, going in from the right. We'll follow a bit later, from the left. Everyone keep your weapons at the ready and stay sharp. Remember, this mission is everything. If one of us falls, don't stop. Just keep going. There is no room for sentimentality in war. Whoever frees Skuld, get her out of here and don't look back. Understood?"

When everyone nodded, Freya looked at Quinn. "Let's go."

Skye and the Earth soldiers moved in one direction, while Quinn, Freya, and Archie climbed higher in the sky and started to move in the other direction toward the Great City.

With the cover of night to shield them, they passed silently over the villages. The giants' homes glowed with the light of their flames. Occasionally they would see a giant out on the street, glowing like a beacon in the dark. Freya sensed a strange calmness in the air, as though the giants living below didn't know about the war their leaders were waging on Asgard.

The second town was a similar sight: elderly fire giants going about their normal lives, as though nothing had changed. Were they so confident of winning that they weren't prepared for any attacks on Muspelheim?

The giants didn't appear to sense them high in the sky

above them. Although they were very much like frost giants in size, their senses weren't as acute. This filled Freya with hope. Perhaps their mission stood a slight chance of success.

Late into the long night they flew over small and then larger settlements. Soon they reached the outskirts of the Great City. They circled around it and encountered smaller villages that tapered off into single dwellings. It was almost dawn before they approached the edge of the Muspelheim desert.

"He knows I'm coming," Freya called. She tried to suppress a shiver but couldn't. "I can sense Dirian's excitement. He's waiting for me."

"Good," Quinn said. "Let's hope he stays focused on you while the others get to Skuld."

Archie looked over to her. "I still don't like using you as bait."

"*Me neither,*" Orus agreed. "*There has to be another way.*"

"There isn't," Freya said. "But we're not going in unprepared. I have my sword, and Quinn his magic. Together we can fight him."

"*And what about all the other Dark Searchers or fire giants with him? He won't face you alone, and you know it,*" Orus said.

Freya did know it, but she didn't want to comment. She had a feeling this wasn't going to end well for any of them. She buried that thought and focused on what she had to do—draw Dirian away from Skuld.

They started over the crimson sands of the vast desert. The temperature soared, even in the predawn light, and warned of the heat of the day to come. Saying nothing, Quinn pressed on and carried them deeper into the desert.

Skye had given Freya another dose of the liquid that would dim her pain. But as the heat of the sandy desert rose, her skin seared and burned.

"You okay, Gee?" Archie called. "You're looking really pale."

Freya nodded and gritted her teeth. "It's just getting hot."

"We passed hot long ago," he commented. "This is volcanic!"

As they ventured deeper into the desert and with the sun's glow starting to peer over the horizon, Freya began to regret her decision. She was in far too much pain to fight properly. She could barely focus, let alone wield her sword with any accuracy. But they'd come too far to stop now. The others were counting on them to draw Dirian and the Dark Searchers away.

"There," Quinn called as he pointed into the distance to a large keep sitting alone on the crimson sand.

"It looks just like the Dark Searchers' keep in Utgard!" Orus cawed.

"Maybe it's the same one," Archie called hopefully. "If it is, we know a hidden way in."

As they drew near the tall stone structure, Freya's hopes

sank. The stone used to construct this building was deep red. The Keep of the Dark Searchers in Utgard was solid black.

"It's not the same," Freya said, failing to hide her disappointment. "But if we're lucky, the layout might be similar."

"I hope we can get in there without much trouble," Quinn said. "That sun is no friend of ours. If we're still outside when it climbs higher in the sky, we'll be roasted alive."

Freya nodded. "We'll get in. Dirian won't want me roasted outside the keep. He wants to kill me himself."

"You make it sound like we've already lost," Archie said.

Freya looked at him and smiled sadly, knowing she wasn't up to this. It was taking all her strength just to keep moving. She didn't have the energy to fight Dirian. Her only hope now was for Skye's team to make it in and out safely.

"Be careful, Freya," Orus cawed. *"If you let yourself be captured too easily, it will raise suspicion. We must enter as though we're attacking."*

"Have you been reading my mind?" she asked.

"No, but I know you better than you know yourself. You're giving up."

"No, I'm not—I just know my limits."

"Hello . . . ," Archie said. "I'm here, remember? I haven't trained all this time at Valhalla just so you can surrender. What about Quinn and his bag of magic tricks? This fight isn't over till it's over. You got that?"

Freya smiled again. "Got it." She looked over at Quinn.

"Take us down to the balustrade. He may know I'm here, but we're not going to make it easy for him to catch us."

Quinn maneuvered in the sky and brought them down to the imposing keep. On closer inspection, it was larger than the one in Utgard, with four large towers at each corner and a wide patrol balustrade running along the top.

"There's no one up here," Archie said.

"And I know why," Quinn answered. "In a short while the sun will be up fully. Anyone still out here doesn't stand a chance."

"Over there." Freya pointed to one of the tall towers. She spied a large door that led to the balustrade. "We'll go in through there."

When they touched down on the roof, Freya drew her sword. "Quinn, can you magic yourself a sword? And perhaps a cape to hide your wings? We don't want you to be recognized as Vanir. I want you to conceal your magic until we really need it."

"And a sword for me, too, please," Archie said. "Crixus trained me well. I'm not too shabby at all."

Quinn cast a spell, and two shining silver swords appeared on the ground at their feet. Quinn picked his up and inspected it. "I've never used a sword before."

"Hopefully, you won't have to. It's just for effect. Let me go in first. Use your magic if you must, but hold back if you can. I'm hoping that with your wings covered, they'll assume you're human like Archie."

"*Be careful,*" Orus cawed.

"You too." Freya pulled the handle on the door. She stole one last look at the rising sun, wondering if she'd ever see it again. Taking a deep breath, she entered Dirian's keep.

23

FREYA SWITCHED HER SENSES TO FULL ALERT. SHE COULD
feel Dark Searchers inside, but no fire giants. Scanning further, she felt something else—another presence: a very old
and powerful presence.

"I can feel Skuld," Freya said. "She's down in the dungeons. But she's surrounded by Dark Elves, dwarfs, and I
think I feel some trolls."

"So where's Dirian?" Archie asked.

Freya frowned. "I'm not sure. I can feel him, but it's like
he's all around us. It's really strange."

Quinn nodded. "I feel it too. He's using Dark Elf magic
to amplify himself—wait . . ." He inhaled sharply. "No, it
can't be!"

"What?"

His intense gray eyes settled on Freya. "Do you feel that? She's here."

"Yes, Skuld is here. We know."

Quinn shook his head. "No, not Skuld. I'm talking about Vanir-Freyja—she's here too!"

"Freya?" Archie asked, sounding confused.

"Not our Freya, the Valkyrie," Quinn corrected. "I mean Vanir-Freyja, twin sister to Vanir-Freyr."

"Wait," Archie said. "Are you saying there are two Freyas?"

Freya nodded. "Okay, quick history lesson. Remember I told you about the ancient war between the Aesir and the Vanir and how hostages were traded? Well, the Vanir sent the brother-and-sister twins, Freyr and Freyja. They've lived in Asgard ever since the war but are never seen. My mother named me after Vanir-Freyja, but changed the spelling." She inhaled. "It makes sense now—probably because I have a twin brother."

"But she didn't name your brother Freyr; she called him Kai," Archie pointed out.

"Yes," Freya agreed. "But she might not have been allowed to call him Freyr because he was to be given to the Dark Searchers." She turned back to Quinn. "Is Vanir-Freyr here too?"

Quinn closed his eyes. After a moment he shook his head. "No, just Vanir-Freyja."

"That's strange," Archie said. "You'd think Dirian would capture both—double the magic."

A rock settled in the pit of Freya's stomach as she recalled the stories about Vanir-Freyja. "He's not using her for magic—he could have taken any Vanir for that. No, his intentions are much worse." She looked back at Quinn. "Do you remember any of the stories about her?"

"Not a lot. Just that she's supposed to be the most enchanting woman in all the realms."

"Exactly," Freya agreed. "It's a part of her magic. Men fall instantly in love with her the moment they see her. Throughout the ages, the giant kings have tried to possess her. Dwarfs have used their magic to create jewelry for her, just to see her smile. That's why she went into hiding. It's even rumored that she was the very first Valkyrie, but I don't know for sure."

"No one could ever be that beautiful," Archie said.

"She is," Freya said. "What if Dirian is offering her as a gift to the giant king who defeats Odin?"

Archie shook his head. "That's crazy! Maybe he took her because he's in love with her himself."

Freya shook her head. "I don't think so. He's too evil to feel anything but rage and hatred."

Quinn caught on to Freya's line of thinking. "You're suggesting Vanir-Freyja is the giants' incentive to go to war?" He paused and rubbed his chin. "I've heard they don't care about power or ruling the other realms. . . ." He snapped his fingers. "Of course, it makes perfect sense! Dirian is clever. He's using Skuld as a weapon and Vanir-Freyja as the reward for the giants."

"That is wrong on so many levels," Archie said. "We've got to save her. We can't let Dirian give her away like some kind of prize in a game. It's evil."

"But we must be sure," Quinn said.

"What other proof do you need?" Freya challenged. "No one, not even Dirian, would have the power to unite the giants unless he could promise them something big in return. Our history is filled with stories of how the giants have tried to get hold of her. They even stole Thor's hammer to exchange for her. Now she's here? That can't be a coincidence. Dirian must be using her as a prize."

Freya looked up at the rising sun. "This changes everything. Quinn, get out of here now, before the sun rises fully. Find Skye and the others and tell them what's happening. Send one of the soldiers back through the tunnel to Midgard. We must get word to Thor and the others. Vanir-Freyja is even more important than Skuld."

Quinn shook his head. "I can't leave you; you're in no condition to fight. You can barely stand!"

Freya shook her head. "Don't you understand? I'm not important. None of us are. Only Vanir-Freyja and Skuld matter. If you're captured with us, the others will never know how Dirian is controlling the giants. Don't you see? You must go!"

"*She's right,*" Orus cawed. "*Go now, before Dirian sends his Dark Searchers up here.*"

"I—I," Quinn started. "I don't want to leave you."

"If you don't go now, you'll be roasted by the sun!" Archie pushed Quinn toward the door. "Just get out of here and warn the others!"

Freya felt Quinn's conflicted emotions and realized she didn't want him to go either. But this was bigger than all of them. "Forget about us and go. Archie and I will do what we can to distract Dirian and the Dark Searchers. You and Skye must work with the soldiers to get Vanir-Freyja out of here. Don't you see? If she's no longer the prize, the giants will stop attacking Asgard. That's how we'll do it! That's how we'll stop Ragnarök!"

24

FREYA WATCHED QUINN DISAPPEARING INTO THE distance and felt a pang of disappointment.

"Earth to Gee . . . Hello?" Archie's voice shook her back to the moment. "Wow, you've really got it bad."

"What?" Freya frowned.

"You heard me." Archie smiled and shook his head. "You and Quinn?"

Freya stole a final look into the sky. Quinn was gone from sight. "Archie, this isn't the time. We're about to face Dirian alone. The chances of us surviving this are nil."

"I know that," Archie said. "Which is why you shouldn't deny your feelings. You like him; there's no crime in that."

"We're at war! I don't have time for these feelings."

"But you do feel them," Orus added. *"I've seen it too, Freya."*

"Not you, too," Freya said to the raven on her shoulder. "Can we please focus? Vanir-Freyja is in here somewhere. Until Dirian catches us, let's see if we can find her."

Freya stormed down the tower steps, which ended any further discussion. Of course they were right. There was something about Quinn that she really liked, and she regretted that he had to leave. . . . But this wasn't the time to let feelings distract her. There was too much at stake.

With her senses on high alert, Freya felt Dark Searchers all over the keep. So far, none were making moves to come after them. The tower stairs wound down through each level. At the ground floor, Freya paused before a tall, dark-red wood door. Dirian. She could feel him close by.

"He's through there. What's he waiting for?"

"He's toying with you," Archie whispered. "He must know you're expecting him to move, so he's teasing you."

"No, he's waiting until we get deeper into the keep, where we stand no chance of escaping," Orus cawed softly.

"There's no escape for us anyway," Freya said. "I can't fly."

"But he doesn't know that," Orus finished.

Freya nodded. "Forget him. We must find Vanir-Freyja and Skuld. I can feel them; they're beneath us in the dungeons."

Freya's senses picked up on at least four Dark Searchers entering the stairwell from above. The sound of thudding feet storming down the stairs confirmed her senses.

"They're coming for us—run!" Archie cried, but in the tight confines of the round tower stairs, they were trapped with nowhere to go but down.

Freya forced her aching body to move. Each step was like a hammer pounding on her tender skin as her damaged wings rubbed against her blistered back.

"Faster, Gee," Archie called. He ran past her and caught her by the hand, dragging her along.

At the bottom of the steps they faced a large, closed door. Archie grasped the handle and cried as the metal burned his palm. He pulled his sleeve down over his other hand and grasped the door handle again. It gave without resistance, and they ran through it into a dark corridor.

With the pursuers close behind them, Freya looked around, working out what to do next. She could feel that Vanir-Freyja wasn't on this level, but she sensed an older presence to her left. "Skuld is here—come on!"

They ran down the dark corridor and straight into two large, imposing Dark Searchers. They turned to run back, but the Dark Searchers from the tower stairs were waiting for them.

They were trapped!

Freya and Archie stood back-to-back, holding their swords high.

"Does the foolish Valkyrie really believe she can fight her way out of this?"

The Dark Searchers from the tower steps parted and a Dark Elf walked between them, wearing a forest-green cape and a mask. As it approached, it removed its mask, revealing a green, pinched elfin face and elliptical black eyes.

"You!" Freya gasped. It was the same female Dark Elf who had exposed them in Utgard. If it hadn't been for her, they would have escaped the city with no one knowing about it.

"Oh, I see the Valkyrie remembers me," the Dark Elf said. Her eyes narrowed and focused on Archie. "At least the dead human has stopped pretending to be an elf."

"So you've joined Dirian," Freya challenged, holding up her golden sword.

The Dark Elf shook her head. "Foolish Valkyrie—I have been with him all along. Dirian is the one true leader of all the realms. He will see us into a new and glorious age— seated on Odin's throne."

"He's starting Ragnarök," Freya challenged. "If you can't see that, you're as demented as he is!"

The Dark Elf screeched and tried to run at her. But the hand of a Dark Searcher shot out and caught her by the shoulder. He shook his head.

The Dark Elf struggled for a moment and then became still. "You're right," she said. "This one belongs to Dirian. It is not my right to seek pleasure in her pain." She focused on Freya again. "When Dirian is through with you, you will wish you'd never been born." She motioned to the other

Searchers. "Take their weapons and put them in the cells."

Freya looked around and assessed the situation. She and Archie were completely surrounded. They could fight, but it wouldn't last long and would end with them hurt or killed. It wouldn't give Quinn or Skye the time they needed to get to Vanir-Freyja.

Freya put down her sword and looked over at Archie. "Drop your sword."

"But we can fight them!" Archie swung his weapon at one of the Searchers.

Freya reached out to grab his arm. "Not now," she insisted, hoping he would understand.

Archie looked at her and held her eyes for several heartbeats. Finally he nodded and surrendered his weapon. She could see the message in his eyes saying he hoped she had a plan.

When the Dark Searchers came forward and seized them roughly by the arms, *she* hoped she had a plan as well.

The first thing the Dark Searchers did was separate them. Orus cawed and bit into the Searcher that tried to take him from Freya. He finally launched into the air, flew down the dungeon corridor, and disappeared around the corner.

"I'll get him," the Dark Elf called. She shot a cruel look at Freya. "I may not be allowed to hurt you or the dead human, but I have no such orders for the bird. I'm feeling particularly hungry for roast raven!" She cackled with laughter and took off in a run after the raven.

"Go, Orus!" Freya shouted. "Get out of here. Don't let her catch you!"

"Fly, Orus!" Archie called. "Keep going!"

The Dark Searcher holding Freya shook her into silence. But Freya looked defiantly up into his visor. "He's fast. She won't get him. You'll see. He'll get away from you!"

Deadly silent, the Dark Searchers dragged Freya in one direction while Archie was taken in the opposite. At the end of the corridor, she was shoved into a dark cell. It was almost identical to the one at the keep in Utgard. There were no windows and nothing to sit on but the red stone floor.

The walls and door were newer, but the feelings of dread they instilled were the same. Freya stood at the door, waiting for Dirian. He would come. She knew he would. And when he did, she would face the end with dignity.

After a time she gave up waiting, walked to the corner of the small cell, and lay down. The drug Skye had given her was wearing off, and the pain from her burns was back. With nothing left to do but wait for the end, she closed her eyes and tried to sleep.

It felt as if she had only just dozed off when she heard a key entering the lock. Freya rose and watched the cell door swing open. Standing at the entrance was a Dark Searcher and a troll.

"Come, come," the troll ordered, wagging a crooked fin-ger at her. He was small, round, and gray. Freya couldn't tell whether this was his natural color, or dirt. More than likely dirt, she decided, when she took in his tattered, smelly rags.

The troll could barely walk, but that didn't mean he wasn't dangerous. Freya felt pure evil emanating from him. He stumbled forward and caught her by the arm. "Don't keep the master waiting." Freya had to muffle her nose with her hand to stifle his vile smell.

She snatched her arm from his grip. "If Dirian wants to see me, he can come down here and get me himself!"

The troll squeaked his displeasure and punched her in the midsection, knocking her back and slamming her against the wall. Freya cried out as her damaged wings pressed against her burnt back.

Trolls may be small, but she quickly discovered they packed a vicious punch. Freya righted herself and kicked the troll across the cell. The foul creature squealed as he hit the opposite wall.

"You touch me again and I'll break your arm!" she warned. Freya turned on the Dark Searcher. "Well, what about you?"

He stood staring at the troll. Eventually he drew one of his black swords. "Move . . . ," he rasped with his broken voice. "I cannot kill you, but I have no orders not to harm you. I will if you don't come."

Freya stood defiantly before the Dark Searcher. The troll

had climbed to his feet and took this opportunity to charge at her again. But Freya was too quick for him. She turned her back and struck out with her right wing, smacking him hard in the face. The troll smashed against the wall a second time and fell to the ground, unconscious. Freya sneered at him. "I've never liked trolls!"

"Valkyrie!" the Dark Searcher commanded. He loomed above her with his imposing height. "I am no troll," he said. "You would be wise not to try that with me."

"No, you're a Dark Searcher—and I don't care for them either!" Freya was baiting him. It was dangerous, but at this point she had little to lose.

The Dark Searcher balled his hand into a fist but held it back. "Do not try my patience. I *will* hurt you."

As Freya stood before him, weaponless and wounded, there was no way she could hope to fight and win. She walked toward the door.

Two Dark Searchers, a dwarf, and a male Dark Elf stood waiting for her in the corridor, ready to escort her further. She sensed they'd been testing her, to see how much she would resist. She looked at the Dark Elf. "Sorry to disappoint you. Looks as if you won't be the one to kill me today."

"The day is yet young," the masked elf said lightly, "and I remain hopeful."

As they walked toward the tower steps, Freya stole a look back to see if Archie was being brought with them. He wasn't.

Making it up to the ground floor, Freya looked around. Again, it looked similar to the old keep in Utgard, but somehow it was even darker, as though the evil from the occupants was driving away any light. Their steps echoed as they walked through the wide, empty corridors. They entered a chamber where the ceiling high above their heads gave the large, desolate room a lonely, cavernous feeling.

In the center of the chamber was a long rectangular table with scrolls sprawled across it. Around the table were a few stools. As they walked past the table, Freya saw the papers were maps of the realms and diagrams showing the giants' military movements.

Freya immediately recognized this as a war room. It was here that Dirian was conducting his fight against Odin. There had been no attempt to hide anything from her eyes.

As she tried to get a closer look at the maps, a sound of rattling broke her concentration. She turned as another Dark Elf and a troll came toward her, holding a metal collar and a chain lead.

"If you think you're putting that on me, you'd better think again," she warned the elf. Freya instinctively took a step back, but the Dark Searcher standing behind her blocked her retreat.

The Dark Elf laughed, exposing his tiny, pointed teeth. "Oh, please do try to stop me. I would love to take on a

Valkyrie. I've heard of your fighting skills, Freya, but never witnessed them personally."

"Come closer and I'll show you."

That comment only made the elf laugh harder.

"Enough!"

Freya's heart sank. She knew that broken voice all too well. It was the voice that haunted her nightmares and made her wake in the night covered in a film of sweat. Every nerve in her body told her not to move—to simply close her eyes and await the end. But she couldn't obey. She turned and saw Dirian striding into the chamber.

The Dark Searcher was as terrifying as always. He was wearing his helmet and full armor, with his two black swords strapped to his sides. She couldn't see his face, but she could feel him, could feel his hatred mixed with joy at having her as his prisoner . . . but worst of all was his anticipation. It was all there, offered for her to feel. He held nothing back.

Dirian stood before her—unmoving and silent. Only the slight change in the pitch of his breathing revealed he wasn't a statue.

"Well?" Freya managed. "Come on, get it over with. . . ."

Freya expected many things, but she never imagined she'd hear him laugh. His deep, fractured voice choked on his mirthless laughter as he stepped closer to her. His visor stopped mere inches away from her face.

"I am sorry to disappoint you, *Freya*, but you will not

die this day or any day in the near future. You are to be my special guest for a very, very long time. You alone will bear witness to the defeat of Odin. You will watch Asgard fall to my giants and see all the realms bow to me. You will be there as your Valkyrie sisters are enslaved and traded like coins. I promise you will see it all and will be helpless to stop any of it."

"You're insane!" Freya cried.

"I am only what *you* made me," he replied. "Actually, I should thank you. Were it not for you, I would still be a slave to Odin—blindly serving his every whim. Now I know what it is to be truly free." The large, imposing Dark Searcher slowly turned his back to her. "See how I have freed myself? Odin removed one of my wings. I chose to remove the other."

Freya was horrified by the sight of his smooth, wingless, armored back. "Why would you do that?"

"It was what I chose!" he spat. "Now, to show my gratitude to you, I will share with you that same exhilarating freedom."

Those words chilled Freya to the bone. She tried to deny their implication, but when Dirian ordered his men to grab her and pry open her wings, Freya realized the meaning was clear.

The tall Dark Searcher slowly drew one of his black blades. "Now, you can make this easy on yourself, or you can make it hard. The choice is yours—but have no illusion, I will take your wings."

"No!" Freya cried, struggling in the Dark Searchers' grip. "You can't do this!"

Dirian took a step closer and rasped, "Good. You're going to fight."

He stepped back and pulled his second sword from its sheath. Dirian threw it onto the ground at her feet. "Release her. Let's see if this Valkyrie has learned anything new."

When the two Dark Searchers let her go, Freya snatched up the black sword and faced Dirian. Her eyes scanned the room wildly. Other Dark Searchers, elves, and dwarfs were filing in, blocking her only exit.

The choice was simple. Surrender to Dirian and let him cut off her wings. Or fight, knowing she stood no chance against him. But every moment she delayed, every second she had his full attention, gave the others time to get to Vanir-Freyja.

"Come on, then, Dirian," she challenged bravely. "You want my wings? You're going to have to take them!"

Freya moved first and lunged toward the demented Dark Searcher. But her burns slowed her movement. Dirian easily deflected her sword thrust.

"You can do better than that," he teased.

She sensed his pleasure. He was toying with her, and they both knew it. But each moment bought more precious time for the others to arrive. She would give him the fight he wanted.

{ 232 }

Dirian made two halfhearted swipes that Freya easily defended. She could sense he was holding back, not wanting to end the fight too soon. In anger, she launched her own attack, a fraction of a second faster than him. Her blade cut across his breastplate, slicing into his leather armor. It didn't touch his skin, but it was enough to surprise him and make him jump back.

Immediately Dirian's mood changed and the game ended. His swipes became more aggressive. While his blade moved in one direction, his free hand moved in the opposite and struck Freya across her burnt and blistered face with a blow that knocked her off her feet.

Freya opened her wings to slow the fall. The next thing she knew, Dirian's blade flashed faster than she imagined possible. So fast that Freya didn't feel the actual cuts—what she did feel was both her wings coming away from her body and falling to the floor beside her.

Moments later, pain arrived. Sharper than anything she'd felt before. So intense, it sucked the wind from her lungs, leaving her unable to breathe, let alone scream.

Freya was in too much pain to think. She tried to climb to her feet, but Dirian was there, pushing her back. When she hit the ground, he moved in for a final, bone-breaking kick that sent her flying across the room. She hit the wall, her senses overwhelmed. She welcomed the coming darkness and surrendered gladly to oblivion.

25

MAYA AND KAI RAN THROUGH THE TUNNEL TOWARD
Muspelheim as fast as their legs would carry them. They had
to catch up with Freya.

Soon they felt the realm slip from Midgard into
Muspelheim and saw something ahead in the tunnel. As
they moved closer, they made out the bodies of the five soldiers who had been reaped, slumped against the wall. They
looked as if they were napping peacefully.

"What kind of person would ask to be reaped?" Kai said,
studying the soldiers.

"The kind who are devoted to the service of their realm,"
Maya answered. "They knew they couldn't go on any farther,
but they didn't want to give up. It was an extreme but honorable decision."

"Would you have reaped them?"

Maya considered for a moment and then nodded. "Considering what's at stake, I would. I'm sure no one will condemn Freya or the soldiers for what they did."

As they prepared to get moving again, they heard footsteps running toward them. A young soldier emerged from the darkness ahead.

"Can you see me?" he gasped, bending over to catch his breath.

"Yes," Maya said. She immediately recognized him as one of the dead soldiers.

The young man stole a quick look at his body against the wall and then turned away. "I—I'm Private Cornish. I have an urgent message from Freya."

"I'm her sister, and this is Kai, her twin brother," Maya said. "What's the message?"

Taking a couple more breaths, the young private started to speak. He passed on the message he'd been given from Quinn. He went on to explain Freya's plan.

"Freya is handing herself over to Dirian!" Kai cried. "Is she crazy?"

The private shook his head. "She's trying to keep him distracted long enough for the others to free Vanir-Freyja and Skuld."

Kai's eyes were wide and wild. "But he'll kill her!"

"She knows that, but she went in there anyway. In the

short time I've known your sister, I've discovered that she's one selfless but very stubborn Valkyrie."

"She's an idiot if she thinks handing herself over to Dirian can help," Kai said.

The soldier continued. "Quinn ordered me to get back to Earth to try to find your people to ask them to help us. If we can free Vanir-Freyja and Skuld, it will end the war and save Earth."

"We're on our way to Muspelheim now," Maya finally said. "I won't let Freya sacrifice herself. Not to him. But Quinn is right. Thor must be told." She looked back down the tunnel to Earth. "Private, I need you to keep going. Get to Earth and, even though you will be a spirit, do what you can to find Thor and the others. Tell them what you just told us."

The private nodded. "I should warn you, Muspelheim is hot and very dangerous. It's essential that you don't touch anything." He held up his burnt palm. "Everything there burns at the touch. I picked a berry and this is what happened. Freya was caught in the rain and has burns all over her body. Quinn has made extra protective shoes out of the root of Yggdrasil. He has left them farther down the tunnel for you—put them on or your feet will burn to a crisp. And one other thing: The air is corrosive and will eventually destroy your feathers. So be as quick as you can."

Maya looked at Kai. "No wonder Brundi called it hell." She finally turned to the young soldier and took his hand.

"Thank you, Private Cornish, for the message and for your sacrifice in this. With your help, we can move this war away from Earth and take it to where it belongs—the very heart of Muspelheim!"

With each pounding footstep, Maya's head was filled with visions of what could be happening to Freya at the hands of Dirian.

"Faster!" Kai called, as he put on more speed.

Maya's heart felt as if it were about to burst as she kept up with her brother. The air in the tunnel was heating up and burning her lungs, but the urgency to reach Freya was driving them both on.

Soon the tunnel began to tilt up and they slowed to a jog. Up ahead they saw the pile of shoes that Private Cornish had told them about.

They were too tired to speak as they pulled on the shoes. Kai also found a stash of weapons and copies of a map leading to the keep.

"I must meet this Quinn," he said as he strapped several swords to his waist. "He thinks like a Dark Searcher."

Maya scanned their dimly lit surroundings, searching for a way out. She felt a soft, hot breeze on her face and looked up. Her eyes settled on a hole in the ceiling above them. "That's our way out. I can feel fire giants, but they aren't close. Now's the time to move."

They flew through the hole and emerged into darkness. Stars twinkled brightly overhead. Maya looked around to get her bearings and then pointed toward the Great City. "It's this way. . . ."

Kai's sudden screams shattered the stillness around them. He arched his back and then fell to the ground between tall blades of grass.

Maya landed beside him. "Kai, what's wrong? What is it?"

Kai writhed in agony. "I feel Freya," he gasped, barely able to speak. "She's hurt. It's her back. . . ." He struggled to reach the center of his back where his wings joined his body. "Something's wrong with her back."

Maya reached out to her brother. "Listen to me—suppress your connection to Freya before it cripples you. Do you hear me? Break the connection! Do it, Kai. Do it now."

Kai lay on his side, moaning and panting. After a moment he spoke softly. "I—I'm all right now." Maya helped him climb shakily to his feet. "Can you tell me what's happened? What has Dirian done to Freya?"

When he looked at Maya, all she could see was rage. "I'm going to kill him—do you hear me? I swear, nothing is going to stop me from destroying him!"

"Just tell me what he's done."

Kai turned away from her. "That soldier was right—her body's burned and it's agony for her. But what that monster has done is worse."

"Enough!" Maya caught him by the arm and spun him around to face her. "Tell me what's happened!"

Kai balled his hands into fists and then drew his sword. "Dirian has cut off Freya's wings!"

26

FREYA LAY IN A BALL ON HER SIDE. SHE'D NEVER KNOWN such pain. Her burning skin was nothing compared to the searing agony of the stumps on her back where her wings had been severed. She was unsure how long she'd been lying on the stone floor, or even how long she'd been conscious after she'd blacked out. All she knew was pain.

Freya could barely remember the fight with Dirian. Though, she knew she'd never forget the sound of his coarse laughter right after he'd sliced off her wings and kicked her in the side. . . . That memory she would keep for the rest of her life, however short that might be.

Lifting her head, Freya tried to look around, but moving made the pain worse. She could just about make out that she was chained to the floor of the War Room. The heavy metal collar she'd seen the elf holding was now secured around her neck, and the thick chain attached to it was locked to a large metal clamp buried deep into the thick stone floor. Above her, mounted to the wall like a prized trophy, were her severed wings.

Freya retched at the sight of them.

She put her head back down, and silent tears trickled down her cheeks.

"Don't let him see you cry, Freya," a soft, light voice called. "It will only give him pleasure. Just stay still and heal."

Freya's eyes followed the sound and peered across the vast, dark chamber. A young girl was chained to the opposite wall. From what she could make out, the girl was no more than eight or nine.

"Who . . . ? Who are you . . . ?"

"I am Skuld."

"Skuld . . ." Freya tried to sit up, but she was overwhelmed with dizziness and fell back down again.

"You must lie still and heal," Skuld called. "I'm counting on you—we all are."

Freya's head was spinning, and she had to shut her eyes to keep from throwing up again. Her broken ribs hurt almost as much as her wing stumps. She became aware of the tight, thick bandage around her midsection. Her breastplate had been removed and her wounds treated, but they had given her no pain relief. Dirian wanted her kept alive, but suffering.

Each breath she took threatened to bring back the blackness of unconsciousness. But knowing it was Skuld chained to the opposite wall, Freya forced herself to stay awake.

"Where is he . . . ?"

"Resting," Skuld said. "It's night."

Night? Freya tried to focus. Nothing seemed to make sense anymore. How could she have lost so much time?

"Do—do you know why I'm here?"

"Yes," Skuld said. "Please say no more. Evil ears are listening."

"Let them," Freya muttered softly. She lifted her head again. "Whoever's listening, know this—I am going to get away from here, and when I do, I swear you'll pay for what you've done. Do you hear me?"

"Strong words from a broken, wingless Valkyrie." The female Dark Elf appeared from the shadows and crept closer to her.

Pain had blocked Freya's senses, leaving her unable to feel the others around her. But it didn't keep her temper in check. She pushed herself up into a sitting position. "Come closer, Elf. I'll show you how wings don't define a Valkyrie—our strength does."

The Dark Elf snorted with a high-pitched laugh that hurt Freya's ears. "I must say, I do like your new look. Have you thanked Dirian yet? Now you can sleep on your back and wear clothing better suited to you. With a bit of soap and water and a proper dress, you'll be a pretty little addition to his trophy collection."

"I'm no trophy," Freya spat.

"Oh no? Why else are you alive, but to please the master? Have you seen your wings lately? They're his most prized possession!" More laughter followed. "It's too bad the rain damaged the feathers before Dirian cut them off. They would have looked so much nicer on the wall if they were intact."

Freya knew the elf was baiting her to look up at her wings again. But Freya refused. She'd seen them once—that was more than enough.

"This isn't over, Elf. Soon I will be free, and you and the others will be punished for your crimes."

The elf moved closer, but stayed out of Freya's reach. "That's what I like about you, Valkyrie. Even in complete defeat you are too stupid to realize that Dirian has won. Soon all the realms will kneel before him."

"I don't understand," Freya said softly. "Why did the Dark Elves join him? What's in this for you?"

"Nothing much. Just a sweet little realm we've had our eyes on for some time. I'm sure you know it. It's called Midgard."

"You want Earth?"

"Yes, and Dirian has promised it to us. Soon humanity will be our slaves. There will be no more warriors for Valhalla. And you, Valkyrie, will be there to see it all!" Her cackling laughter filled the chamber.

Freya was about to respond when her sense caught hold of her brother. It was only a brief flash before he suppressed their connection. But it was enough. Kai was in Muspelheim, and he was coming for her.

"Oh, Elf," Freya said as she lay back down. "I will see things, that's true. But what I'll see is something that will give you nightmares for the short piece of life you have left."

"Pain has made you delusional." The elf snorted as she returned to her guard post.

"We'll see," Freya muttered as she settled down again.

Kai's arrival did more for Freya than all the healing potions in all the realms. If Kai was here, the others were too. All she had to do was keep Dirian distracted long enough for them to reach the keep and free Vanir-Freyja and Skuld.

She closed her eyes and blocked out the ranting Dark Elf. Freya needed to rest, to heal as much as she could before she faced down Dirian in their final battle.

The sound of voices roused Freya from her troubled sleep. The moment she woke, the pain swooped down on her as a constant reminder of what Dirian had done.

"Do it," the Dark Searcher's broken voice commanded. "Do it or I will make you suffer again."

Skuld was whimpering softly. "Please, no more . . ."

"Do it now!" Dirian commanded.

Freya lay still but opened her eyes. Dirian was standing

with his back to her, leaning over Skuld. The youngest Norn was curled against the opposite wall and weeping as a parchment and quill were thrust into her hands.

"Cross them all out . . . ," Dirian commanded. "Or must I once again prove my absolute power over you!"

Freya was unable to see what Skuld was doing, but by listening to the exchange, she had a pretty good idea. This was how Dirian was ending his enemies. He was having Skuld cross out the futures of those whose names were written down.

After a moment she heard Dirian inhale deeply. "Very good. Now you may eat."

He turned and faced Freya. "I know you are awake," he rasped malevolently. "I can feel you."

Despite the protests from her broken ribs and the screaming from her wing stumps, Freya pushed herself up into a sitting position. She considered trying to stand but knew she didn't have the strength. The last thing she wanted was for him to see her fall.

"Is that how you amuse yourself," Freya said to him. "Tormenting children and cutting wings off Valkyries?"

"I did enjoy taking your wings," the Dark Searcher said as he strode casually toward her. "And there is yet more pleasure to be had in your pain. Let's start with a bit of early-morning reading. . . ."

"You can't read," Freya spat, determined to keep him occupied. "You're too stupid. You can barely even speak."

The only reaction her comment caused was Dirian turning the parchment around and lowering it enough for her to see. "I can read and write well enough to draw up a very special list of names. I'm sure you'll recognize them. These are the names of those who have no future. The moment my giants kill them, they will stay dead."

Dirian bent down closer. "I did this especially for you. It took me a great deal of time and effort to discover all these names. Tell me, have I missed anyone?"

Freya didn't want to see, but she couldn't keep from looking.

~~Brünnhilde of Skiir—Valkyrie~~

~~Eir of Brünnhilde—Valkyrie~~

~~Gwyn of Eir—Valkyrie~~

~~Skaga of Eir—Valkyrie~~

~~Kara of Eir—Valkyrie~~

~~Maya of Eir—Valkyrie~~

~~Kai of Eir—Dark Searcher~~

~~Giovanni Angelo of Brünnhilde—Dark Searcher~~

~~Kris of Brünnhilde—Dark Searcher~~

~~Myriam-Elizabet of Giovanni Angelo—Valkyrie~~

Freya's hand flew up to her mouth as she read the names of her family. A bright red line crossed through each of their names. Her senses told her that the red line wasn't ink. It was Skuld's blood. That was how the Norn would destroy the future of everyone Freya loved.

"Of course, your raven and dead human aren't on the list—yet. But there will be plenty of time to add them later, after I take the throne. As for you, Freya, you don't need to worry about appearing on any list. No, you and I will have a very, very long life together."

Freya tried to snatch the parchment away to destroy it, but Dirian was faster and pulled it from her reach. "Temper, temper," he teased.

The Dark Searcher rose and walked toward the chamber door. He reached into his cloak and pulled out Freya's flaming sword. Pinning the list on the end of the blade, he stabbed the sword tip into the wood of the doorframe—posting the list for her to see.

"You're a monster," Freya uttered.

Dirian's broken laughter echoed behind him as he stormed out of the War Room.

"I am sorry." Skuld wept miserably. "He made me do it."

Freya heard the pain in the Norn's voice but couldn't look at her. Her eyes were locked on the list. Dirian had condemned her entire family.

There was only one thing left for her to do, and Freya hated herself for having to do it. "Azrael," she softly called. "Please, come to me. I need your help."

Freya waited for the arrival of the Angel of Death. Last

time she'd called his name, he'd appeared immediately. This time there was nothing. "Azrael, please, I need you."

More time passed and still the angel did not appear. Horrible thoughts went through her head. Had he fallen in battle? Could he not hear her on Muspelheim?

Freya lay down again—crushed by despair. In all her life, she'd never felt so alone.

27

MAYA AND KAI FOLLOWED THE MAP TOWARD THE KEEP, flying high, above the prying eyes of the fire giants. The small villages they flew over grew into towns and then into the massive Great City. Past the city, the terrain gave way to villages and small settlements again. They soared lower in the sky as they approached the vast red desert rolling out before them.

As they flew near the desert edge, the heat rising from the sand hit Maya like a protective wall, designed to keep them out. Grazing against it was like sticking her wing into a blazing fire. It burned her skin and seared her feathers. Just as she was about to warn her brother, her senses picked up on dead humans and the Vanir.

"Kai, wait—I feel something." Maya started to descend.

KATE O'HEARN

"Yes, it's the heat from the sand. It's reflecting and magnifying the sun's rays. I've heard about this desert. It's deadly. We have to find another way in."

She shook her head. "I'm not talking about the desert; it's something else. Follow me." Tilting her wings, Maya continued down through the sky. She followed her senses to a single dwelling on the very edge of the red sands. "There," she called to her brother. "The two Vanir are in there. Human soldiers are with them."

They touched down lightly at the back of the dwelling. Maya pulled in her wings. Flying all night and into the day had taken a heavy toll on her feathers—especially her left wing, which had grazed over the edge of the desert sand. The feathers were frayed and tinder dry. If she touched them, they actually snapped.

Feathers weren't the only problem. The intense rays of the sun had burned her arms and hands and any exposed skin. Muspelheim was everything she'd been warned about, and worse.

"I'm not sure how much farther we can go," Kai said, making his own inspection of his wings. "My feathers are ruined."

"Mine too," Maya agreed. "I've heard the Vanir are very powerful. Maybe they can restore them."

Raised voices came from inside the single-story hovel. It was too small to be a giant's home. Low and squat, it looked as if it had been built for a dwarf or a troll. Maya approached the back door and forced it open.

"Help me," cried a troll when he saw Maya and Kia enter the single room.

Maya welcomed the cooler air in the shady hovel as she and her brother entered. A troll was tied to a chair, while two figures stood before him. Maya could make out their beautiful wings. One of them turned around—a boy about Freya's age, with a broad build and finely sculpted features.

"Valkyrie . . . ?" the Vanir boy asked, staring at her. He finally drew his eyes away, and they landed on Kai. "I don't know what you are."

Kai stood to his full height. "I am Kai, a Dark Searcher."

The boy inhaled. "You're Freya's twin brother!"

Kai nodded. "And this is our sister Maya. Are you Quinn?"

The boy nodded, smiling at Maya. "This is Skye." He presented the Vanir girl. She was about the same age but with raven hair and bright, worried eyes. "And these soldiers are from Midgard."

"What are you all doing here?" Maya asked. "Private Cornish found us in the tunnel and told us you were moving in on the keep. Why have you stopped?"

Quinn shook his head. "The desert. I was nearly roasted alive when I flew from the keep. It was still early morning, but the flight nearly killed me. It took all of my magic just to make it out of there alive."

"Same with us," the sergeant said. "When we tried to reach the keep, the sun came up and drove us back. Look how it damaged Skye's wings."

Skye showed them the burnt edges of her delicate butterfly wings. They were tattered and scorched. The skin on her arms and legs was peeling from intense sunburn. "Dirian positioned his keep well. No one can survive that desert during the day. We have to wait until the dark before we can risk going in again."

Maya frowned. "But you're Vanir. Surely your magic is strong enough to combat the sun?"

"Sadly not," Quinn admitted. "I've never known such intense heat. Vanaheim can get warm, but not like this. It's too much for us."

Kai exploded. "This isn't good enough! We must get to the keep *now*. Dirian has hurt Freya. He's cut off her wings and broken her bones. . . ."

"What?" Quinn cried. "Is she alive?"

Maya nodded. "But she's in so much pain, Kai had to break the connection to her just to be able to move."

Quinn's face contorted with rage. "I'm going to kill him!"

"Get in line," Kai said darkly. "I grew up at the keep in Utgard and I've hated Dirian all my life. But now he's gone too far. He will feel the cut of my blade!"

Maya took a moment to smile as she felt their deep feelings for her little sister. "You can both kill him—but first we have to get there."

"She's right," Sergeant Romin said. "You can do whatever you like to him *after* we free Vanir-Freyja and Skuld." He turned his steely eyes toward the troll tied to the chair. "And this guy here knows exactly where they're holding them."

He stepped up to the whining troll. "Listen, little buddy, these people mean business. They won't stop until you tell us where they're holding the others. If you value your skin, you'd better start talking."

The troll shook his head. "I know nothing of what you speak. I am a humble troll."

"Humble?" the sergeant said. "I don't think so."

"I am, dead human, I am. . . . I know nothing of the war."

"Really? And I'm sure you have no idea what we're talking about."

The troll nodded. "It's true. I am innocent. I don't know Dirian or anyone at the keep. I've never even been there."

"Oh no?" the sergeant said. He reached inside the tattered, ragged shirt of the filthy troll. Hanging on a long, leather cord was a single black feather. The edges were singed and fragile. "And I suppose this isn't one of Freya's feathers. . . ."

"Feather?" Kai stormed forward and yanked the cord from around the troll's neck.

The troll squealed and snatched at the feather. "That's mine. Give it back!"

"This is Freya's!" Furious, Kai turned on the troll. "How

did you get it?" When the troll said nothing, Kai slapped him across the face with the back of his gloved hand. "Answer me!"

"Kai, stop," Maya called. She caught hold of his hand before he could strike the troll again. "Torture doesn't work on trolls. You know that."

Kai was panting heavily, fighting to contain his rage. "I must try. He's going to tell us about Freya."

Maya nodded. "He will—"

"No, I won't!" the troll squealed. He spat at Kai. "You can kill me and I still won't speak. The master knows I am loyal."

"Oh, yes, you will, little troll," Maya said darkly. "You'll tell us everything we need to know and more."

"How?" Quinn said. "Nothing we've tried has worked. He doesn't care if we hurt him or not."

"Fear of pain isn't an incentive for them, but I do know a way," Maya said softly.

"If you do, I'd sure like to know about it," the sergeant said.

"There is a dangerous weapon here that you didn't have before. And that will make all the difference."

"Really?" the soldier said. "Would you care to enlighten us and tell us what it is?"

Maya sighed unhappily. "It's me. . . ."

* * *

Maya shooed everyone out of the hovel and asked to be left alone with the troll. When they were outside, she walked back to the smelly little creature.

"What will you do to me?" the troll asked fearfully.

"What I must." Maya retrieved a second chair and placed it before the troll. Turning it front to back, she straddled the chair and sat. She recoiled as the smell of the filthy troll hit her. But she had to focus. She had to do this to get to Freya. "I hate you for making me do this. . . ."

"Do what?"

Maya started to sing.

All Valkyries have the power to charm with their songs. But Maya's family was unique among the Valkyries and possessed even greater powers than this. No one knew why, and throughout their lives, the family had tried to hide their extra abilities.

Freya had been born with unique black feathers and was the fastest flyer in all of Asgard. Her older sisters were the strongest, most powerful fighters among all the Valkyries.

But Maya had an even more extraordinary power— though it was something she had fought against and tried to suppress all her life. She had been born with striking beauty and great power to enchant. No one could resist her when she turned it on. Until now, she had never used it fully—to her, it was a curse, not a blessing. But to save her sister, she would do anything.

Maya poured all that power into the song to cast a spell over the troll. The troll's eyes began to glaze over until he couldn't stop staring at her with complete adoration.

Maya shook her head and rose. She went to the door and called the others in.

"Thank heavens," Tina said. "I thought I was going to melt out there. Being dead isn't much fun when you can still sweat!"

"Well?" Skye said. "We heard you singing—what happened?"

Maya was disgusted with herself. "The troll will answer our questions now."

Kai stepped up to the chair holding the troll. "So, now, troll, you'll give us some answers."

The troll looked at Maya and smiled. "Will I?"

Maya nodded. "Yes, you will. You will answer truthfully, or I will be very displeased."

"No, no, please don't be angry at me," the troll whined. "Ask me anything. I swear I will tell all. . . ."

28

AS THE SUN PASSED DIRECTLY OVERHEAD, THE TEMPERA-
ture in the hovel became almost unbearable. Maya stood at
the small window, watching the waves of heat rolling over the
sand like malevolent living things searching for something to
devour. Nothing could survive in that lifeless, cruel desert.

They spent all morning interrogating the troll. He didn't
hesitate to tell them everything he knew. They untied him
from the chair, and Skye magically produced a quill and
paper, and the troll was instructed to draw up plans of the
interior of the keep.

Nothing was omitted. By the time the troll had finished,
they had the full layout of the keep, including the location
of Vanir-Freyja's cell in the lower dungeon and Archie's cell
on the next level.

The troll went on to tell them that he had seen Freya face Dirian and had personally witnessed him cut off Freya's wings. She was now Dirian's prized possession and was chained in the War Room across from Skuld.

At this point, Kai slammed his fist down on the only table in the room and shattered it to pieces. "I swear he's going to suffer for that."

Quinn nodded. "I will be there with you when he pays."

Maya faced the troll. "If Freya is his prized possession, what are the orders regarding her?"

The troll stared at her adoringly. His voice became dreamy. "No one is to touch or harm her. It is death to anyone who does."

"Good," Maya said.

"Good?" Kai cried. "Didn't you hear what Dirian did to her?"

"Of course I heard," she snapped. Her sister was hurt, the war was raging, and the heat in the small hovel was unbearable—seeing the loving expression on the troll's face only exacerbated her already foul mood. "But didn't you hear what he said? No one is to touch her. That means if we free her, no one can go against her. Freya is safe. Yes, she's suffering. Yes, she's broken—but she's safe!"

Kai and Maya glared at each other for a moment. Finally Kai nodded. "You're right. As much as I hate what he's done to her, Dirian's hatred of Freya will protect her from the others." He turned back to the troll. "You, tell us about all the entrances into the keep—those known and used and those that are hidden."

"Why would they need hidden entrances when they have a large desert out there to protect them?" Quinn asked.

"Because fire giants are immune to the heat of the desert," Kai explained. "And like the frost giants, they can be unpredictable and dangerous. In fact, the keep in Utgard had many secret ways in. They were used as emergency escapes in case the frost giants ever attacked. Dirian may be many things, but he's not stupid. This is the fire giants' realm. He wouldn't have built the keep without a hidden way out—especially now that he's wingless."

"So," Kai barked at the troll. "Tell us how to get in."

Within moments they were staring at the map the troll had drawn. Indeed, there were two hidden tunnels that had been built. One entrance sprang from the lowest level in the keep, crossed the desert deep beneath the deadly burning sands, and exited in the Great City. The other was on the dungeon level and also ran under the desert. It exited through a hidden door in the floor of the hovel—directly beneath their feet.

"Of course," the sergeant said, slapping his forehead. "Why didn't I think of that? This stinky little critter couldn't have walked through that desert on those stubby legs. It would have killed him before he made it three steps from the keep!"

"We all should have thought about that," Quinn said.

"It doesn't matter now," Skye said. "We know about the tunnels. So let's get ready to go before this war destroys all our realms!"

After the troll revealed the entrance to the tunnel, they drew up a plan. Again, they would split into two groups. Maya, Skye, and Tina would access the dungeon to free Vanir-Freyja while the troll would lead Kai, Quinn, and the remaining soldiers to Archie's cell and then make their way up into the War Room to free Freya and Skuld.

Though their weapons were checked and rechecked, Quinn also issued daggers to the soldiers in case their weapons failed in the harsh Muspelheim climate. Once those were secured, they started down the stone steps into the tunnel. The air became much cooler, and everyone breathed a great sigh of relief.

The tunnel was wider than Yggdrasil's roots. Kai stepped forward and opened his blazing white wings. "It's wide enough for the Dark Searchers to fly through. We must be on our guard. They might try to engage us down here."

"And we'll be ready," Skye said.

Quinn and Skye cast a spell to lift them off the ground and carry them swiftly through the long, torch-lit tunnel. Eventually the tunnel slanted up and Maya began to feel a dark presence. "Be careful, everyone," she whispered softly.

"There are Dark Searchers in there. I didn't realize just how many followed Dirian, but it's got to be at least forty."

"Forty?" one of the soldiers cried. "I saw the Dark Searchers on Earth—they're unstoppable!"

"Quiet!" Sergeant Romin ordered. "What did you expect? That we'd just stroll in and take the keep without opposition? We're in for the fight of our lives. And each of us must realize that there's a strong possibility we won't be coming out again."

"But we're already dead," Tina said.

"True," Maya hushed. "But your body can be killed again. So we must all be on our guard."

"This is what we signed up for," the sergeant reminded them, "so let's get moving."

Before they separated, Maya gave the troll his final orders. "Remember, you will do everything Kai and Quinn tell you to. Then, when you find Freya, *you* will keep her safe. Do you understand?"

The troll nodded. "As you command."

Maya said to her brother, "I emptied his mind and altered his loyalties. He is to serve our side now. But be careful in there."

"You too," Kai said.

They approached the hidden entrance to the keep. It was a thick stone arch, supporting the weight of the keep far above. Built into the arch were two tall doors, cut of the same stone.

As Quinn used his magic to open the doors, Kai turned back to Maya and whispered, "Remember, the moment you free Vanir-Freyja, get her out of here and go back to Midgard. Don't wait for us." His eyes settled on Skye. "I want you to use your strongest magic to seal these doors after you leave here."

"But you'll be trapped."

"Yes," Kai acknowledged. "And so will the Dark Searchers. They won't be able to follow you through this tunnel, and the other one will take them only to the Great City. It's too hot for them to fly after you when the sun's out. It will give you time to escape."

"What about you?" Maya said.

"We'll free Freya, Skuld, and Archie, and then Quinn will open the doors again. But even if we don't make it out, Vanir-Freyja is the most significant hostage."

Reluctantly, Maya nodded her head. Vanir-Freyja was the most important part of their mission. She would have to trust Kai and Quinn to save her younger sister.

The moment Quinn raised his hands and cast his spell, the two heavy stone doors swung open and a blast of hot, dry air blew into their faces. Powerful evil emanated from deep inside the red stone keep, causing Maya to shiver despite the heat. Freya was trapped in there with it. Maya also sensed a presence older than she'd ever felt before: Vanir-Freyja.

They entered the secret passage and followed the low

tunnel to a crossroads. "That way goes to the tunnel beneath the dungeon." The troll pointed and then turned his filthy finger in the opposite direction. "The stairs going up into the keep are that way."

Maya nodded to her brother a final time as he and his team drew their weapons and disappeared down a dark, arched corridor. She motioned for Skye and Tina to keep low and follow her as they walked in the opposite direction.

Senses on full alert, Maya freed her sword and padded softly down the dimly lit corridor. She held up her hand as she neared the first bend. "There are two Dark Elves and a dwarf just ahead," she whispered.

They paused and listened to the slurred voices of the Dark Elves mumbling before one called out loudly, "Where have you been? We've been waiting ages. . . ."

A dwarf's voice responded, "This barrel is heavy. If you two had stopped drinking long enough, you could have helped me carry it down here. . . ."

The drunken argument continued as Maya looked back at her team. "Tina, don't use your gun just yet—we don't want to alarm the keep. Let's keep it quiet. Skye, you use magic, and I'll use my sword."

Skye nodded. The wide-eyed, butterfly-winged Vanir reminded Maya of Freya. She was young, determined, and ready to surrender her life for the protection of others.

With a final nod, the three crept around the corner.

Maya pulled in her senses and tried to suppress her powers to mask her presence from the two drunken Dark Elves, but it didn't work.

The Dark Elves felt her and turned. Maya and Skye had no choice but to charge at them. There was no time for the elves to give alarm or even draw their weapons before Maya cut one down with her blade and Skye obliterated the other with magic.

The dwarf squealed in rage and ran at Maya. Even before he could raise his sword, Tina stopped him with the dagger Quinn had given her.

Maya nodded to the human soldier—acknowledging her ability with the blade.

"This way." She motioned as she led her team deeper into the keep. Maya followed her senses, taking the sandy trail toward the keep's most important prisoner. After turning down another, narrower corridor, she stopped and looked up at the ceiling. "Vanir-Freyja is directly above us. Skye, any chance you can cut through the ceiling to get into her cell?"

When Skye nodded, Maya looked at Tina. "Vanir-Freyja is surrounded by female Dark Elves and trolls. More than I can fight with my sword alone. I hate the noise it's going to make, but you must use your weapon. We're going to need all your skills as a fighter. After we get Vanir-Freyja, we'll bring her back down through here and out of the keep the way we came in. Understood?"

"I'm ready," Tina said.

"Me too," agreed Skye. "I'll open a hole above us and lift us up through it. Be prepared—it's going to happen quickly."

Skye closed her eyes and started to whisper. Moments later, a large hole appeared in the ceiling and two trolls fell through it. Maya silenced them with her sword before the three of them shot up through the hole.

They arrived in a heavily secured cell. Within a fraction of a second, Maya took in the entire scene. She saw a still, shrouded figure lying on the bed against the far wall. At the head of the bed perched a Dark Elf, whispering a spell. Maya's senses told her the figure on the bed was Vanir-Freyja. The actions of the Dark Elf suggested that she was being kept in a deep sleep by some sort of magical charm.

The rest of the cell was filled with more female Dark Elves, trolls, and dwarfs serving as guards for their ancient, powerful prisoner.

With no time to think, Maya flashed her blade and cut down the Dark Elves charging at her. A loud explosion of gunfire burst to life behind her and echoed through the dungeon level. Tina was taking on the guards outside the cell who were working to get in through the door.

"There are too many!" Tina cried. "Skye, seal the cell door!"

After the final Dark Elf fell to Maya's blade, Maya ran forward and killed the elf keeping their prisoner asleep. Maya scooped up the ancient Vanir in her arms and was shocked to discover that the wings on Vanir-Freyja's back were feathered like the Valkyries' and not insectoid, like most other Vanir.

Maya turned and watched Tina shooting through the bars and taking down guards while Skye used magic to secure the cell doors. Moments later three large Dark Searchers appeared outside the cell and roared at the sight of the intruders.

"Come on!" Maya clutched Vanir-Freyja close and jumped through the hole.

A second later, Skye landed on the sandy ground beside her. She looked up and immediately closed the hole in the ceiling.

"Where's Tina?"

"The Searcher threw one of his swords at her through the bars," Skye cried. "She's dead. They're sounding the alarm—we have to go!"

For an instant Maya felt conflicted. Freya was still trapped in the keep, but Vanir-Freyja was safe in her arms.

"Please forgive me, Freya," Maya whispered up to the ceiling.

With Skye by her side, they headed toward the exit.

29

THE ONLY WAY FREYA COULD TELL THE DIFFERENCE between night and day was through the temperature of the War Room. It was hot at night but stifling during the day.

She passed in and out of sleep as her body slowly healed, with the pain from her back and ribs a constant reminder of her loss.

Lying on her side, she tried her best not to reveal the emotions raging through her. Dirian's latest torment had been the most effective yet. His words cut more than anything he could have done with a sword.

The rebel Dark Searcher had taken great pleasure in informing her that his giants had broken through Asgard's outer wall and were now marching on Valhalla. He was preparing to leave the keep and join his generals there to capture the throne.

"This won't take long." Dirian leaned in close to her and rasped, "When I return, I will bring a special gift, just for you. . . ." He rose and headed for the door but paused before passing through to look back at her. "I will bring you Odin's head."

When he was gone, Freya lay her head down. Part of her wished Dirian had killed her, so she wouldn't have to witness Odin's defeat and the destruction of her home.

"Do not cry, Freya." From across the War Room, Skuld's voice was like a soothing lullaby in the long, terrifying night. "Things seem their darkest now, but the future is in flux. Nothing is set. Many things can happen, and fortunes can still change."

Freya raised her head and sniffed. "How? Dirian will march on Asgard with the giants. He'll kill Odin. How can the future be anything but awful?"

Skuld leaned back against the wall. "Because nothing is ever as it appears. Just as you are not as you appear—"

The arrival of a Dark Elf guard interrupted her midflow, and the change in the Norn was instant.

"Release me, you wretched creature!" Skuld screeched. "Never in my life have I been treated so disrespectfully. If you do not free me this instant, I swear I will erase you from existence!"

Freya watched in stunned silence. This was the first time she had heard Skuld raise her voice, and the Norn sounded a lot older than she looked. Every word dripped with threat. Freya's senses told her that the young Norn meant every- thing she said.

"Erase me from existence?" the elf repeated. "Those are powerful words from a child, especially one chained to a wall. Tell me, Skuld, how do you hope to achieve my demise?"

"I have my ways. Do not doubt . . ."

As they argued, Orus flew silently into the War Room. He landed unseen behind Freya and was hidden from view by her body. "Orus!" Freya was so relieved to see her friend. "What's happening—do you know what they did to Archie?"

"Don't worry—Archie has not been harmed. He remains here in the keep, but Dirian and his generals are on the move—they're heading to Asgard!"

Freya nodded. "It's awful," she whispered. "The giants have breached the boundaries of Asgard and are pouring in. Soon Odin will fall. . . ."

"Don't give up yet," Orus cawed softly. *"He won't be easy to beat."*

Freya was about to speak when her wounded senses picked up on something she'd never thought she'd feel again. She inhaled sharply. Maya and Kai! They were in the keep— deep down somewhere below her. And then she felt the pres- ence of Quinn and Skye.

"You!" the Dark Elf called, hearing Freya's gasp. She

stepped away from Skuld and walked closer to Freya. "What are you up to over there?"

"Careful," Orus whispered. *"Don't let her know I'm here."*

"If you must know," Freya shouted, wincing at the pain it caused her, "I'm in agony. What do you expect—me to sing with joy? Every time I breathe, it is like Dirian's blade cutting through me again." She knew that would please the evil elf, and her senses told her it had. "I need something for the pain."

"The Valkyrie is in pain? Good!" the Dark Elf cried with glee. "You deserve it, and much more. Why the master spares your life is a mystery to me. But I am sure he has more plans to make you suffer."

Freya's lips went tight. "You're the one that's going to suffer. . . ."

The Dark Elf laughed as she made her way to her seat—a posting where she could keep an eye on both Freya and Skuld.

Freya became silent and unmoving as the Dark Elf's beady eyes kept their watch on her. She kept her emotions well hidden while she inwardly celebrated. Across the room, Skuld gasped and started to smile. She too must have seen the arrival of the rescue team.

"What is it, Norn?" the Dark Elf demanded suspiciously. "What have you seen?"

"Leave her alone!" Freya shouted, forcing herself up

into a sitting position. She was still weak and dizzy from her wounds, but feeling her family close was giving her strength to keep fighting.

"What is this?" the Dark Elf shrieked. "Is the Valkyrie giving *me* orders?" She ran across the room and tried to kick Freya, but despite her wounds, Freya's reactions were faster. She caught hold of the Dark Elf's foot and twisted it back so quickly, she felt the delicate bones snap.

The elf cried out in pain and fell to the floor. Freya kept hold of her foot and pulled her close, quickly finishing her off.

"That's for threatening to eat Orus!" Freya spat. "I hope your head really hurts when you rise again."

"She won't rise again," Skuld said darkly.

Across from her, the Norn bit the end of her finger and was writing the Dark Elf's name on the stone floor in her blood. She swept her finger through the name, as though to wipe it out. "There, you horrible creature. You deserved that!"

Freya stared in stunned silence at the small Norn. The youthful expression had vanished from her face to reveal a powerful, ancient being with more than a trace of malice. Just as quickly, this disappeared and Skuld sat back, looking as innocent as ever.

Moments later an alarm bell started to chime from far above. Shouts filled the corridors of the keep. Stomping feet could be heard just outside the War Room.

Freya felt her sister somewhere beneath them; she was with Vanir-Freyja. She could feel Maya's excitement— this was a good sign. Suddenly there was hope that not all was lost.

"*Freya,*" Orus cawed, drawing her attention back. "*Check the elf's pockets. Does she have the keys to your collar?*"

"Don't," Skuld called quickly. "We only have a moment before the others discover what's happened in here. When I told you the future was in flux, I meant it. I have just seen something and must share it with you. You are no ordinary Valkyrie. You have power way beyond your knowledge, but you don't know how to use it. You must learn as quickly as possible—the future depends on you."

"I don't understand. What power?" Freya cried. "What are you talking about?"

"The power of the Vanir."

30

MAYA AND SKYE CHARGED THROUGH THE NARROW corridor deep in the bowels of the keep. Clutching Vanir-Freyja protectively, Maya navigated her way back to the tunnel entrance.

Just as they passed through the doors, Maya felt an unwelcome presence. "Searchers are coming," she cried. "Skye, seal the doors!"

Skye nodded and waved her hand. The thick stone doors started to swing shut just as the Dark Searchers arrived and began to pound and push against them.

"Seal them!"

"I'm trying!" Skye cried as her hands moved quickly through the air to cast the locking spell. "But the Dark Elves are using their own magic to force them open. They're too strong for me—the doors won't hold!"

Maya shifted Vanir-Freyja to one arm and pulled out her sword. Just as the heavy stone doors started to give, a hand shot out from under the shroud and grasped Skye's arm.

"Calm yourself, child. Focus your powers and let me help you . . . ," a soft voice said.

Skye inhaled sharply and recast her spell on the door. The heavy stone doors slammed shut.

As Maya started to put Vanir-Freyja down, the ancient Vanir's soft voice spoke again from beneath the shroud. "No, Maya, take me away from here, please. . . ."

How did Vanir-Freyja know her name? "Of course," Maya said respectfully. "Anything you say." She settled Vanir-Freyja in her arms again and spread her wings wide. She looked back at Skye. "I hope you can keep up with me."

"I'm right behind you," Skye said, casting her magic to lift off the ground.

Maya flapped her large white wings and took off through the deep tunnel running beneath the burning sands of the desert. She flew harder and faster than she'd ever flown in her life. Before long the tunnel ascended, and Skye lifted them through the hidden entrance in the hovel. When they were safe, Maya kicked the trapdoor shut. She looked around the small room for somewhere to lay her charge.

As if in answer to her thoughts, Skye waved her hand, and a narrow, soft bed appeared.

Maya lay Vanir-Freyja down gently. She reached for the shroud and pulled it away. Maya gazed down into the face that had the power to start wars. She was too stunned to speak.

Beside her, Skye was doing the same. Her mouth was hanging open as her eyes passed from Vanir-Freyja to Maya and then back to Vanir-Freyja again.

"Maya, she looks just like you!"

Vanir-Freyja's ice-blue eyes fluttered open. When she saw Maya, she smiled gently. "No, Skye. My great-great-granddaughter looks just like me. . . ."

Maya fell backward and landed awkwardly on her wings as Vanir-Freyja sat up. Maya's mirror image fluttered open her white wings and reached out to Maya. "Come, my child. Take my hand."

Struck silent by the sight, Maya climbed to her knees and crawled forward. She took Vanir-Freyja's hand.

"I'm so sorry that you've borne the curse of my image," she said softly. "But you are my blood, my direct descendant, and it was too great a power to lay dormant for very long."

"I—I don't understand," Maya mumbled. "How is this possible?"

"In Asgard, anything is possible," Vanir-Freyja said. "When my brother, Freyr, and I were traded as hostages in war, we settled in Asgard. It became our home and we flourished there. But when I arrived, I was already with child. I had one daughter, the first Valkyrie—a full-blooded Vanir, but born in Asgard. And then she had a daughter, and so on.

"As each new generation came, my brother and I cast a spell that would stop most of our powers from being inherited. But recently we've felt the tension in the realms growing, and we realized that Asgard needed special defenders. When you and your sisters were born, we did not cast the suppression spell. You all have our powers, and you, my dear heart, are the closest to me in looks. But your beauty has been a curse, hasn't it?"

Maya lowered her head.

"Of course it has, especially in Valhalla with all those warriors. I have seen how they've all fallen in love with you."

"You have?" Maya whispered.

Vanir-Freyja smiled, and it lit her whole face with a beauty that Maya had seen reflected in her dressing mirror many times before.

"Oh, my sweet child, I never left Asgard. I live there still and have watched over you and your family—my family—closely. I have seen my namesake, Freya, and her restless, unstoppable spirit. I've watched Gwyn's, Skaga's, and Kara's fighting skills develop, and I've seen you grow into the powerful beauty that you are."

"How can this be?" Maya asked. "Surely we would have seen you?"

Vanir-Freyja waved her hand over her face. Suddenly her beauty vanished and an old crone in a thick, tattered cloak was sitting before her. The cloak hid her wings and gave the appearance of a painful hump. Her voice cracked with age. "This is the only way I could ever find freedom from my curse."

Maya instantly recognized the sweet-seller from the market her family regularly attended. For as long as she could remember, the old woman had given her and her sisters treats whenever they visited. "You're Old Maave?"

The old crone nodded. "It was the only way I could see my family without causing mayhem. How I have longed to hold you all and tell you who I am. Your uncle Freyr has felt the same. You know him as Rathgar."

Maya didn't think anything could be more shocking— but finding out that her great-great-grandmother was Vanir-Freyja and that her great-great-uncle was actually the old blacksmith working at the stables of the Reaping Mares was almost too much to take in.

"Rathgar," she repeated softly. "He's always been so nice to me and takes extra-special care with my Reaping Mare when he makes her shoes."

"Of course. He loves you. He loves all of you as much as I do, which is why we stay close and do what we can to protect you."

"You know everything about us?"

Vanir-Freyja nodded. "Everything and everyone. Including the birth of Vonni's baby."

Skye was sitting beside Maya, listening in silence, but finally reached out. "I am sorry to break this up—but the war. We must stop the war."

"What war?" Vanir-Freyja said.

Maya shook her head and focused on the immediate. "Of course." She turned back to her ancestor. "Don't you know about the war? What Dirian has done?"

Vanir-Freyja shook her head. "I know nothing. From the moment the Dark Elves discovered my secret and caught me in Asgard, I have been kept under a sleeping spell." She looked around the hovel. "I can see and feel that we're in Muspelheim, but I don't know why."

Maya told Vanir-Freyja everything she knew, including the giants' arrival on Earth and how Dirian had caused it all. She finished with what he'd done to Freya.

"He cut off my baby's wings!" Vanir-Freyja raged. "I'll crush him!"

"There are many of us waiting to do that," Maya said softly. "But before that, we must stop the war in the realms from turning into—"

"Ragnarök," Vanir-Freyja finished.

Skye nodded. "We believe Dirian has been offering you as the prize for the giants when they help him defeat Odin. You are to be given to their kings."

As the news sank in, the crone facade slipped away and was replaced by Vanir-Freyja's outstanding beauty—beauty tinged with pain. "It's this cursed face of mine," she said miserably. "Because of it, war in the realms has started."

Tears rimmed her eyes, and seeing her pain was almost too much for Maya to bear. She shook her head. "Listen to me. This isn't your fault, and it's not Freya's either, though she still argues it is. Dirian is doing this, no one else. It's obvious your face hasn't captured his heart. He was going to give you away to those who served him. So it's his crime, not yours. But *you* are the only one who can stop it."

"Me? How?" Vanir-Freyja said miserably.

Maya rose and reached down for her distant grandmother's hands. "By coming with us to Earth and showing the giants that you are free and will never be anyone's prize."

Vanir-Freyja nodded. She stood and wrapped her arms and wings around Maya. "We will do this together. You and I, my great-great-granddaughter and mirror twin. We will use our beauty like weapons and lead the giants away from Midgard and send them back to their realms."

Maya smiled. "For most of my life, I've resented how I look and been envious of my sisters' fighting skill. But that ends today. If beauty started this war, then together we will use our beauty to stop it!"

31

THE KEEP WAS IN UPROAR AS DIRIAN AND HIS GENERALS charged back into the War Room. Freya didn't need to use her senses to know how furious the Dark Searcher was. He stormed over to the table and slammed both his fists down. The enormous table buckled beneath his rage, and the maps went flying and then settled on the floor around the room.

"Find me the map with the tunnels to all the realms!" Dirian shouted to his men. "If Vanir-Freyja thinks she can find sanctuary back home, she's in for a rude surprise. We'll unleash fire giants on Vanaheim—and as their realm burns, they'll plead for mercy and surrender her to me!"

The map was found and Dirian called his generals forward. He stole a glance over his shoulder and caught Freya watching him.

"You!" he raged, taking three long strides to reach her.

The body of the Dark Elf was still beside her. Dirian took one look at it and kicked it aside as though it meant nothing to him. "That sister of yours has stolen my prize! But it won't save her or your realm. I will find Vanir-Freyja, and when I do, Maya will pay for her crimes—and I will make you watch!"

"You've lost, Dirian!" Freya shouted.

"Freya, stop!" Skuld warned frantically. "Say no more!"

Freya knew she should keep her mouth shut, but she couldn't. She was in pain, and hearing that Maya had freed Vanir-Freyja was the best news possible. Even if Dirian killed her now, she could die happy.

"Without Vanir-Freyja, you have nothing to offer the giants. They'll turn on you and squash you like the insignificant bug that you are!"

Dirian's fury soared and washed over her in waves. He drew his black blade and lifted it over his head.

Freya closed her eyes. This was it. She would not live to see the end of the war. Archie, Orus, and her family would be lost to her, and she'd never learn who her father was. It would all end now—and she was ready. . . .

Freya waited one heartbeat, and then two, but nothing happened. She opened her eyes. Dirian had put his weapon away and knelt down close to her.

"Thank you . . . ," he rasped with his fractured voice.

"Thank you, Freya. Once again you have made me see things clearly. Were it not for you, I would have made a terrible mistake and followed Vanir-Freyja. But now I realize I don't need the giants anymore. Asgard has already fallen. Only Odin stands in the way of my ruling all the realms."

He reached out to her, and Freya flinched back. But instead of striking her, Dirian patted her lightly on the head as though she were a young child being praised by a parent. "You will make an excellent part of my war council."

Dirian rose and walked back to his men, his whole demeanor changed. He pointed at one of the generals. "I want you to take a team of Searchers and go after Vanir-Freyja. The giants don't know she's free yet—use that to your advantage. Take a group of fire giants with you to Vanaheim. I want her found and brought back here. Now that Vanir-Freyja has sealed our primary tunnel, it's useless to us. Take the secondary one. It's longer, but you will come out in the Great City. Go from there."

He turned to the others. "You're with me." Glancing back once more at Freya, he said to his men, "While they go after Vanir-Freyja, we will go to Asgard. Before another day has come and gone, Odin will be dead!"

"*Freya, what have you done?*" Orus emerged from his hiding spot.

Freya was shaking her head, trying to understand what had just happened. "I wanted to make him really angry, to distract him and give Maya time to get Vanir-Freyja away from here. I was ready to let him kill me."

"Dirian is too clever for that," Skuld called. "I tried to warn you."

"I know. I'm sorry," Freya said, bowing her head. She looked miserably at Orus. "Why don't I ever listen?"

"It's not in your nature," the raven said sadly. *"Most of the time your instincts work."*

"Not this time," Freya said. "I've made things worse."

"Then you are going to have to fix it," Skuld called.

"How?"

"By acknowledging your mistake and moving on."

Freya looked at Skuld, chained to the opposite wall. She appeared to be so young, but she sounded older than anyone else Freya had ever met before.

"Freya, hear me," the Norn continued. "You are alive, and while you are, there is hope. I told you, the future is in flux. Many things are happening at once. Nothing is clear, not even to me. Remember what I told you. You must summon a part of you that you've never used before. You have strength, and power. Now is the time to use it before it's too late."

"What power? I just don't understand."

"Yes, you do," Skuld said cryptically.

Freya cast her mind back to the beginning—when they were still in Midgard, preparing to leave for Muspelheim.

What was it Quinn had said after she'd helped them lift the stone altar? Something about her Valkyrie blood having a lot of power in it.

Was that what Skuld meant?

Did she have Vanir powers? There were times in her life when things had happened that she couldn't explain—when she'd achieved things and she couldn't possibly understand how or why, like defeating the much bigger and stronger Dirian at the Ten Realms Challenge. And being the fastest flyer in Asgard. She'd always believed it was her wings carrying her forward, but perhaps there was more to it.

Freya sat very still for some time, considering Skuld's words and all the occasions in her life when strange, unexplained things had happened. She closed her eyes and pushed back the pain from her severed wings and broken ribs. Taking a deep, cleansing breath, she reached out with her senses. She could tell that all the Dark Searchers had now left the keep as they made their final push in the war.

Apart from one. Kai was still alive, somewhere in the keep. She could feel him. As she reached out further, she felt Quinn and the soldiers with him too. There weren't as many as before, but a couple remained. They were with . . . Freya inhaled. She could feel that they were with Archie!

"Calm," Skuld called. "That's it. Remain calm and breathe deeply. Focus on what you want to do."

Freya took another long, deep breath and ignored the

pinching from her ribs. She reached up and grasped the metal collar around her neck.

Orus moved closer and climbed up onto her knee as she sat cross-legged on the stone floor. *"You can do it, Freya,"* he coached. *"You can do anything."*

With Orus and Skuld offering encouragement, Freya started to pull at the lock securing the collar around her neck. The heavy metal seemed to move a fraction, but when she felt it shift, it broke her concentration and everything stopped.

"Try it again," Orus cawed.

"But it's so hard." Freya panted from the strain. "I can't break metal, at least not this kind."

"Then you are already defeated," Skuld said. "If you don't believe in yourself, how can you expect others to have faith in you?"

Those words stung. "Just because I can't break metal doesn't mean I don't believe in myself!"

"Why are you trying to break the lock?" Skuld asked. "Surely you can't. But what you want to do is open it."

"Open it? How?"

"Haven't I told you already?"

"All you've said is that I have the power of the Vanir. But you didn't say how! If you know so much, why don't you tell me?"

"That is up to you to discover," Skuld said.

"You're talking in riddles now?" Freya fumed. "Just as

Dirian is moving in on Asgard? Skuld, if you know something I don't—and you do, because you're the Norn of the future—for Odin's sake, tell me!"

Skuld's expression dropped as if Freya had struck her. "I can't tell you how to do something I don't know how to do myself." It sounded as though she were on the verge of tears. "All I know is I've seen you use the power. But that doesn't mean I know how to teach it to you."

Freya felt as if she'd stolen a treat from a child. "Skuld, I'm sorry. I didn't mean to yell at you. But this is so important, and I just don't know what to do."

Orus pecked Freya in the leg. *"You're overthinking this. You always do your most amazing things when you don't have time to think about it. So stand up, open that collar at your neck, and save Odin!"*

"How?"

"Don't ask how. Just do it!" Orus shouted.

Freya put Orus down and climbed slowly to her feet. This was the first time she'd stood since Dirian's attack. Her balance was way off because she didn't have the weight of her wings on her back. Everything felt strange and wrong. She leaned against the wall for support until she found her balance and stood straight.

"That's it," Orus cawed, flying up to his proper place on her shoulder. *"Now pull the collar's lock to the front and do like Quinn or Skye would do, and open it."*

Freya was filled with doubt. This was insane. But with so much at stake, she had to believe that deep down inside, somehow, she had the power of the Vanir.

Once again Freya clasped both sides of the metal collar. Instead of straining to use her strength to pull it open, she focused all her thoughts on "wanting" it open.

It was impossible to know who in the War Room was the most shocked as a loud *click* echoed through the large empty room.

As the collar fell away, Freya's eyes went wide. "Orus, I did it!"

"I knew you could all along!" Orus said as he playfully nipped her ear.

Freya reached up, caught him by the beak, and gave him a big kiss. "Thanks, Orus."

Free of her chains, Freya took two unsteady steps forward. Without the weight of her wings for balance, walking felt strange, and she wondered how long it had taken Brundi or even Dirian to get used to being wingless.

Freya could sense that the corridor directly outside the War Room was empty and that they were alone. The first thing she did was walk over to the door where Dirian had posted the parchment with the list of her family names on it.

Catching hold of her golden flame sword, Freya pulled it out of the wall, freeing the list. She caught the parchment in her hands and shivered as she read the names of her family again.

"Skuld, can you take this back? Can you give my family their futures again?"

The young Norn nodded. "Bring the list to me."

Freya never imagined that walking across a room could be so difficult or awkward. But now that she was upright, the wounds on her back were throbbing and her balance was still way off.

As she drew closer to the Norn, Freya was finally able to see her clearly. Skuld did look like a child. But as Freya came closer to her, she saw that Skuld's eyes were solid white.

"Skuld, are you blind?"

"I am the Norn of the future," Skuld said. "I must be blind to the past and present; otherwise I wouldn't be able to see the future."

Freya's heart immediately went out to her. "I'm so sorry. Why didn't you tell me?"

"What difference would it make? Yes, I'm blind and I can't see you right now, but I am no less the person I was before you knew, and you shouldn't treat me any differently."

"Why would I?"

"Some do," Skuld said. "That I am without present sight makes some believe I am less than they are. But I often ask them, 'Can you see the future?' and that makes them think."

Skuld reached for the parchment. "Freya, before I do this, you must know—I can't help those who have already fallen from this list. They will not rise again."

A dagger of fear cut through Freya's heart. "Do you know who's fallen?"

The Norn said nothing, but nodded.

"Please, you must tell me."

Skuld shook her head. "I can't. To tell you would distract you from the trial you must now face. But I will say there have been only two losses. Everyone else on the list is alive."

Freya's heart raced as she scanned the parchment again. Her mother, grandmother, sisters, brother, cousins, and uncles were there—almost everyone she cared for most in all the realms was on that list. To know that two had fallen was unbearable. "You must tell me!" she cried. "Don't you understand? I can't go on without knowing. Please, who have I lost?"

Tears rimmed the Norn's eyes. "I am so sorry, Freya. Your grandmother, Brünnhilde, and your sister Skaga were killed in separate incidents. Skaga was defeated by a fire giant. I promise you; it was quick and painless. She died bravely, surrendering her life to save humans."

The Norn paused and then inhaled deeply. "Brünnhilde and her raven were killed when two frost giants attacked the mountain she and your cousins were hiding in. Myriam and baby Michael are alive. I do see a future for them, but until this war ends, that future is in flux."

At her shoulder, Orus cawed in grief. But Freya was silent. She felt the air sucked out of her body as her legs gave out and she collapsed to her knees. Her amazing sister Skaga was dead for good. Brundi, who had suffered so much and had risen above it all to do great things, was gone.

"You shouldn't have told her, Skuld." A Dark Searcher entered the War Room. "Knowing never helps anyone . . ."

Freya gasped, fighting to hold back tears. The Dark Searchers would never see her cry. Instead she let rage overwhelm her senses as she reached for her sword. Driven mad by fury, she rose and turned.

Silenced by grief, Freya stalked the Dark Searcher. Clear thinking was gone. She felt no pain from her wing stumps, burns, or broken bones. She felt nothing but an overwhelming desire to share with him the agony she was suffering. She lifted her sword, unwilling to wait for him to defend himself. Skaga and Brundi were dead; soon he would be too.

The Searcher stumbled back and held up his hands. "Freya, stop!" Suddenly the Dark Searcher shimmered and melted into a familiar form, standing before her in green armor holding a Vanir staff in one hand.

"Loki?" Freya staggered and dropped her sword, unable to trust her eyes. But her senses quickly confirmed what she couldn't believe. "Is that really you?"

Loki nodded. "I am sorry for your loss—for our loss. Brundi was a very special woman. She meant everything to me."

Tears that she'd fought so hard to hold back flooded her eyes. "You're alive . . . ?"

Loki nodded and opened his arms to her. Freya ran forward and embraced him as though he were the only real thing left in her life.

"Let it out, Freya," he said softly into her hair. Loki held her tight but was careful not to touch her wing stumps as he rocked her like a father comforting a suffering daughter. "Just let it all out."

32

MAYA WAS FILLED WITH MIXED EMOTIONS AS THEY entered the Yggdrasil tunnel and left Muspelheim behind. She had rescued Vanir-Freyja, but leaving her sister, Kai, and Quinn behind was the hardest thing she'd ever done in her life.

Vanir-Freyja cast a spell to carry them through the roots of Yggdrasil to Midgard.

Traveling at speed, Maya was barely aware of passing from one realm to the next. It was only when they rounded the corner and saw a cluster of soldiers before them that she realized they were entering the domain of Midgard.

"Maya! I'm so glad to see you! We didn't know what to do, so we've been waiting here for you."

"Tina?" Maya called. Three other soldiers from their journey to Muspelheim were there as well—including the one whose ghost she'd sent back to Earth to warn Thor about Vanir-Freyja. But as she reached out with her senses, she realized that none of them were ghosts anymore. They were very much alive and healthy.

Not much farther down the tunnel, the body of Sergeant Romin sat against the wall—looking unchanged and alone. Private Cornish scratched his head. "I don't know what happened. One moment I was talking to Thor, passing on your message about Vanir-Freyja, and the next, I was back here."

Another private said, "I was at the keep with Kai and Quinn, and some Dark Searchers came. Then I woke up here."

Tina nodded. "All I remember is entering the cell with you. . . ." She frowned. "But then everything went blank and, just like the others, I woke up here."

Maya remembered perfectly well what had happened to Tina. "You don't remember being killed by the Dark Searchers as they tried to enter the cell to stop us?"

Tina frowned and shook her head.

"Maya," Private Cornish said, "these are our bodies, right? I mean, I know that Freya reaped us, but we're alive again, aren't we? How is this possible?"

"I really don't know," Maya admitted. "You were dead. I know you were. But now you're alive, and I don't understand how."

Vanir-Freyja nodded. "I believe I do. Tell me, when Freya reaped you, were you here in this tunnel?"

"Yes," Tina said. "And our bodies were left right there, just like John's is now. Our ghosts went to Muspelheim with Freya and Skye to try to free you."

Vanir-Freyja nodded. "Your bodies were held in the embrace of Yggdrasil. The World Tree kept them safe for when you needed them again. When each of you completed your task, Yggdrasil returned your spirits to your bodies and restored you to life."

The ancient Vanir came forward and touched Tina's face. "But you have changed. You are no longer a human of Midgard. Nor are you Aesir, or Vanir, or of any one realm. You are part of all realms—you are the children of Yggdrasil. It is a great honor she has bestowed upon you. You must use this gift wisely."

Behind them came the sound of a deep inhalation and a cough. Everyone looked back and saw the body of the sergeant stir. His eyes opened as he took another deep breath. Confusion rose on his face.

"John!" Tina cried. She ran over to him and helped him climb to his feet. "Nice and slow. It takes a moment to adjust."

Sergeant Romin shook his head, and then his eyes flashed open. He ran over to Maya. "I don't know what just happened or how I got here, but we have to go back."

"Calm down," Maya said. "If you are here, it means you must have been killed at the keep. Yggdrasil has restored your spirit to your body."

"I—I'm alive?"

When Maya nodded, the sergeant shook his head. "No, no, I can't be. They need me!" He reached out and took Maya's hand. Nothing happened.

"Maya, reap me!" he cried.

Maya looked down at where they were touching and back up to the sergeant, baffled to see that he was still alive.

"She can't," Vanir-Freyja said. "Yggdrasil has changed you. You aren't human anymore and are immune to a Valkyrie's touch."

Tina approached him. "John, she says we can move through all the realms."

"Is this true?" he demanded of Vanir-Freyja.

"I believe so."

The sergeant nodded. "Good." He looked back at his men. "Just like before, this is a volunteer mission. Those of you who want to come with me, do. Those who want to return to Earth, you can go with no charges or blame against you."

"Come where?" Tina asked.

"Back to the keep. Just before I passed out, Kai, Quinn, Archie, and I were on our way up into the War Room to get Freya and Skuld. Outside the door, we heard Dirian and his men making plans."

"Did you see Freya?" Maya demanded. "Is she all right?"

"I couldn't see her, but I could hear her. Dirian was furious that the exit tunnel was sealed after you left. Freya started baiting him, making him even angrier. It sounded like he was going to kill her—"

Maya inhaled. "No . . ."

"It's all right," the sergeant said quickly. "He didn't. From what I could hear, he actually thanked her for making him think clearly. He sent some of his men to take the other tunnel out of the keep and gather a group of fire giants together. They're going to Vanaheim to burn it down and force you to hand Vanir-Freyja back over to him."

"But we're not going to Vanaheim," Skye said.

"He doesn't know that. They're on their way there now."

"What of Dirian?" Vanir-Freyja asked.

The sergeant's eyes landed on Maya. "That's why I wanted you to reap me. I've gotta get back there. Dirian is on his way to Asgard right now. He told Freya it's fallen and he's going to kill Odin." The sergeant paused and started to frown. He rubbed his neck. "I—I can't remember what happened after that. We—we heard them coming out of the War Room and hid in the tower stairs. I think other Searchers found us. . . ." He continued to rub his neck as though it hurt.

From this Maya was sure he had been killed in the tower by a sword strike to the neck. "Can you remember if Kai was hurt?"

Sergeant Romin's brows furrowed deeper as he tried to recall his final moment. He shook his head. "I just don't know. I can't remember anything after that."

"Just as well," Vanir-Freyja said. "Remembering how you died will not serve you going forward."

"We must go back," Maya said. "Dirian must be stopped."

Vanir-Freyja shook her head. "No, child. Our first priority is stopping the giants from destroying Midgard, Vanaheim, and all the realms in between. When they are on our side, we'll move on Asgard and go after Dirian."

"But he could kill Odin!" Maya insisted.

"It is a risk," Vanir-Freyja said. "But Odin is powerful and resourceful. I doubt many alive today will remember what a fierce fighter he can be. It won't be easy for Dirian to kill him."

The sergeant stepped closer to the ancient Vanir. His eyes were filled with passion. "There is nothing I would love to do more than follow you wherever you go. . . ."

Maya felt the sergeant and all the soldiers in the tunnel reacting to Vanir-Freyja's beauty. They were all under her spell and would do anything she said. Or so Maya thought. She was stunned when the soldier continued. "But with all due respect, Odin must be protected. I've seen what that monster Dirian can do. We have to stop him from claiming the throne."

"Of course." Vanir-Freyja smiled at him, and her smile commanded all the soldiers' attention. "Our paths lie in different directions." She turned to Skye. "The choice is yours, my young, brave friend. You may stay with Maya and me as we go after the giants, or lead these Guardians of Yggdrasil to Asgard to protect Odin."

"We won't make it there without you," Sergeant Romin said. "Skye, only you can help us."

Skye's eyes moved from Maya to Vanir-Freyja and then to the sergeant. Finally, determination rose on her young face and she nodded. "What Vanir-Freyja says is true. Our paths do lie in different directions. I will go with the soldiers and use my magic to help defend Odin."

Maya walked up to the young Vanir girl with the badly tattered butterfly wings. "You remind me so much of Freya. Please, take special care of yourself." She gave her a powerful hug. "When this is over, if we are all still standing, there will be great celebrations in Asgard and we will all know such joy."

Skye nodded. "And all the Vanir will be there."

Maya stood with Vanir-Freyja and watched the brave soldiers departing down the tunnel with Skye. She could sense that the change in realms was not affecting the soldiers. It was true, Yggdrasil had altered them and made them all part of the Great Cosmic Tree.

"Do you think they'll be all right?"

"I hope so," Vanir-Freyja said. "Yggdrasil is counting on them."

"We all are," Maya agreed.

Once again the Vanir used her magic to move them swiftly through the tunnel. Finally, their long journey came to an end when the ground beneath them started to tilt up toward the entrance in the Temple of the Sun in Peru.

"Now, before we start, we must be set on our course." The ancient Vanir took Maya's hands. "This will not be as easy as you might think, my child. We are going to cast a spell that will never be broken. In doing this, we will unleash your greatest power—power that has lain dormant within you until now.

"After this, anyone who hears you—be they giant, human, elf, or Asgardian—will become as obsessed with you as they are with me. The life you knew will end. You will know no peace, freedom, or respite from their pursuit. Not in Asgard, Midgard, or any realm. They will always be looking for you—not to do harm, but to love and possess you. Trust me. This is a great burden to carry, much greater than you have known. To find peace, you will have to do as I have done and live the rest of your life in hiding."

Maya considered her words carefully. "If we do this, will it end the war?"

Vanir-Freyja nodded. "I believe so. When the giants are

enchanted, they will do our bidding and return home. All that will remain will be to stop Dirian and his men from taking the throne. Even if they succeed in killing Odin, they must never rule. If needs be, we will command the giants to stop them for us."

"I understand," Maya said somberly. She took her great-great-grandmother's hand and nodded. "Let's do this."

33

KAI, QUINN, AND ARCHIE RAN INTO THE WAR ROOM BUT
stopped short when they saw Loki holding Freya.

"Loki?" Archie cried. "What are you doing here? We saw
you die in Montreal."

"Get away from my sister!" Kai demanded, charging over.

Loki gave Freya a final squeeze and whispered gently,
"Dry your tears and don't tell them about Brundi or Skaga. It
can't help them to know just yet."

He turned on Archie. "You might wish I had died, ghost,
but it will take more than a few giants to end me. So what
took you so long to get here? Or were you hoping Freya and
I would take Dirian down by ourselves?"

That set Kai off, and he furiously explained what they'd
been through.

While Kai talked, Archie approached Freya. "Gee, are you all right?"

Freya nodded, still unable to speak without breaking down and telling him what had happened to her family. Instead she stumbled into his arms, grateful that he was unharmed.

"It's gonna be all right. I promise," he reassured her. "I know what Dirian did to you. But you're alive—that's all that matters."

Freya nodded and pointed to the place where she'd been chained. Posted on the wall were her black wings.

"That monster! He's mounted them like a trophy!" Archie left Freya and ran over to the wall. Jumping up, he caught hold of her severed wings and wrenched them down. "I'd rather see them burned than left up there for him."

"I'm so sorry." Quinn approached her cautiously. "Do you want me to get rid of them so Dirian can't have them?"

When Freya nodded, Quinn put his hand on her shoulder and gave it a squeeze. "You're sure?" he asked gently.

Was she sure? Her wings . . . They were so much a part of her life. How was she going to live without them? "They're not really mine anymore. They're just useless wings that will never fly again. Yes, please, destroy them."

"*Your beautiful wings . . . ,*" Orus moaned.

"They're gone," Freya whispered to him.

Quinn took the wings from Archie and frowned.

"They're much heavier than I expected," he said. "No wonder you could fly so fast—you had an unfair advantage when we raced. No one could beat these!"

Archie shook his head. "Not now, Quinn . . ."

"Archie, it's all right," Freya said, knowing Quinn was trying to make her feel better. As she watched Quinn put her wings down on the floor, Freya realized that was another thing she would grieve over for the rest of her life. She wondered how long it would take to get used to being grounded.

"You might want to look away," Kai warned.

"C'mon, Gee," Archie said, taking her by the hand. "Let's check on Skuld."

When they walked over to the Norn, Kai looked back to where Quinn was casting the spell that would destroy Freya's wings. "I swear I am going to kill Dirian for doing that to you."

"We all are," Archie agreed.

Freya wiped away the last of her tears and swallowed down her pain. There would be time enough to mourn later. She took a deep breath. "If we're going to find Dirian, we'd better get moving. He and his men have gone to Asgard to kill Odin."

"We heard," Archie said, still holding her hand tightly. "And we will . . ."

"Just as soon as we get you and Skuld to Vanaheim," Quinn added as he rejoined them.

Freya stole a quick look back, but there was no longer any evidence of her wings. They were gone. Just like Skaga and Brundi. "I don't want to go back to Vanaheim. . . ."

"You must," Quinn insisted. "They'll take care of you and help you heal. And Skuld must be returned to her sisters."

"I'm afraid there's no time for that," Loki said. "Dirian and his men already have a good head start. If we have any hope of getting to Asgard before he does his worst, we must all go now."

"No. You're wrong," Quinn said. "Freya and Skuld must be taken to safety first."

Freya could feel that Quinn cared for her, and it warmed her heart. In this—the worst moment of her life—she realized she felt the same for him. But this wasn't the time for emotions. Freya shook her head. "After *everything* Dirian has taken from me, I want to be there when we stop him. I *have* to be there. All I need is a bit of that potion of yours—the one that takes away pain. Then we can go."

"But it's too dangerous," Quinn insisted.

"*She has to do this*," Orus cawed. "*And for once I agree with her. Freya must face Dirian one last time if she's ever to get past this.*"

"It'll be all right, Quinn," Archie said. "Nothing's ever too dangerous for our Gee. Just give her the potion. We don't have time to argue."

"Finally the ghost has something intelligent to say!"

called Loki as he knelt beside Skuld. "And when you're fin-ished making the potion for Freya, get over here and open Skuld's lock."

Once Skuld was free, she looked even younger and more vulnerable—standing no higher than Freya's shoulder and staring forward blankly. Despite her seeming youth, she was the oldest among them, and the expression on her face made it clear that no one was going to tell her no, or risk angering the tempestuous Norn. "I will go with you to Asgard," she said firmly. "There will be no arguing with me."

"Of course," Loki said. His expression made it clear he was cautious around the ancient Norn.

They headed out of the War Room and entered the corridor.

"Freya, look out. It's the troll that attacked you!" Orus cawed in warning.

Freya simultaneously realized two things. One, she wasn't in pain anymore and could move quickly again. Two—and perhaps most important—although Quinn's potion did relieve her pain, it dulled her senses. She hadn't felt the troll lingering in the corridor.

Freya raised her sword to dispatch him.

"Gee, no!" Archie cried, grabbing her arm. "Don't. He's with us."

"With you?" Freya frowned and looked from the troll to

Archie. "He attacked me when I was in the dungeon. He's no friend of mine!" She pulled her arm away. "Let me do this!"

"Freya, stop!" Skuld commanded. "He has a purpose to fulfill in the future. You must not harm him."

"But—"

"I swear he's with us now," Archie said. "Maya reprogrammed him. He's here to protect you and will show us the way out."

The troll nodded. "Maya told me I had to protect you. I am your slave. . . ."

Freya felt pity mixed with disgust as she watched the sniveling, round troll appear to be happy to be her slave. She took a step back. "All right. All right. You can protect me— but you're not my slave, and you're never to call yourself that again! Do you understand?"

The troll nodded. "I do. I do understand. I will be a good slave."

Freya sighed and shook her head. "How did Dirian get out of here?"

"I will show you!" the troll squealed, jumping gleefully to his stubby feet. He caught Freya by the hand. "Come, come, this way. It will be faster, and I can keep you safe!"

Freya was repulsed by the touch of the troll, but she let him lead her forward. The silence was disturbing as they walked through the long corridor. Where was everyone? Surely their escape couldn't be this easy. Not too long ago, the keep was teeming with Dark Searchers and Dark Elves. When she asked the troll, he shrugged. "They're with Dirian on his mission to kill Odin. Only a few were left, but we've killed them to protect you."

Freya looked back at her brother.

Kai nodded. "We encountered a couple of Dark Searchers and a few Dark Elves and dwarfs. They killed Sergeant Romin before we could stop them. But it seems the keep is now empty."

Freya wasn't sure if this was a relief or a worry. Just how bad was it in Asgard?

"This way," the troll cried, leading them to the tower stairs. "We all go down."

Everything about the keep was eerily quiet. Only the sounds of their footfalls on the thick stone steps disturbed the overwhelming silence.

When they reached the next level, Freya saw the remains of the Dark Searchers and elves Kai was talking about. By the looks of things, the fight had been quick but deadly. As she studied the bodies, she couldn't see the sergeant. She also noted that some of them had no obvious wounds and wondered if Quinn had used magic to dispatch them. She looked back at the Vanir. Quinn simply nodded, confirming it was true.

At the bottom of the stairs, the troll led them forward into another dark, low-ceilinged tunnel. They walked single file, Quinn keeping close to Skuld and acting as her eyes as they reached a narrow archway, with an even narrower corridor beyond it. At the end of that corridor, they faced another set of steps going down. The air around them felt stale and the temperature seemed to be rising, despite their being underground.

"This was only to be used in emergencies . . . ," the troll said. "But now that the other tunnel is blocked, it is the only way out during the hot day."

The potion kept most of her pain under control. But the heat of the still air around them made Freya's burnt skin prickle. She didn't like this one bit. As the troll started to descend, she had no choice but to follow.

At the bottom, they stood before two wide double doors.

Kai tried to push them open but failed. "There's magic keeping them sealed." He looked back at Quinn. "Can you open them?"

Quinn left Skuld in Loki's care and came forward. He brushed past Freya, smiled, and reached for her hand. "With a bit of help, I can."

Freya blushed under the intensity of his stare and took his hand.

"Oh, please," Loki cried. "I think I'm going to be sick. Just open the doors already."

"You ready?" Quinn asked.

Freya nodded, recalling how she had unlocked the chain

around her neck. She took a deep breath, forcing down all her grief, pain, and rage, and focused only on finding calm. She closed her eyes, breathed softly, and thought of nothing but opening the doors.

Holding tightly to Quinn's hand, she felt his presence so close, it was almost as though they were one person. His powers flowed into her, and her own power entered him and then came back into her again. Merged together, their combined powers were directed toward the doors.

The doors didn't just open; they exploded into tiny bits that rained down into the exit tunnel.

"Wow," Archie cried. "That was awesome!"

Orus cawed and flapped his wings. *"You did it!"*

Quinn kept hold of Freya's hand. "Someone's been practicing."

"Freya, is there something you should tell us?" Loki asked with a raised eyebrow.

"It's nothing," Freya said quickly. She released Quinn's hand, suddenly feeling awkward, and stormed into the tunnel.

"Freya, calm down," Orus said. *"You should celebrate what you can do."*

What could she do? That was the question. Until now she'd been just a plain Valkyrie. Yet there was no denying that she possessed the power of the Vanir. Nothing in her life made any sense anymore.

She looked up at the raven on her shoulder. "Orus, stop. I don't want to think about this or anything else!"

Archie ran to catch up with her. "Gee, what is it? Something's wrong—and don't tell me it's just your wings. I know you too well. It's more than that."

Freya refused to look at him and kept moving. Archie was her best friend and knew her better than anyone else. She wanted nothing more than to share with him her grief over the loss of her sister and Brundi, and her confusion over her Vanir powers. Instead she said, "Please don't ask me now. I can't tell you; it hurts too much. Ask when this is over."

"Okay," he agreed reluctantly. "But you know, don't you, when you're ready to talk, I'm right here."

Freya stopped and gave him a sad smile. She nodded. "I know."

"Enough chatter," the troll called. "Come, come, we must move. It is a long walk to the Great City."

"We're not going to walk," Quinn said. He cast a spell that lifted them up and carried them swiftly through the tunnel. They were moving so fast, the torches posted on the wall flashed by them like twinkling candles.

They stopped when they reached the entrance to the Great City. "We're going to need a disguise, and I know just the thing." Quinn magicked clothes for them out of thin air.

"Dark Elves again?" Archie moaned as he held up a mask and cloak. "We're going to cook in all this clothing."

"It's better than being roasted alive by the fire giants," Quinn said. "Just imagine what that would be like."

His words stabbed through Freya's heart like a dagger as she thought of Skaga being killed by a fire giant. It took all her strength to fight back the tears that lingered painfully close to the surface.

"He couldn't have known about Skaga and didn't say that to hurt you," Loki whispered to her as the others were busy changing into their disguises. "You'll get through this, Freya. I know you will, and you'll be stronger for it."

Freya looked up into his dark eyes and for a moment saw beyond the troublemaker she had known her whole life. So this was the man Brundi had cared for and called family. As he winked at her and walked away, she wondered if this was the real Loki, and whether the mischief-maker of Asgard was just the mask he wore.

Kai pulled the Dark Elves' cloak over his white wings and took the lead going up the steps. He reached a closed trapdoor and drew his sword. "I can feel others are up there. Wait here. I'll call when it's clear."

Kai shoved open the trapdoor and disappeared through it. They heard the sound of a scuffle and then two loud grunts.

Kai appeared at the trapdoor again. "All clear—you can come up now."

Two Dark Elves lay in a heap. Kai reached for one elf

and called to Archie, "Grab the other one. We'll hide them behind this barrel."

Freya looked up at the high ceiling and enormous doors around them and realized that they were in the cellar of a fire giant pub. Just across from them was a stack of enormous kegs of mead. The stench of the strong drink in the intense heat was almost overwhelming and threatened to make Freya sick. From above came the loud sounds of drunken laughter and heavy dancing.

"What is it with secret tunnels and pubs?" Archie demanded, brushing off elf blood. "This is just like the one in Utgard."

"Pubs and inns are the best places to hide tunnels," Kai said. "Most of the patrons are too drunk to realize the tunnels are here."

Quinn looked up at the noise from the merrymaking. "It sounds like they're celebrating."

Freya nodded. "Yes, the fall of Asgard," she said darkly. "Dirian told me they'd broken through the defenses."

"Then we'd better hurry." Loki walked over to the giant-sized stairs leading up to the main floor of the pub. The first step rose high above his head. "It's going to take a giant to get you out of here safely without alerting the others to our presence."

"Why?" Archie asked. "We're dressed like Dark Elves. We can just walk out of here."

"You may look like an elf, but you stink like a dead human," Loki said sarcastically. "Don't you ever wash?"

Archie took a step closer. "I've had it with you, Loki. We didn't ask for your help and we don't need it. We were doing just fine without you!"

"Yes, I can see. You were doing so fine, Dirian cut off Freya's wings!"

"Loki, Archie, stop it," Kai said. "We're facing enough danger already. We don't need to hear you two bickering as well."

"Then tell the ghost to keep his mouth shut," Loki spat.

Archie opened his mouth to reply, but Freya stopped him. "Let it go, Archie. We don't have time for this."

"Exactly," Loki said. He turned to Quinn. "Can you work some of your magic to protect everyone from the heat and flame of a fire giant?"

Quinn nodded. "I could, why?"

"Because you're all going to need it if you're going to travel in my pocket." Loki stepped away from the group and started to shimmer. "You'd better start casting that spell now. It's about to get very hot in here. . . ."

Freya took Skuld's hand and escorted the blind Norn back a safe distance from Loki as he started to grow in size. His color changed to bright orange as his clothes started to burn.

"Quinn, hurry with that spell!" Orus cawed. *"My feathers are roasting!"*

"Everyone, grasp hands," Quinn cried.

While Loki turned into a full, flaming fire giant, a bubble of protection formed around the others, very similar to the one they had traveled in under the frozen sea. Inside the bubble, the air was refreshingly cool, even though just outside it was scorching.

Loki now stood high above them, looking very much like a fire giant version of Loki, with a bulbous nose and exaggerated features. His long dark hair was ablaze and his clothes were a raging inferno. His hands were huge, and each finger was on fire.

"I really hope he's on our side," Archie said.

Freya looked up at Loki. "He is. He just doesn't always know how to show it. But Loki isn't the one I'm worried about." Her eyes settled on the troll who was holding Kai's and Archie's hands. "You, I still don't trust. If you let go and break the spell, the moment we feel the first bit of heat, I swear I'll use my sword on you!"

"No—no—no, I am your guardian," the troll whined. "Maya told me to protect you and I am."

"Maya isn't here," Freya said.

"But I promised. And I always keep my promises."

Loki bent down and put his hand on the floor, inviting them into his palm.

"Remember," Quinn said. "No matter what happens, we must keep hold of each other to keep out the heat. Does everyone understand?"

They all agreed and walked as one onto Loki's hand. As he lifted them up to his enormous giant's face, his now golden eyes indicated his pocket.

Freya nodded and called, "Go ahead."

Being surprisingly gentle, Loki pulled open the breast pocket on his tunic and placed them inside. Before they disappeared into the burning depths, he brought a massive finger to his lips and hushed them.

"Say nothing, but hold tight to each other," Quinn whispered. "The spell will hold, but being this close to his burning clothes means it will get hot in here."

It was already getting hot and very uncomfortable for Freya as her burnt skin protested and wing stumps throbbed under the heat and tight confinement. Every nerve in her body screamed to be freed from the confines of the pocket. Freya closed her eyes and leaned her head back, forcing herself to remain calm. At her shoulder, Orus pressed in tight and lightly closed his beak on her earlobe, to let her know he was with her and understood better than anyone else what she was suffering. Beside her, Quinn squeezed her hand reassuringly.

They felt each step Loki made as he climbed the cellar steps and made it to the main floor of the pub. Loud music played, and people sang and danced.

As Fire Giant Loki moved through the crowds, he was being bumped and shoved by the other giants around him. The mood was boisterous as the fire giants celebrated the fall of Asgard. A large hand slapped Loki on the back, and they all jolted inside Loki's pocket.

"Everyone keep still," Freya hushed, and they each held their breath as the fire giant embraced Loki.

"Have you heard, my friend?" a voice boomed. "Asgard has fallen—soon it will be ours!"

"I have, friend," Loki's giant voice replied. "Odin will die and we will know a new and prosperous age!"

The fire giant laughed, and they could hear his breathing getting louder as he leaned in close to Loki's ear. "After Odin, we will conquer Utgard and the frost giants, once and for all. Fire giants will rule all the realms!"

Freya inhaled and looked at Kai and Archie. She had never imagined that the fire giants had such ambitious plans.

"We've gotta stop them," Archie whispered.

Giant Loki started to cough and pounded his chest, nearly crushing his pocket. His message to them was understood. *Keep quiet.*

Soon the music faded and they heard sales traders calling out offers of goods at reasonable prices—so they knew that Loki had stepped safely out of the pub and was now walking the crowded streets of the Great City.

Time stood still in Loki's pocket as he moved through the city streets and eventually out of town. When all they could hear was the crackling of burning clothes and Loki's heavy breathing, they knew they had made it.

Loki stopped. Light poured in from above as he opened his pocket. "Quinn, lift everyone out of there." His voice boomed like thunder.

The bubble of protection floated out of the pocket and drifted toward the ground. By the time they touched down, Loki had changed back to his normal form.

"I'm sure you heard," Loki said. "They're already celebrating Asgard's defeat."

"And they're planning to attack the frost giants next. If we don't stop this now, it really will be Ragnarök," Kai said.

"We have got to get moving before it's too late." Loki stepped up to the troll. "You, tell us, where's the tunnel Dirian is using to get to Asgard?"

The troll looked back to Freya.

"Speak," she ordered.

Within minutes Quinn had them in the sky and on their way to the tunnel. The sun was high overhead and mercilessly hot in the clear, cloudless sky. Freya's skin seared under its scorching intensity. If they somehow managed to survive this, she swore she would never return to this wretched realm again.

As day turned into early evening, there was only a slight respite from the heat. They passed over the flatlands and a large, steaming lake. In the distance rose a series of mountain ranges covered in red- and orange-leaved trees—their destination.

The troll directed them to touch down by a hidden cave. The entrance was almost completely obscured by giant leaves that grew on the thick vines draping down before it.

"Look," Quinn said as he walked to a small area of cleared vines. "They've been here. This vine has been recently cut. . . ."

Kai stepped forward. "With a hole just large enough for Dark Searchers to fit through. This is the right place."

"Then what are we waiting for?" Freya asked as she held Skuld's hand and led the blind Norn forward. Just before she passed under the cut leaves, Freya warned Skuld to keep her hands and head down. "Don't touch anything," she warned. "The leaves here will burn you worse than fire."

"I understand," Skuld said as she pressed closer to Freya. "You lead and I will follow."

Freya raised her sword and passed through the opening into the dark cave. Immediately the temperature dropped and she breathed a great sigh of relief.

"Ah," Archie sighed when he entered. "That's much better. Gee, remind me never to come back here."

"I will," Freya promised. She looked up at Orus. "And I want you to bite me if I ever suggest we do."

"Don't worry, I will."

"You never will come back here," Skuld said cryptically.

Freya looked down at Skuld and wondered what the Norn of the future meant. Was it that Freya would never return? Or was it that she had no future left in which to do it? They were about to head into a war zone. Would that spell the end for her?

"What have you seen?" she finally asked.

Skuld smiled, and there was a sense of mischief about her. "That's for me to know and you to find out."

"Freya, do you and Skuld want to stay here and talk and maybe have a picnic, or are you coming with us to Asgard to save Odin?" Loki challenged.

Freya smiled, grateful for his sarcasm. It gave her the first trace of normalcy she'd known in a long time. She held on to Skuld with one hand and raised her sword with the other. "Oh, don't you worry about me not coming. I've got a very special date with Dirian!"

34

"REMEMBER," VANIR-FREYJA WARNED MAYA AS THEY rose through the opening at the Temple of the Sun in Peru, "sing as loud and as strong as you can." Vanir-Freyja had taught Maya the song that would unleash her powers fully. They were now back in Midgard and ready to cast their spell over the giants.

The moment they emerged from the temple, Maya felt her new powers affecting the people who greeted them. Vanir-Freyja had had to lift them high up into the sky to keep the crowding soldiers from touching Maya and being reaped.

"When you finish the song, start over again. Just sing and fly—that's all you need to do. Your powers will do the rest. And when you reach the tunnel entrances that the giants are using to enter Midgard, sing even more. And when they are yours, command them to return to their realms. Make them love you, child, and they will do anything you say.

"If we fly at our top speed and circle the globe, we should finish quickly. Then I will meet you at the tunnel entrance to Asgard—the one in northern Canada. If I am not there, wait for me. Together we will return to Asgard and stop the giants."

Maya felt the weight of responsibility pressing down heavily on her. "I understand."

Vanir-Freyja hugged her tightly. "I am so proud of you. Asgard will sing of your bravery and Odin will bow to your beauty."

Maya shook her head. "I don't care about that. I just want this war over."

"Indeed," Vanir-Freyja said. "Go now, my mirror twin. Go and do as you were born to do."

Maya opened her wings and lifted off. She looked back and watched Vanir-Freyja fly in the opposite direction. They had been together only a short time, but already Maya felt the anxiety of separation from her powerful ancestor.

Rising high above Machu Picchu, Maya started across the Andes, keeping alert for any giants. It wasn't until she headed farther north that she felt a familiar prickling on her skin. Giants. Taking a deep breath, Maya started to sing. At first the words of the song were unfamiliar and awkward, as they were from an ancient language unknown to her. But then a strange wave of heat and a kind of calmness washed over her, and everything changed.

Like a dam bursting, powers that Maya had been unaware of were released. She understood the ancient words she was singing and felt the full power of the Vanir coursing through her veins.

This power fed her voice, and the song that sprang from her became louder and reached farther. She was calling to others, enchanting them—commanding them to love her and do as she bade.

By the time she reached the tunnel entrance from Utgard in the Florida Everglades, Maya was heartbroken. The area had been reduced to ruins. The main cities of Florida were gone, trampled under giants' feet and revealing a steady path of destruction leading north.

Circling over the tunnel entrance, Maya sang her heart out.

"Come to me. . . ." Her haunting notes were filled with yearning. The frost and fire giants halted their northern march. They turned and looked back at her longingly.

It was working! The giants were drawn toward her and were calling her.

Maya put even more of herself into the song. "Come to me . . . ," she sang. "Love me. Serve me. . . ." They reached up, trying to catch hold of her from the ground.

Drawing them back toward the tunnel, Maya changed

the song. As Vanir-Freyja had taught her, she kept up the melody but changed the lyrics.

"You have been used as weapons of war!" she sang to them. "But that is over now. Go home. Return to your families and tell the others in the tunnel that they will please me by leaving this realm forever. . . ." She sang of Vanir-Freyja's freedom, and how she had never been a prize for the kings.

One by one, as though in a trance, the giants started to descend into the tunnel.

Heartened by success, Maya kept singing. Following the path of devastation, she flew farther up the coast and called the giants home. She soon learned that she didn't have to escort them back to the tunnel. At her command, they went on their own.

Along the route, Maya saw signs of fighting. Defeated frost and fire giants lay on the ground, waiting to rise—but her heart sank when she saw the number of military vehicles and soldiers who lay among them. The humans had fought hard to defend their realm, but had failed. There would be no rising again for them, as they had been taken by the Angels of Death.

Farther up the coast, where human soldiers were still fighting the marching giants, Maya's song halted everyone. Giants and humans alike paused to listen. As she passed overhead, the humans called to her, while the giants turned around and followed her commands to go home.

After Maya reached as far north as she needed, she

KATE O'HEARN

changed direction and headed back toward California and the tunnel entrance out in the Pacific Ocean.

"Follow my words," she kept singing. "Return to your realms and make war no more. . . ."

Day turned into night, but still Maya kept singing. She crisscrossed the United States and ordered the giants home.

By dawn, Maya's voice was breaking and she was exhausted from the exertion, but she was overjoyed. A simple song was the most powerful weapon they had against the giants. She had to keep going. As she made her way north, Maya kept singing and watched the steady stream of creatures heading south. Male or female, frost or fire giant, dwarf, elf, or troll, it didn't matter. They all moved as though in a dream—reaching up to her, calling out to her, but always obeying her command to go back home.

As Maya crossed into Canada, her voice was weakening and she needed to rest. She glided down into the ruins of a small northern town. Touching down in the center of the street, she spied an abandoned diner that had somehow survived the giants.

Once her senses assured her that she was alone, Maya entered the diner. The place was eerily silent. Food and drinks lay abandoned on tables. Some meals were partially consumed while some lay untouched by those who had ordered them. Maya took a seat on one of the counter stools and reached for the abandoned food.

In all her life, she had never felt so exhausted. Her body was shaking, her wing muscles were sore, and her throat felt raw. But it was worth it. The giants were leaving Midgard.

Maya lay her head down for just a moment. Before long, she drifted into a deep, much-needed sleep.

"Maya . . ." Someone was shaking her arm. Groggily opening her eyes, she saw the face of her mother hovering above.

"Mother?"

Tears filled Eir's eyes as she pulled Maya into a tight embrace. "My beautiful girl, you've come back to us. We feared the worst!"

It had been a long time since she'd seen her mother cry. "I'm all right," she soothed.

"Maya, I don't understand," Eir said. "I heard you singing, and then felt compelled to find you. What's happened?"

As Maya looked at her mother, she sensed a deep grief coming from her. Her mother had been through a lot; she could feel it.

But before she could find out more, the door of the diner opened. For the first time in a long while, Maya smiled as the familiar faces of her sisters Gwyn and Kara appeared, followed by her uncle Vonni, who was being supported by Kris. Vonni's left leg was wrapped in a thick bandage and his arm and face were cut. It felt as if she hadn't seen them in a thousand years.

Behind them were Dark Searchers. When their eyes landed on Maya, they rushed toward her, trying to get as close as possible.

"Please, stop!" Maya cried, pushing the Dark Searchers away. They were pressing in so close, she couldn't breathe. "What you're feeling isn't real. It's a spell, that's all. Please, stand back."

The Dark Searchers immediately obeyed her command and took a step back. But their emotions didn't change. They loved her.

"How did you find me?" Maya asked, reaching back for her mother.

Vonni's eyes were glazed, staring at her. "You called to us and we had to obey."

"It's just a spell," Maya explained. "You must get past it. Asgard needs you."

Vonni shook his head. "What kind of spell? Why do I feel this way?"

Maya took her mother's hand and started to explain. "Our family are the direct descendants of Vanir-Freyja and Freyr. For generations they've used a spell to suppress the power in our family line. But for our generation, they didn't. We possess the powers of the Vanir. I inherited Vanir-Freyja's beauty and power to enchant. That's what you're all feeling. I cast a spell to send the giants home, but it's affecting you, too. Vanir-Freyja is here in Midgard and is doing the same thing in Europe and the rest of the world. It's working. The giants are leaving."

Vonni shook his head to clear it. "You're defeating the giants with magic?"

Maya nodded. "Vanir-Freyja warned me that using magic would have a price. I've enchanted everyone." She looked at all the Dark Searchers beginning to get close to her again. "That's what's happening to you. It's not real. You must fight past it."

"What of Freya? Have you seen her?" Her mother's voice shook.

Maya dropped her head. "Mother, Dirian has Freya. He's cut off her wings and is holding her in his keep in Muspelheim."

Her mother gasped, and the shock of hearing what had happened to Freya broke part of the spell over everyone.

"I—I swear I didn't want to leave her there," Maya implored, "but freeing Vanir-Freyja was the only way to end the war."

"You did right, my daughter. Freya knows that too. This war has cost us all dearly. . . ."

Once again, Maya was struck by her mother's suppressed grief. As she pressed further with her senses, she felt something terrible. Maya's eyes shot up to her sisters. "Gwyn, Kara, where's Skaga?"

Tears rimmed her sisters' eyes. "A fire giant killed her and—and . . . she didn't rise again," Gwyn struggled to say.

Maya inhaled sharply and shook her head. "No . . ."

"Your grandmother is gone too," Vonni added with a pain that ran deep. "The frost giants attacked the mountain in Colorado. I've been told Mims and the baby are safe, but the military has moved them. . . ." His voice broke. "I know what happened to my Sarah. Eir says because you and Mims reaped her, she is still with Mims, but I don't know where they've been taken."

"We'll find them," Kris rasped with his broken voice. "It will be a grave mistake if the humans try to keep them from us."

Maya couldn't breathe. So much pain and loss, all because of Dirian. She rose from her stool and staggered, finally overwhelmed. Two Dark Searchers darted forward to support her. But their touch only added to Maya's distress.

"No, I'm all right." She pulled away and looked at the large gathering of Dark Searchers and her family. "This isn't the time for our tears. Come, we must go."

"Where?" her mother asked.

"Vanir-Freyja told me to meet her at the tunnel the giants are using. We're going home to declare war on the giants in Asgard!"

35

QUINN'S HEALING POTION WORE OFF SOMEWHERE IN the tunnel between Muspelheim and Asgard. But Freya found the pain wasn't as bad as it had been. Her burns were healing, and her bones felt stronger. It was her wing stumps that still throbbed and stung. She wondered if that pain would ever end.

But with the clearing of her head, her senses returned. She could feel Yggdrasil all around them as they moved within its root. But something was wrong—the vibrations from the tree had changed and were becoming sporadic. The green lichen that grew on it was turning pale and its glow was fading. The Cosmic World Tree was in distress.

"How much farther?" she asked the troll.

"Not far now. We will be there soon."

"I miss Bifröst," Archie grumbled from beside her. "I don't ever want to travel through a tunnel or root again!"

"Me too," Freya agreed.

"I've heard Bifröst is beautiful and filled with the colors of the rainbow," Quinn said.

"It is," Freya agreed. "That's why they call it the Rainbow Bridge. If we manage to survive this, I'll take you there."

"Well, aren't you just a little ray of sunshine," Loki teased. "What do you mean, 'If we survive this'? Of course we will. Soon everything will get back to normal."

When Freya looked at him, he winked at her. They both knew things could never return to normal. But she appreciated him saying it. Freya hated to admit it, but she liked this new version of Loki.

"We are here," the troll called excitedly.

As Quinn slowed them down, Freya felt the presence of other Valkyries, citizens of Asgard, and Light Elves, and was filled with hope. But her heart sank when she also picked up on a large number of frost and fire giants.

"It's true," she said. "The giants have broken through the defenses. I can feel them here. I also feel Dark Elves and more dwarfs and . . ."

"And Dirian," Kai finished. "I feel him too. He and all his Dark Searchers are here."

"Then what are we waiting for, a written invitation?" Archie said. "C'mon, let's go kick some Dark Searcher butt!"

"Hear, hear!" Loki cheered as he led them forward.

They climbed up the incline that led into Asgard and exited through the base of a large, fallen ash tree. Freya stood in stunned silence as her eyes took in the sight of her home realm. They were in the Asgard forest, just outside the city. Before them, the wall that surrounded the city had been partially knocked down. In places it was gone completely.

Beyond the wall, plumes of smoke rose in the air above the many buildings. In the distance, she spied the damaged spires of Valhalla. The flags were down and smoke billowed from its windows. She was sickened to realize that the Great Heavenly Hall was burning.

"*They breached the walls,*" Orus cawed, as stunned as she was. "*The walls have stood for thousands of years and now they've fallen. Asgard is burning!*"

"Look at it," Archie said in shock. "How long have the giants been here?"

"Too long," Freya cried. "C'mon, let's get them!"

Forgetting herself, Freya took three long strides and leaped into the air.

"*Freya, stop!*" Orus cried. "*You can't fly!*"

Just before she hit the ground, Freya stopped and floated in midair for a moment, before being lowered to the ground by Quinn. "You must remember your wings are gone."

Freya's spirit crashed to the ground, even if her body didn't. The horror of her new life cut as badly as Dirian's blade. She was grounded and felt helpless. "I can't believe I just did that," she muttered softly.

Skuld reached for Freya. "It is understandable considering the circumstances. It will take time for you to adjust."

"Time we just don't have," Kai said. He opened his wings and drew his black swords. "Quinn, can you bring the others with you? I'm going ahead to find Dirian."

"No, Kai. Wait for us!" Freya called. But he was already in the air, winging his way toward Valhalla.

"Kai's not going to be the only hero here." Loki started to shimmer and grow. "I'm going to fight fire with fire." Soon his staff and clothing started to burn as he turned back into a fire giant. Loki bent down and he smiled at Freya. "See you on the other side!"

As Loki started to run toward the destroyed wall around Asgard, Quinn lifted them in the air and carried them toward what was left of the walled city.

"Freya, where's Dirian?" Quinn called.

Freya cast out her senses until she started to shake. She felt Dirian's evil presence like a foul touch on her burnt skin. "He's that way." She pointed. "Moving toward Valhalla from the opposite side."

When they passed over the damaged outer wall and reached the outskirts of the city, they encountered the worst of the fighting. The reaped human warriors from Valhalla were fighting side by side with Light Elves and faeries as they took on renegade dwarfs and Dark Elves.

"We trained for this at Valhalla"—Archie gazed around himself in awe—"but I never imagined it could happen. I hope Crixus is okay. He's the toughest warrior in Valhalla—and crucial to our fight."

Freya tried to take it all in but couldn't. Her home realm, everything she'd known, was being destroyed.

The sounds of battle were coming from every direction. Everywhere they looked, they saw Asgardians and friends from other realms fighting to defend Odin.

"Gee, look up there," Archie cried.

Freya followed his gaze and saw a cluster of Valkyries taking on a frost giant. Their swords flashed as they went after the giant's head. Despite the enormous size difference, working together, the Valkyries quickly defeated the giant and he fell to the ground with an impact that rattled buildings. Not stopping to rest or celebrate, they flew like a squadron toward the next giant.

The sounds of thunder and lightning rose in the air. For a moment Freya hoped it was Thor, back from Earth, but as she listened, she could tell the sounds were different. "That's Odin!" she shouted. "He's still alive!"

Freya strained her senses to feel Odin. "Quinn, forget Dirian. Head in that direction as fast as you can. Odin's in trouble—we must protect him!"

While they flew over the battleground that had once

been Asgard, Freya caught hold of Skuld's hand and placed it in Archie's. "Stay close to Archie," she said. "This is going to get very dangerous. and I don't want you hurt."

"It is you I worry about," Skuld said. "You have so much rage in you; it might make you reckless."

"I'll be careful." Freya looked at Archie. "You have your sword. Be ready to use it. Skuld must be protected until we can get her back to her sisters."

Archie nodded. "Don't worry about me—Crixus trained me well. You just focus on protecting Odin."

"And I will protect you," the troll added.

Freya had almost forgotten about the troll. She fought to hide her revulsion of him as they approached the partially destroyed Valhalla. She gazed down to the large training field surrounding it. Not too long ago, that field had hosted the Ten Realms Challenge, where members of the realms competed against each other in friendly contests. Now some of those same participants were back, fighting against each other for real.

"*It's a nightmare,*" Orus cawed mournfully. "*How can we hope to beat them?*"

"We don't have any choice," Freya said grimly.

Thousands of human warriors were gathered on the field, battling against the invaders. As they moved closer, Freya was overwhelmed by the number of fighters on Dirian's side. Apart from the giants, Dark Elves, dwarfs, and trolls, there were also faeries, Dark Demons, and creatures she'd never seen before that must have been dredged up from the deepest depths of the darkest realms.

Large spiders, snakes, and serpents fought alongside the giants. Freya's eyes landed on Sif among the throng. Thor's wife held two swords and fought with bravery and expertise as she stood back-to-back with another Asgard fighter. Freya also spotted Heimdall, the bulky Guardian of Bifröst, fighting against a frost giant. Though the giant was bigger, he was felled by Heimdall's might.

Freya took it all in, realizing that this fight was bigger than just Dirian's bid to dethrone Odin. They had to stop it from becoming Ragnarök—or none of the realms would survive.

As they scanned the immense battlefield and listened to the sounds of roaring voices and clashing swords, Freya's eyes landed on a group of Dark Demons, Dark Elves, and Searchers moving in on a Valkyrie and one other fighter she couldn't quite make out. Despite her fighting skills, the Valkyrie was taken down swiftly by demon magic. When she hit the ground, the dwarfs pounced on her, tearing out her feathers and breaking her bones.

The other figure tried his best to defend himself against the attackers. His back was to her, and Freya saw him for only a flash before he was swamped by the invaders. But she'd seen enough. The flash of a gold eye patch, blazing red hair, and familiar armor, now dented and covered in the many shades of elf, dwarf, troll, and giants' blood, made it clear who it was.

"Odin!" Freya cried.

"Where?" Archie asked. "I don't see him."

"Down there!" Freya pointed. "Near that fallen Valkyrie. They've overwhelmed him and somehow captured his staff. Without Gungnir, he doesn't stand a chance!"

"Freya, give me your hand!" Quinn cried as he reached for her.

Using their combined powers they blasted away Odin's attackers and lifted the leader of Asgard off the ground. A large serpent launched itself into the air after him—as it went for Odin's foot, Freya reached down and cut off its head with her sword.

"Freya!" Odin roared when he saw his rescuers. "What are you doing here?" His shock grew more intense when he saw Skuld. "What's happening?"

"Great Odin," Freya cried. "We're here to protect you. Dirian is behind all of this. He's back in Asgard and coming for you. He plans to kill you and take your throne."

"He'll never take the throne!" Odin boomed. "Take me into Valhalla. I will face him there!"

"No, sir, you can't," Archie cried. "It's too dangerous. The giants will capture you in there. We must take you away from the danger."

"Abandon the battle?" Odin cried furiously. "Never! I am more than the leader of Asgard—I am its protector! If it falls, I fall with it. Do as I command and get me inside Valhalla—now!"

Freya looked at Quinn. "We'll take him into the banquet hall. It's in the very center of Valhalla and looks like it hasn't been damaged."

Quinn carried them over the raging battle secured in the magical bubble. Swords, spears, and weapons flew at them from below but were deflected away. When the group approached a large, gaping hole in the side of Valhalla, they had a close-up view of what the giants had done to the Heavenly Hall. The entire front had been torn open by giant hands. Towers lay in rubble on the ground, and many of the doors had been ripped off.

Most of the roof had been burned away, as well as all the warriors' sleeping quarters. Acrid smoke billowed out of the windows and holes from the parts of Valhalla still on fire.

As they drifted down to the ground, Freya was left speechless.

"In here," Odin commanded. His one blue eye focused on Freya. "If you really want to redeem yourself, Valkyrie, follow me." Just as he was about to move, Odin frowned. He caught Freya by the shoulder and roughly turned her around.

"Who took your wings?"

"Dirian," Freya said. "I was a prisoner at his keep."

"He held me and Vanir-Freyja there as well," Skuld added.

Odin was stunned by the news. "Where is this new keep?"

"*In Muspelheim,*" Orus cawed.

Freya continued. "He's been forcing Skuld to end the futures of fallen warriors and using Vanir-Freyja as a prize for the giant kings who served him."

Skuld nodded. "He had me cross out your name, Odin, but I restore you now. He cannot keep you dead."

For the first time in her life, Freya watched Odin bow deeply. "Thank you, Skuld."

"It is not me you must thank. Freya, Archie, Quinn, and many others have served and sacrificed for you without you knowing it. They are the ones deserving of your thanks."

Odin was looking at Freya as if seeing her for the first time. His one remaining eye lost its hardness. "Where is Vanir-Freyja now?"

"In Midgard," Freya answered. "Maya and a Vanir called Skye rescued her from the keep. They took her to Midgard for safety."

Odin took in the information but gave nothing away. He turned and started to climb over the rubble outside Valhalla.

"Come," he commanded. "It's time we faced Dirian!"

36

THEY FOLLOWED ODIN THROUGH THE RUBBLE.

"*Valhalla is gone,*" Orus moaned.

"It can be restored," Odin said.

They wound their way deeper inside and reached the banquet hall. Tables were overturned and chairs toppled, but the walls and high ceiling were intact. On the dais, Odin's throne remained standing.

"Up there," Odin said. "If Dirian wants my throne, he's going to have to take it from me!"

They followed Odin up onto the dais and took protective positions on either side of his throne. The sounds of the battle raging outside echoed through the ruins of Valhalla.

No one spoke. They all knew there was nothing left to say. This was it, the final confrontation. Soon they would have to fight Dirian and his Dark Searchers for ultimate control of the realms.

"My sons, Thor and Balder, are dead . . . ," Odin said softly, breaking the silence.

"Dead? When? How?" Freya cried.

"They went to Utgard to learn of the giants' plans. They were killed at the keep just before the war started."

"Wait," Freya said, shaking her head. "They weren't at the keep at the start of the war. They were with us in Midgard."

Odin's head turned sharply to her. "What are you telling me? Speak!"

"Thor and Balder weren't killed at the keep. They and a few loyal Dark Searchers followed us to Brundi's farm."

"My sons are alive?"

Freya nodded. "The last time I saw them, they were planning to fight the giants in Midgard. I promise you, they were very much alive."

"And they still are," Skuld added.

Odin roared in joy and jumped to his feet. He scooped up Freya in his massive arms and nearly squeezed the life out of her. Freya was too stunned to cry out that he was crushing her wing stumps and fragile ribs.

"I was told they were no more," Odin said in disbelief, and put Freya down.

"I assure you, they are unharmed," Skuld said. "They still have a future. I can see them in it."

"I don't understand. What were they doing in Midgard?"

Freya dropped her head. "They were coming after me and my twin brother, Kai. We were . . ." She stopped as she felt as if her stomach had been punched. It was Kai. Her brother was in pain and struggling. Then Freya felt something else pull at her. She forced herself to block Kai's pain for the moment and focus. She stepped down from the dais and raised her sword. "Dirian and his Dark Searchers are approaching."

Among everything she felt, Freya also sensed Odin's renewed energy. Hearing that his sons were alive put the fight back in him. "Let him come. I'm ready for him," he roared.

Then Odin held his hand out to Quinn. "Vanir, give me a sword, a large one."

Quinn nodded and cast a spell to create a large broadsword that looked almost too heavy to lift. Odin picked it up as though it weighed nothing and nodded his head. "Very good, thank you."

Kai staggered into the banquet hall, his white wings covered in blood. He had a deep wound on his side, and he was limping from another gash to his upper thigh.

In moments Freya was by his side. "He's hurt," she called to Quinn. "Please! We need more of your pain potion!"

"I'm all right," Kai said. He lifted his head to see Odin standing before his throne. He pulled himself up with Freya and Archie's help.

"Odin." Kai struggled to bow before him. "I am at your service. My swords are yours."

Odin's one eye moved from Freya to Kai and back again. "The twins are united."

Freya nodded. "And we'll never be parted again."

"Agreed," Odin said.

Quinn helped Kai drink the potion, but there was little time to pause.

"ODIN!" a broken voice rasped.

Freya turned and watched Dirian enter the hall with a troop of at least ten Dark Searchers. They were followed by a stream of Dark Elves, dwarfs, and demons. She felt a large number of giants encircling Valhalla on the outside, poised to strike at anyone who tried to flee.

They were trapped.

Dirian came closer and focused on Freya. "You? How? I left you chained and broken in my keep."

"You can't stop me from protecting my realm or my leader!" Freya spat.

Dirian's visored head nodded. "It seems I made a mistake in letting you live. I should have taken your head, not your wings. I won't make that mistake again."

The troll squealed and ran at Dirian. "You won't hurt Freya!"

The Dark Searcher cut him down with a single blow. "You have trolls fighting your battles now?"

Freya looked at the troll that had sacrificed himself for her. His death fed her anger. She handed Kai over to Archie and raised her golden sword. "It's over, Dirian."

Dirian slowly drew his two swords. "Over? Not quite— Odin is still alive. You know, Freya, I may actually miss your sense of humor. But not enough to let you live!" He ran at her with murder in his heart.

Freya tossed Orus into the air and released her own rage to meet him halfway across the floor. Unlike their last fight, she felt stronger, and this time, there was more at stake. Odin had to be protected at all costs.

Freya charged into his attack, her sword flashing. Her Vanir power coursed through her veins as she defended against Dirian's every blow.

As she fought, Freya became aware of the others fighting around her in the banquet hall. Odin was taking on all the Dark Searchers at once, while Quinn and Kai fought against demons and elves. Archie remained with Skuld, fighting two Dark Elves who were trying to reach the ancient Norn.

"Freya, be careful!" Orus cawed as he flew at Dirian to block his vision.

This move had worked at the Ten Realms Challenge, but now the Dark Searcher was ready for him. As Orus dived a second time, Dirian's blade flashed, cutting Orus out of the air.

The raven fell to the floor.

"Orus, no!" Freya howled.

"Your raven is dead," Dirian rasped. "Soon you will follow him!" His swords flashed against her even faster. One cut sliced across her abdomen, but Freya kept fighting through her mounting pain.

With grief and fury driving her on, Freya matched Dirian move for move as they fought all through the banquet hall. Seizing an opening, she thrust forward. Her sword hit its mark and cut into his chest. She immediately followed with another slice across one of his arms.

As Freya went for a third, lethal strike, Dirian lunged forward and caught her in his arms. They encircled her and started to squeeze. "This ends now," he rasped.

Freya felt as if she were caught in a dragon's mouth as Dirian's arms gripped her, tighter and tighter. She couldn't move, couldn't breathe, and bones snapped as he slowly crushed her. Freya's head felt as if it were going to explode under the pressure, but still Dirian squeezed tighter.

Just as she felt herself slipping away, Dirian whispered into her ear, "No—not yet, little Valkyrie. I won't free you until you've witnessed my victory! Watch, Freya. Watch your beloved Odin die!"

He released her, and Freya collapsed to the floor. Gasping for air, her ribs broken again, it took all of Freya's strength to lift her head and see the deadly Dark Searcher advancing on Odin.

The leader of Asgard was displaying every fighting skill

he possessed against the Dark Searchers. He was able to duck and dive against the blades that cut at him, while simultaneously cutting down Searchers one by one. When most of the Searchers were defeated, the Dark Elves and demons moved in, casting their magic. The sword was ripped from Odin's grasp, and a blow from one of the remaining Dark Searchers knocked him to the floor. Freya focused on Odin until she felt her brother fall in battle at the blades of two Dark Searchers. She couldn't imagine a pain worse than losing Skaga—until now. Kai was more than her brother. He was her twin, a living extension of her. As Kai died, a big part of Freya died with him.

Across the hall, Dirian stood triumphantly over the restrained Odin, his two swords hovering above him and poised to strike. "You have lost, Odin of Asgard," Dirian rasped. "I, Dirian of Utgard, claim the throne and all the realms, in the name of the Dark Searchers!"

Freya raised her head as a blind rage overwhelmed her. She climbed to her feet and charged at Dirian with every ounce of energy she had left.

Cutting her way through the Dark Elves and demons, Freya dashed under Dirian's blades as they started to move. She pushed Odin behind her and turned to face the Dark Searcher. As her golden sword thrust up and into Dirian's heart, his blades cut down into her.

"Gee!" Archie howled.

Freya felt no pain. There was nothing.

With their swords interlocked, Freya and Dirian fell as one. They hit the floor together and lay sprawled beside each other.

As the world around her started to fade, Freya felt Dirian go first. The enemy she had made so long ago and had fought so hard, was finally dead.

Freya was barely aware of the fighting going on around her. First she heard gunfire, which made no sense to her fading mind, as there were no human weapons in Asgard. After that, she was sure she heard the boom of Thor's hammer.

Just as her mother reached her side and called her name, she was swallowed into oblivion.

37

FREYA WAS DRAWN SLOWLY BACK TO CONSCIOUSNESS, only to taste a bitter liquid at her lips that drove her back into sleep. This happened many times before she was allowed to rise to the surface for a moment.

There was pressure on her chest. Opening her eyes, she saw Orus lying on her. Her raven was covered in bandages and unconscious—but his faint breaths told her that he was alive.

She looked up to see that she was lying in a tent. Loki was standing beside her bed. With his arms crossed casually over his chest, he was grinning at her. "Welcome back."

Freya's lips were dry and her throat too parched to speak.

"Don't try to talk." Loki knelt beside her and brought a cup of cool water to her lips. "What a journey we've been on, you and me."

"Wha—what happened?"

"We won," he said, gently brushing hair back from her face. "If you tell anyone I said this, I'll deny it. But I want you to know, I'm proud of you."

He rose. "Now, get back to sleep and heal—it's no fun picking on you when you're down." Loki grinned, shimmered into a bumblebee, and buzzed his way out of the tent.

Freya tried to follow him with her eyes, but they were too heavy to keep open. She surrendered to the draw of sleep.

It was two more days before Freya woke and stayed awake. This time Archie and Quinn were at her side.

"Orus, you're alive . . ." Her feathered friend was perched on Archie's shoulder, looking a little rough, but very much alive.

The raven cawed and flew to sit on Freya's stomach. *"We both are!"*

"Freya, it's time to get up. You mustn't put pressure on your wings any longer; they need to be exercised."

Freya followed the voice and saw Maya on the other side of her bed. There was a man beside her who looked like an older version of Kai or even Vonni—with dark, neatly styled hair and eyes of blazing sapphire blue. His features were finely sculptured, and he had a dimple in his chin. If it were possible, he was even more handsome than her uncles.

"Maya, my wings are gone. Dirian cut them off."

"Gee, that's not Maya." Archie started to grin. "It's Vanir-Freyja and her twin brother, Freyr. They're your family. They saved your wings and were able to reattach them."

Freya heard the words, but they made no sense. Vanir-Freyja? But she looked exactly like Maya! And what had Archie said about her wings?

Now that she thought about it, she became aware of the discomfort she always felt when she slept on her wings too long. "Wings?" she cried.

"Freya, get off your wings," Orus cawed as he limped up to her shoulder. *"You don't want to break them when you've only just gotten them back."*

Freya was helped to her feet by Archie and Quinn. She felt weak and dizzy as she stood for the first time in days. She smiled as she felt the familiar weight of the wings on her back. She opened them and fluttered them lightly. "H-how?"

Vanir-Freyja smiled and walked around the bed to embrace her. "Quinnarious didn't destroy them in Muspelheim. He hid them and brought them back to us. Our Vanir magic restored them to you."

Freya could hardly believe what she was hearing, but the black wings on her back proved it true. She looked at Quinn. "You did?"

Quinn grinned. "Course I did. I wasn't about to destroy a perfectly good set of wings. Yes, the feathers were a bit burnt, but otherwise they were beautiful—just like you."

Lost for words, Freya threw her arms around Quinn and held him tightly. "Thank you!" she wept into his long brown hair.

"Come, my little Freya." Her uncle Freyr gestured to her. "There are a lot of people outside waiting for you."

It was only then that Freya looked around and saw she was the only patient in the private healing tent. "The war?" she quickly asked.

"It's over," Archie said. "Maya and Vanir-Freyja enchanted the giants and sent them home. You killed Dirian." He paused and frowned at her. "But you and I are going to talk about that stunt you pulled with him. I've never been so scared in all my life!"

"In all your death, you mean," Quinn teased.

Archie punched Quinn and chuckled. "All my death . . ."

"What happened to Dirian?"

"You mean after you killed him?" Archie asked. "Skuld wrote down his name and crossed a big line through it. She really enjoyed doing that."

Freya was almost too frightened to ask. "And Kai? Is he all right? Why isn't he here?"

Vanir-Freyja nodded. "Like you, he rose again. He's been with Odin and Thor, giving his full report. He'll be here shortly."

Freya felt as if she were asleep, in the most wonderful dream. Her brother was alive, her wings were back, and Dirian was dead. If it was a dream, she didn't want to wake up.

Her great-uncle Freyr smiled. "No, little Freya, it's no dream," he said, reading her thoughts. "You're very much awake."

"C'mon, Gee," Archie said, taking his rightful place at her side. "Let's not keep everyone waiting."

With Archie supporting her on one side, and holding tightly to Quinn's hand on the other, Freya walked toward the entrance of the tent. Once she was outside, her eyes flew open and she couldn't take it all in. Everyone was there, including Vonni and Sarah—bearing the mark of Mims on her hand. Then there was Mims with Skaga's raven nestled on her shoulder. She was grinning and holding her baby brother. Beside them stood Skye and her team of human soldiers from the tunnel. . . . Her senses told her they were alive, but not human anymore.

Archie started to laugh. "You should see your face! Breathe, Gee," he teased. "Keep breathing."

Her mother was standing with Freya's surviving sisters. When Freya's eyes landed on Maya, she welled up and ran to her.

"I felt you in the keep," Freya said, holding her tightly. "Thank you for saving Vanir-Freyja!"

Maya's eyes misted. "I didn't want to leave you. . . . It was the hardest thing I've ever done."

"I know," Freya said, as they laughed and cried together. "You did right."

As the two sisters embraced, their ravens, Orus and Grul, started to argue about who had the worst wounds and who had suffered the greatest.

"Yes, well, a frost giant broke my back," Grul said. *"I was completely paralyzed! I nearly died!"*

"You call that suffering?" Orus cried. *"I did die. Dirian cut me in two! The healer almost failed putting me together again!"*

"Too bad she didn't keep your beak shut. . . ."

Freya looked around at the gathering of those she cared for most and was completely overwhelmed. She didn't know who to hold or talk to next.

Suddenly a hush fell over the gathering and everyone parted. Kai, looking pale but very much alive, was walking toward them with Odin and his wife, Frigg, and Thor and Balder. Odin was out of his armor and displaying his new battle scars proudly.

"Freya," Odin said informally. "We have much to discuss, but for today I want only to say thank you—thank you for saving Asgard."

"I—I," Freya stuttered. "I didn't save Asgard. It was you."

Odin's eye darkened. "Even now you wish to argue with me?"

"No! I'm sorry, Great Odin," Freya rushed to say.

Odin held the stern look for a moment longer but then burst into laughter. "You will never change," he said, shaking his head.

"And I hope she never does." Frigg smiled. "We have a gift for you. It is our way of thanking you for everything you've done." She stood back and motioned for someone to come forward.

Freya recognized the dark hair, blazing eyes, and muscular build of the strongest warrior in Valhalla. It was Archie's gladiator trainer, Crixus. He walked forward and nodded to her.

Frigg said formally, "Normally, this is forbidden, but today we will make an exception. Freya, daughter of Eir, twin sister to Kai, I would like you to meet your father, Crixus of Midgard."

Freya inhaled sharply. Her eyes flashed over to her mother, who was smiling and nodded her head. Kai was also nodding.

"Gee," Archie breathed. "Crixus is your dad? That's awesome. . . ."

For so long Freya had yearned to know who her father was. Now that he was standing before her, she didn't know what to say or do.

Crixus opened his arms. "Daughter . . ."

Freya ran into his arms.

"How I have longed to tell you it was me," he whispered into her ear. "All these years, watching you grow into a powerful, accomplished Valkyrie and I was forbidden to say anything or claim you as mine. All I could do was train your best friend and hope that he would help you when I couldn't. I am so proud of you. . . ."

"Father . . . ?" Freya whispered.

Crixus nodded and held her tighter.

With her arms around her father, and all her family about her, Freya finally felt whole.

EPILOGUE

THE FIELDS OUTSIDE OF VALHALLA WERE ONCE AGAIN decorated with colorful banners, as all Asgard welcomed the end of the war. Though the Great Heavenly Hall lay in ruins, plans were already under way for its restoration.

Invitations were sent to Vanaheim, and many of the Vanir traveled to Asgard via the newly opened Bifröst to join in the celebrations and renewed union of the two realms.

Urd and Verdandi arrived, and for the first time in recorded history, the normally somber Norns laughed and danced as they were reunited with Skuld.

Over the following days, Freya and Orus stayed close to their family. Vonni, Sarah, Mims, and the baby moved into their large home in Asgard, while Vanir-Freyja and Freyr also took their place among the family. Plans were being set for

Maya to spend time away with her great-great-grandmother, to learn to use and control her newly released powers.

"Gee," Archie called to her. Skye and Quinn were with him with big grins on their faces. "We need you to come with us for a minute. Someone needs to speak with you urgently."

"Who?"

"You'll see," Skye said as she put her arm around Archie and lifted him lightly into the air. Her butterfly wings had recovered from their burns and fluttered lightly in the blazing blue sky.

"This way," Quinn said.

Freya looked at Orus on her shoulder and shrugged before launching into the air behind them to fly to Valhalla. When they landed, they crossed over the rubble and into the Great Heavenly Hall.

They led her to the banquet hall. Just outside it, Archie nodded. "In there."

"What's in there?" Freya asked.

"You'll see."

"Why don't you guys come in with me?"

Quinn grinned but shook his head. "Because it's for you."

"*That's right,*" Orus said as he flew off her shoulder and landed on Archie's. "*We'll be right here.*"

Freya frowned suspiciously at the raven. "What are you up to?"

"Me?" Orus cawed. "*Why do you always blame me?*"

"Because it's usually you." She laughed and stroked his smooth black feathers.

Then Freya turned and entered the banquet hall alone, curious as to what awaited her.

"Azrael!" she cried.

The Angel of Death threw his arms around her and wrapped her in his stunning white wings. "I'm so sorry I couldn't help you in Muspelheim. I heard you calling for me, but I couldn't come. It tore at me to know what Dirian did to you."

Freya held him tightly. "It's all right."

"No, it's not. I promised I would always help. But Muspelheim is the only realm we angels can't survive in. To know that you were there and suffering . . ."

"Azrael, I understand. I really do," Freya said. "I'm just so glad you're alive. When I didn't see you again, I feared the worst."

"Never fear for me. I will always come for you. . . ." He grinned and playfully tweaked her nose. "Unless it's in Muspelheim again."

Freya shook her head. "I have no plans to go back there."

"Good." Azrael's face became somber. "Freya, with all you've endured and lost, I can't bear to see you grieving." The Angel of Death waved his arm in the air and a beam of light appeared. Freya squinted until she could make out two figures emerging from the center of the beam. Dressed in the same brilliant white as Azrael, Skaga and Brundi appeared.

"Skaga!" Freya cried.

The two sisters greeted each other noisily. When Skaga released Freya, Brundi bundled her into her arms.

"I don't understand. How is this possible?"

Azrael started to chuckle. "Skuld isn't the only one with powers over people's destiny. When Skaga and Brundi were killed, there was no returning them to their lives as Valkyries. But there was nothing to say that I couldn't claim them for my angels."

Skaga started to laugh and opened her angel's robes. "Can you believe it? Look, they let me keep my Valkyrie armor!"

Freya laughed with her sister. "A Valkyrie Angel of Death . . . only you, Skaga, only you."

Skaga held on to Freya's hands. "Heofon is so beautiful. I hope you can come and see it."

"I hope so too," Brundi said. She smiled and opened her new white wings. "Look at this. I can finally fly again." She looked up at her raven. "And did you see who came with me?"

"Pym!" Freya cried, reaching to stroke her grandmother's raven. "I'm so glad to see you again."

"*And I you, child,*" Pym said.

Freya looked at Azrael. "Can I tell everyone? Mother and Vonni are really suffering."

He nodded. "Of course. I'm sorry we can't stay for the

celebrations. Earth still needs us. It took quite a pounding in the war, and people are suffering. But when our work is finished, we'll have a proper reunion."

Azrael gave Freya a final smile and then disappeared with her sister and grandmother.

Freya stood watching the empty place where her sister and grandmother had been standing. She was overwhelmed. So much had changed in her life. Loved ones lost and new friends found. Would anything be the same again? Did she want it to be the same?

Probably not. After a few minutes, Quinn and Orus entered the banquet hall. Quinn used his dragonfly wings to fly to her. "Are you all right?"

Freya nodded. "I am now." She looked past him. "Where are Archie and Skye?"

Quinn grinned. "Archie is giving Skye a personal tour of Asgard. Those two really like each other."

Freya nodded. "Archie and I went shopping earlier. He bought a necklace to give to her."

"*Archie has got it bad for her,*" Orus said.

Quinn tilted his head to the side. "What do you think about that? I mean, Archie bears your mark. He should be with you, shouldn't he?"

"No, it's not like that. Archie is my best friend, and nothing can ever change that. But he's free to be with whomever he wants."

"Just like you?" Quinn asked.

"Exactly."

Quinn stood beside her and smiled. It lit up his whole face and started Freya's heart racing. With so much happening, she hadn't allowed herself to feel anything. But now that the war was over and they were here alone, she realized how much she cared for him.

"Want to go back to the party?" Quinn asked.

"In a minute," Freya said. She lifted herself up on tiptoes and gave Quinn a tender kiss. She smiled shyly and knew that this was just the beginning.

"Freya," Orus cawed. *"What is your mother going to say about that?"*

As Quinn took her hand, Freya looked up at the raven on her shoulder and stroked his smooth feathers. "Orus, I think she'll be fine." Her eyes trailed over to Quinn. "We'll all be fine now."

A GUIDE TO THIS WORLD

Norse mythology is old. It's not just old; it's really, really old! It's also known as Scandinavian mythology and was created, retold, and loved by the Vikings. The Vikings, or Norsemen, settled most of Northern Europe and came mainly from Denmark, Norway, Sweden, Iceland, the Faroe Islands, and Greenland.

As you get to know the Norse myths, you might notice there are some similarities to the ancient Greek myths (including flying horses—but not my sweet Pegasus). Here's a simple comparison.

In Greek mythology, you have the Olympians and the Titans. The "younger" Olympians, in fact, came from the "older" Titans, and yet, there was a war between them and the Olympians won.

In Norse mythology, you have the Aesir and the Vanir. The "younger" Aesir came from the "older" Vanir, and yes, there was a war! But the difference is, in Norse mythology, neither side won—they called a truce.

Here's a big difference. In Greek myths, you have the place called Olympus. But in Norse myths, there are in fact nine worlds, or "realms" as they are sometimes called. In each of these realms, you have some really weird and wonderful creatures. And you know what? *We* are part of those nine realms. We're in the middle bit. And instead of Earth, our world is called Midgard.

Now, some of you may think you don't know Norse mythology at all. You do, but what you have learned may not be correct.

What's the biggest mistake I hear all the time? Okay, here is a really big one. I mean *big*. He's huge. He's green and has a bad temper. Yes, I'm talking about the Hulk. He is *not* part of Norse mythology. Neither are Iron Man, Hawkeye, Black Widow, nor many of the other characters from the Avengers movies. But no matter how many schools I visit, the moment I mention Thor or Loki, the students immediately think that the Hulk and the other characters are part of Norse mythology.

Trust me, they're not.

Don't get me wrong: I love the Avengers and Thor movies as much as anyone. But they are the creation of Marvel, Paramount, and Disney. The real Norse myths are much older and have a much richer history.

So, as you enter the world of Valkyrie and Norse mythology, I would like to introduce you to some of the characters you may meet along the way.

Some will appear in this book; others will appear in the

later books in this series. But I also encourage you to go to your local library or bookstore and check out more books on Norse myths. Believe me, with all the heroes and monsters you'll meet, you will soon love them as much as I do!

—Kate

NAMES AND PLACES IN NORSE MYTHOLOGY

YGGDRASIL—Also known as the Cosmic World Tree, Yggdrasil sits in the very heart of the universe. It is within the branches of this tree that the nine realms exist. Yggdrasil is supported by three massive roots that pass through the realms. It is said that the fierce dragon Nidhogg regularly gnaws on one of the roots (when he's not eating corpses—don't ask). The Well of Urd, where Odin traded his eye for wisdom, sits on another root. Water from that well is taken by the Norns, mixed with earth, and put on the tree as a means of preventing Yggdrasil's bark from rotting. They also water the tree. It is said that a great eagle sits perched atop the tree and is harassed by a squirrel, Ratatosk, who delivers insults and unpleasant comments from the dragon Nidhogg, who resides at the base. Yggdrasil gives the nine realms life. Without it, they and we would cease to exist.

AESIR—This is the name of the group of younger gods, like Odin, Thor, Loki, Frigg, and the Valkyries. These are warrior gods who use weapons more than magic.

VANIR—This is the name of the older gods. Not much is known about them, but there are some familiar names. Vanir-Freyja and her twin brother, Freyr, are two well-known Vanir who were traded to Asgard in a peace exchange after the war. The Vanir are more earthen/forest-type gods who deal with land fertility and use a lot of magic.

ODIN—He is the leader of Asgard, the realm of the Aesir. A brave, strong, and imposing warrior, he presided over the war with the Vanir. He has many sons, most notably Thor and Balder. Odin carries a powerful spear, Gungnir, and wears an eye patch. It is said that Odin journeyed to the Well of Urd, where he exchanged his eye for wisdom. Each night Odin can be found in Valhalla, where he celebrates with the fallen heroes of Earth's battlefields. His two wolves sit loyally at his side.

FRIGG—The devoted and very beautiful wife of Odin, she is the mother of Balder and is known for her wisdom. Sadly, not a lot more is known about her, other than that she knows everyone's destiny. In later mythology, she is often confused with Vanir-Freyja and their deeds are mixed.

THOR—The son of Odin, he is known as the thunder god and is often compared with Zeus from the Greek myths. Thor is impossibly strong, with flaming red hair and a raging temper. He is known for being a fierce but honorable warrior. Thor is a sworn enemy to the frost giants, but calls Loki (who is part frost giant) a friend. They had many adventures together. Thor is also known for his mighty hammer, Mjölnir, which was created by the dwarf brothers Sindri and Brokkr on a mischievous bet with Loki. After its creation, they gave it to Thor, as he was one of the few strong enough to wield it. (By the way, Loki lost the bet and the two dwarfs sewed his mouth shut.) Thor is actually a married man—his wife is Sif, and they have three children. Note: We use the name Thor every week, as Thursday was named after him. Just think: Thor's day.

BALDER—Son of Odin and Frigg, he is known as the kindest of Odin's sons. Balder is a devoted brother to Thor and can calm his brother's fearsome temper. Sadly, within the mythology, Balder died, and it is widely believed that Loki caused his death and was responsible for keeping him dead.

LOKI—He is the trickster of Asgard. His origins are a little unclear, but it's said that both of his parents were frost giants. He is by turns playful, malicious, and helpful, but he's always irreverent and self-involved. Loki likes to have fun! He enjoys getting Thor into trouble, but then he helps Thor out of the same trouble. Loki is a shape-changer and appears in many disguises. For all his troublemaking ways, it is written that Loki is tolerated in Asgard because he is blood brother to Odin.

HEIMDALL—Ever vigilant watchman of Bifröst, Heimdall has nine mothers but no father. He is a giant of a man and amazingly strong. Heimdall requires less sleep than a bird, and his vision is so powerful, he can see for hundreds of miles, day or night. His hearing is so acute that he can hear grass or wool grow. It is written that he carries a special horn, Gjallarhorn, that he will sound at the start of Ragnarök when the giants storm Bifröst.

VALKYRIES—Choosers of the slain, the winged Valkyries are an elite group of Battle-Maidens who serve Odin by bringing only the most valiant of fallen warriors from Earth's battlefields to Valhalla. There, the warriors fight all day and feast all night, being served food and mead by the Valkyries. In early mythology, the Valkyries could decide who would live or die on the battlefield, but later this was changed to only collecting them for Odin. The Valkyries arrived on the battle-fields riding blazing, winged horses, and their howls could be heard long before their arrival. It is written that the Vanir goddess Freyja, who was traded after the war, was in fact the very first Valkyrie. Again, within the mythology, she gets to keep half the warriors she reaps—but it's not written what she does with them. The other half go to Odin.

FROST & FIRE GIANTS—Throughout the mythology, the frost and fire giants often appear, and there are many stories about Thor's encounters with them. Fearsome, immense, and violent, they each live in their own realms. Frost giants are from Utgard in Jotunheim, and the fire giants come from Muspelheim. Though there are some peaceful giants, most seek to conquer Asgard. To offer an idea of size, there is one story in which Loki, Thor, and two humans venture to Utgard to meet the frost giant king, but get lost in a maze of tunnels. It is later discovered that these tunnels were, in fact, the fingers of a frost giant's glove.

DWARFS—Both good and bad, dwarfs play a large part and fill an important role in Norse mythology. They are the master craftsmen and architects of the building of Asgard. It was dwarfs who created Thor's mighty hammer, Mjölnir, and Odin's spear, Gungnir. There are many stories of the dwarfs and their amazing creations.

LIGHT & DARK ELVES—These are the two contrasting types of elves. Dark Elves use dark magic, cause a lot of trouble, and can be very dangerous; they are hard to look upon and seek to do harm. Whereas the Light Elves are fairer to look at than the sun, use their magic for good, and help many people.

MIDGARD SERPENT—Also known as Jormungand, the Midgard Serpent is the son of Loki and his giantess wife, Angrboda. The Midgard Serpent is brother to the giant wolf Fenrir and Hel, Loki's daughter and ruler of the underworld. It is written that Odin had Jormungand cast into the ocean, where he grew so large, he could encircle the Earth. There is an ongoing feud between Thor and the Midgard Serpent. It is written that Jormungand is big and powerful enough to eat worlds.

RAVENS—Ravens play a large part in Norse mythology, and Odin himself has two very special ravens, Huginn and Muninn, who travel through all the realms and return to Odin at night. They sit on his shoulder and tell him everything that is happening in the other realms. They are known for their wisdom and guidance.

VALHALLA—Odin's Great Heavenly Hall for the heroic dead has a curious problem. In the mythology, there is a question of where Valhalla actually is. Most say it was part of Asgard, but others suggest it is in Helheim, the land of the dead. One thing is clear: Valhalla is a wondrous building where the valiant dead from Earth's battlefields are taken. Here they are served and entertained by the Valkyries who delivered them there. They drink and feast with Odin and continue their training until the day comes when they are called back into service to fight for Asgard during Ragnarök.

BIFRÖST—Also known as the Rainbow Bridge, this is a magnificent, multicolored bridge that links Asgard to Midgard and some of the other realms. It is said to have been created by the gods using the red of fire, the green of water, and the blue of air. Bifröst is guarded by Heimdall the Watchman.

THE NORNS—There are three Norn sisters who dwell at the Well of Urd at the base of Yggdrasil. The oldest is Urd, the middle sister is Verdandi, and the youngest is Skuld. These are the goddesses of destiny, similar to the Greek Fates. Urd is able to see the past, while Verdandi deals with current events. Skuld is able to see everyone's future. It is said that they are weavers, weaving people's destiny. If a thread is broken, the life ends.

RAGNARÖK—Also known as the apocalypse of the Norse gods and the end of everything, Ragnarök (in the mythology) is said to have been started by a very insane Loki and his wolf son, Fenrir, along with the frost and fire giants. They took on Asgard, and during the war all the gods were killed. Odin was killed by Fenrir, who was then killed by another of Odin's sons. Thor and the Midgard Serpent fought a battle to the death in which they managed to kill each other. Heimdall was the last to fall at the hand of Loki. It is during Ragnarök that Odin called on the warriors of Valhalla to fight for Asgard—but there were no winners. And it was from the ashes of Ragnarök that a new world was formed from the survivors—the world that we inhabit today.

DARK SEARCHERS—The Dark Searchers did not actually exist in Norse mythology. They are my creation because, in all my research, I couldn't find a mention of Odin's police force. So I created them for that purpose.

AZRAEL & THE ANGELS OF DEATH—Now, some of you may already know that Azrael and the Angels of Death don't come directly from Norse mythology. That's very true. But as they are known all over the world in almost every culture, and since they do similar jobs to the Valkyries and have wings just like the Valkyries, I thought it would be fun to mix things up a bit. To avoid confusion, I set it up so that the Valkyries only deal with the most valiant warriors reaped from Earth's battlefields, who are then taken to Valhalla— thus staying true to Norse mythology. Azrael and his Angels of Death deal with everyone else—thus staying true to many other cultures.

ACKNOWLEDGMENTS

Life is filled with many challenges.

This was never more evident to me than when I was writing this book. I had only just started it when two of my brothers (one here in the UK, the other in New York) became unexpectedly but gravely ill. One came out of it—scarred but alive. The other didn't. I lost my oldest brother, Pat, before Christmas 2014. And for the first time in my life, I found I couldn't write. The words were gone.

This is why I want to thank my editor, Naomi Greenwood, and everyone at Hodder Children's Books for their patience and for letting me take the time I needed to heal—so the words would return. They did. This book was so late being delivered, but not once did I hear a word of complaint from my publisher.

My wonderful agents, Veronique Baxter and Laura West, were equally supportive during this dreadful time, and continue to be just as supportive as the rough waters finally start to calm.

This just goes to show the resilience of our hearts and spirits. Terrible things do sometimes happen, but somehow we get through them—even when we think we can't.

ACKNOWLEDGMENTS

Should you, my sweet readers, ever face these terrible times—and a lot of you will—just know the days do get better. I promise. You are not alone.

Normally about now, I would start talking about protecting horses, dogs, marine animals, all endangered species, and doing all you can to protect our Mother Earth. But for now, instead, I will leave you with a few words to my brother. I have never claimed to be a poet, but for you, JP, I will try.

Seek Me Not

Seek me not, where the seabirds fly,
Or tempest ocean crashes to lonely shore
Do not look for me on a windswept cliff
Or where caverns sing, or rain will pour.
I am there with you, no further than a whisper
Not lost, or hiding behind eternity's door
So search no further than your own wounded heart
For there I reside, forever more.

HUNTING IN HARLEM

HUNTING IN HARLEM

A NOVEL

MAT JOHNSON

BLOOMSBURY

For Meera

Published by Bloomsbury, New York and London
Distributed to the trade by Holtzbrinck Publishers

Library of Congress Cataloging-in-Publication Data has been applied for.

ISBN 1–58234–272–5

First U.S. edition 2003

1 3 5 7 9 10 8 6 4 2

Typeset by Hewer Text Ltd, Edinburgh
Printed in the United States of America by RR Donnelley & Sons, Harrisonburg

ORIENTATION

THREE EX-CONS CAME to Harlem looking to become something more.

Bobby Finley drove up in a rented truck from New Carrellton, Maryland, his boxes of books stacked to the ceiling in the back, what few other possessions he had riding in the passenger seat next to him. Cedric Snowden took the train north from Philadelphia with just a backpack and a boom box, figuring if this turned out to be a scam he could grab both and just as quickly head back toward the Schuylkill. Horus Manley was going to take the plane from Chicago but then realized he could pocket the majority of his travel allowance *and* bring his guns if he took the bus instead.

These were the men recruited by Horizon Realty for their Second Chance Program, selected for the opportunity to rebuild their lives in a neighborhood trying to do the same. Regardless of mode of travel or point of origin, all three new interns soon found themselves in the same basement classroom in the city they would be asked to call home, identical orientation packets on their child-sized desks and looks of confusion as they tried to make sense of the man standing behind the podium before them.

"You have yet to realize the creative brilliance of this path Horizon's founder Congressman Cyrus Marks has blazed for you," their host informed them. "You know this is an internship program, that you'll be provided with real estate training and opportunities for advancement, but gentlemen, you don't yet know the *majesty* of this venture. The Second Chance Program isn't simply

about acquiring job skills; this isn't the Learning Annex. This is about you receiving your destiny!"

The man speaking was Horizon's manager of operations, Lester Baines, a name and title the three recruits recognized from their correspondence. It was everything else about the man they found decidedly alien: the lunar pockmarks of his face, the greased tidal wave breaking perpetually inches above his brow, that there was such a thing as pink corduroy, and that a sane man would actually wear a three-piece suit of the fabric. They were expecting Cyrus Marks, the owner, the man Lester insisted everyone refer to as "the congressman" even though it had been years since he'd left the office.

At Lester's feet, an odd, off-breed dog barked its approval. The mutt's jaw was heavy and wide and clashed with its long dachshund body, giving the impression that some sadist god had grabbed its head in one hand and ass in the other and yanked the beast like taffy.

"The congressman, he contains multitudes," Lester continued. "You may have wondered why your applications had to come through parole officers. The congressman was once a PO. He was mine, actually. Oh yes, this was quite a long time ago, but he molded me into a man, as he will you," he told them, glancing at each member of his audience individually in search of appreciation for this proposed manipulation.

"I assure you, there will also be other, more material benefits awaiting you. As you know from our promotional materials, the person who most impresses us during this inaugural year will be chosen to oversee the Second Chance Program for the years to follow, promoted to the public as the symbol of Harlem's phoenix-like spirit, and of course get a brownstone townhouse of his very own as a bonus. Know, however, that you will all be transformed by this experience. The congressman will see to that."

Lester leaned forward across the podium like he had a secret and was going to tell it. "Our greatest ambitions, our loftiest goals – that's just where the congressman *begins*. I'm sure you know about his glorious tenure representing the Fifteenth District, of course, most

do, but then to start over as a businessman and in a mere twelve years create this empire? Last year, I had a dark time, I lost someone I loved. I thought life was over, I really did, but he gave me an even higher purpose. That's part of why you're here. I ask you, how do you not bow to such a man?"

Firm the muscles in your lower back and remain vertical, Snowden thought, but grumbled monosyllabic declarations of awe with the rest of them. Looking to his side for sympathetic cynicism, Snowden examined his fellow intern Bobby Finley, the long, emaciated man whose limbs shined black and thin like licorice. Bobby was actually squinting at the front of the room like there was something to see, had already filled one long page on his yellow notepad as if there was something specific being said to remember.

For these first days before their formal initiation into the Horizon fold, the three recruits of the Second Chance Program's sole assignment would be to walk every street of Harlem twice, one time for each side of the street. Special attention was to be paid to the Mount Morris Historic District, which they were in, as this would be the center of Horizon's activities. To this end, the three men were handed maps, along with the caveat that it was unwise to be seen using them on the street, particularly in areas marked in red, such as the Polo Grounds.

After this week of casing out the neighborhood, the recruits of the Second Chance Program would start their internship as moving men for the company's relocation service, helping new buyers move in to their new homes. It was not simply manual labor, it was a chance to begin learning the business from its most basic vantage. The recruits of the Second Chance Program would proudly wear the neon yellow workmen's coveralls with Horizon's logo on the back while on duty, a conspicuous symbol to all that a new day for Harlem had arrived. The recruits of the Second Chance Program would have to get over the fact that their uniforms looked just like the ones they wore in prison.

"Hold on there, let me get this straight," the recruit introduced as

3

Horus Manley interrupted. Horus's thick, muscle-swelled body leaned back so far in the little elementary school chair that he was nearly horizontal. He sat in the row behind the other two contestants, one foot sprawled out under each of their seats. Horus Manley reminded Snowden of a guard dog, the kind whose grizzled snout poked out of junkyard fences or who barked unseen from ghetto basements, beasts bred for irrational violence and fed hot sauce and cayenne pepper until they instilled fear even in the brutes who owned them.

"You say we ain't going to meet the boss man himself or get started till the end of the week?" Horus questioned with disbelief. "I'm saying, how you going to let a resource like me go to waste all that time? My man, I could be out there hustling for you now. Come on. Don't you got some houses for me to sell? Or maybe you got something heavy you need lifting." The man seemed genuinely confused when Lester told him his services were not yet needed.

"Excuse me." Bobby Finley waved his notepad to attract Lester's stare, the ink-scarred pages crinkling over his head. "In honor of our generous benefactor, I've composed a salutary poem focusing on this neighborhood the congressman has selected us to serve. Just a little memento, if you would be so kind to give this to him for me. It's a ceremonial piece, really, with references to great Harlem artists, as well as a salute to the bright fut – "

When Snowden first heard the sound, saw the movement as Bobby Finley went crashing to the linoleum, he thought the man's chair had simply broken. Then he noticed that Horus Manley's foot was still tangled in the chair's wire undercarriage, and that the instigator was smiling.

"My bad. You all right, chief? Good." Horus answered himself before waiting for one. As Bobby attempted to get off the floor, Horus chuckled, shook his head from side to side. "Y'all got to admit that shit was a little funny."

Snowden rose from his seat, went over to help Bobby untangle

himself. Back on his feet, Bobby turned for a second to say something to his attacker, but on getting a better look at Horus Manley turned quickly away again. Approaching the front of the room instead, Bobby pulled an orange envelope from his shirt pocket and placed it into Lester's hands. "A gesture of gratitude is all," Bobby said lightly, sitting down once more.

"Oh isn't that wonderful?" Lester asked, holding it up to look at it. Snowden thought the question was directed at him since he was the only one not taking part in the conversation, but then saw Lester repeat it staring down at the dog. "Wendell, isn't that just a lovely act of respect?" In response to this direct question, the wiener mutt pulled his jaws from his behind, slapped his tail to the concrete floor in a code Lester could apparently understand.

"The congressman is a great lover of art." Lester looked back up at the humans to explain. "Congressman Marks is a board member of several prominent Black Arts organizations. He is, you must understand, a man of grace, and as such has the ability to empathize with grace in all of its forms. So are there any last questions, comments, or offerings before we break? One more?" Lester rose a gold-circled finger to the room.

"I'm sorry," Snowden prefaced, "I couldn't find the answer in any of the handouts we've been given. But if we win, how long do we have to keep working for Horizon before we can sell the house and go back home?"

Snowden turned at the sound of Bobby gasping at the crassness of the inquiry, met the joyous grin on Horus's face past him at the misstep of openly expressing greed. Lester, for his part, seemed merely amused by the naïveté of the query.

"Mr. Snowden, listen to me. This isn't about cashing in on a boom market, it's about making something. Horizon does welfare-to-work training, offers all kinds of loan assistance, provides schooling for local children. In Harlem, the congressman spreads love like it was peanut butter. Horizon is his dream. Once you understand his

5

vision, you won't want to leave. So trust me, the question is moot. He'll make you a believer too."

Snowden was not a believer. Snowden didn't believe in anything at all. This of course was an exaggeration; there were some heartfelt views that were integral to Snowden's understanding of reality: that the Los Angeles Clippers would never win a title, that most people in this world were not to be trusted, that he would sooner die than let himself be locked behind bars one night more. These tenets, however, Snowden invested in with such certainty that he saw no faith involved. To be a believer, in Snowden's mind, was to agree to be blind, to see only what you wanted to and ignore what contradicted it. It was to be a fool, or even worse to be like his father, a man who wasted his life raising banners no one wanted to read, following his conscience wherever it led him — even though that was usually jail.

Snowden's earliest memories of his dad were from the day of his father's first release from prison: the bullhorned speeches in Fairmount Park and the crowd that yelled in response to them, so much food that casserole bowls sat on seats while people stood balancing paper plates in their hands. By his last release from a federal penitentiary twelve years later, the reception had been reduced to a bucket of drive-through chicken and Snowden's uncle in the front seat saying, "It's 1983 and nobody gives a damn about that shit no more, so just shut up and stop hogging all the white meat." The movement had moved on, without leaving a forwarding address behind. The only things Snowden Sr. could point to for all his sacrifice were the parts of him that were clearly missing. A bitter, drunken husk of a man whose life ended the moment his son finally had enough of his taunting and punched him as hard as he was asking for it. By the time Snowden made the mistake of swinging on his father, knocking him to the floor and into the coma that would eventually take him, there really wasn't much left of the man that hadn't already died anyway.

Having read the Horizon literature, Snowden understood that they were looking for someone a bit more evangelical and, to keep his bid competitive, he was willing to accommodate them – within reason. Snowden was willing to let faith guide him, as long as it didn't walk too far ahead. Searching within himself in the days after his orientation meeting, he found that there were several things he was agreeable to believing in. That he could win this Second Chance contest, for instance; that he could beat out the brute and the beanpole if he applied himself and stayed out of trouble; that if he won, he would take that promotion for just long enough to show his gratitude and then cash in and sell that one single-family brownstone for enough to buy a whole apartment building back in Philly, a big one. Snowden believed that in his Philly building he could live in poor man's luxury, survive off the rents into retirement, his only duties being to call the plumber and carry the trash to the side of the road.

The night after his initial Horizon orientation, spurred on by these first visions, Snowden vowed to rise early the following morning, grab his map of Harlem and set forth walking around this neighborhood to see the world it would be his job to champion, to do what he could to make his hopes a reality. Drifting to sleep when exhaustion finally overcame the excitement of it all, Snowden saw himself treading sidewalk in the days to follow, converting the unknown to the familiar one blister at a time, and loved the image of it all.

Oversleeping that following morning, Snowden rose with all his intentions in place. Walking down his building's stairs he saw Jifar, the little boy from the apartment directly below. The kid reminded him of his own youth, his own canned innocence, and Snowden chose that as a good omen. He felt good for a moment, descending those last few flights, then he walked out his front door only to have to make it through the handful of men who had decided his building's stoop was their new living room. It was eleven A.M. and they already had beer in hand, brown paper bags covering their forty bottles like condoms. The building door opened and they

7

stopped talking and looked at Snowden like he insulted them just by leaving his home, like he should have climbed out his window and down the fire escape, jumped the ten feet from the metal to the pavement out of politeness. Snowden looked at their faces, looked quickly away again. There were blocks in Philly where you could get shot for meeting a hood's eyes. There were other blocks in Philly you could get just as dead if you didn't.

On 125th Street, Snowden wasted time at a book vendor's table before walking farther, shelled out the twenty for the new Bo Shareef book, *Shuckin' 'n' Jivin' Down Lenox*, and managed not to admit to himself that in the next few days he was going to have time to read it.

135th between Lenox and Fifth was also known as Astor Row, one block of wooden, country-style houses that there'd been a blurred photo of in Horizon's pamphlet. The homes looked misplaced in the picture, architecture meant to be surrounded by barns, not bodegas, but it looked less surreal in person, mostly because at least a third of the houses were as devastated as the rest of the neighborhood. Some with soiled bedsheets hung in windows as curtains, others with no windows at all, just punctured holes where frame once held glass. A quarter of the way down the block, Snowden saw that one of the houses had been destroyed by fire, long enough ago that a treelike weed reached from the top floor up through the hole in the roof, but recently enough that a charred couch still sank into the mud on the front lawn. At the far end, trying to admire the absurd architecture, Snowden noticed a brown flash that poked out and disappeared again in an attic window of an abandoned building just past him. Aside from that one small lookout, the building was sealed, sheet metal nailed over every opening and covered in graffiti for good measure. Snowden tried to calm himself, ignore the sight, but was overtaken by fears of crackhead snipers and looked back up at the window. The head was there, staring down at him. The woman's hair shrieked from her scalp, her eyes as empty as the room behind her. Her face was negative space: the hole of her mouth, the hollow of her cheeks and

8

sockets. The only thing that kept the woman from looking dead was that she was rocking back and forth, moaning.

Snowden did a U-turn and blew off his quest right there. It took an hour underneath the fluorescent lights of the nearest McDonald's to convince him that he had returned to the rational world once more.

It turned out, Harlem was a ghetto. It turned out, Harlem was loud and overcrowded and there was a lot of trash on the ground. That Harlem fit into this category should not have been a surprise, as Harlem was perhaps the most romanticized ghetto in the world, the endless tour buses packed with European and Asian voyeurs that rattled brownstone windows every Sunday attested to that fact. Nor should the specifics of ghetto life have been alien to Snowden either, as he had grown up in an environment that fit firmly within that category. What Snowden realized, as he walked bemused down Lenox, was that Harlem was not *his* ghetto. Snowden looked at the faces flooding by and knew none of them, felt no attachment beyond one of basic humanity. This city was naked to him, stripped of personal attachment and familiarity. Without the haze of anecdotal past affecting his vision, Snowden saw chaos: buildings and people crushed together and crumbling from lack of air, poverty and the destruction of the soul it perpetrates. Snowden knew this was only a larger-scale version of the place he grew up in; it angered him that this should be the world he was saddled to, so he escaped back to his shelter. Got into bed and took Bo Shareef's vision of Harlem with him. It was a safe one, orderly, trapped in ink and constructed from accepted ideas and understandings. It had a pretty lady in it, earnest people, jazz. The only conflicts were caused by money, sex, and other people's racism.

The best thing about a Bo Shareef novel was that you knew what to expect from it.

"Arson, in the second degree," Bobby confessed.

"First-degree manslaughter," Snowden offered.

"One count of attempted homicide. Three counts of first-degree manslaughter, sentences served simultaneously. Two counts assault with a deadly weapon, and a couple of them racketeering charges – but that was just some tic-tac shit thrown in because of my gang affiliation," Horus assured. "They even tried to hit me with vehicular homicide, but it didn't stick since the car wasn't moving."

The other two hadn't realized it was a competition, but Horus's voice said it was and that they had lost. The three recruits of the Second Chance Program were waiting at the back doors of P.S. 832 as instructed, their formal induction into the Horizon Realty fold only moments away. The stoop smelled of malt liquor and urine, its corners filled with leaves and windblown trash.

"Arson. Don't you know better than to light shit on fire?" Horus laughed in gasping barks, holding his stomach tenderly like the sound hurt to make it. "What happened, little man, you get busted playing flame thrower with your mamma's hairspray?"

"He doesn't have to tell you nothing." Snowden meant this statement as a warning, a defiant stance, but after staring into Horus's dull eyes and smelling his cheap cologne like it was menace, the words came out as a polite offering of minor information. Even still, Snowden looked at the way Horus was looking back at him, then quickly checked his watch to make sure it wouldn't be long before Lester would come to the rescue.

"No, no, really, I don't mind," Bobby interrupted. "I don't mind at all. It's good to get these things out in the open – identifying the problem makes it that much more avoidable, don't you agree? Well, my mom's boyfriend, I burned his house down. The whole thing. Actually, I burned down his house, and I burned down his garage, and also his car, which all should probably count separately since the garage was detached and the car was parked three blocks away at the time. He did something that upset me, not that that's an excuse though. Neither he nor my mother speaks to me now, but that's penance, right? Penance is important," Bobby offered, eyebrows raised and head bobbing like it was a novelty they should try.

"What'd you do hard man? What'd they stick on your ass?" Horus didn't ask Snowden the question, he pushed it into him, shooting his thick arm forward and slamming his open palm into Snowden's shoulder. Caught off guard, Snowden fought to keep his body rigid and balanced, worked even harder to make this look like no struggle at all.

"I killed a man," Snowden said back to him. It sounded hard. It was supposed to sound hard. Snowden didn't say it was his father, that it was a mistake, or that it was one punch and the man's drunken fall had been more responsible for the hemorrhage than his son's initial action. Immediately overwhelmed by the guilt of act and omission, Snowden turned directly to Bobby and said in a different tone, "It was an accident."

"That's good when they can't prove it was premeditated or nothing," Horus mused behind him. "That's what got me out early. There was four of them and just me, so wasn't no way they could prove I started shit. Could have gotten self-defense too, but I got a little carried away, y'know, with that blunt instrument and all." Horus paused, inspected his shoes as he waited for a question that never came. When the back door finally opened, Lester stepping aside to let them in and instructing the men to climb the stairs all the way to the roof's access door, Horus waited until they were two flights up before continuing.

"I would tell you what that blunt instrument was," Horus said like someone had pleaded with him to share this information, "but when people find out it tends to get all sensationalistic. Me, I'm more the subtle type."

There was a hedgehog floating ten yards above them, dropping greetings below.

Not really. It wasn't a hedgehog, it was a man. It was the man who brought them here, the one whose name was his former office. He was floating, though, up there in the air in the round basket of the hot-air balloon he'd rented for the occasion. Men with shirts and

11

hats that said ROSEDALE AMUSEMENTS surrounded a crane, working it around to pull the air monster down by its cabled tether. Slowly, the balloon dipped to the roof the recruits stood on, bringing former Congressman Cyrus Marks down with it.

Snowden looked to his side in disbelief as Bobby joined Lester in waving joyously in the air, as if something great and improbable had been accomplished by this entrance. Next to them, Horus wasn't even looking up, stretching his arms behind his back and pulling his knees to his chest like he was going to jump the remaining distance to their new boss.

"Boys. Neophytes. I was just like you once," Marks began yelling over the edge of his hot-air balloon's basket. "I too did careless, destructive things like you have done. The only difference was that I was smarter than you ever were. I didn't get caught. You are nothing now and you know it, but follow me where I say to go, do what I say to do, and I'll make you something! You have my word, and that's like gold."

"It's like solid gold!" Lester repeated on the ground next to them.

Even standing far below, looking straight up into the air at the man, the congressman appeared squat to Snowden. Compressed, crushed, as if gravity had taken it upon itself to push this full-grown man into as small a physical space as possible. Snowden kept looking up instead of around, trying to ignore the fact that he was standing on a bare roof, with loose gravel underfoot, the only thing keeping him from falling off the edge being friction and willpower. When the basket holding his new boss finally tapped down, Snowden smiled broadly with relief as Cyrus Marks made to exit, unhinged the nest's door like he was preparing to leave the balloon behind. When Marks stepped back from the open gate and gestured instead for his new employees to climb aboard, Snowden fixed his grin into place and made a point to get on last, as if that would save him a moment's horror.

The balloon operators quickly diminished from reassuring figures to smudges of color you had to squint to differentiate. They were high

enough that both the East and Hudson rivers could be seen as mirrored strips all the way south toward their meeting, glancing north that wet slash that separated Manhattan from the Bronx looked like a fresh cut, like the freed island was moments away from floating over toward New Jersey.

Snowden gripped the side railing so fiercely he became certain he was going to break a piece off, counting down from twenty and looking at his feet when the urge to roll up in a ball threatened to overcome him. It was several minutes into his own drama before he noticed that the other two participants in the Second Chance Program were holding the edge with equal vigor. Even Lester, dressed in a patchwork suit that expressed every shade between pure white and dark brown, had wrapped himself tightly around one of the cables that attached their basket to the floating ball above, his other bejeweled hand resting atop a gentleman's cane, a hesitant nod to fashion. The only one not holding on was the congressman, and that was Snowden's first impression that the man was insane. Even when they came to the end of the balloon's tether, the tension sending them swiftly east and bouncing from the wind's pressure, the congressman just bent what little legs he had and remained standing, hands in his pockets.

"The Second Chance Program will make you real estate agents, but you'll become more than that, much more. I'm giving you the biggest thing you never had, what every man needs if he's going to accomplish great things in his life. I'm giving you a mission." Marks walked forward, stopped in front of Lester and held his hand out without looking, pausing until his subordinate figured out what he wanted and put the cane into it.

"See that down there at the bottom, that cluster of skyscrapers off to the left?" Marks pointed the stick south. "That's Wall Street. There used to be a real wall there, hundreds of years ago in the seventeenth century. The whole of New York City fit below it, on that tiny tip of land. The rest," the congressman made a sweeping

motion with the cane that included all the eye could see in its entirety, "was trees, brush, and Indians. The first blacks on this island were forced to live right by that wall, on the woods side, unprotected. Allowed to farm and mind their own only because they'd serve as a buffer in case the natives attacked. The sounds of their slaughter as an alarm system."

Congressman Marks shook Lester's cane over the edge as he talked, his grip light and floppy. If that thing fell, somebody far below would die a painful and posthumously embarrassing death, but Marks clearly wasn't thinking about this, too focused ahead to see the world around him.

"They've always done us like that. As the city's grown, they've always displaced us, pushed us to the periphery. See the dome of Madison Square Garden? That land was ours. Used to be the Tenderloin District, but now it's the Garden, the post office, Penn Station. That complex farther up there, that's Lincoln Center. It sits on land that used to be part of a black neighborhood called San Juan Hill. Do you know what happened to the community that lived there? We were evicted. These were people who'd spent their whole lives there, entire families, an entire neighborhood destroyed, but the developers didn't care. Central Park, the same story. Used to house us and some poor micks, the rich whites seized the land and threw everybody out on the streets to make that park happen. Always pushing us farther to the perimeters. You see, that's why we have Harlem. We had nowhere else to go. It was the only place they would let us live anymore: past the park, all the way at the top of Manhattan island where they hoped they could forget about us." Marks was pointing Lester's cane down at 110th Street, the northern edge of Central Park, leaning so far forward that it seemed he might jump out the basket to get there.

"This used to be a nice place," the congressman pleaded, his tone casually defensive, righting himself and walking away from the edge once more. "It was far from perfect, but we had our own doctors, our own services, our own stores. There was money here, circulating.

Then desegregation came, and everyone who could afford to leave, did. Poverty and their own racism were the only things that kept the whites from coming in and seizing the place, but even that's changing now. They're running out of space once more, prices are so high everywhere else that they're even prepared to ignore their fear of us. So that's were you come in."

Snowden watched the man's ring as he lectured. It was as thick as a chestnut, gold dark enough that it held a red hue. Every time he made a point he felt particularly important, Marks had the habit of slamming that ring into the nearest hard service available, the clang reinforcing his punctuation.

"You, my handpicked warriors, are needed. Harlem is more than a place, it's a symbol. It's our Mecca, it is our Jerusalem, the historic cradle of our culture, the ark of our covenant as Africans in this Western world. It must be protected, by any means necessary," Marks declared, ring banging. "This is our last chance. If we don't get this place together, attract our own people to come back and make it vital once more, history will repeat itself. Gentlemen, we at Horizon Realty are not going to stand by and let them push us out this time. So it stops here!"

"It stops here!" Lester repeated, nodding, smiling. A gust of wind sent the balloon dipping sharply to the right, but Lester merely gripped a cable with both hands and kept grinning, undaunted.

"It stops now!" Marks called, this time all but Snowden loudly responding, Snowden himself having only just enough sense to mouth the words.

"This is where we make our last stand, great black warriors of the new millennium! Together, and with the help of all the people we'll recruit to stand among us, we'll bring back the renaissance that once defined this place. We shall not be moved!"

"We shall not be moved!" repeated the chorus.

"Harlem is ours!" Marks yelled, spittle shooting forward, tears dripping straight down.

"Harlem is ours!" the others responded. Snowden closed his eyes,

unsure if Harlem was his, or if it was if he really wanted it, and began praying aloud for a safe landing. Cursing aloud that this was his last chance at something better. Nobody noticed, though, with all the clapping.

MOVING UP

IN THE WEEKS of moving Horizon's clients into their newly acquired homes, Bobby made a practice of going to the back of the truck and selecting the biggest, heaviest beasts – things Snowden spent the morning looking at and thinking, *If I can just get through this day without lifting that, I just might make it* – and trying to lift them, carry them down the little ramp and into the property all by himself. Bobby Finley looked like a skeleton dipped in chocolate; his strongman spectacle was intensely unnerving to watch. Snowden would be standing behind him cringing, offering unaccepted help, sure the skinny man's arms would simply distend from the strain, that his femurs would snap in two from the struggle.

The most disturbing thing about Bobby's behavior, in Snowden's opinion, was that he wasn't even doing it to win the house or job at all, that there was no spur of competition driving him. Bobby didn't care about the brownstone, never brought it up. His only comment if someone else did was, "Fate will decide who's best suited to lead us." Bobby didn't care because Bobby actually believed in what Lester and the congressman were telling him, bought into all of it from the start. Horus was the same way, never questioning, never complaining, but Snowden found this far less remarkable. Having seen Horus eat, Snowden doubted the man questioned what he consumed at all.

Originally, Snowden assumed Bobby's faith was nothing more than a clever ploy, a work of performance art meant to create the impression that he was the most committed of the three of them, but after weeks of testing this façade with conspiratorial cynicism, Snowden conceded defeat just to get him to shut up. Bobby used

17

the slightest doubtful whisper as an excuse to spew Horizon propaganda back. Fevered, ecclesiastic ramblings that could often be interrupted only by running away from him, which on two occasions Snowden had literally been forced to do. Bobby Finley could spin firm logic from the mist of romance. Both times Snowden had chosen to run were because Bobby was starting to make sense to him.

Bobby was good with words. He was a writer. Not a very successful one even by his own admission, but a published one nonetheless, a novel he'd called *The Great Work*. One of these copies Bobby Finley presented to Snowden, who out of a sense of grudging obligation tried to read it, and after several motivated assaults did manage to push through to the third page. This fact irritated Snowden, as it was his habit to take pride in his assertion that he loved reading everything: romance, mystery, science fiction, sometimes even the newspaper.

Not only did Snowden fail to get beyond the very opening of *The Great Work*, he also realized — as he struggled for some polite compliment to offer Bobby afterward — that he had no idea what he'd read. The book's sentences seemed to make sense individually. They had verbs and adjectives and nouns, but reading one after another only compounded his confusion. The sole blurb to grace the back cover said " . . . creates an emotional response . . . ," which Snowden had to agree with, as his emotional response had been to scream and want to hurl it across his apartment. Instead, upon reuniting with Bobby, Snowden smiled and said, "I've never read anything like it!" to which Bobby's response was to snatch the book out of Snowden's hands and start frantically wiping away imaginary fingerprints from its cover.

Bobby Finley was a passionate man, obsessive, covetous. The most absurd proof of this, in Snowden's opinion, was Bobby's take on love and women, or rather *the* woman. The one: the mythical creature that was Bobby's other favorite obsession, his imagined soul mate. Snowden discovered this particular delusion while the two

were stuck in traffic on the BQE and he asked the skinny man, "Have you ever been in love?" It was a question simply meant to throw Bobby off guard, to get him to stop quoting from the Horizon-recommended *Social Construction of Community* just long enough to let the ringing that had started to vibrate in Snowden's skull subside into a light hum. The question was fortuitous, fateful even. It revealed the only subject guaranteed to distract him.

At some point in his lonely life, fermented by years of awkwardness, rejection, socially and governmentally enforced isolation, Bobby Finley had decided that the reason things between him and every woman he'd ever been interested in had gone horribly wrong was that he was destined for one perfectly matched mate and no other. Bobby shared this with Snowden like it was simple fact, swatting it away as if it was merely one more annoyance fate had burdened him with. Despite the casual manner of his revelation, it was quite a while before Bobby himself changed the subject again. About two weeks. Sometimes even tempting Snowden over to his apartment with promises of free beer just so he could continue his monologue.

In that time, exhausted but amused, Snowden had actually grown attached to the emaciated man, and having shared the company of several women and fallen in love with something about each one, tried in moments of sympathy to dissuade him. "Promiscuity is good," Snowden explained to his surely less experienced compatriot. "Variety isn't just the spice of life, it's the point of it." It was an argument destined for the disproportionately large yet deaf ears of Bobby Finley.

"Complementary, you see? We'll be like one of those gold necklace sets in the Penney catalog, the ones shaped like two jagged sides of a broken heart." Bobby was thirty-four years old and usually wearing a banana-colored work suit when he said things like this. Snowden was so embarrassed for the man he wished it were true.

Snowden spent the morning getting his physical at the company doctor's office up on Striver's Row, didn't get out until half past noon

and only went straight back to work because that's what the other two guys had done when they went for theirs in the weeks before. He found the Horizon truck at the address given, already returned from picking up the day's customer from Connecticut, its back gate open and a quarter of the haul already removed. Walking up its narrow metal ramp to get inside, Snowden found Bobby, too, nearly obscured in the rear among the shadows of boxes and dressers.

"She's here. Piper Goines, our client, the lady we're moving. She's *her*. She's *the one*."

Bobby was talking in near whispers. Until he stepped farther out of his hiding space, Snowden wasn't certain Bobby had even been talking to him, nor was he entirely sure after. Bobby's usual plum skin seemed drained, ashen. There was a cigarette in his fingers that he dragged on, then shook his head like someone had just defecated on his tongue.

"Then why do you smoke?" Snowden asked him.

"It's the only thing I'm allowed to light on fire anymore."

This was not the first time that Bobby had suspected he'd found "the one," not even in the few weeks since he'd revealed his mythology. There'd been the woman Bobby'd been in line behind at the Jamaican take-out place on 125th, the one he'd followed for four blocks before realizing she couldn't possibly be "the one" from the vagaries of her gate. There'd been the woman glimpsed momentarily standing at the 79th Street station platform as Bobby'd whisked by on the 2 express downtown. By the time he'd taken the local train back up, she was gone. This had provided conversational fodder for days. These past events, however, had always left Bobby in a cheerful mood, elated, prone to say really pathetic things like, "It must mean I'm getting closer," or to go into his theory that the reason he had never met her before was that he was destined to come to New York City to do so.

In response to Snowden's glare, Bobby said, "I'm not hiding, I'm preparing. First impressions are of extreme import. Being characterized negatively, or incorrectly, could have devastating results

down the line. I am trying to avoid a tragedy here." Snowden noticed the yellow notepad sitting on the chest-high pile of boxes as Bobby put his cigarette back in the side of his mouth and lifted a pen from behind his ear.

Snowden climbed aboard, looked for something to carry, even considered grabbing a good-sized television for the chance to peek at what Bobby was writing before choosing a large teddy bear instead and just asking.

"Notes. I'm writing out possible conversation directions so that I'm prepared with something that demonstrates my capacity for witty banter."

"Why not just be yourself?" Snowden smiled, shrugged to him.

"Because that is a cliché," Bobby sighed. "Look, this is no . . . 'round-the-way-girl whose affections can be bought with a *howyadoin'* and a Pepsi. Piper Goines is clearly a person of refinement. A woman of sophistication and substantial beauty," Bobby said back to him.

"The boy's right, Snowball. You should see the ass on this bitch," Horus declared coming up from behind. Snowden turned to catch Bobby's reaction, but the skinny man had disappeared deeper into the truck behind the stacks of furniture.

"Straight up dog, I'm about to get me some of that!" Horus continued. "I'm going to be all up in that booty, you watch me. I'm going to bang it *hard*. I'm going to bang it *greasy*." Horus crinkled his nose above his smile as if even he was somewhat disgusted by the image. After he'd hoisted a bookshelf onto his back, Horus trudged off again, cursing in delight with every step. Snowden turned around and grabbed the teddy bear with the intention of following him into the house, and Bobby was standing exactly where he was before, same footing and everything.

"Dear God you have to stop him." Bobby's face had lost so much blood Snowden imagined it tingled.

"Me? What's this got to do with me?"

"If that animal goes in there and starts slobbering over her, he

won't just ruin my chances, he'll disgrace the honor of Horizon Realty itself! Besides, he'll listen to you. He respects you more than he respects me," Bobby insisted.

"Now why the hell would you think that?" Snowden asked incredulously.

"You know. Because you killed someone."

Piper Goines was moving into the condo on the third floor of the brownstone. The couple who owned the rest of the townhouse stood on the main floor guarding their domain, entwined at the bottom of the steps like dried vines, wearing matching sweatshirts and overalls as if they were doing the lifting. Behind them this place, Snowden walked slowly just to get a better look at it. Most of the brownstones they refilled were shells, houses scraped out and abandoned, cut into single-room-occupancy flophouses decades ago. Places of construction, dust and drywall, their architectural details hidden or stolen or replaced with modern finishings by the returning middle class. But this townhouse was how they all were supposed to be: intricate woodwork angling through the double doors, spinning lattice icicles above the archways, fireplaces snug in tile, cake-tin moldings along the ceiling above, the stained-glass mosaic of the back window, and all of it original. Snowden the agnostic saw it and couldn't help but think for a second of God. That God had made them build mansions for millionaires who never came, so that there was no one but their slaves to fill them. That this was his reparation. That Harlem was God's gift to black people.

Snowden walked up the ornate stairway with the stuffed bear in both hands, Bobby straining behind him with his arms wrapped around a narrow armoire. The wall going up was lined with paintings and Snowden was admiring them when he heard their owners yelling up from below.

"They're originals. Including the frames. Why don't I just get those out of your way." The brown and blessed, moneyed and

mobile, Snowden couldn't remember if he'd moved this couple in or just so many of their type he could no longer see individuals. The female of the breed sprang into the narrow space alongside him, started taking the artwork off the wall before they could even get by.

"Negroes get a couple Henry Ossawa Tanners, think they running the Met," Bobby offered when they finally made it to the apartment, closed the door behind them. This was Bobby Finley: If the people they were moving had more blue-collar tastes, Bobby would make fun of their prints and assembly line African sculptures. If their possessions were more sophisticated, Bobby would attack them for their bourgeois pretensions. Bobby was militant about being middle of the road. "She probably thinks Monet is 'the root of all evil.'"

"First of all, that's my big sister you're dogging," a woman's voice responded, its owner following it out of the kitchen. "Second, even if I agreed with you – which I do – it wouldn't be right for me to say so since she's also flipping your bill. If it was up to me, I would have just got some bums off the corner to do the job for beer and pizza." The comments came coated in good humor, but Snowden could still see Bobby acting shaken, his lips fluttering before his words started bouncing through.

Standing before Bobby Finley, Piper Goines seemed like a separate species: better bred, better fed, better raised. Apparently taller than Bobby (he stooped so much, it was hard to tell even with him coiled next to her), Piper was round in face and arms, making her look both soft and strong at the same time. The curves below her waist that Horus coveted were lost in the folds of Piper's mud-cloth skirt, material as thick and wrinkled as elephant skin. Her beauty was in her face, the nose that dripped down into a smile of bright teeth and dark gums, but her strength shone all over her.

It seemed obvious to Snowden that Bobby Finley, who fit in his uniform like one french fry in a potato sack, was not in the same league as Piper Goines. Literally, figuratively, she seemed too much for him. If this was Bobby's ideal partner, Snowden deduced his

concept of the perfect human relationship must be based on the model set by the praying mantis.

"Hey, don't worry about it, my sister's a freaking Republican," Bobby responded. This might have been a good return, had Bobby not nearly said "fucking" and only caught himself after the first syllable, or had a sister at all. The last bit was immediately revealed as false when Piper asked, "Oh yeah? Is she older or younger?" and Bobby answered, "Medium."

Snowden broke in only to save him. "Madame, you got some nice furniture and all, but oak? Don't you think it's a little . . . how do you say . . . heavy? You know, Wal-Mart does some lovely things with plywood nowadays."

Snowden just got the first laugh. So that's how that started.

"See, this brother knows how to get a good tip," Piper Goines pointed out to Bobby. "He understands you have to *charm* a client." Her hair hung in soft bush behind her head, too much Euro in her blood to make a proper Afro.

"Ms. Goines, you have my humblest apologies. I'd like you to have this as a peace offering," Bobby leaned forward, *The Great Work* in hand. Snowden hadn't noticed it on him, but with the way his outfit fit, Bobby could have concealed a whole library inside its folds.

"Oh. OK. Is it any good?" Piper reached out and took it from him, inspected its front and back, flipped the pages like that would tell her something.

"I hope so. I wrote it." Bobby beamed back at her.

"Cool. I write too. I just started as a staff reporter for the *New Holland Herald*," was Piper's response, and Snowden looked up to see Bobby's earnest reaction, as if they hadn't sat around his apartment on several occasions drinking while Bobby read the rag aloud and goofed on it. "What the hell, you go put this on the window ledge in my study and when I get a chance, I'll read it."

From the look on Bobby's face, Snowden could tell he was confused. He seemed to think Piper just said "I love you" from the way his lips quivered, his eyes instantly teared. Bobby's speed in

disappearing down the hall to perform the task was the only thing that saved him from melting down completely before her.

As soon as Bobby was gone, Piper Goines turned to Snowden, grabbed him by his wrist and smiled, "OK, muscle man, I've got another task for you to do besides standing there and looking cute."

"You want me to sit down?" Snowden asked. There was guilt over flirting with Bobby's latest obsession, but it was reduced considerably by his certainty that he would take it no farther.

"I got some heavy boxes in the living room I want you to help me peek into, figure out what's inside so we can move them to the proper room before you abandon me."

"Ah, but my Nubian queen, that's why you're supposed to mark your boxes when you pack them," Snowden smiled back at her as Piper began to drag him toward the front of the apartment.

"You're right, moving man, I could have done that, but that would take away the thrill of surprise," Piper told him, squeezing Snowden's arm and winking over her shoulder on the last words.

Horus Manley was on his knees facing the wall, head in his hands. Bobby walked quietly behind him to drop off *The Great Work* by the window, thought Horus was praying until he turned around and saw that he was actually holding something to his face. It was a shiny emerald fabric, poking out of the spaces between his fingers and rumpled in a bunch around his snorting nose.

"What the hell are you doing?" Bobby demanded. When Horus took the cloth away, Bobby saw a look of pure joy, an innocent, ecstatic excitement as Horus quickly stuck a finger to his mouth, lightly shushing him.

"Yo kid, this box, it must have got crushed open in the ride. It's all panties in there! Victoria's Secret and everything. And guess what? They're *dirty*," Horus added with clear glee, throwing the pair he had down and reaching for another.

"Put that back!" Bobby insisted, stepping forward to yank them away from Horus's face. Horus snarled and butted his head forward

and Bobby remembered himself, pulled his hand back, unsure if Horus had just tried to bite him.

"Don't do this, Horus. What do think the congressman would say if he found out?" Bobby asked him. Horus responded to the threat by further snarling, but a few seconds later the pose disappeared completely, was replaced by a disappointed sigh and the comment, "You're no fun, man," as he shoved the panties back in the box before him. Emboldened by the passive stance, Bobby continued.

"Look, as long as we're on the subject of our hostess, Piper Goines, I want to ask you a little favor. I know we all just met her, OK, but I'm really interested. Long term, you know what I mean. I think . . . I think I could have something special with her and I would really appreciate it if you gave me a clear path on this chance."

Horus really thought about it. Cocking his head to the side and squinting his eyes a bit in consideration before nodding his head. "That's a good trade. The bitch for the drawers. Then I'm trying to find me a thong," his hands shooting back in the box, pulling out another pair and inspecting them.

Bobby Finley was not a strong man, but he was a quick one, flying across the room to grab Piper's undergarments out of Horus's clutch before he could shove them in his pants pocket. Bobby was good at leverage too – it's what helped him carry all that heavy furniture – and by placing his foot on Horus's thigh and pushing off with his full weight, he was able to effectively counter the larger man's advantage. It was the equal grips, Horus with one hand and Bobby with two, fabric wrapped around his back fist, that made the tug-of-war a draw, stretched the garment out like a flag for those seconds before Piper Goines herself walked into the room and broke the standstill.

"You shiftless bastards," Piper spit at them. When Piper stormed over, Horus let loose his grip first, leaving a mortified Bobby holding the panties when Piper snatched them from him. Stomping away, each footfall an assault, Piper almost made it out of the room before she turned around again. "You know what the worst part of this shit is? My sister *told me* not to hire a black company for this move, and I

made a big fuss too about using Horizon. Then you no-account Negroes had to go fuck things up, didn't you? Why can't we ever do a goddamn thing proper? Be *ashamed*, you hear me?"

They did. Piper charged forward, her finger pointing, sending Horus scuttling away from her wrath and Bobby spewing frantic explanations.

Piper ignored Bobby's excuses, screamed louder to drown them out. "Be ashamed for yourselves. Be ashamed for your people."

Snowden, who'd trailed into the room on Piper's heels, was too stunned to follow them back out or make any comment at all. Even Horus didn't say anything until Piper had slammed the door behind her, then turned to Bobby to yell, "Look what you did! You had to go mess things all up. After work, punk, you're getting a beat down."

"Stop threatening him." Snowden stepped forward. "He doesn't have to take that shit from you."

Horus seemed surprised, even amused at Snowden's defense, walked close enough in front of him to whisper, "That's cool, dog. Then you can just take my shit instead. After work, when the truck's unloaded, don't go nowhere. Because I just scheduled you in for an ass whupping."

Snowden took his time working for rest of the day. Walked slow, took breaks, asked far more questions than he needed to. Piper Goines herself was no longer available for answers, so irate her sister was keeping her down in the back of the lower house so she didn't do something stupid and make them all vulnerable to a civil suit, putting her husband on guard in the apartment instead. Regardless of all the stall tactics, a point came when the back of Horizon's truck was empty, the receipts had all been signed, and the sole tip for the evening had been placed discreetly in Snowden's hand.

Fighting was stupid, there was nothing to be gained from it, it put both their bids for the lead candidate in jeopardy. This much Snowden told Horus when he approached him on the sidewalk

halfway down the block, but Horus's response was just, "Yeah, you might got some points there, but what can you do? I got disrespected, so somebody's got to pay for it."

Horus popped every knuckle in his right hand individually, One, Two, Three, Four, Five, before going over to his left hand, Six, Seven, Eight, Nine, Ten, and then cracking his neck sharply left and right, Eleven, Twelve. Snowden stood waiting patiently to be beat up, but Horus seemed in no particular rush, like he wanted to do things right. Finished his stretching, Horus began unbuttoning the length of his Horizon uniform, from his neck down to his groin, revealing a pair of blue and green striped boxer shorts. It was Horus's very flesh, however, that made the biggest impression on Snowden. Not his prison muscles, taut tributes to boredom and vanity, nor the tattoos Snowden recognized as having been etched into his skin with sewing needles and the ink of cheap pens, but Horus's unintentional ornamentation. It was the scars. The flock of thick, keloid slashes from all the knives that had tasted his blood. The dark, dimpled caverns from all the bullets that had failed to kill him.

"What are you doing?" Snowden asked nervously.

"I don't want to get any blood on my work clothes," Horus told him, balancing on one leg to pull his booted foot through the outfit's cuff.

Snowden sought his own anger, that electric green rage that was always begging him for freedom. It was still there, but its hate was focused on Snowden himself for getting into this situation. When Horus was pulling himself out the sleeves, both arms tangled behind him, Snowden sprung forward and punched his opponent in the stomach with all his might. It was a cheap shot, free even, one Snowden would have never considered if he wasn't fairly sure it would be his last chance at a shot at all. Horus collapsed to the sidewalk, gasping, spending a few seconds learning to breathe again.

A sucker punch was a shameful thing, completely without honor, so little face could be lost succumbing to one. It was Snowden's hope that Horus would realize this, give them both an out from this

situation, and keep his ass down. It was a faint hope, quickly dashed when Horus's hand shot out and grabbed a broken half of brick discarded by the curb, one of those blunt instruments he was so fond of.

In one move, Horus was on his feet, the look on his face saying whatever rage had dissipated over the last hours had now been completely replenished. His arm pulled back, brick in hand, and it was very clear what Horus's intentions were. Horus was going to bash Snowden's skull in.

"Cease!"

The command came from behind Snowden. Snowden didn't move to see the source because Horus froze when it was yelled so Snowden assumed the person had a gun and worse, a badge that would actually let him shoot it. Tai chi slow, Horus dropped the rubble and let his arms glide up into a Y.

"Mr. Snowden, at ease," Lester ordered. *I've never been fired from a job by gunpoint,* Snowden was thinking, but when he turned around it wasn't the snub-nose he'd seen in the truck's glove compartment. Lester held a hundred-dollar bill over his head with both hands.

"Mr. Manley, I do believe we can resolve this in an immediate and nonviolent manner, don't you?" Lester shook the note before him, the bill was crisp and new, and it crinkled as it flapped. Lester in lavender, immaculate with jacket and purple shoes on. A grin exploded across Horus's mug, erasing all trace of the homicidal mask of moments earlier. Coming closer, Horus snatched the money out of Lester's fingers like it might be a trick, gave a victorious yelp before offering his thanks, examining the C note up to the sunlight as he walked off.

Lester made the dazed Snowden sit in the truck's cab while making sure everything was OK with the customer. It took that smell of brave Wendell to reacquaint Snowden with his senses, an entirely uncalled for, overdone remedy in Snowden's opinion. Wendell had all the regular canine odor expected from such an active dog, but his

more disturbing smell was of cologne. It lay on him so thick you could smell the alcohol in his fur. This was not a new discovery, Bobby had mentioned it weeks ago and the two of them had a running bet on what brand it was. The wager was doomed to remain unresolved. Neither one would dare ask Lester about it, let him know they had the image of him down on his knees, spraying his ridiculous dog. Snowden was in the process of trying to roll up the window when Lester yanked the door away from him, pulled on the fabric above his knees before bending his legs up and inside.

"Mr. Finley called me, told me what was happening. I was waiting here in the cab, I wouldn't have let it get too far." Lester scratched at Wendell's ass as he talked. Wherever you put your hand on Wendell, he always moved so that it was soon on his ass.

"If you know what happened, then why'd you just give Horus that money?" Snowden asked.

"Sometimes you have to throw a dog a bone," Lester told him, falling into a baby voice right after to ask Wendell, "Isn't that right?" repeating this until the dog licked his face in response.

"Protecting the weak, taking a stand against the odds, that's what Horizon's all about. The congressman would be very proud. So as a reward, I'm giving you a special project from now on. It'll provide you an additional opportunity to learn the business and earn some extra dough," Lester said, Snowden's acceptance of the offer assumed. "Tomorrow, six A.M. Not in front of the office, but at the lodge entrance. This is *your* special project, so keep this to yourself. And you don't wear your uniform for this job."

CLEARING OUT

NOTHING RAGED LIKE a Harlem night. There was no quiet acceptance of the day's end, no dying of streetlight. Through his shades, an orange, hopeless glow landed in strained parallelograms across Snowden's walls and ceiling, keeping his room lit like it was dusk till dawn. Harlem at midnight was louder than some parts of Midtown during the day. Noise as consistent as boisterous, a seamless stream of audio pollution, poor people loud because sound was the only thing they could afford in quantity.

Snowden had a game. Lying sideways in bed, pillow pulled over the ear exposed upward, midnight hours behind him, the goal of his game was to count ten seconds of silence to fall asleep within. Hours of reaching to three or four before being halted by conversations yelled from one end of the street outside to the other, honking livery cabs too lazy to ring a bell, kids screaming in joy or horror. One, two, three, four, then something. Always something. It was almost magical, how one sound would die down always to be replaced by another, just as piercing, just as inconsiderate.

Snowden preferred obsessing about the literally disturbing sounds outside his window. If he got angry about them, made them the focus of his frustration, he was less likely to notice the sounds emanating from the apartment below. The vibrations of shrieks that rose through the ceiling, through insulation to floorboards, trailed up the post of Snowden's bed to tremble his mattress in sympathy. The beatings. Lying there, Snowden waited for the next percussion of skin on skin, for it to shut up the yelling or ignite more. Eyes closed, wishing ears had the same option, Snowden's mind could provide

information his senses couldn't. From the sound of the hit, Snowden could tell impact location, force, and source. In his mind he could clearly see Jifar, the boy who lived down there, taking the blow. Snowden could differentiate the resonating smack of open hand to the side of the face from the quick thud of a palm thrust to the back of the head, and remember exactly what it felt like to be something small and confused as someone impossibly large and inconceivably hostile assaulted you.

Worse, the sounds that followed. The father, Baron Anderson, made a habit of singing to his karaoke machine in the shower after most skirmishes, belting out canned tunes with a guilt-free and joyous enthusiasm. Pleased, wailing vocals over music caught and gutted of voice and harmony. Snowden hated Baron Anderson for being tone deaf, felt it was deliberate, felt it was gloating. A list of music Snowden was slowly beginning to detest as much as the man who mangled it: every single track of Marvin Gaye's *Forever Yours* (despite himself), all Smokey Robinson's post-Miracles creations and even some before that ("*People say. . .*" People say shut the hell up it's two o'clock in the morning), every top ten hit between 1981 and 1987.

Snowden awoke at five-thirty A.M. to the sound of crickets. They weren't really there, but with the window closed and rain muting the neighbors outside, his room was quiet enough to hear the sound of home on a summer morning, light chirping of crickets in his mind. After over a month in Harlem, Snowden's Philly seemed in contrast impossibly southern, spacious, slow, and behind him. Out his front door half asleep, his waking mind lost in memory, Snowden nearly tripped over the bundled body lining the top of the stairs in the hallway, clutched desperately at the rail to keep from falling over it, through the wide stairway shaft, and five stories down.

The memories of a child's screams that had plagued Snowden's dreams were understood as he kneeled next to the little figure, lifted off the cloth at the end he assumed was covering Jifar's head, just like he always did when he found the boy sleeping in the hall.

"Little man." When Snowden lightly squeezed Jifar's cheek, the boy's eyes began to open, looked up at him blinking, pupils barely lifted from lids. Jifar yawned, the hot smell of morning blowing across Snowden's face.

"I was camping. You woke me up." Maybe it was the light lisp of his voice that doomed the boy, maybe it was that simple. Maybe the sound reminded the brute who was his father of the wife Snowden deduced had left him far behind. Or maybe Jifar's father was one of those people who didn't need a reason, just enough drink to bring out his character. Maybe he was just bad, like there are some people who are just good in this life.

"You can't stay out here like this, somebody's going to trip over you and fall down the stairs, break their neck."

"Somebody did fall once, right before you moved here. The woman who used to live where you do, she jumped right down," Jifar said, staring at the stairs beside him. "She was lonely. And mean."

"You want to go back downstairs and get back in your bed? He's probably passed out by now." Jifar pulled his blanket over his head again, its cartoon pattern faded and dotted with fabric pills instead of pixels. Snowden looked at his watch, thought of Lester doing the same in front of the office, pulled his keys out and into Jifar's hand.

"Now listen. These are yours. Anybody gives you trouble, you ever need to get away, you use these. This apartment is your safe place, OK?" Snowden told him, wishing there was someone he could call instead, wishing that he hadn't been through the foster care ring himself and could believe it was that simple. That this was a world in which you could pick up the phone and then find yourself in a better situation than the one you were already trapped in.

Jifar glanced down at the keys before pulling them within the blanket without comment. If he'd bothered to shrug, even that message of ambivalence was lost in the folds of the cloth.

*   *   *

Lester and Wendell paced in circles in front of the lodge, the man absentminded and heavy footed, the dog intense and intent on finding a square foot of concrete good enough to poop on. The dog was surrounded by young admirers, children in maroon blazers with gray shorts and skirts who called Wendell by name as he ignored them. Lester shooed them off as Snowden approached, and the children shot up the lodge's steps, the last boy making a great effort to close its towering door without slamming it.

The lodge was also Cyrus Marks's home, in addition to being Lester's and the property the Horizon storefront was connected to, so Lester made sure to get his newspaper down before Wendell's feces landed so as not to leave the slightest stain behind.

"Who are those kids? Are they visiting from a Catholic school or something?" Snowden asked, but Lester ignored him, focused instead on the dog crap being excreted, carefully bagging and removing it when Wendell was done. The storm grate on Horizon's façade was still down, locked. Compared to the other buildings on the block the lodge was not only much larger but also immaculate, as if some local superstition protected it from vandalism.

In the truck, Wendell sat on the floor beside the stick shift, staring at Snowden. Snowden couldn't figure out if the dog was looking to be entertained or was considering lunging at him. Lester began making a series of sudden, fast turns that forced Wendell to lie down, his paws outstretched for balance. After ten minutes of driving, Lester had managed to put only six blocks between them and the office, and Snowden was about to ask if they were lost when, before a red light at Adam Clayton Powell, Lester pulled the gear into park.

"We're being followed." Lester's hand shot in front of Snowden to reach in the glove compartment. Even Wendell was surprised by the action, bouncing to his feet to get away. Removing a heavily rumpled brown paper bag, Lester slammed the little door shut again.

"Listen, when I jump out this car, you get in the driver's seat. As soon as I get back in, you pull off." Then Lester jumped out, slammed the door behind him.

Snowden scooted over, looked out the side mirror. Lester was talking to the second car that was stuck on the narrow street behind them, the passenger responding with motions of misunderstanding and denial. Snowden watched as Lester lifted the brown paper bag and pointed it right up against the driver's head.

There was no job on earth, no dream Snowden could imagine, that would keep him from hitting the gas if he heard a shot ring out. It was a one-lane road, cars parked on both sides, and there was a little Toyota in front of the truck that he'd just have to roll over. Wendell started barking and then Snowden couldn't think straight, told him to shut it, please just shut up. When Snowden looked back in the mirror, Lester was gone. The driver still sat in his white Taurus, wiping the sweat from off the top of his bald pink head, his other hand dialing a cellphone.

"Drive to 345 East 117th Street. Between Park and Lex." Wendell stopped barking. Snowden jumped, but when he turned and saw Lester sitting at his right he played it off like he was adjusting his seat. Snowden pulled out halfway into the intersection before checking to see if the light was green. In the rearview mirror, the white car screeched into a right and was gone.

"These real estate agents from downtown, they have no ethics, no morals. He thought he was going to ghost us, cherry pick some new properties for his clients downtown. Just an opportunist. There's no love there." The explanation was unsolicited and pretty unwanted. Snowden's only desire was to drive, to get to fresh air to cancel out Wendell again.

"My man, you hungry? You need some breakfast before we get busy today?" The affection, concern, Snowden didn't for a moment think Lester was talking to him. Out of the corner of his eye, Snowden was almost sure he saw Wendell nodding yes. Lester reached in the brown paper bag just as Snowden was stopping at the next red light and removed his weapon from it: a shiny glazed cruller, already bitten into. Lester ripped another bite away, pulled the piece

out of his mouth and threw it to his dog. Wendell ate it in desperate, choking gulps, immediately begging for more.

The apartment building was much like Snowden's own, a four-story tenement with kids and debris blowing around outside. From the look of the block, its narrow street of renovated townhouses, the shining doorknobs and newly stripped doors of the recent arrivals, Snowden knew that this was the building they all looked over at and wished they could blow up.

The only buildings in the world dirtier than New York City tenements didn't count because they were made from dirt itself. Floors, ceilings, and walls encrusted in thick, multilayers of scum, the product of a century of tenants too busy and exhausted to take care of anything beyond their own apartment doors, a testament to supers who were so in name only. That's why this building looked so dramatically different inside, why Snowden's neck rotated from awe. It was simply clean.

Lester on its pale white marble stairs, hand on the freshly painted rail, turned to see the frozen figure behind him.

"You look shocked. This is what it's supposed to look like." Lester kept climbing, his voice reverberating in his wake. "This is Horizon property now. You're looking at the new Harlem."

"What's up with it? We upping the rent?" *We.* Always use first-person plural when you refer to Horizon, a habit encouraged since training day. For Snowden, a lifelong *I*, it was more uncomfortable than wearing the banana outfit. It said, *Erase the border between your own objectives and that of the company, loose your individuality in the sentiment of the many.*

"Rent stabilized. Even if we wanted to up the rent, we can only do it by the allotted citywide percentage for the year, understand? Even on new tenants, we can only raise it fifteen percent of the existing rent." His suit was the color of dried roses, his shirt and tie variations of lighter petals. Lester wore many suits but was always a champion of scorned colors. "Even if random evictions were legal, we still

36

wouldn't make money off of them. But see, it's not about the money." If they said it wasn't about the money, they were either lying or they wanted something even more valuable from you, Snowden thought. Dreams, time-shares, God, whatever they were pushing, salesmen always inspired in Snowden the same feeling of revulsion.

Lester stopped in front of a door on the third floor, dropped his tool bag and started unzipping it.

"You want I should ring the bell?" Snowden put his finger on the black button, looked over in anticipation of clearance.

"You can if you want to, but he won't be able to hear you." Snowden did, so did so, hearing the stiff chime echo on the other side.

"Why's that, he deaf?"

"No. *He dead.*" Lester stood up with a crowbar in his hand, poking its bucktooth into the minute separation between the doorknob and jamb.

"Oh shit. I'm sorry." Snowden heard himself and immediately wondered who he was apologizing to.

"Don't be. He was an asshole. He wasn't supposed to change the locks," Lester strained as he leaned into the metal. The sound of his actions and words echoed from the tin ceiling to the marble floors around them.

Snowden took hold of the middle of the crowbar, leaned his own weight into it as well. The wood around the lock began to splinter along with the doorframe it was attached to. Before they could get theirs open, another door unlocked and opened three yards to the right of them. The head was so close to the knob, Snowden thought at first the person was elderly, but when a voice called behind her, a moment of distraction let the door drift inches farther. Though a child, the first stages of puberty had already begun elongating her legs out of proportion with the rest of her body, the man's T-shirt that already hung far above her knees would clearly cease to serve as a nightgown by the following summer. Her braids were the long elaborate strands of a woman, but the yarn woven in, its pink and

37

primary colors, was more representative of the girl who wore them. Lester said, "Horizon Property Management, nothing to worry about," but the girl was already closing the door, disappointed by the sight of them.

Snowden felt weird being in the dead guy's apartment, guilty for thinking of him as just that, "the dead guy." These are the dead guy's condoms on the coffee table, note the deceased's optimism. This is the dead guy's remote control, its batteries would outlive their owner. This thing they were both sitting on, this was the dead guy's couch.

"The deal is, a lot of people die in Harlem." Lester removed his Cigarillos tin from inside his breast pocket, lit one. His cigarillos lasted longer than regular cigarettes, stunk worse than regular cigars. "A lot of people die everywhere – everyone dies, to be truthful – but when they die in Harlem, in a Horizon property, we have to clean up afterwards. We got a license with the City of New York Sanitation Department, a special-use permit for the industrial cleaners you can't get over the counter."

"Is the dead guy in the apartment? Is that what you're going to tell me?" Snowden felt weak, not for what he just asked but for the way Lester laughed at him.

"Relax, this is an easy one just to get you started. He didn't die in here. It's just, this is your special project with Horizon. You'll be paid bonus money for these hours, since Tuesday's your day off. There's a lot of older folks in Harlem, a lot of people living risky lives, we get jobs like this pretty regularly."

"I can handle it." Snowden nailed the point home with nods.

"Good. Thing is, this has also got to be low profile. We have all these people coming back to Harlem now, real estate market booming, vibrant, but it's fragile, see? A lot of it's PR, public perception. Death, that's not something people want to hear about. Especially people looking for a place to live during a housing crunch. Who wants to know they're moving into the home of someone that just kicked it?"

"No one. So I'll keep it quiet."

"Exactly. The other two, your coworkers, don't even tell them. The point is, Snowden, to protect the client, the neighborhood. People are always looking for bad things to say about Harlem, let's not even give them an excuse."

When you die, it shouldn't be like this, a stranger and a brightly dressed man breaking the silence of your abandoned home to go through your things and throw most of them in the trash. Lester leaned a chair against the splintered front door to keep it shut, started giving out his orders. They were so specific, so mundane. Clear a room at a time, you start from the back, I'll start from the front. Place all electronics and small appliances in the center of the living room, all books in the bathtub, all photos and official documents in white kitchen bags, clothes in the green trash bags, the rest in the black lawn bags to be thrown out. Glasses, dishes, silverware: trash. Double-bag them.

It was a two-bedroom. In the back was the kitchen, behind that a small room being used for storage. It was amazing how fast it was possible to clear away someone's life when you threw it in the trash. A couple of full arm sweeps into open bags and the kitchen was nearly barren. Snowden was even more impressed with how much was obvious from the trash he was dumping. The dead guy was Carlton Simmons (cable and electric bills stuck to the freezer door identified). Mr. Simmons had family in Buffalo: Rena Simmons, whom he called for brief minutes during the week, longer on holidays and weekends (Verizon). If Mr. Simmons cooked, it was fast and simple: spaghetti or an occasional burger. Of all the pastas available to him on the grocery shelf, the only one he'd bought was angel hair, probably because it cooked fast and he was impatient. The frozen burgers were bought in prepackaged bulk, the meat mechanically shaped into CD-thin wafers. Carlton Simmons must have liked the idea of health because there were greens in the crisper, but he wasn't completely invested in it, because each individually bagged bundle was completely untouched and rotting. What this

brother really liked was Chinese food. Evidence lined every shelf in the refrigerator as proof of a daily habit. Fried and breaded pieces of dark meat glazed red or brown on beds of yellow rice. Imported bottles of blistering hot sauce in the cabinet a nod to some West Indian or African ancestry.

Snowden the detective, Snowden the archaeologist on a dig into the permafrost lining the freezer, searching for artifacts. The more mundane the job, the more his imagination took over, the more fun it became.

In the back bedroom, Snowden lost himself between his janitor motions and his detective dream. The clues were endless, heavy, the garbage much the same. Carlton Simmons ate fatty foods and dreamed of the skinny days he'd long deserted. Nearly all the worn pants were forty-two waist, disregarding a few scarred and veteran forties, and then on the top shelf of the closet Snowden found a stack of pants size thirty-six waist. They were different colors but all the same brand, all new with their retail folds undisturbed and starchy, a purchase for a waistline that would never return until the fat decomposed off of him, and then he wouldn't need pants anyway.

One large box remained at the back of the closet floor when all the clothes had been evacuated. Inside, obscured underneath a pile of video game magazines, was a beige metal safe the size of a dictionary and a paper grocery bag. Snowden pulled at the safe, played at cracking its combination for a bit before growing bored, and took the bag. Pictures, loose and organized in books. Snowden decided it was time for his break, took a seat on one of the fully packed bags of clothes.

Carlton Simmons, his face in repetition. They were the same age, Snowden and the dead guy, had shared the same era of childhood. Snowden recognized the clothes, the hair, fell into the past and saw the other there as if he had known him. Carl had been to Atlantic City, there was a picture of him leaning back on a bench with the Sands behind him. Carl had been to the Washington Monument. Carl had a daughter. Her pictures, from newborn to infant, joined his own.

Trying to pile the loose photos together, Snowden noticed a white envelope lying at the bottom. It held a key inside, one he soon found out worked on the beige safe. The safe had no money in it, just another, older envelope inside.

In the span of time it had taken Snowden to clear out most of the kitchen and what amounted to a large closet, Lester had cleared out the living room, the bathroom, and was sweeping up the debris from his assault on the master bedroom. Along the far walls of each room were stacked layers of blank brown boxes, topped by trash bags, plush and shiny and full. It was the precision of repetition, of muscle memory of countless other jobs like this one. For Lester, this duty seemed to have the meditative value of pulling a rake through a Japanese rock garden. The only thing that brought him out of the action of moving the straw broom across the wooden floor was the way Snowden sounded at the door.

"What am I supposed to do with this?" Before him Snowden held out the white envelope like someone had just hit him with it. The thing was so worn, the paper so dirty, uneven and stiff in his hand, it was like it had been left out in the rain for an entire season. Lester removed the plum kerchief from his jacket's breast pocket and held the envelope with that by its corners. When Lester took it from him, Snowden looked relieved to not hold it anymore. Inside, Lester found Polaroids with their stiff white borders, took them in a stack and let their packaging drop to the floor with the rest of the trash.

The first picture was of a woman naked, leaning back on the couch of the room he'd just cleaned. Even if Lester was attracted to women, he doubted this one could excite him. You could see the dark brown blotches on her legs, the even darker flesh under eyes as wide and dead as deviled eggs. Around her skull a legion of hair had reverted to chaos, rioting in neglect. On her breastbone was the wrinkled line of a pulled-up shirt, at her calves matching crumpled pants, both articles ready to be pulled back into position as soon as the flash had dimmed. Lester looked at the track marks on the arm,

tried to locate the fresh one. The second photo was of a mother and her infant child, whom she held on her side as she leaned forward to fellate the cameraman. The third was of a little girl, dressed only in her colorful braids. It took a moment for Lester to recognize her as the one who'd just peeked out at them from down the hall, the one Snowden had been talking to. What Lester noticed the most about this photo, as opposed to the ones of her that followed, was that you could clearly see the dollars in her hand, gripped fiercely in discomfort.

There were at least a dozen more photos, but Lester reached for the dirty envelope on the floor, stuck the contents back inside, took a roll of packing tape off the bed to seal it up thoroughly before reopening a trash bag along the wall and sticking it deeply inside.

"Is that all we're going to do?" There was indignation in Snowden's voice, but there was relief too.

"There's nothing else that needs to be done. He's dead now."

"How did he die?"

"He had an accident." Lester picked up his broom and started sweeping again. Snowden needed to sit down. He walked over to the bare mattress, became nauseous at the sight of it and opted for a bare wall and floor.

"Someone like that, someone like that deserves worse than that."

"I don't know. Apparently, his brakes went out on him on the FDR. From what I hear, it was pretty gruesome. Couldn't stop, knew he couldn't stop. Speeding to begin with. A lot of sharp turns on that thing, heavy, fast traffic. Very narrow lanes. Must have made for some pretty scary minutes." Lester's tone was casual, calming. It was like none of the facts present were new to him.

"You knew about this?"

"What?" The way Lester said it, Snowden immediately regretted the question, was about to apologize when Lester continued. "I knew he was a registered sex offender. We found that out after we bought the property. Specifics? Of course not. But there's only one cure for people like that, isn't there?"

Lester stopped sweeping, looked over at Snowden for him to take over the exercise, then took his seat against the wall.

"Well that's the thing, am I right?" Lester continued. "You take almost any block in Harlem, almost any apartment building, and out of every hundred people, ninety are basically decent, hardworking folk just trying to take care of their own. But that ten, the drug dealers, the thugs, thieves, and rapists, those that abuse their children directly and through neglect, the ones who have no respect for others, civilization, society, all of these parasites set the tone that everybody else has to live by. 'The Terrible Tenth,' I like to call them, that keeps everybody else down."

"At least, with this bastard's death, it's down to 'The Terrible Nine Point Nine Nine Percent' now," Snowden said, immediately regretting the callousness of the statement. Lester just smiled though, sat there puffing on his cigarillo, watching his smoke rise around them.

The night ended with beer, two forties held one in each of Snowden's arms like he was headed for a party. Walking up his building's steps, Jifar was in his path. The boy was laid out on his dirty landing with paper and crayons. It was one o'clock in the morning.

"What are you doing?" Snowden asked him.

"What's it look like I'm doing? I'm drawing."

"Drawing what?"

"I'm drawing the Chupacabra." The paper had been cut from the side of a brown paper bag, on it was the image of a green fanged thing with too many arms.

"You got school tomorrow, you need to be in bed. What's a Chupacabra?"

"It's the monster eating people in Washington Heights. Mannie Ortiz knows someone who saw it. If I do this good, we're going to give it to the police so they can catch him."

"Why aren't you in bed, little man?"

"I'm locked out, and I left your key in my room, in my hiding space," Jifar admitted.

43

There was music vibrating the door of Jifar's apartment. After a while, Snowden gave up on knocking, just started kicking it until the sound stopped and the peephole darkened.

"Come get your boy," Snowden said into it. The door began unlocking.

"Nigger, you woke me up." Baron Anderson in his gray WEL-COME TO NEW YORK, NOW GET OUT T-shirt and wrinkled Y-fronts. Snowden attempted to continue the discussion but Anderson walked out in the hall in his bare feet yelling, "Get the fuck in here," grabbing his boy by his arm and disappearing again, the door slamming in back of them.

The final sound sent other doors along the floors slowly unlocking, other heads leaning out doorways to stare at Snowden as if he was the villain. Snowden ignored them, reached down and rolled up the picture, forcefully shoved each crayon back in the box, imagining he was cramming them up the father's nose instead.

BOBBY FINLEY,
THE GREAT WORK

AFTER CLASS SNOWDEN would go over to Bobby's house and they would get drunk. The game was to go to a new bodega each time and get 160 ounces of the cheapest beer they could find. They called it a game because to acknowledge that it was all they could afford was depressing. Then they would spend seventy-five cents on the *New Holland Herald* and Bobby would read the misprints and more egregious grammatical errors out loud. At first, Snowden didn't know what the big deal was, at least the paper was trying, but some of these bloopers were just too ridiculous and after a while they were both laughing until they just couldn't anymore because it hurt too much. This would usually be followed by a discussion on the future of black people, hopeful or pessimistic. Both had majored in African-American studies during their college careers, one of many similarities they were discovering. If you added the amount of undergraduate credits they had together it was enough for one bachelor's degree, which gave them a bit of confidence in putting their heads together, even though they were pretty drunk heads by the time they really got into it.

Once they had been peeing clear for hours, when simple things like balancing a bowl of cereal in their hands became nearly impossible, the conversation often reverted to simple primal confessions. This is when Bobby slurred that he'd burned down his mother's boyfriend's house after the man raped her, that the man was alive but probably wished he wasn't. This was when Snowden talked about all the foster homes, told the funny stories he could

about the quirks of each one, how he had been returned to his father in ninth grade, how even he was surprised at the way his father's nose disappeared into his face when he punched it. How he couldn't even remember the last thing the man had said to him that had pissed him off so much, but would never forget the smell of the adrenaline-rich blood that filled his own nose, the orgasmic bliss of momentarily giving his anger free reign.

Bobby's place was smaller than Snowden's, made even more so by the books in milk crates that lined the walls. Aside from the ones on the shelves in the bathroom, every single book in Bobby Finley's house was a hardcover first edition of *The Great Work*, a novel by Robert M. Finley, all signed and numbered by the author himself. He had so many that he used them for furniture, laying a wooden plank and cushions over crates for his couch and bed. Bobby started this collection four months after the publication of *The Great Work*, three years before, picking up the first editions at near 85 percent discount on the remainder shelves of large bookstore chains. They seemed so forlorn sitting there, each his dream incarnate, rejected, abandoned. That was how the collection began.

The Great Work received only two reviews, both by publishing magazines pretty much obligated to review anything with pages and a spine. Both were dismissive, seemed confused and not a little hostile, as if the text that had been given to them was not printed on paper but instead tattooed on the shaved flesh of a large and bemused grizzly bear. After reading them, it took two weeks for Bobby Finley to stop fixating on burning the buildings that housed the critics, the magazines, and the distributors, in that order.

Later, Bobby managed to douse those desires with the knowledge that both critics had been white and unfortunately had proved themselves unable to separate themselves from their preconceived notion of what to expect from an author of African descent, and therefore had blinded themselves to the genius *The Great Work* really was. This perspective was reinforced by the fact that both reviewers

had made major factual errors when describing the plot, errors that coincided with a misprint in the summary on the dusk jacket, leading Bobby to determine that at best they'd given it a sloppy, rushed read or, as he suspected, hadn't read the whole book at all.

Unfortunately, *The Great Work*'s reviews proved a harbinger for the reaction of the few readers it managed to attract. Though no readings were ever actually conducted for *The Great Work* (several were arranged, but no one showed up; even the bookstore clerks called in sick), Bobby Finley was still able to determine this by months of long hours of searching newsgroups on the Internet. Bobby Finley took no solace from the fact that all three people who mentioned *The Great Work* lacked the imagination to use any descriptor other than a conjugation of the verb *to suck*.

The purpose of the author's own collection of *The Great Work* changed dramatically after his first and only signing. A clerk at the black bookstore in the New Carrellton Mall put an accidental zero on the order form and after seven months local author Bobby Finley was called in an effort to move the twenty copies. In an attempt to assist him in this endeavor, the owner had booked Bobby Finley, author of *The Great Work*, to appear on the same day, at the same time as Bo Shareef, best-selling author of *Datz What I'm Talkin' 'Bout*.

The two sat at opposite ends of one long fold-out, a fortress of *Datz What I'm Talkin' 'Bout* piled across the table, floor, and back wall on one side, twenty copies of *The Great Work* in two neat piles on the other. Shareef's publisher had outfitted him with blown-up images of the book and the author big enough to shame Mussolini. In the brief moment Bobby had a chance to speak with Mr. Shareef, he did find him friendly and charismatic, but it was the last chance they would have to talk as Bo Shareef was quickly swallowed by a mob of women Bobby had previously assumed to be the assembling of a large gospel choir.

Three hours. It seemed as if every black woman in the DC Metro area had been bused in for the occasion. Shocked by the display,

Bobby Finley faked a cough, reached back to his bag for his water and then leaned over and vicked a copy of *Datz What I'm Talkin' 'Bout*. A far cry from *The Great Work*'s dignified all-white cover with the title in black twelve-point Courier font, the cover of *Datz What I'm Talkin' 'Bout* looked like a panel from a self-published children's book. Upon inspecting the first sentence, first paragraph, first page, and first chapter, Bobby found prose with the originality, sophistication, and poetry of the instructions that came with Happy Meal toys. Yet the crowd kept coming. "You are the greatest, Mr. Shareef," they said. "Oh my God, I can't wait for your next one," they told him.

Bobby read *Datz What I'm Talkin' 'Bout* in its entirety, right there at the table, too numb to be embarrassed. Of the handful of people that did stop by Bobby's side after the long wait for Bo Shareef's signature, few refrained from making a face when Bobby explained the plot of *The Great Work*. One said, "Alaska? There ain't no black people in Alaska." Those who didn't tried to get him to give them copies for free. One brother with what looked like a queen-sized bedsheet wrapped around his head demanded to know what his "thesis" was.

Years had gone into crafting *The Great Work*. Years had gone into crafting single sentences within it. Authors' entire life works were reread just to inspire certain paragraphs.

Bobby felt like a chef who had dedicated his life to the study of the greatest culinary techniques, practiced for years to perfect them before presenting his finest dish to the public, only to be outdone by a guy who walked in off the street, shit in a tortilla, and deep-fried it.

Reeling from the public's failure to recognize the genius of *The Great Work*, Bobby Finley resolved to determine the reason. That's when he decided that the readers were dung beetles. That they didn't just consume crap, they liked it. That the critics, of course, were much less than that. That there was no one worth writing for.

Snowden, who'd already made a point of admitting he thought Bo Shareef was "the bomb" before Bobby's story unfolded, could take no more. "Dude, did you ever even ask yourself if it ain't the other

way around? Like, oh, I don't know, maybe every other human being in the world is right and you're the one that's wrong. Maybe *The Great Work* just sucks. You ever think of that?"

"Yeah, I thought about that for a minute. But then I reread it. It's brilliant, they're dung beetles, trust me on this one."

The world didn't deserve *The Great Work*, at least not in this century. So with renewed effort, Bobby spent what little money he had reacquiring every one of its three thousand copies. Besides Harlem and Horizon, Bobby's favorite thing about New York City was its used bookstores, the Strand and Gotham Book Mart, where he spent his money and free time. Also, that there were several Ikea furniture stores in the area, as *The Great Work* could often be found being used as a bookshelf prop in their faux living room sets. The books weren't for sale, but that was OK because those he stole on principle.

Snowden, having been unimpressed with the three pages he'd managed to plow through of *The Great Work*, didn't care if it remained Robert M. Finley's only published novel. What annoyed Snowden, particularly since they'd decided to become drinking partners, was that once he got his blood alcohol level up, Bobby Finley never stopped talking about the world he'd abandoned, particularly his theory on the way it worked. Since his mall-front "awakening," Bobby had determined that there were only two roads to success for a male writer of African descent, such as he was. The first was to write a romance novel with an illustration of three or fewer attractive black people on the cover, preferably done in a comic book style so as not to scare off the illiterati. One written in flat descriptions of every action so that the prose was completely subservient to the plot, even though that plot was invariably predictable, as close to the readers' expectations as possible so as not to scare them. This type of book was basically for a readership looking for melaninized, low-tech versions of their afternoon soaps.

"If I wanted to, if I just gave up on humanity completely and wanted to sell out, I could make a million, no problem. I'd just excrete some story about a guy dating four women, but then they

find out and get even with him, maybe he ends up married to one, some dumb shit like that. I'd give it a clichéd title spelled with a bunch of useless Ebonic abbreviations. I could write it in a weekend."

Even more insidious, Bobby liked to declare, was the path toward black male literature. At some point it had been decided that the role of a black male writer was to create a work in the vein of Richard Wright or the great Ralph Ellison, not in the sense that the works be original and energetic, but that they focus on inner-city strife and racism. Whites, who made up the majority of sales in the literary category, felt their own writers could handle the other issues in the universe just fine, they just wanted the black guys to clarify the Negro stuff. The author would do best to deal with those issues in a predictable, derivative manner, as these readers were looking for confirmations of their viewpoints, not new ones. Bobby insisted that works were reviewed, awarded, and hailed based on this principle.

"Snowden, believe me when I say this, if I wanted to, I could produce a critical hit, full-page rave in the *Times*, TV interviews, no problem. I would just pump out another thing about this poor black person struggling to overcome white racism, inner-city violence, or poverty or, even better, all three. Are you kidding? That's a whole cottage industry. Dung beetles love that stuff. I'll even throw some hip-hop references on top, *'cause you know dey want it all authentic 'n' topical 'n' shit*. Nobody ever went broke giving people what they think they want."

This obsession infected every part of Bobby, even his bowels. The man insisted on calling his toilet Irving Howe, after a critic he particularly loathed, just so he could take pleasure in shitting on it daily.

"Look, the problem is you're writing the wrong things." Snowden enjoyed baiting him. Rarely was something so easy, so rewarding. "People don't want books, man. They want movies. Even the bad ones get hundreds of thousands in the seats."

"Bullshit! They only want movies because the film industry

spends a couple million dollars on each one to tell them to! If I had a couple million dollars, I could get a hundred thousand people to read anything, but books don't get that. The only way I could get people to read *The Great Work* would be to do something huge and crazy, create some spectacle for free publicity."

All this was not to say that Robert M. Finley had stopped writing. Bobby's newest work, *The Tome*, was just not meant for public consumption. With no readers, Bobby had intentionally started writing for no one. The only other person who got close to the 478 pages of *The Tome* was Snowden, who liked to use its pile to rest his beer on. *The Tome* was the first example of the principles of the "Robert M. Finley Emulsion Literary Theory," a theory that Bobby himself had invented. To any he could engage in a discussion upon the concept, Bobby often remarked that he was nearly twenty pages into its treatise, but that he would not reveal it until it was completely ready, and then as a mass E-mail. At its simplest (and despite hours of detailed explanation, the simplest version was more than Snowden could comprehend), it was about not actually writing, but showing, highlighting, and amplifying the poetry of the universe around us. Something about humans being imperfect, so avoiding themselves as a source. From what Snowden had heard of *The Tome* during impromptu drunken readings, it seemed to be collections of random conversations, stream-of-consciousness, and chapter-long descriptions of street noise. His second forty ounce near gone, Bobby would talk about the line between genius and insanity, the importance of walking close to it. Snowden just wished he would walk on the other side. Bobby swore, though, that with the right drugs opening your mind, you could dance to it.

At moments, Snowden found the intensity of Bobby Finley inspiring, something he could just sit and drink in front of for hours, and Bobby's intelligence gave it both a voice and elegance. After a while, though, it could get plain boring. Sometimes Snowden feared that when Bobby got excited (as he did) and pulled out a copy of *The Great Work* to quote, the thousands of others on the shelf

would come collapsing down as well, crushing them. Just another fatal accident, and then Lester would be in here cleaning up, blank faced, except this accident would get press for the sole reason that it was so absurd. The earnest cream puff anchor on Channel 9 news would run the teaser, "Man Crushed by Dreams," during commercials only to offer the story as an almost lighthearted piece slipped in after the sports and weather. Snowden's own apartment was only a block away, and Bobby had even suggested that they go there sometimes, but since Snowden had already given Jifar his own set of keys it didn't seem right, the boy there, them drinking. If the kid wanted to see that, he could stay downstairs.

Those keys had been meant for Bobby in case Snowden got locked out. However, drunk, resting on the space cleared off Bobby's makeshift couch, Snowden didn't see the use anymore in getting another set made for Bobby. Not only would they most certainly be lost in the debris that blanketed every surface and floor, but there were other, even more compelling reasons not to. The most obvious was that while Bobby had implied that the burning down of his mom's boyfriend's house was a one-time incident, and while the fact that he was walking a free man certainly testified to the fact that a judge and jury agreed so, the burnt crap that emerged from beneath the surface anytime Snowden adjusted the mess around him contradicted that. While the majority of it seemed to be charcoaled packs of matches, black and flailing, the variety of what Bobby chose to ignite was nearly impressive. Plastic silverware, just the eyes in an entire issue of *Talk*, a collection of small colored plastic dinosaurs. Snowden began hunting for new finds, curved round and twisted by the heat, every time Bobby went to the bathroom. Based on one of his findings – an entire collection of male doll heads apparently disfigured and guillotined before melting in some postapocalyptic revolution – Snowden began to believe that Bobby was actually going out and buying things specifically to burn them.

LEARNING

A LOT OF people died in Harlem. This didn't surprise Snowden, it was a big place. What surprised Snowden was that almost once a week one of them died in a Horizon property. Sometimes it was a preexisting condition finally taking its toll, but often it was just a matter of one little misstep, a simple accident, and those that were living, weren't. Snowden's Tuesdays were booked with the special project from then on, going in and bagging it up to take it away. Bike riders without helmets or reflective gear, residents who chose to avoid the pedestrian route underneath the scaffolding of renovating buildings, commuters who ignored the plea to buckle up in the back of taxicabs. Snowden would ask the cause and Lester would tell him and then Snowden would spend the rest of the day imagining the end the person came to, piecing together his or her life before as he shoved its remnants into the Dumpster.

In an attempt to prove to himself that sudden death was not this random, that these people had brought this fate upon themselves (and therefore it was avoidable), Snowden looked for clues of moral or discipline lapses that preceded their demise. Snowden wanted reasons. When they were cleaning out the sty of the guy who croaked in his bed from diabetes, Snowden found two cases of Pepsi underneath the sink and caught himself pumping his fist to himself in victory. This was a rational universe. This guy was huge too, his mattress bowed like a hammock from the springs he'd crushed while sleeping. The whole thing had acted like a sponge. It wasn't the smell of the bed that made Snowden vomit, it was the layer of maggots on top of it, the sound of a thousand dry worms in agitated orgy.

Together, he and Lester wrapped it in plastic, had to take it straight to the sanitation department and come back because it stank so bad. The man's room was a collection of empty ninety-nine-cent boxes of snack cakes, gun collector magazines wrinkled and stained, and cheap black porno. Videotapes were strewn across the floor of his bedroom, their boxes discarded beneath the bed, images of the poor, tattooed, and desperate covered in a layer of gray dust and the congealed remnants of their late owner. When Lester and Snowden finally unscrewed all the locks on the narrow closet in his hallway ("You can't bust a door like this, that oak woodwork's irreplaceable"), the final evidence in the deceased's damning was the strongest. Shotguns, wood and black metal, some barrels already sawed off by the same hand that had rubbed out the registration numbers, but mostly handguns, piled in boxes according to make, caliber. A cardboard barrel with the letters *SNL!* written on it was the biggest, the visibly cheap six-shooters piled on one another like so many crabs.

The next posthumous eviction was a woman who'd lived in the second-story floor-through on 126th, right around the block from Sylvia's, the victim of a hit-and-run walking back from a bar all the way over on Amsterdam. It was a nice building too, even for a Horizon property, fully renovated the year before. There was a literary agent making an office of the garden apartment, the third floor held a thick bit of brown-skinned cuteness who smiled at Snowden in the hall as he carried up sheets of boxes to be unfolded. Lester said she was playing the role of a dancing plate in *Beauty and the Beast*, turned back to caution Snowden not to bug her for tickets to the show.

Back to work, walking down the apartment's hall for the first time, Snowden saw the children's room. This was a shock because usually, when they showed up to clear a place out that had housed children, that presence could be felt immediately just by the collage of toys, books, and drawings they left behind. This apartment was spotless. A sparse, mature space without a sign of anyone below legal drinking

age. Yet here it was, this kids' room, a narrow area with two bunk beds on either side, barely enough room for an adult to walk between them. Four name tags handwritten in crayon, one on the frame of each mattress. They must have built them in there, that was the only way they could have fit, and now he was going to have to take them apart just to get them out. As always, Snowden packed the children's things separately in the specially stamped boxes. On Lester's request, Snowden also created a different box for each child. They were now enrolled in Horizon's Little Leaders League and Lester intended to relay their possessions to them that night.

Finished, joining Lester in the master bedroom, Snowden was amazed at the contrast in size. The bed was a king yet looked like a little island in the center of the vast room. The mirrors on the walls and ceiling made the space seem like a loft. Lester caught Snowden looking at the costumes lying out on the dresser: a full-body skin of latex with holes for the head, hands, feet, vagina, anus; a leopard leotard whose tail erectly saluted; the mandatory French maid outfit but in red leather this time; countless others obscured below them and shackles straight out of *Roots* on top.

"She was a whore," Lester clarified, throwing the bulk into a fresh lawn bag, stomping it down with his purple snakeskins to make room for more.

Back to God. It was as if he existed. It was as if he was making up for a century of hands-off management, was considering a new policy of snatching up the unjust and using Harlem as a testing ground. It was a source of comfort, that the bad would be punished. It explained things: Maybe, when Snowden swung on his father and the man just died, maybe that was why. Maybe God was a brain hemorrhage sometimes. It offered solutions to unsolvable problems: This fate could await Jifar's father as well, some moisture on the bathroom tiles and faulty high-voltage wiring ready to claim victory for a vengeful lord, and then one more child would be free of a monster.

More troubling was the universal implication of the theory Snowden had begun to imagine. It wasn't long before he began judging himself and his own actions.

Weeks into his special project, Snowden went up on the roof, unhooked the line he had less than two months before connected, then called Time-Warner to get his cable legally this time. The DMV tickets for the rental car, he paid them. He cursed the City of New York Transportation Authority for their contrived alternate-side-of-the-street parking, but he admitted his sin and paid them anyway. Snowden's entire collection of *Black Tail* (April/May, August/September, October/November, and the double-size Juneteenth Collector's Edition) went in the trash. Snowden even found himself keeping his apartment unusually orderly, fixing the stopper on the Irving Howe so you didn't have to hold the handle to flush, replacing the shower curtain with a plain, mildew-free print, hanging up the framed pictures that had from the day he'd moved in been resting on the floor against the wall. Eventually he would die and someone would be in his apartment as well. The saddest thing, those little tasks undone.

This rest of the world could not be controlled. In light of his new awareness of death's proximity, its random appetite, Snowden looked for safety, found none. On the job, carrying large, visually impairing objects down the steps, Snowden lost the confidence that if he simply dropped a foot blindly to the space below, there would be a stair there waiting for it, ready to carry his weight and the weight he was carrying.

Bobby: "You look like a little girl trying to figure out if the water in the pool's too cold."

Undaunted, Snowden kept dipping down his right foot only, testing for purchase with his toe before investing the rest of his weight on the platform. The last step on any flight, the one right before the landing, was particularly worrisome to the newly spooked Snowden. His view blinded by whatever crap he was forced to lift at the moment, he kept fearing that he would confuse the final stair

with the landing, or the landing for the final stair, and that this miscalculation would result in a fatal fall. One could drown in a thimble of water (or cereal bowl – Brian Lane, 853 East 134th St., Apt. A19). One could break one's neck just by landing headfirst on a steel-toed shoe (Pernell Harris, 432 East 116th St., Apt. E4). Uncertainty guaranteed, Snowden walked slowly. Horus, twice the boxes in hand, just pushed by, calling Snowden a "pussy" when the laggard cringed at contact.

It was nearly ten weeks before they got to do anything as a group besides lift furniture, then training began, late but as promised. Lester announced the change in schedule before handing out checks in the back of the van. "Come to the lodge front door at nine A.M., dressed like a real estate agent." During nearly every coffee and lunch break for at least two weeks before, Horus had been putting forth his personal conspiracy theory that the whole program was a big scam, that they would never promote ex-cons to agents, that there was no townhouse to be awarded, that they just wanted the cheap labor and to make the sick joke of the banana uniforms. It began as an obvious ploy to throw the others off, but every time Horus made mention of it Snowden found himself succumbing to that delusion as well, despite the contradiction that there was no reason to import cheap labor to Harlem.

The Horizon Property Management office was just one small storefront in a converted stable; the corner brownstone it was attached to was originally built for the Slang Berg Explorers League, a short-lived gentlemen's club that derived its name from the original Dutch title for Mount Morris. While the lodge was built in the same architectural style as the other brownstones of the Mount Morris Historic District (as all were the product of architect Richard Morris Hunt, better known for his contributions to Carnegie Hall), it was obviously too big to have been intended as a regular home, bulbous around its edge like it was pulling away from a block it had outgrown. There was an abandoned cinder-blocked shell attached

to it, but the contrast just added to its grandeur. They all knew it was Cyrus Marks's residence, they all hoped to get a chance to be seen by him. Bobby had even practiced bending down to shake hands so it looked more like a bow than an acknowledgement of how much shorter the old man was. It made sense that Marks should live there. If you could have your pick of any house in Harlem, and were not burdened by modesty, this would be the one.

Wednesday morning, ten to nine, they stood outside, ready for the next phase in their ascension. Snowden had bought his suit the day before at Sutter's, Nineteenth between Fifth and Sixth. It was black, a retired tux rental, he wore it with a red tie and hoped the others didn't notice the strip on the outside of the pant legs. It was the best he could do for under $150. Bobby's suit was expensive. Snowden could tell, but Bobby bragged about it anyway. It was his reading suit, the one he'd bought to wear standing in front of bookstores, award ceremony podiums, glossy magazine shoots, and in the darkened room of a coveted interview show. That didn't happen and now it didn't fit anymore. It was baggy. Bobby'd forgotten to wear a belt so kept the coat buttoned even though it was hot and June, kept his hands in his pockets to keep his pants up while attempting an air of confidence.

Horus was dressed in a some sort of military formal wear, but it was not an outfit someone actually in the military would own, rather the type of uniform a doorman or the guy who takes the tickets at a fancy show would be forced to wear. Its felt material was Astroturf green, the rope that lined it gold metallic. Horus saw Snowden looking and, smiling, brushed off absolutely no lint from the glowing rope that lined the shoulders, arms, and five-inch cuff links.

"How much did you pay for that?" Horus asked Snowden. The question was nonjudgmental, but the way Horus nodded to Snowden's suit, with his nose leading, Snowden could sense the distaste in it. Snowden adjusted his own shoulder pads, both of which seemed to be determined to emigrate south and get jobs as elbow pads.

"One forty," Snowden told him. Pissing contests were tax-exempt.

"Snowman, you should have gone with me to the warehouse. I told you." Horus spread his legs, slight and stiff, held out his arms for inspection. "Eighty bones, my son. That's what I'm talking about. Forty for the coat, forty for the pants. Check this out." Horus leaned into Snowden, glanced over at Bobby for mock privacy. "It buttons all the way up the neck so I don't have to waste money on a shirt or tie neither."

Their first training day set the schedule for the rest: At exactly eight A.M., a man appeared, a Mr. M. R. Linden. M. R. Linden was white and bald except for his beard, which disappeared over his ears and was brown with an oval albino patch on the left side of his face as if he'd fallen asleep in a shallow pool of Clorox. He looked like a genetically modified pig, but he wore a much nicer suit than they did so his students listened intently. Day one was the basics: the difference between rent controlled ("a set rent price that increases slowly for the length of the rental") and rent stabilized ("a controlled rent price that can be raised by a citywide certified percentage each year"). From there Mr. Linden flew without pause into the particulars: Rent control is over, the only people who have it are the elderly or live-in descendants who inherited the robbery; rent-stabilized status applies to an apartment regardless of the owner, and even when a tenant leaves the rent can be raised only by a controlled percentage. The first postlecture discussion topic: Are rent control and rent stabilization the cause of Manhattan's exorbitant real estate prices?

Snowden leaned forward in his chair just to get a look at Bobby. Bobby the preparer, Bobby memorizer of manuscripts, dark prince of data. Bobby, who in less sober moments had confessed that since he was long and weak his best chance at proving himself to the powers of Horizon was to intellectually dazzle, was preparing to use this opportunity to display the depth of his knowledge of the ruling argument of New York housing questions: whose fault were the

prices, the realtors or the renters? Snowden could tell Bobby was reciting his speech in his head, raising his hand with no intention of waiting till he was called on. Brushing off one of the techniques that got him through high school, Snowden quickly excused himself to the bathroom, tried to make it to the door before Bobby could start talking.

The hall outside was poorly lit, the lights were on but were too weak to manage the cavern. During the building's second incarnation as the Upper Manhattan Guild of Hebrew Men, the basement floor had been lowered ten feet to serve as a respite from Prohibition for the distinguished gentlemen of Judea. The bathroom was porcelain, tiled and equipped to facilitate a regiment struck by incontinence at once, but unfortunately a sign on its door said all of its services were temporarily unavailable, so Snowden headed instead for the WC on the second floor as the text instructed.

Snowden had never been up there before and the action of climbing the wide wooden steps felt both naughty and one of employee entitlement. The hallway off the balcony had the same institutional feel as the basement, the same oak-lined walls and porcelain doorknobs, but the colored glow of the animal-shaped night-lights plugged intermittently along the floorboards gave the space a life missing below. Also missing: the bathroom. It had been Snowden's expectation that this floor would be built on the same grid as the one he knew, but much to his disappointment there was not even a doorway where he'd expected the bathroom to be. What doors he could find had signs on them, but they said things like TV and PLAY SPACE instead of MEN or WOMEN.

Congressman Marks's voice came from down the hall after Snowden was already walking back, resigned to the thought that he would just have to hold it in for as long as it would take for Bobby to shut up and class to end. Moving toward the sound, Snowden wondered for a moment if he would be chastised for his intrusion, but then he located the door it was coming from and the sign above it said BOYS. Snowden, relieved to relieve himself, burst right in.

Marks sat in a rocking chair dressed in a smoking jacket of green satin, Wendell's lump of brown canine flesh was snoring on the floor beside him. There was a book in the man's lap, one Marks stopped reading aloud as he turned up to look at Snowden. So did all the kids. From where Snowden was standing, it looked like at least twenty bunk beds filled the length of the room. Each one had a boy in a maroon blazer and short pants sitting on top of a mattress, looking over his shoulder to get a view of the intruder.

"We have a special guest, one of Horizon's future leaders come to tuck you in for your nap. Say hello to Snowden, men." The bored, elongated welcome of children directed in unison. Snowden waved to them. A hand waved back. It took Snowden a moment to recognize that the boy it was attached to, probably around ten as most seemed in the room, had a question for him.

"Yes, Mr. Godfrey?" Cyrus Marks asked, smiling.

"Is Snowden your first name, or your last name, or is that a made-up name?"

"Last name," Snowden told him. He looked over to Cyrus Marks, expecting some sort of explanation for the scene he was witnessing, but the man just sat there, legs folded, finger holding his place in his book, waiting for Snowden to answer like the rest of them.

"My first name's Cedric," Snowden continued. "I just don't use it."

"How come?"

"Cedric was my dad. I'm just Snowden."

"Junior!" a child's voice came from the other end of the room, the laughter it emitted from the other boys was what finally got Cyrus Marks out of his seat. The discomfort of stifled urination and the sound of Wendell farting: the only things that kept Snowden positive this vision wasn't his creation, staring over his shoulder as the congressman grabbed him by his shoulder and pulled him politely out of the room.

"Mr. Snowden, so good to see you." Cyrus Marks in the hall, whispering, door closed behind him. "I really wish I could spend

more time with our men of the Second Chance Program. You can use their rest room up here, but I wouldn't suggest sitting down: One of the boys seems to like urinating on the seats. I'm still trying to find out which one."

"I'm sorry, sir, but what was that? It looked like a boarding school in there."

"Are you pulling my leg? Lester hasn't informed you three about the Little Leaders League? I'm surprised. Lester is very thorough."

"I knew there was a tutoring program, but those boys look like they live here."

"Oh yes, of course they do. And you should see our strong little ladies, on the third floor; they've done a lovely job decorating their room. We're just starting to expand, take in more of them. Hale House used to have the same kind of services, but less so since Mother Hale died – God bless her, she was a lovely woman – and all their financial troubles. This is the first time many of these children have had a peaceful, orderly home. You should volunteer sometime! Lester says wonderful things about your work, I'm sure you'd be perfect for it."

"Forgive me, sir, but how can there be so many? This won't be a permanent situation for them, right?" In response to the question, Cyrus Marks pulled on his shiny lapels, smirked amused disappointment.

"Mr. Snowden, Mr. Cedric Snowden of 124 Winona Street #2, Philadelphia 19144. I'm surprised, really. I've read your file. You've experienced the alternative: multiple foster families, chaos. Do you think these children have ever had more stability than they do with us?"

The entire journey seemed impossibly long, and yet somehow, when Snowden returned, Bobby was still talking.

" – so while the popular theory among New Yorkers may be that the cause of the high price of apartment rentals is due to property owner greed . . ." Bobby squinting. Bobby tilting his head to the right

and lifting his hand for emphasis. Snowden saw him doing the same thing the night before when they were drunk and aping the president on television. Bobby Finley looked more sincere doing the move than the man he stole it from. Practice is cheating. "The true reason is that owners are forced to compensate for income lost due to unrealistic price fixing."

"We charge as much as we do." Like a Jamaican DJ, M. R. Linden liked to start it up only to stop and bring it back again, beginning anew once he was sure he had complete attention. "We charge as much as we do because we can. For every fifty people who won't pay twenty-four hundred for a four hundred-square-foot one-bedroom four-story walkup with no windows, there's some asshole with good credit who will, who'll smile when you drop the keys in his hand because 'it's only five blocks to the express subway.'" The last bit M. R. Linden offered in his own interpretation of a New York homosexual. Snowden's body tightened in response to the entire presentation. Horus began applauding. Bobby took notes. His handwriting was so small it was like he was hiding something even from himself.

"M. R. Linden is a troglodyte," Lester said after the first lecturer had departed. "But he is very talented at what he does. Listen to what he says. Take his skills and apply them to your own agenda." Bobby wrote that down as well, Snowden watched him.

It was always like this. Linden would lecture and then, ten minutes after disappearing into the Town Car waiting outside for him, Lester would take his place and spend the first minutes of his teaching time discrediting the other's opinions. The first day it was: "That is the difference, that is what Horizon is about and that's why you're here. Horizon is not about building profits, it's about building a community." It was the kind of thing that every company said, a hint of social agenda worn like perfume to make the business that much more enticing. Even McDonald's bragged about paper wrappers. Snowden found it disorienting to actually believe Lester meant it.

Lester went with it, this theme he was pushing. The second segment of the day Lester called "context." Specifically, how power brokers like Alain Locke created the Harlem Renaissance out of almost nothing, contacting artists and intellectuals nationally and telling them to come here because there was a vibrant community. And because they came, there was.

Lester in lime. Lester in a glowing lime suit, matching shoes and tie, socks and shirt in lemon. This was where he looked most comfortable, a book and lectern in front of him, a blackboard behind. Wendell entered the room and sat in the corner staring at him, panting to the rhythm, tongue hanging to the side in awe.

To wrap up the first day of school, Lester pulled out an old record player on a wheeled cart in the corner. The voice within the scratches was that of Alain Locke himself, talking about the influence that period of old Harlem had on black America. An hour on, while the three waited for their pizza at Slice of Harlem, Bobby did an almost dead-on impersonation of Locke by sticking two fingers up his nose and humming the words out the top of his palate. His slices of sausage and mushroom gone before the others had managed three bites, Horus used the silence created by full mouths to share his sole commentary about the day's proceedings. "That Locke dude, the one he was playing? I bet you could tie both my wrists behind my back, and make a rule that there was no kicking, and I could whup his ass real good. Just with my head, no hands."

What was stunning about this remark was not just that this was the one and only thing Horus would say about the six hours of intensive study, but that he would offer nearly the same solitary observation in the weeks that followed. From Lester's lecture on W. E. B. Du Bois's identification of the educated middle class as the Talented Tenth and how their post–civil rights flight to the newly integrated suburbs sent Harlem into its ghetto tailspin: "Definitely. That Doobie brother. You could tie, like, my left hand to my right foot, and give the dude a large, wooden club, and I could whip his ass. Probably in less than a minute, if he got close enough."

Even when Lester delivered his surprisingly moving sermon about Horus's own former stomping ground, the Cabrini Green projects, where the city gave half the apartments to working families as condos to break the culture of poverty, create an environment where people worked, invested in their homes. By the time Lester got to the end of it he was sweating so hard beneath his shirt that even his tie was soaked to his chest. He said, "Imagine what we could do for Harlem following that model," but his voice was hoarse, wasted. After putting the needle down on a old record of Langston Hughes reciting "Low to High," "High to Low," Lester collapsed on the pulpit, exhausted by his performance. Snowden could smell him from his seat, the scent stronger as the service went on, but he didn't care. Snowden was too moved to be bothered, too jealous of the passion. Even for a cynic, it was easy to get drunk on the dream of Horizon, to imagine one's life no longer without reason.

Despite his earlier emotion, when the lesson was over and the three were waiting for their lunch to heat up in the ovens at Slice of Harlem, Snowden found himself playing the rational counter to Bobby's evangelism.

Snowden: "I'm just saying, wait, see. It's always about money. If this ain't, that's great, but it's always about money."

Bobby: "That's your problem. You don't know what to believe and when to do it. You've got to have fire."

Snowden: "Even if Lester's for real, the way he talks about a new community in Harlem, what's going to happen to the people here who don't fit into that? We just going to kick them out on somebody else's streets every time we get a chance?"

Bobby: "That's a shame for them but it's not about what's best for some individuals, it's about what's best for everybody. Malcolm X said, 'By any means necessary.' People like that drug dealer Parson Boone, you don't worry what happens to them. Morally, the purity of the goal is all that matters."

Horus: "That Hughes dude, that's not even a challenge. It'd be

like, two hands handcuffed behind my back, one set of cuffs linked through to my right ankle, and still, I whup him, no problem. On one leg. My left one. I still whup his ass in a minute twenty."

It wasn't that Horus was dumb, nor was it that he hadn't been listening. It was that he simply had no questions. Aside from, "When we going to eat?" and "When we getting paid?" Horus never had questions. You just told him something and he moved forward with it in mind. It was a wonder no army besides the Black Stone Rangers had ever recruited him.

After lunch, Snowden returned from work to find his door vibrating with the sound of the television on the other side. He got depressed. Jifar hadn't been over in days and he'd begun hoping his secret dream had come true, that God had taken the time to reach down and smite the boy's father.

Inside, the television was still on, but Jifar was gone, probably to bed. After turning off the set, Snowden collapsed on the couch, almost immediately beginning the process of gathering the willpower to rise once more, accomplish that long list of things like take off his shoes and brush his teeth that suddenly seemed so monumental. The sound of his own labored panting lulling him to sleep, Snowden tried the motivational tool of holding his breath and refusing to let it go until he forced his body to at least get up and microwave something. It was the sound of heavy breathing continuing from behind the couch that shot him up and over. When Snowden's blind fist slammed into a cast-iron frying pan flying nearly as fast in its same direction, he was as awake as any narcotic stimulant could possibly manage.

When Snowden experienced a sharp and sudden pain, it was his habit to hold the afflicted area and jump up and down. He wasn't sure if he did this because he had grown up watching Chuck Jones cartoons, or if Jones himself had just called attention to a innate quirk in human pain management. Either way, this is what Snowden did, and this is what he was doing now. Jifar, for his part, had

dropped his culinary assault weapon and was jumping up and down with Snowden, in time and sympathy, offering "You should have knocked!" over Snowden's primal "Ow."

"What were you thinking, boy?" It was his own father's voice Snowden used. This he knew from the timbre – it came on first deep and argumentative then got even lower, turned to a rage-filled scream on the last word. This Snowden knew also because Jifar turned his head to the side, tensed his face to counter the expected blow. He didn't run away, he didn't raise his arms to guard himself because he had learned, like Snowden had at his age, that that just brought more blows, harder ones.

"I'm sorry. You don't be sorry, I am. Just, what were you thinking, little man? Were you going to try and kill me?"

"I didn't know it was you. Honest."

"Who the hell else is going to put a key in the door and come in here? Huh?" Snowden could hear the anger start to build again in his voice, tried to extinguish it by talking slowly enough to give himself the chance to control the emotion in each word. "You give my keys to anybody to make copies?"

"No. I don't do like that. I'm a man."

"You're a man. Great. Then who the hell else was I supposed to be, then?"

"I don't know. Maybe you the Chupacabra or something," Jifar admitted.

"The Chupacabra. That monster." Snowden looked at the boy and could see who that monster was. The one with the gray mustache stained brown at the bottom from smoking Dominican cigars, the one with the endless supply of novelty T-shirts, like the one that said JUST SAY NO TO CRACK with the illustration of a woman's anatomically impossible cartoon ass swallowing a helpless man. That monster. Snowden could see the monster's claw marks on Jifar, in a line along his biceps at the same place on both arms; they were the ones you get from being shaken really hard. Jifar's skin was the light brown of fall leaves, the dotted bruises a dull green. They looked like tattoos of olives.

67

"The Chupacabra," Snowden confirmed. Jifar stared up at him for a few moments to decide if he was being believed or taunted, decided he didn't care and started nodding vigorously in the affirmative.

"I thought your boy said he only went after people in Washington Heights. He's coming down below 145th Street now?"

"Mannie Ortiz says he started all the way up Inwood, like 220th Street or something."

"So he's working his way down."

"Yup. Mannie Ortiz says Harlem's just lunch. He's going to have dinner on the Upper West Side."

"Why not the Upper East Side? They're richer."

"He's following Broadway. Mannie says he sleeps along the tunnel of the one and nine trains during daylight."

"Little man, can I tell you something? Mannie's your friend, but he's full of chocolate. You shouldn't believe everything Mannie Ortiz has to say about the world. There's no such thing as a Chupacabra. It's a story, a myth. It's like . . ." Snowden was going to say Santa Claus but caught himself, unsure where Jifar stood with that phenomenon. "Like Spider-Man. It's just made up." The look Jifar gave him, the incredulousness, the pity, made Snowden fear it was a reflection of his own face moments before.

"No, lots of people talking about it. Lots of people thinks it's the Chupacabra, not just Mannie Ortiz. Adult people. His big brother Vernon, he's in the eighth grade, and a boy in his class saw it running around 135th Street station. They shot at it."

"But they didn't hit it, did they?"

Jifar shrugged a no.

" *'Cause it ain't real.* Don't worry about monsters, or anything else. You want to be safe in life? Just stay happy, try not to stay poor when you grow up, and watch your step, and you'll have nothing to worry about. It's that easy," Snowden told himself as well.

BOBBY FINLEY, POET, ROMANTIC

"**I** WROTE PIPER a poem," he said.

It had been three months since they'd moved her in. The weeks after were peppered with Bobby's territorial talk about his apologetic calls to her answering machine, laments that he was never home to receive her call in case she was shy about leaving a message on his, and then mention of the woman ceased. Snowden knew from this that Piper Goines had never called Bobby back; the thin man was not the type for quiet victory. So then two months went by and Bobby started up again and Snowden realized he hadn't conquered his obsession, just his need to talk about it.

"It's totally her poem, too. It's her; I used her actual voice for it."

"Where you get her voice?"

"Off the phone."

"So you've been calling her."

"Oh yes, I told you she gave me her number." By this it should be noted that Bobby meant that he'd taken it off the back of the Horizon receipt form she'd signed. Snowden had given it to Bobby on his request, as well as a pen and his own back as a writing surface. Snowden was impressed with the intensity of Bobby's fixation, that not only could he ignore that fact, he could also ignore that Snowden knew the truth as well.

"Damn, boy. Congratulations. You finally got to talk to that woman."

"Yeah, right? Well, not in person, I left a message. Then I got recordings of her voice off her answering machine, she changes the

69

message all the time. I just mixed the words together on my computer."

Bobby's contention was that showing up unannounced at her office at the *New Holland Herald* the next day was not stalking, it was just being practical. He had several reasons for this, the most creative was that if she received an unsolicited package with a tape inside it, as a reporter she might think it was a lead on a kidnapping, and he didn't want to disappoint her. By coincidence – one of those amazing coincidences the universe doles out to keep its inhabitants on their toes – Snowden had been instructed by Lester just the day before to place two ads at this very same paper. This was less of coincidence when you considered that Bobby had overheard Lester's instructions and apparently planned to tag along for moral support.

The ads, handwritten in Lester's small linear script along with font instructions, sat in Snowden's breast pocket with the message:

Folk of Harlem!
Are you considering moving away from the area? Retiring? Going back down south or to the Caribbean? Whether you're a home owner or a renter, contact Horizon Property Management to assist your transition. Cash bonuses for all referrals.

and

Folk of New York!
Coming back to the dream of old Harlem? Let Horizon Property Management help you make it a reality. Buyers or renters, call now.

Rereading them, Snowden wondered if a white person would get the meaning of "folk" and realize they were being excluded. On further thought, Snowden wondered when was the last time any white person had gone to a newsstand and bought the *New Holland Herald*. There was no reason for them to read it. With blacks writing at the top newspapers in the country, with endless glossies devoted to

African-American interests and life, there didn't seem too much reason for black folks to read it either. That's why Snowden never felt embarrassed by how bad it was, or guilty at taking pleasure reading it aloud. Snowden felt confident in the assumption that no one else was listening.

The walk to the *New Holland Herald* became eventful once the two came in sight of the new Disney Store on 125th and Frederick Douglass. The state of righteousness Bobby'd been stuck in for weeks, Snowden knew it would set him off, but since the paper's office was on the other corner, it was unavoidable. In preparation, Snowden had attempted to ensnare Bobby into the more nuanced debate about the corruption allegations involving the Apollo, the other landmark they were passing, but the smaller man would have none of it.

"Fucking bloodsuckers. Fucking mind-numbing smiley-faced Jim Jones Kool-Aid bloodsuckers up here to siphon what little money we have with their poison blankets shaped like plush corporate logos," Bobby started chanting. Snowden found the worst part of talking to Bobby when he got like this was that Bobby would take Snowden's own opinions but become so froth-mouthed fanatical that Snowden felt forced to claim the opposition for the sake of keeping the discussion in the realm of sanity.

"Well, they've provided some jobs up here, and it looks good for the one-two-five, as far as attracting investment," Snowden said and immediately resented Bobby for this, for making him defend the mouse.

"Right, like six jobs at eight dollars an hour. Up, you mighty race!" It was amazing how he could do that, hyperventilate and talk at the same time. Several women paused with their bags in front of Lane Bryant and McDonald's Express to take in the licorice blur vibrating past them, his voice modulating with each word between stage whisper and scream. Snowden was waiting for somebody to offer a wallet to stick in Bobby's mouth so he didn't bite his tongue off, "Goddamn leeches, riding up in their Trojan horse to suck the green

71

right of the place, then they'll go back to Anaheim and do a *Pocahontas* on Sally Hemings, turn that into a love story too."

"It will attract people to Harlem. That's the point of what we're doing, right?"

"It attracts white people to Harlem. That's the point of it. It says, 'Look, no broken windows, the canary's alive and well.' Then they take over the last bit of the island that they're not in the majority. That's the plan. We'll all get pushed to Newark and they'll get this back again, and to them it will just be a loaded name and a bunch of cool brownstones. They'll even open some jazz theme clubs to remember us by, like they do with fake villages on the lands they got from the Indians."

Snowden said, "Healthy canaries are a good thing. They send the message that the air's all safe to breathe," but nothing more. Snowden took the talk of race as a sign to shut up and just keep walking. Snowden always took the talk of race as a sign to shut up and keep walking because he'd never figured out how to discuss the subject without stating the obvious, sounding bitter, or like a sellout, doomed however he approached it. Talking about race was like trying to have a serious argument about the existence of the Easter Bunny: No matter what position you took, you always ended up sounding either thick or mildly insane.

By the time they reached the office of the *New Holland Herald*, Bobby was so worked up that he was forced to lean against the wall of the abandoned building next to it in order to regain his composure.

"I should burn that bastard down," Bobby wheezed. "It would probably take out most of Harlem USA with it but, you know, 'by any means necessary.' " He tried to light a cigarette but was breathing too hard and ended up in a coughing fit, limply cursing the class warfare of the tobacco companies as he put it out against his foot, pocketing the filter so as not to litter. Inside, the two men parted when Bobby was directed to the offices upstairs and Snowden to the classified desk on the first floor. Bobby parted with, "Don't wait up

for me," managing a wink before succumbing to another fit of coughing, pausing on the long wooden stairway as others quickly went around him.

The clerk behind the counter seemed ecstatic to see Snowden, looked so relieved to have a break in the monotony of the otherwise empty room, its dust, its faded furniture. The guy didn't even take his money, he held it for a moment, yes, but then when he read the copy he smiled and nodded as if he'd been the target of a harmless joke and handed it back. Piper Goines stood in the room behind him, looking good like that. Snowden smiled, she smiled back, remembered him and came over.

"Excuse me," she said. "Does that guy Robert M. Finley still work with you? Because I've been getting these calls on my phone from Robert M. Finley ever since I moved in, he doesn't even leave messages anymore, he just keeps calling and then hanging up on my machine."

Bobby was upstairs leaving Ms. Goines a surprise. Snowden was downstairs, trying to convince Ms. Goines to associate the word *persistent* with the name "Bobby Finley" instead of the word *psychopath*, not making any headway with his argument until Piper realized that Bobby was the one who looked like a human snow crab and not the creepy one with a head like a rottweiler.

"Bobby's a really smart guy, funny. It's just that we're not from here, we work a lot, he was just trying to reach out. We're from out of town, don't really know anybody in the area, you know how it is. He's good people. He gave you his book, right?"

"That's right, that's right. Actually, I tried to read that thing but couldn't get past the first page. It didn't seem to make any sense, like there'd been misprints or something. I probably just didn't read it close enough," Piper was the one making the guilty face now. Snowden nodded at this like a mistake had indeed been made, staring at her, trying to think of a way to tell her that the man they were talking about was at this moment at her desk. Piper watched as Snowden struggled to say something and got tired of waiting.

"So you don't know anyone. You kind of know me," Piper told him. "You've already been to my place, you might as well come back over and we can have dinner sometime. I'm on my way to Ephesus to cover the protest meeting about the Mumia Abu-Jamal Memorial Halfway House, the one the state's trying to open by Mount Morris Park, but there's tomorrow."

"Memorial House? Mumia Abu-Jamal hasn't even been executed yet."

"I know! Sick bastards."

In moral law, there was definitely an edict about dating your friend's obsession.

"If you're worried about your buddy, I'm sure he's a nice guy, but I'm never going out with him. That just ain't happening."

Snowden appreciated Piper's plucky initiative, her persistence. It meant that every time he felt a pang of guilt for accepting her invitation he could tell himself he'd been forced into doing so, take some of the bite out of it.

PIPER GOINES SPEAKS

T HE THING THAT really pissed Piper off about living in the apartment above her sister and brother-in-law was that she had to walk through three floors of their home to get to hers, and even though she loved them they were materially driven intentional archetypes of the bourgeoisie, something Piper once even said to their faces months before their wedding only to have them high-five gleefully in response, dancing circles together in their boutique clothes as they waved their status symbol watches in the air in victory. Their home was a museum of all the class accoutrements they'd collected in just seven years working as a tag team: rich woods, fabrics, and leathers placed on rugs so expensive that having them on the floor was indulgent insolence. Piper kept redecorating but it didn't matter, by the time she reached the top floor her home seemed a slave quarters in comparison.

They were like twins, her sister and her mate, one identical mind-set compensating for the fact that they looked nothing like each other. As obnoxious as they could be in tandem, Piper had produced more tears at their wedding than the collective attendants. It was the natural order of it that got to her, that maybe there was somebody out there to perfectly match each individual. That maybe there really was one person out there perfect for her.

Piper's sister and brother-in-law were arrogant about their relationship too, but equally arrogant, so it took nothing away from the symmetry. If they were the type, they would have used the term "soul mates," but they weren't so called themselves "power couple." Since moving in, Piper came to call them Tweedle Dee and Tweedle

75

Dumbass. In response, Dumbass, or Brian as he was known to the others in his life, usually referred to Piper as Assata Shake'n'Bake, Rosa Park Avenue, or Sister Soul Food, depending on how the spirit moved him. Dee, known to all as just that, preferred to call her sister Audre Lorde Have Mercy. It wasn't that they hadn't read the books, they just didn't feel them like that.

Tweedle Dee and Tweedle Dumbass, Tweedle Dee and Tweedle Dumber. Dee born in New Haven, Brian in Providence. Dee the vice president of Jack and Jill's Connecticut chapter, Brian the treasurer of the Rhode Island contingent. Brian and Dee trading locations so one could be a Bulldog and one be brown at Brown. Two memberships to organizations named with three Greek letters, both with two *A*'s bookending them. Three years apart, but how many early encounters until the First Friday where fate connected them? A shared hotel, Virginia Beach, spring break weekend? A shared ferry from Hyannis Port? Piper wondered. Piper wondered if the narrowness of Shark Bar hadn't made their world even smaller, how long those uneventful encounters would have continued. Piper stopped wondering if her own counterpart was entering her life, repeatedly and unnoticed: It was too painful.

Piper: impeached as bacillus from the NAACP Youth Group after calling former leader Walter White a "bleached coon" during the introductory address at the Teen Summit in Niagara Falls, a painful event compensated by years of bragging rights. Earlham College, class of '92, *Fight, Fight, Inner Light, Kill Quakers, Kill.* The best editor B.L.A.C.'s newsletter would ever claim. Greek affiliation: once sucker-punched by a Kappa Sweetheart at a Ball State step show. Ten years later and single, some false alarms but no children, no furniture that cost more than a day's salary. A job she loved and was good at. Hope. In painting, an art freed from ambition. A refusal to ever buy a cat as a companion, or let herself get to the point where she'd be tempted to.

Dee, Dumbass; hers an artistic and slightly cool career that didn't really pay for her lifestyle, his a dull career playing with money that

paid for them both. For fun they bought things and went to foreign resorts that called themselves "spas," hung out with other finance men and their creative wives. At night they planned to breed others just like them. For fun Piper went downtown, paced bright openings and got just drunk enough that her work looked better than theirs, took a cab home and hoped secretly that the driver would complain that her destination was Harlem so she could fight a little injustice on the way. If they were away, Piper would simply come in the front door and go to sleep in their living room, look around at how beautiful and comfortable it was and admit that she was as jealous of their lifestyle as she was disgusted by it. They never got too sad because they were sure about life, and as bankrupt as their value system was, it would never force them to accept its insolvency. It was impossible to own everything, and as long as there was more to acquire they would have faith that further acquisition was the key to happiness.

Piper got happiness doing, not buying, which worked out well because her job gave her a lot to do but hardly any money to buy anything with. If evenings were disheartening, it was in morning that she found her victory. Just waking up and being happy about your life when you remembered it was a damn good thing, but actually being excited about the work in the day to follow was the richest possible blessing. She loved her job and the moments it gave her: when she was typing and felt like the mute were given the ability to scream through her to the page, later when it was on the newsstands and she could look and see her own mark on the world. Seeing her name in print made her feel alive, made her feel immortal. She was connected by a continuum of newspaper issues going back week by week to the time when this paper brought news of Jim Crow and lynchings, called for boycotts of the whites-only-staffed department stores on 125th Street. No handmade Persian rug felt better underneath you than a purpose.

While Piper liked to think that she rose an hour early just for the opportunity to whistle past Dumbass on the stairs as he tried to

numb himself for another dehumanizing day of numeric servitude, getting to the paper before her coworkers served a more practical purpose. The *New Holland Herald*, the last great lion of the pre-integration news media, was a paper of many distinctions. Unfortunately, its most current was the fact that it had to be the only twenty-thousand-plus periodical in a major urban area to have only one computer in the entire company. Copy was manually typed in the office by staff writers, submitted by fax or in person by freelancers. Corrections were made on the page, or for the occasional major changes the writer was forced simply to rewrite the work. The publisher Mr. Cole's recited response to requests for computers was, "If James Weldon Johnson didn't need one when he was writing in this very room, then neither do you." On Wednesday all of the articles were taken to a printing service, where typists rewrote the entire edition word for word and laid it out into a template that had been created years before. Often, the section titles failed to match the copy below them as articles were arranged in random order. It was a standard sight to see an article on poor nutrition in public schools under the header DINING OUT complete with the illustration of a man and a woman in formal wear, martinis in hand. The edition was quickly copyedited because the whole thing had to be done by four-thirty P.M. or the paper was forced to pay overtime, which was a sin worthy of dismissal. Since the typists were going so fast that they were not even reading what they duplicated, it was impossible to catch every mistake. In the past this practice had led to several rather dramatic copy errors, the greatest one of Piper's tenure being the obituary headline that read MR. GAVIN WYATT, 79, LIES, which resulted in a two-week campaign of irate phone calls from his descendants, all of whom insisted he was an honest man.

Mr. Cole was impossible to shame and that was his most impressive attribute; his claim to fame was that he had run 342 continuous "Special Report" front-page editorials, 176 of which contained the exact same headline: IMPEACH GIULIANI. The columns were always in a darker, bolded shade than the rest of the

edition and sometimes covered nearly half the front page. The majority of sentences ending in exclamation points gave the impression that Mr. Cole was constantly screaming at the reader with incredulity! This was accurate! The column was the only thing he cared about. Piper had seen him in the office receiving the first printing of the new issues and he rarely cracked it open unless his own editorial was continued inside. As long as his regularly occurring "Special Report" was uncut and errorless, Mr. Cole was unmoved. Mr. Cole looked liked an aged orangutan, was old, belligerent, and eccentric in equal measure. When Piper was hired she was pulled aside by several people and told that at times he acted committably insane, and on such occasions she should just nod at everything he said and, if he got violent, go home.

So Piper arrived early with notes and wrote out and printed the articles she'd researched and outlined the day before, then spent the rest of the day preparing articles for the following morning. It wasn't that anyone else would need to get on the computer later, just that it was in the executive editor's office and, although he was pleasant, the space was simply not big enough for two people. The executive editor shared Mr. Cole's name plus a Jr. to go with it, was hired for the position for his inability to stand up to Mr. Cole Sr. and to provide a front to allow his father to say whatever the chemicals in his head dictated and pass it off as a "letter to the editor" when the paper was inevitably sued for libel in response. Whole days went by when the executive editor kept his door closed, which was appreciated by his staff because watching the graying thirty-five-year-old Junior get yelled at was nearly as uncomfortable as when Mr. Cole chose one of them for belittlement.

In addition to Piper, the *New Holland Herald* had three full-time employees, Segun Diop, Bill Sims, and Gil Manly, two other part-timers, Carleen Wilson and Shandy Gomes, and a rotating legion of freelancers willing to pump out four-hundred to eight-hundred word stories for thirty-two dollars a pop. Piper was the only staff writer under forty, the only one more accustomed to a monitor's windy

hum than the insect percussion of the manual typewriter. Carleen and Shandy spent their moments in the office slumped nearly level to their desks, in turn harassing and being harassed by the writers who wrote their sections. Aside from Mr. Cole, the fact that the writers were paid so little was enjoyed by no one. The writers, obviously, found this an annoyance, particularly when much of their work was printed with far too many errors to be used as clips to entice other, better-paying publications. (The *New Holland Herald* was not a premiere African-American periodical, such as its fierce competitor the *Amsterdam News*, the *Philadelphia Tribune*, or Washington, D.C.'s renowned *News Dimensions*.) For the editors it was extremely difficult as well, since the freelancers invariably tried to compensate for the low wage by hacking out the fastest pieces they could manage. This technique the writers would employ with greater and greater desperation until they were submitting paragraphs of disjointed gibberish. When asked to rewrite the piece and read it at least once before handing it back, the freelancers would do so but then quit, refusing to invest any more time in their submissions in the future.

Charlie Awuyah and Gil Manly were two of the main reasons the entire paper wasn't trash. Charlie Awuyah ate red pistachios all day and had been at the same desk for twenty-five years, before Mr. Cole even bought the place. In each issue he filled the last three pages of the paper with some of the most intelligent sports writing done anywhere. Gil Manly was barely in the office, was sixty, and dressed like reporters did when he was a boy, always kept a yellow pencil in his mouth in the building and a cigarette in it outside. Gil got to cover every single news event that didn't involve a press release. Piper wanted his job. She thought he was good, but each week the first thing she did was pore over his work and tell herself that she was better, or at least she would be some day soon. That was what Piper would do: stare at his desk, calculate how long it would be till he retired. Two years – there was no way he could hold out more than that; Piper'd caught him resting halfway up the long straight

stairs that went from the ground to the third floor. Then, really, how long would it be until Mr. Cole Sr. would follow? His rage, his hatred, his obesity. If the man lived another five years it would be due only to his other bad habit, his stubbornness.

In particularly optimistic moments Piper imagined one day taking the helm, gathering investors, maybe Dumbass and his friends, restoring the paper to its former glory. Or maybe she would just follow the pattern and get a dumbass of her own for security, be his artistic wife, a trophy to hold up, breed with, and eventually cheat on. Conquering conformity by complying with it completely. Piper was surprised at her lack of discomfort with the notion, until she thought of the look of smug affirmation etched in the wrinkles that had grown to accentuate her mother's expressions. Piper knew just the face she would make, too, the one that always formed when some event unfolded as she had contradicted it would, positive or negative. It was such a jarring image, her mother sitting in the front pew at some Episcopalian church in her wedding lace, the hat and everything, that face that said, "See, I told you, is it so bad really?" and Piper would realize that it was, but it would be too late not to say "I do."

The image was so clear, so alarming, that Piper left the copy room with it floating behind her, and when she happened to notice the cute guy who'd helped her move into her place months before she went right up to him and asked him over for dinner. Her boldness, which intoxicated her on the long ride to the ribbon cutting at the new CVS in Bed-Stuy, started haunting her with remembrances of sentences like "get to know you better," which seemed absurd without that guy before her, not quite looking at her in the face like he was alternately threatened by and ignoring her, both of which made the attraction stronger. His hands felt so thick with calluses that Piper was sure he could juggle live coals, the arms swollen and rounded from repeated use, making her giggle aloud at the irrationality of her desire to be lifted by him. If they never kissed that would be fine, but not if she never got to

feel what it was like to be lifted from the earth in those hands, held in those arms from it.

Piper's idea of housekeeping was to keep all her papers on raised surfaces like the counter, dining room table, and lid on the toilet basin, and all her clothes in piles on the floor, organized by the place she was standing when she took them off. There were no dishes to wash because she used paper plates and plastic forks, and couldn't cook. She walked to the take-out counter at Bamboo and they said, "Piper, you should really get the greens with that, you're not eating enough vegetables." She dialed their number from memory. There was a place on her tongue that was lobbying heavily for Thai, but what Piper wanted even more was a dish she could pour into her own cold pots and claim credit for. While Piper was quick to brag that she couldn't cook, she was equally willing to passively pretend she had. Not cooking Creole food was her speciality.

When Snowden arrived, Piper was laid out on the sofa, the effort of removing half her debris from sight rendering her unconscious. It was after nightfall and the light coming through the glass door to the outer hall pushed her toward waking, but it was the sound of Dee knocking on the door as she pushed through it (a fascist trait inherited from the mother, Abigail Goines) that brought Piper completely to reality. From a quick glance at her sister, the ever astute Piper could tell several things: that the food had arrived, that Dee had paid for it but not brought it up till now, that in the short walk up the stairs Dee had found time to ask Piper's guest his occupation (because she would surely not recognize random help) and he had told her, because she was wearing that face (one their mother created as well). It seemed that on 122nd Street, for all intents and purposes Dee was Abigail Goines.

Snowden was gracious, smiling and nodding to Dee until she closed the door behind her. His pacing of the room before seating himself was polite, complimentary. The curiosity Snowden displayed was in the acceptable manner of casually walking over to Piper's

paintings along the back wall, smiling with polite befuddlement before heading over to the bookshelf to see what titles were in the mind of the person he was dealing with. Piper encouraged this by drawing out the process of microwaving the dinners because that's what that bookcase was for. All the junk that would give him any real insight, the seedy true crime stories and painfully embarrassing personal growth memoirs, were carefully hidden in the bedroom within a trunk, beneath several sedimentary levels of dirty laundry, exactly where they belonged.

His politeness and respect were not a total façade either, because when Snowden went to the bathroom Piper listened and she didn't hear the crashing sound that would have erupted if he'd attempted to peek in the medicine cabinet. A legion of pill bottles had been placed there specifically to fall out if the door was opened, revealing a handwritten note that said YOU DON'T KNOW WHO YOU'RE MESSING WITH, a homemade novelty item for friends and a warning to dates that her heart had its own security system.

The meal disappeared rather quickly, the bottle of red also, but Piper's mouth kept running. She started with a capsule version of her life story, a set background piece she used with new friends to get it out of the way and provide context, which she followed by more in-depth studies into the more prominent themes and incidents: Abigail Goines's failed attempt at breeding the *über*-Africanus woman, Piper's exchange year in Portugal, the buying of this condo within her sibling's home, and the anecdote that displayed that her brother-in-law's credit wasn't as clean as he liked to pretend it was. The complete *New Holland Herald* breakdown, including employee profiles and her desire to overtake the office and seize control, if possible by armed struggle, the latter confession telling her she was officially tipsy and that she was talking entirely too much. Despite polite (if not overly enthusiastic) efforts to draw her guest out, the only thing Piper'd learned was that he was from Philadelphia and had attended Temple University, a fact that he himself admitted was probably true of nearly half the city's population.

"So you're how old? Can I ask you that, or will you blush and get coy on me?" A slight teasing. This was a major component in Piper's arsenal of seduction. It always worked, and when it didn't it was probably for the best anyway.

"I'm thirty-one. And I'm too dark for blushing," Snowden bantered.

"And so where have you been? What have you been doing since you graduated?" Snowden removed his napkin from his lap in response to the question, accepted that he liked her enough that he would definitely be back and therefore was unable to give his usual lies as an answer.

"I didn't graduate," Snowden said flatly. It was meant as a deterrent, offering a statement of failure as emotional libation while defining a border clearly marked against further trespass. Piper respected no such boundaries.

"College is expensive, half the time it's useless. But that doesn't explain where you've been, what you've been doing, does it?" Piper was smiling. She wasn't pretty, but she was cute and she used this sometimes to excuse her rudeness. She did it so well that Snowden noticed only when he was about to begin confessing, annoyed at the manipulation.

"I was in jail."

Piper didn't even pause before following with the mandatory response, "What for?"

There was the word, *manslaughter*. It was the proper one to use because it was literally the action he'd been found guilty of and sentenced for. It was also the best word there was to say that you killed someone. At Holmesburg State Penitentiary, it meant that this was not to be your permanent residence, and that you'd been smart enough to get a lawyer who arranged a lesser sentence. In this world it implied that there were ulterior circumstances, that the murder might even have been justified in everyday morality but legalities forced this minimum judgment. Its vagaries were one of the reasons Snowden hated saying it, it was a word that demanded questions.

Worse, every time he said it, Snowden could clearly hear both words it was made of. When Snowden said it, Piper didn't bother to ask for more, just waited quietly for him to offer.

"My father – I mean there were problems for a long time, I was in foster care mostly growing up, he was in jail. He was a Panther, then in the BLA, that's the Black Liberation Army; he was nuts. I came home from college winter break, we got in a fight, I just hit him wrong. That's it." That was. There was more Snowden could say, but that was enough.

"Oh shit, I'm sorry, I always push things too far, I'm always screwing up doing that."

"Look, I'm sorry. I'm not used to talking about it. I should be. I mean, it's not like I don't think about it, or don't regret it, it's something on top of everything I do. It's just, you know, something I've been working myself away from. So I got out almost two years ago and I've been struggling to get a good job, but now I do. I got hooked up by my PO in this program with Horizon, you know. Got the chance to make some money, do some good, right?"

"They have some kind of community program?"

"No. I mean, that's what it is, exactly what it is, community work. That's what Horizon is doing, trying to create another era of thriving black Harlem. Things been rough since the black middle class ran off to integration and took the money with them, right? So we're trying to bring them all that back."

"So how is that good?" Piper asked. "Helping the fortunate take Harlem away from the poor people who've been living here all this time?"

"No, that's not it, that's not what I'm saying. What Horizon has planned is better than that. They don't want to displace everybody, they just want to bring enough people back here to make the place healthy again. People to spend their money, create some vibrant retail life like back in the day, create jobs. Straight up, also to have some folks as role models walking around, to show that you can do it."

"Believe me, just because they make money it doesn't make them any kind of role model. Come on, it's just the same old story, isn't it? Gentrification." Piper bugged her eyes out and chuckled bitterly.

"Gentrification? No, no," Snowden shook his head in near confusion. "It's not gentrification when it's black folks moving back into the black community. It's . . . it's housecleaning."

"Great. So you got it all planned out, then."

Apparently Snowden did. Snowden had never really had a plan for anything, one that required sturdy bridges of faith to keep it connected. Rinsed by euphoria, Snowden kept going. Piper looked at him like he was glowing. It just encouraged him to burn brighter. He sounded like Lester himself, worse, like Bobby at his fevered best, but he wasn't channeling. Freed from the role of reluctant skeptic only to find himself a true believer. A dream was a drug. In a world without meaning, belief was an aphrodisiac. Snowden could feel it working on him, working on the woman across from him. So being a dreamer felt like this, having a belief brought this out in others. It made sense that so many dreamers were whores.

"Thing is, it has to be now. We don't have time to fool around anymore. The white people are coming. The island is full, they got nowhere else to go. They're scared to death of us, but that's how bad they need a place to live. If we don't start buying up this area, moving into its apartment buildings and staying there, in twenty years our Harlem will be lost. There's already a Starbucks on 125th Street . . . and it sure as hell ain't for us."

"I'd love to do a story on you guys."

"You should." Snowden smiled, pointed at her. "You met the other guys, Bobby obviously, Horus is the other one. Like I said, not that bad, really, once you know them, like most folks really. Whoever performs best this year is going to be promoted to oversee the whole thing, too, even get a house out the deal. I'm in the lead, I'm pretty sure. My boss has me doing a special project the others aren't even in on, things are going good."

"What kind of project?" Piper asked.

"Well, it's a little morbid, but when people die and nobody claims their stuff, I go in with him and we clean it all up. Mostly it's accidents, and it's just in this little area of Harlem around historic Mount Morris, up to Adam Clayton Powell, rarely above 128th or below 117th."

"That doesn't sound bad. You can't have to do more than one a month, right?"

"No, you'd be surprised. It's a rough city. You got to be careful in this place. Drugs, disease, stupidity. Old age. Mostly accidents."

"So come on, you can tell me," Piper leaned forward smiling, rubbing her hands together. "How often do people around here, y'know, drop off?"

"I don't know. I guess we're doing people almost once a week," Snowden said.

Piper pulled back, stopped smiling. "You mean that in this little area – what, a square mile, maybe two – there is at least one death a week, accidental?"

"Yeah, crazy right?" Snowden looked over the last of his platter for a discarded sliver of bass to nibble on.

"That's insane. You're pulling my leg, right? You're just messing with me." Piper said the last sentence like he'd admitted as much, grabbed the dishes off the table and started piling them for removal.

"Oh, I'm not lying to you, for real," Snowden pleaded. He wanted the smiling Piper back. He was pretty sure that one would kiss him. "I make a lot of extra cash for those days, so I know."

"But it seems like there wouldn't be that many accidental deaths in the whole city," Piper blushed back at him, offering innocent amazement. "That's so wild. Just out of curiosity, what were their names?"

BREAKING STORY

"**S**HE'S AN AWFUL . . . awful person," Bobby decided. He was drunk, lost his way after the third word of the sentence, found it again. Snowden agreed with him. Piper seemed all right to him, but for the purpose of this discussion, yes, she was an awful person. To jilt the person who loves her without even giving him the respect of acknowledgment makes her an awful person, in that moment. We are all awful people when we do that. Snowden raised the nearly dry remains of his own jug of malt liquor in salute to the truth of it, was reminded by its lightness that to go further into oblivion he needed more, but his tragedy was that he was too drunk to get up and get some.

"She was . . . there should be another word for rude. Something like callous, but harsher."

"Asshole," Snowden offered. Bobby burst out laughing at the joy of it, that the language hadn't failed him, that he wasn't going to have to learn French or create his own collection of syllables to give voice to his emotions. Bobby stumbled across the room to slap the hand of the man who pointed this out to him. They slapped bottles instead. The glass broke. Neither one acknowledged it, or looked down to where the shards had fallen, because neither one felt like being bothered to pick them up.

"She was an asshole," Bobby continued, getting a little more comfort from taking this woman who'd inexplicably consumed his mind, dumping her in the past tense and leaving her there. The two actually had more than a bit in common, Snowden registered. The passion, the moral certainty, the disastrous attempt at art. To his eye,

Piper's work looked like she subjected herself to paint colonics, squatted over the canvas and let go. Snowden burst out giggling at the thought. Emboldened by the sound of laughter, masculated by his protest, Bobby continued.

"I was lucky! She was an evil whore!" The last word Bobby screamed. Snowden sat with it for a little while and got uncomfortable. There was no form of torture that had been invented yet that would get him to disclose that he'd had dinner with her the night before, that she had in fact chastely escorted him at evening's end to the door, so Snowden protested on more general grounds.

"Dude, I don't know about that, man. I mean, you can't really say she was a whore, can you? I mean, it doesn't really apply here, does it? If she was a whore, she would have given you some, got you all worked up, then dissed you. This one, she didn't even bother calling you back."

"Hey man, I'm not talking in a literal sense! I'm talking in the sense that, I don't know, I'm a man and she's a woman and she did me wrong, right? Like, I can use it that way." Registering that the other was clearly unswayed, Bobby tried another vein of reasoning. "Okay, she was a whore in the sense, in the sense that she was nice to me that day, right? Real nice, so in a way she was kind of promiscuous with her . . . her politeness."

Both of the men became silent. Bobby's last comment sounded so stupid, Snowden felt as if it lessened him just to hear it. He just stared at his feet, watched the alcoholic optical illusion of the ground swaying beneath them. After a few minutes this way, Snowden accepted the fact that the snorting, gasping sound coming from the other man was crying, but he couldn't bring himself to look up and face it. Snowden literally couldn't, he was so drunk he felt like his head had been filled with BB pellets when he wasn't looking.

"The word *piper* means 'crackhead' in Philly," Snowden offered, head bowed.

"There you go!" Bobby pointed across the room, energized. "That's what I'm talking about!"

*   *   *

Just because every metal sidewalk door you've ever walked on has held your weight doesn't mean they all will. Some become concave from years of pedestrians and simply fold beneath that one foot too many. Sometimes there's rust, underneath where you can't see it, making it brittle like metal matzo. Step on the wrong one and you could shred an ankle, a kneecap as you loose the ground beneath you. Step on the wrong one and you can, your whole body, go right through. Who can say how far down it will be before you reach ground again? You can't. You don't even know how long it would be before they found you. It could even be one of those grates you tread over every day without thinking, like it was for Irene Bell of 843 Lenox, #4. One minor step in a day of many, the context changes and it's the final one. They find you two weeks later only because it smells so bad the Con Ed man checking the meter next door to the abandoned building thinks it's worth calling the cops over. Think of how bad that's got to stink, that a man would call the police in response to it. So many ways to die. If you don't choose one, a method will be appointed to you. Life's only guaranteed service.

Snowden wasn't exactly feeling sorry for Ms. Irene Bell. Part of this was due to the fact that when he opened the trunk she used as a stand for her small black and white TV he saw that it was filled nearly three feet deep in other people's wallets. The collection ranged immensely in size, color, and quality of craftsmanship. The ones at the top of the pile had stubs to recent movies inside them, the ones at the bottom held licenses that had expired years before. She deserved to die, Snowden decided. She deserved to die because everyone deserves to die, so really what was the point, which was Snowden's new attitude to death in general. There didn't seem to be any other way to deal with it.

There were moments still, like when Lester had him run an envelope down to a buyer on Fifty-first and Madison during the lunch hour, when he saw all those people and thought somebody must have figured out an escape. Staring at the thousands pushing forward, each one a part of the crowd he wished to avoid, Snowden

could believe that in the millennia of humanity surely someone had figured out how to avoid mortality. But that mix of optimism and paranoia never lasted long. No matter how many people, no matter how decent they were or how much money they acquired, the odds were still the same. Everyone was going to die. So how could you feel sorry for Ms. Bell, probably miserable in her dirty little apartment, going out into the city to ride the crowded subways in search of someone to lean against and steal from, to plant some of her misery into his or her life?

Snowden crumpled her designer dresses into balls and shoved them in one more trash bag and this time thought of how many days would be better without her. How many men would pat their inside pockets and women check their purses and see that what they worked for was still there and not even know they had a rusty basement grate and a twenty-foot fall to thank for it. Life has many stories, but one ending. Snowden decided it wasn't always a sad one.

Ms. Bell's apartment was done by one-thirty P.M. It was small, and Snowden was getting good at what he did. Sometimes Lester didn't even stay around anymore, just let him in and came back around the time everything was ready to be loaded, and Snowden didn't mind. Lester always put the soft rock station on the radio, and with him gone Snowden could listen to whatever he liked. In addition, Snowden had decided that all coinage on the floor (or not already in a purposed container) was his tip money, and isolation made the acquisition that much easier. Also, Snowden sometimes caught Lester staring at him.

At first Snowden thought it was to make sure he was doing the job right, and when he caught the older man doing it he would ask politely just that, and the answer was always pretty much the same: yes, that's it, good job, that's right. Then Snowden would pass a mirror and Lester would be in it, looking at the back of him like Snowden had a movie projected between his shoulder blades.

There were so many Lesters, Snowden began to feel, and some-

times all they seemed to share was a fashion sense. The regular workday version of Lester barely talked, only smiled for the customer, spent his time either off showing properties or showing up late and falling asleep in the back of the cab while the work was getting done. Not just naps, full-fledged sleeps, some going six or eight hours if the time allowed, waking up just before the sun went down again. The classroom Lester was a set persona as well, the interpreter of the real estate portion, the pulpit inferno for the historic and philosophic conclusion. Tuesday's "special project" Lester Snowden found a bit more laid-back, casual clothes that still managed to cover his body completely: turtlenecks with elbow-patched sports coats, slacks. On especially hot days, sandals. For some reason, Snowden found the site of Lester's hairy feet parti-cularly disturbing, perhaps because it was the only part of him approaching nudity. This Tuesday Lester had, on more than one occasion, referred to his charge as "Snowball." Even Wendell seemed more informal on their Tuesday encounters, walking over to Snowden's legs and leaning his weight into him as he slowly pushed pass. At night, Snowden's calves reeked of the mutt.

When Lester came back that afternoon, Ms. Bell's life had become orderly. She had gone to her grave, the clothes worth saving in the bags to the Salvation Army off Third Avenue, electronics in a box to the 135th Street Y, the personal items in a long plastic storage container just like the others, ready to be retrieved by whoever they held meaning for. The furniture was in two piles on opposite sides of the room, the larger of which was headed for the Dumpster, the smaller one to the prop warehouse on Twenty-fifth and Tenth, proceeds going to the rent Ms. Bell had apparently intended to catch up on before her fate caught up with her. The rest, which was most of it, garbage. Wendell immediately located the bag that held the former contents of the refrigerator, took a long snort, and walked away without being told to. When Snowden returned from his first trip down to load the truck, Lester was standing over the pile of wallets that Snowden had dumped in the bathtub pending further

instruction. Snowden watched as the older man churned the pile, searching.

"Crazy, right?" Snowden asked. "She must have been cleaning up for years. You should see some of the Afros in the pictures of the older ones. A lady, too. From what I saw in her pictures, looked perfectly normal, like a schoolteacher or something. Has to be a thousand of them there. Not one credit card in the bunch; she must have sold them. Can you believe that shit?"

Lester offered nothing in response. He kept shoving his hands in and up the pile like he was tossing a salad. After a minute, Snowden began wondering if he'd actually just said anything at all.

"I saw her," Lester offered. Snowden replied with a polite affirmative; the woman had framed pictures of herself all over the house.

"No. In person I saw her. Just a little while ago."

"You know what, that's funny because I definitely think I saw her too, probably when we moved that guy in on the third floor two doors over a couple weeks past."

"I saw her then, but before that," Lester said, still looking, still churning. Wendell was pushing up against him, annoyed that the expected hand with scratching fingers didn't come. "I was at the Schomburg, in the reading room. I was at the shelves. I saw her reach right into a man's blazer and remove his billfold from its inside pocket. Right there, in the Schomburg Library of all places. You'd think that all those books, all that history and knowledge, that it would keep the ignorant at bay, wouldn't you? That it would just repel a nigger like a church would a vampire." Wendell, either in agreement or impatience, started barking. The bathroom was small, lined with graying tile, amplifying the sound and sending both men's hands to their ears in unison. "Fucking bitch," Snowden heard Lester say as he reached for Wendell's mouth, but he was pretty sure it wasn't the dog he was talking about.

When everything was dumped and loaded, Snowden suggested they drop the licenses in the mail, that someone had done that for

him once and he was sure the former owners of Ms. Bell's booty would be just as appreciative. Lester loved the idea and took it even further, ordering that Snowden pack up the lot of them, wallet and all, and mail each one to the address listed. Snowden spent the first moment proud that his input was being respected, the next pissed at what the job would entail, and then the next six hours doing it.

After Lester dropped off the box of envelopes, he left Snowden there in the apartment of the recently departed. All the furniture was gone, so Snowden sat on the toilet as he worked, discovering the mailing address of each bit of stolen property and repeating it on the manila, sealing the package and throwing it in one of the white postal crates. Dizzy from the repetition, Snowden forced himself to speed up as the night approached, feeling increasingly certain he didn't want to be in the dead woman's apartment when it was dark.

By the time he got out the door and turned the final lock behind him, he was determined to start smoking. Its promise was the only thing that got him through the hours before. He would start smoking, not just an occasional puff, he would buy his own pack and take it up seriously this time. He would not fear the valley of death, he would buy a ticket to it, bring a reclining lawn chair, two towels, a Bo Shareef book.

Lester insisted that Snowden deliver the packages to a post office downtown. He did not want the reputation of Harlem to be sullied when the recipients saw the 10027 zip code, and Snowden agreed. Snowden pulled the lumbering truck onto the narrowness of the FDR, driving as slowly as he safely could in the newborn fear he would die with this cargo and be posthumously blamed for each of Ms. Bell's crimes, getting off at the first exit he could in midtown. After the job was done, Snowden double-parked in front of a kiosk on Fifty-seventh, still enamored with the idea of his new hobby. What better way was there to be rid of one's fear of death than to just embrace it and be done with the matter? Snowden stared solemnly at the packs lined topside out behind the attendant, understanding that the first pack would probably solidify a lifetime of brand loyalty and

addiction. Momentarily overwhelmed with the feeling of incompetence, Snowden banished the fear with the firm declaration, "A pack of True Greens."

The statement came from memory, in which it was accompanied by himself barely as tall as the counter at the corner store, a dollar and a quarter hot in the tight grip of his little fist. It was a later time, and these cigarettes cost more than those did, but when the guy handed the pack over to him, Snowden recognized them as his father's brand. He knew he'd asked for them, he knew that the guy inside the wooden box was not his dad but just another fathead man, but for a moment it was like he had asked for a smoke and his father had reached out and given these to him. A gift, or revenge. Snowden asked for matches.

Imitating the ghost, Snowden slapped the little box's ass four times before taking his teeth to the cellophane and folding the lid back. Looking off for a distraction from the meaning of his actions, he found one in the newly arrived edition of the *New Holland Herald*. The stack still had its white packing strips lying loose around it where they'd been cut. Snowden was looking at it, trying to discern what it was that made the front page look odd, and realized that the letter from the editor, the consistently well-written and intensely insane column that was one of his favorites, was missing, the absence of its always bolded text giving the tabloid a naked quality. Then he saw her name, and he thought, *I shouldn't have tried to kiss her.* They'd been at the door downstairs, and even though Piper Goines seemed a bit distant at the end, he'd gone for lips during the parting gesture, she to his cheek, both landing at an awkward place in the middle. Snowden scratched that spot like it itched him, saw the title ACCIDENTS HAPPEN? above Piper's byline, and that same hand shot out to bring it closer. HISTORIC HARLEM EXPERIENCES DISPROPORTIONATE NUMBER OF ACCIDENTAL DEATHS.

Snowden would never find a better time to begin his new hobby. Back in the truck, he was through his second cigarette and on to his

third when he got the strength to pick up the paper from his lap, shake off the ash, and turn it over.

The first skim was just a hunt for a name, his own, a blissfully unsuccessful one. The facts that presented themselves on the second read were actually less painful than the dread with which Snowden anticipated every word. It made the damaging point that life was a little shorter above 110th Street, the coroner's office was quoted as saying on examination that the number of accidental deaths in the last year in Harlem were almost as much as the number of similar fatalities in the rest of Manhattan, Brooklyn, and Staten Island combined, but the commentary that he sounded "surprised" was provided by the author herself, not the source, and the piece didn't depict the anomaly as anything more than what it was. It was certainly nothing to promote the real estate renaissance of Harlem, but it didn't seem to be anything to destroy the fragile boom either. It wasn't like they were muggings, rapes, drive-by shootings, or any of the other man-made calamities that would fuel the imagination of the outside world that Harlem was the hellish ghetto they feared it to be. The people there were just clumsy.

Inching back up the FDR with the rest of the late rush-hour traffic, Snowden felt relief replace the hollow flash of anxiety. By the Seventy-second Street exit, he was glad that this was all he had shared with Piper, that he hadn't had any more sensitive information for her to expose. By the time he'd reached the Ninety-sixth Street exit, Snowden was overwhelmed by a feeling of betrayal, all of Bobby's drunken admonishments flooding back to him. He was sure he had given Piper Goines his number, and even if days had gone by without him calling her, he wasn't the one with the reason to. Turning left onto the exit for 125th Street, it was this that stuck with him, that she'd used information from their private conversation, information given in an informal and confidential setting, and had used it to further her own career, her own ambition at getting a front-page story, and hadn't even bothered to give him notice of her actions. Snowden wasn't the type of person to feel justified indulging

in self-righteousness that often, so as such relished the novelty of it, drove straight to Piper's home instead of dropping the truck off.

The brother-in-law answered the door, the one she obnoxiously referred to as "Dumbass." Snowden recognized him, smiled, then recognized his reluctance to open the door. Relieved that Snowden was there to speak with Piper and not sell him something, the man's response was a quick smile and wink before turning around to yell a name Snowden didn't recognize. Flopping down the stairs, barefoot and pajama-bottomed, two feet on every step before going to the next one, was Piper. There was no rush, and when she finally got to the door she didn't open the screen for him. She didn't even ask, "What?" just her face did, and it didn't do it particularly politely, either. Snowden the Pious used this as motivation.

"I saw your article," Snowden challenged. Piper said nothing. She just kept looking at him, mouth closed, a big woman in a tall doorway.

"I can't believe you – "

"No!" Piper barked back at him. Snowden stopped, startled. He waited for her to say something else. She didn't. For a moment he was glad there was a screen door separating them; she was like a bear.

"What do you mean, 'No!'?" Snowden demanded.

"I mean, no. I'm not arguing with you. I'm not going to accept being yelled at at the moment."

"But I don't think you understand. I have the right to be upset here. You took what I told you in intimate conversation! You even pulled me along to get more, and then you published it for the world to see without even telling me. I could have lost my job! I'm the wronged party here."

"Fine. You're a wronged party. How about you come over in about three days, how about Saturday night, maybe? You can yell at me then. I'll set time aside, I'll make sure nobody else is home so you can really get loud if you want to, and then you can come over and yell at me. We'll make a date of it. I'll order pizza or something."

"But . . . I don't want to yell at you in three days. I want to yell at you now." It didn't seem true anymore. She'd exhausted him, derailed the passion he'd mustered. Now he was just thinking she looked cute like that: the man's white overshirt loose except at her breasts' roundness, the red plaid pajamas below. She had chipped paint on her toenails and for no reason that could make sense to him Snowden found that immensely exciting.

"Look, I'm not saying you don't have a right to yell at me. I should have told you, I wasn't sure if I'd go farther with it when you were telling me. It wasn't supposed to be on the front page. It wasn't even supposed to be printed at all; the typists, they picked it up by mistake during production and nobody caught it. I've been getting yelled at all day, three different people chewing me out. So if you want to yell too then you're too late, I'm completely numb now. You can come up, relax with me, because I'm in the process of getting drunk, but if you just came by to yell, then come back Saturday."

They made it as far as the entrance hallway just past Piper's apartment door, then spent the next hours on the long strip of rug there. The light in the hallway leading up to it was out and Piper held out her hand for Snowden behind her. It was small but strong, the plains of skin holding his fingers hard and round. Piper opened her door with one hand and in response to the darkness Snowden pulled his own back to him. Piper didn't let go, turned around and pulled him in fast, and Snowden's reaction was to kiss her. Snowden stepped back to check his libido with reality, save himself further misunderstanding and a potential parole violation and ask her if he should apologize for the gesture or offer more, but Piper didn't open her eyes, just leaned her head in for more.

On it, in it, during the moment. They could have easily gone left to the couch or right to the bedroom but they were on the hall rug and their knees were already bending, going down, and where was the drama in practicality? Piper thought, *I need this right now, I deserve*

this distraction, he is a pretty man, I am a woman, and don't I deserve to just once use a pretty man?

When Snowden awoke, Piper was at the windows, the ledge starting at her knee and rising nearly to the ceiling. Her pajama pants were on her and not inside out and in a ball next to him anymore. The way the streetlight came in through the blinds, hung in yellow bars on her and created a silhouette with the stripes of light on the wall behind, made Snowden want to go over and pull those pajamas off again, throw them in the same ball where they had fallen the first time. He got up with that intention, walked over to her, saw the stiffness in her stance, and remembered that she was a stranger, that no moment had been guaranteed beyond the one they'd just had, that if he touched her and she pulled back or was immobile the loneliness he was already starting to feel would crush him and he didn't even have his pants on.

"You know your friend Bobby sent a cassette tape to my job, I just listened to it today. There was a poem on it. I got really creeped out – it was my own voice from my answering machine spliced up, the words rearranged."

"I'll talk to him about that."

"Don't," Piper told him, her head leaning on the windowpane like she wanted to stick it through the glass. "The crazy thing was the poem wasn't that bad. It was about destiny, the importance of seizing your destiny, I think. It was actually really good. Once I realized that, I wasn't freaked out anymore. Mitigating circumstances."

"What are you watching down there?" Snowden stepped closer to follow her eyes to the street below.

"Do you see them? You should have heard them going at it. Is that what woke you up? Can you believe that? If he hits her, I'm going to call Giuliani's goon squad, I swear to God." Snowden saw the couple. The woman had her arms crossed, staring across the street at nothing. The guy was pacing like he was trying to wind himself up. Piper kept her arms crossed around her body but leaned

back into Snowden. Relieved, Snowden placed his arms around her. Looking below he saw the other couple and thought, *What's the difference between us and them? Three months? So let's enjoy this point now. Let's make this stage last and that stage as brief as possible.* Snowden smelled the oil in Piper's hair and wanted to pull her back to the couch, stared down and wished he believed in God so that he could pray that the other couple would clear off and let them enjoy their good moments.

"They were so loud they woke me up. I was having a good dream, too, and then they started. I think he hit her already, I do. I just want to see it before I call the cops. I don't want anybody to get shot for no reason."

In seeming response, the guy stopped his pacing for a brief moment, then sprang at her. His arms were straight up in the air to show his exasperation, so he was totally unprepared when she punched him right in the mouth, a full-bodied right hook that sent the man to his knees, trying to keep his jaw from coming off his face by holding it with both hands.

"Should we call the police now?" Snowden asked. She kept hitting him. From his knees the man collapsed forward, tried to hold her arms, but she just started screaming, so he gave up, rolled himself into a ball and let her pummel him. The woman screamed, cried the whole time like it was her that was on the receiving end.

It seemed to Snowden another half hour before the couple joined each other arm and shoulder and dragged their heels over to Lenox so that he and Piper could do the same to the couch a few feet away. The scene had outlasted Snowden's arousal. Piper went to the kitchen, took a bottle of bourbon off the counter and two glasses, so they went down that road instead.

"That's the thing about living in the city, you see everybody's business up close. Whether you want to or not. At least here they're all strangers." Piper sat down on the couch's end, guided his hand to her side. Tall water glasses sat on the coffee table, both filled with an inch of alcohol.

"I hate the city," Snowden told her. "Harlem's OK, and I'm going

to try to do this, try and give to it for a while, but when I get my nest egg I'm going to get a nice place way outside the city, someplace cheap where the money will last." Snowden was always tempted to discuss nesting after new sex, even in cases where he doubted it would go much further, like this one.

"No. You don't want to go out there. There's nothing outside of the city limits. It's like Mississippi out there. Upstate New York, New Jersey, Connecticut, Pennsylvania? Mississippi. Just rednecks. All looks the same, too, north, south, it doesn't matter. Nothing for black folks. This is all we have. That's why making this place livable is so important."

"Not that far out. Like, the suburbs. They got folks in the suburbs. Shit, like the place you grew up, that's what I'm talking about. Start my own family out there, kids running around – "

"Running around, draining the energy out of you with every step, taking a year off your life for every one they get. Selfish, destructive, constantly demanding vacuums, that's what kids are," Piper spit. "And talk about loud, your little suburban world sounds about as quiet as a school bus."

"Rather hear that than this four-fifteen in the morning argument in the street stuff. In the suburbs, summer is nice and calm like it's supposed to be, relaxing." Snowden was smiling, hands before him like he was holding the dream up for Piper to get a look at. She wasn't looking at it, she was looking at him like he was a madman. Like a madman had sneaked into her apartment and had sex with her.

"Summer in the suburbs isn't relaxing. Don't believe that. Suburban summers are not relaxing. It might be stiller at night, just the hum of a hundred air conditioners, but all day, you never heard anything like it. Lawn mowers, constantly. Not a lot of grass, just people mowing their little lawns, going over the same patches over and over. So scared something's going to grow, something wild, they're out there all the time, wasting fossil fuels, creating smog. Weed whackers, hedge machines, blowers, it's crazy. Then you've got

all those damn ice cream trucks. So loud you can have all the windows closed, the air conditioners going, the lawn machinery roaring, and you can still hear their electric music box sound playing the same four bars over and over, because that's how they want it. Not just one truck, either, a fleet of them, one showing up before the last one can disappear. Can you imagine how insane you have to be to work in one of those? Or how nuts it drives them to hear that same song, over and over, every day for months? Sure, they're selling ice cream, but that's not what it's about. The ice cream, that's just to support their real agenda, to drive you as crazy as they are."

Snowden looked at her in awe. She was Bobby's soul mate, he was suddenly sure of it. She was just as crazy, in just the same way as he was. Snowden couldn't even look at Piper, the guilt of his betrayal so palpable. Maybe there really was someone out there for everyone. Maybe Bobby had found his one, that one person in the world who would put up with his combustible insanity. Maybe the woman Snowden had screwed on her hallway floor without a moment's consideration really was Bobby's one chance at happiness.

"I'm sorry," Piper said. She'd hopped closer and laid her hands over his own. Snowden looked at her and couldn't figure out what transgression she was referring too. "I should have called you, told you I was working on it. I just got so excited, and I didn't even think it was going to be published this week, it wasn't supposed to be. But I don't know if I would have told you before next week's issue, either. I might have, but who knows? But I wasn't trying to use you. I certainly wasn't trying to single-handedly destroy the real estate market in Harlem."

Snowden shrugged before responding. "Look, lady, I'm going to ask you something, but y'know, it's not based on anything but my own paranoia." Snowden paused, tried to think of a good way to ask his question, but couldn't find one. "It's just . . . everything is kosher, right? It's not like there's some psycho killer walking the streets they don't want us to know about."

"Oh my God, wouldn't that make a great story?" Piper mused

wistfully. "Sorry. People like that, they kill in patterns, similar ways, similar people. I looked, trust me."

"So there's not like a Chupacabra monster running around?" Snowden asked. He tried to laugh at the question but it just came off like a nervous tic.

"Wow. That would be cool. Can you imagine how many *Herald* copies we could sell? But there's nothing. Totally different people, obvious circumstances. I mean, there's dumb things. Like, I got all excited because I noticed in the coroner's reports that a bunch of them all had five-dollar bills in their pockets, at least twenty bucks' worth. But then, some didn't, and there's always some stupid stuff like that, some little coincidence that if you look hard enough you can connect. That doesn't mean it's not meaningless."

Don't carry any more five-dollar bills, Snowden told himself. He could do that. The key to irrational fear and superstition is getting them to work for you. It wouldn't be hard to get rid of all his five-dollar bills; Snowden always considered himself more of a one-dollar-bill man.

Snowden leaned forward, started kissing on her neck, wanting to make sure that if another night like this one didn't happen he had covered every inch of her.

Snowden tired. Snowden drunk. Snowden left Piper's and was back at his building as the sun's first rays streaked across the sky. Not caring about previous arrangements or responsibilities, just that he had to pee, and then he had to go to bed, and hopefully in that order. Snowden ran into Jifar sleeping across a step on the flight that separated their apartments and thought, *Come on, man, not now, give me a break,* but didn't register much more until he unwrapped the boy's blanket and saw the child's unconscious face, its new symmetry with a swollen eye on one end and a busted lip on the other. Snowden said his name, crammed in a progressive number of grim conclusions before Jifar blinked back at him. "What's wrong with you?" the boy managed. Snowden lifted the boy up, kept walking. First it was just

the weight of Jifar in his arms that kept him from going back down and banging on the door so the father would come out and Snowden could pound even harder. Then, after he'd laid Jifar on his couch and was forced to pause in contemplation for those two minutes standing before the porcelain bowl, it was a combination of exhaustion and rational thought. Snowden allowed himself to walk out of the bathroom and continue straight to the bedroom by pledging, *I will take care of this. I will do whatever I have to to change this situation, tomorrow.*

THE MUSIC MAN

S NOWDEN WOKE UP late because he didn't want to do it. Then he heard the bastard singing "Super Freak" from his bath as the water pipes whined, and he'd had enough. Two sets of knocks and then Baron Anderson answered the door.

A bathrobe nearly as worn and frayed as he was, both of them dripping. Jifar walked between his father and the door, the plastic shopping bag of ice cubes Snowden had given him discreetly removed from his face. Anderson didn't ask where his son had been, gave no more than a casual glance noting Jifar's presence and appearance. If there was guilt, if there was concern there, it was not being offered for public consumption. Just annoyance. Just a motion to close the door that was aborted with the look at Snowden still standing there, shoulders squared.

"What?"

"Could I talk to you?"

"I got work to do. I got things I got to accomplish." The door seemed leaden, its weight pulling it shut with little resistance.

"Jifar's a good kid."

"That's right, Jifar's a good kid. I don't need you telling me that, I'm his father. I got to go to work."

The door had almost closed when Snowden's foot shot forward to halt its progression.

"Look, I wanted to tell you, I know about this special boarding school. I think it'd be good for him. It's right in the neighborhood. I think I can – "

"Don't think, man. Don't think. That's your problem, you're

107

spending your time thinking about shit that don't got a goddamn thing to do with you." Grunting out the last words, Baron Anderson turned his energies away from polite conversation and toward trying to shove his front door closed despite the sneaker blocking it.

"That boy's face – " Snowden gave up and started pushing awkwardly to keep it open, hoping Jifar was in his own room behind a closed door so at least he didn't hear the grunts of the struggle. Anderson kept muttering "nothing to do with you," like if he said it enough times Snowden would believe him.

"You know what, I got to see that boy in these halls all messed the hell up, so it's got something to do with me. I got to hear you abusing the kid through my floor all the time, then it's got something to do with me. Don't think I won't call the police on your ass." It was the last, hollow threat that got the door to stop shaking.

"What the fuck? Man, I don't need this. I don't need this from the likes of you. Call the police, then. You know what? Call them. I want to know what my boy's doing up in your apartment all the time. I know he's there, I can hear him watching his cartoons through the ceiling. Get them coppers in here looking at you."

Like most smelly, feral animals, when cornered Mr. Anderson could display impressive pugnacious ingenuity. Particularly the ability to locate weakness and exploit it immediately. "That's right fool, and I want to know what the hell he was doing sleeping up there last night. I woke this morning, didn't see him, I was worried sick. That's right, punk. You don't mind your business, I'm a give those cops a call, figure they'll want to know too. You like prison? They sure like your kind in prison, I can tell you."

Snowden had a property to clean later that morning. A tenement, much like his own but farther along in its process of being converted to a decent building. Of its nuisance tenants, three overcrowded apartments' worth had belonged to the superintendent, a grumbling grub of a man who for over a decade had made a habit of demanding bribes to provide the most basic of his duties. He'd

had a verbal agreement with the previous owner to house his entire extended family in exchange for keeping the repair prices down, an arrangement that immediately dissolved when Horizon purchased the building. (Apparently, the entire gene pool was now creating havoc out of a one-bedroom apartment in Paterson, New Jersey.)

The other problem tenant was the guy on the third floor who liked to club and who liked to come back from the club and continue the party back home even louder, speakers in every room as well as aimed straight out the window, and dance or screw at an even louder volume. His greatest skill was his ability to turn off his music and lights as soon as the summoned squad car pulled onto the block. Then one night he went out and a couple of days later the other residents realized they'd had a suspiciously quiet string of restful nights. The only reason anyone finally noticed he'd gone missing was he'd left his shower dripping. After a week it'd managed to swamp the whole apartment and leak through to the one downstairs. It was the middle of the night; firemen had to break in the door with a battering ram. He never came back home. Everyone chalked it up to another victim of the gay life. It was horrible what happened here, Snowden thought. It would take three layers of varnish just to bring the floor's shine back.

Inside the Horizon office, Snowden could tell it was Halloween because Lester wore a black suit, orange shoes, plastic ghost cuff links, and a large pumpkin on his tie with a smirk much like Snowden's own.

"The importance of style is not to impress, nor to conform to the expectations of the masses, Snowman. It is to manifest an aspect of your soul externally."

Lester walked around his office whistling. It made him seem relaxed. Too relaxed, it suddenly seemed, and Snowden was hit with the guilty thought that Lester had seen Piper's article, that he knew where she got the idea and, when he least expected it, Lester would fire him. It was an attractively paranoid thought, but it made Snowden smile to himself at its absurdity almost immediately.

Everybody knew no one read the *New Holland Herald*. It was absolutely dreadful. That was the existential beauty of the paper: It was reading material for illiterates.

"Can any child, or at least one that a Horizon employee recommends, be admitted to the Little Leaders League?" Snowden asked to get his mind off of it. This question had actually been planned in bed that morning, made moot by Baron Anderson soon after, and was only offered to inspire further questions, as it did. Snowden, in the mood for the catharsis of confession, told Lester all of it. What the boy's beatings sounded like through the floor, the shade of Jifar's bruising the night before, how gentle the kid was, Baron Anderson's implicit threat of blackmail, and even a description of what the bastard's voice sounded like singing "Brick House."

Into his folded hands Lester nodded. Snowden was down to the detail that the hairy freak had the nerve to reek of Johnson & Johnson's Baby Shampoo when Lester stood up to close his office door, went to the file drawers behind his desk, and opened one.

"That's the apartment directly below yours. Is that B. Anderson?"

"That's him. That's the guy, Baron Anderson."

"Arrested 1989, Disposal of Stolen Property. Again in '93 and '97, same thing. The guy's a fence. He works at a pawn shop at 117th and 2nd."

"How do you have all that? Did it come up on his credit report when he applied for the apartment?"

"We have information on all our residents with criminal backgrounds. You wouldn't believe how helpful having strong connections with the parole board can be, with a mission like ours. Look here, Mr. Anderson has been investigated twice in the past four years by Child Welfare for endangerment. Two different social workers," Lester read. Snowden kept waiting for something that pointed to some great Explanation, something that would solve the situation and absolve him of further action. "Apparently the man is very neat." Lester looked up, impressed. "Both visited in response to complaints by neighbors. No female relatives to take the boy in, no easy

110

answers. Neither case worker saw fit to recommend difficult ones, either. Very clean, though. They both mentioned that."

"That's great. The geniuses at Child Welfare. See, that's why I would never bother calling those people in the first place, they just make things worse. Cleanliness. Oh, the place is really clean, so . . . whatever. Cleanliness is what matters." In response to Snowden's remarks Lester checked his fingernails, shrugged like it might be possible to argue that point successfully.

"Look, you really want to address this situation?" Lester asked. "You really want to take care of it, like a man, and put this guy in his place? Then it's not a problem. I know how to handle so-called men like this: You put the fear of God in his black ass, if you'll pardon me. If it means that much to you, we'll just go in there and make him understand in his own language that if he doesn't stop taking out his aggressions on the boy, we'll take ours out against him."

Snowden was laughing at it, the image in his mind, the insanity of it. "OK, I like it. No really, it is very good. The only thing is, we're not exactly the type to inspire 'the fear of God,' are we? The fear of gosh, maybe."

"Snowball. Don't underestimate the cowardice of bullies, or the element of surprise. I have keys to all the Horizon properties, correct? Next time he has one of his bathroom concerts, we'll arrive. Tonight, for instance, would be perfect. We're having a Halloween party for the students, just tell this boy to come, get him away from this. It's dirty work, there's no shame in flinching from it. Trust me though, a threat to their own mortal coil is the only thing bad people understand. This will work; it always does. Think of it as property management in its purest form."

Snowden, whose only alternative idea was to get Jifar to shove a couple of five-dollar bills in his dad's pocket to attract the Chupacabra, said, "Sounds like a plan."

It was a bad idea. At the time Snowden agreed to it, it was a bad-yet-tempting idea, but the tempting part didn't last long. After Snowden

had walked an excited four-foot Chupacabra (or four-foot mutant frog – Jifar wasn't married to any one interpretation of his costume) over to the Horizon Little Leaders League Halloween Party, after it had gotten dark outside, Lester's plan no longer seemed tempting at all. It was just bad. Snowden left his boss voice mails hinting at his new opinion, but there was no return call. Snowden was on the phone to give it one more try when he walked from his kitchen to his living room and saw Lester right there. Sitting on Snowden's couch. Legs folded, dime-size embroidered black cats hissing a line up his gray socks. The only changes to his earlier attire were black gloves and a matching hair net that made it look like a giant spiderweb had formed over his head.

"See? I know how to enter quietly. Mr. Anderson does sing a bit loud, doesn't he? I just heard him in your bathroom. You were right, a weak baritone under the delusion he's a tenor. Dreadful. Let's go get him."

Lester's hand on Baron Anderson's doorknob moved slower than the minute hand on his watch. When the door finally cracked open, the whining first bars of "Let's Get It On" jumped out. They walked inside. Lester started taking off his shoes so Snowden imitated him. The stench of sesame oil was so strong it conjured images of sesame seeds as big as almonds. The apartment was dark, nothing but the light from the windows and the illumination coming from the bathroom down the hall. From it, Baron Anderson yelled, "We are all sensitive people / With so much to give!" Lester lined up both sets of shoes along the door perfectly before rising, walking toward the light, the sound, the man.

"There's nothing wrong with me!" Baron Anderson declared into his microphone, and then Lester kicked open the door.

Lester walked into that bathroom like it was a hotel lobby. His first action a deft swat to the power button on the stereo machine by the tub. "We are the ghosts of Halloween past!" he declared into its silence. Baron Anderson covered his genitals. Considering the

situation, Snowden thought this was a rather odd first response. That Lester was smiling as much as he was, that was odd as well.

Anderson noticed Snowden behind the odd man, cursed directly at him as he moved a hand from his groin to grab the side of the tub to lift himself up to attack. He managed to make it to the bent-kneed position of an upright Neanderthal before Lester could remove his snub-nose pistol from his coat and push it to the side of Baron Anderson's head.

It was a bad idea. I don't put myself in the middle of these situations, Snowden assured himself, *these situations hunt me down and swallow me.*

"Now you relax. That's your job right now, relaxing. Lay back down. You ask nice, we can even turn on the hot water if you start to get cold. It is kind of cold in here, isn't it? You cold, ghost?" Lester turned back to Snowden to ask him, pushing his gun farther into Baron Anderson's temple as he did so.

"I'm fine, sir," Snowden told him. Snowden was near the toilet. It called and teased him as every liquid inside Snowden all of a sudden wanted out.

"Good. Now everyone's comfortable so we can talk. See, we got a problem. You know what that problem is? Do you know?"

"I don't know what the fuck your problem is but I'm – "

Lester had large hands for a man his size. Laid perfectly flat and slapped quickly across Baron Anderson's face, his head shooting back as if it had been hit with equal force by a large timber product, oak or elm. Lester's hand, however, was just soft enough that it left no mark beside a moment's blemish.

"No vulgarities, thank you. So, as you might have guessed, our problem is you. Let me explain. You see us here." Grinning, clearly enjoying his own performance, Lester motioned back and forth between himself and Snowden several times before continuing. "We are good people. We are among the people trying to make something for the folks in this community. We are the people who make, you see? You, on the other hand, are of the people who take."

"I didn't take nothing – " Another hit. If Anderson paid better

attention, he could tell when the blows were coming because the gun lifted off of his head slightly right before the impact.

"Metaphorically. You are a drain on our community. Better example: You know the word *nigger*? Do you know why it's so offensive? Because it refers to people like you. People hear the word *nigger* and they get that disgusting image of you in their minds."

"I'm not the problem! That child molester behind – " This time it just took a hand pulled back to shut Anderson up.

"No lying," Lester said before leaning in closer. "We know how you been treating that boy. The beatings. The insults. Evil. It is the moral responsibility, the job, of the strong to protect the weak. How small are you, how weak must you be, to ignore that?" Baron Anderson didn't look weak to Snowden at all. In fact, Snowden found the man rather threatening despite his current situation. All he had to do was imagine the retribution the man would exact later to see him as strong. Of course, there would most certainly be retribution after this performance. Lester was a fool, or insane. The only reason Snowden didn't stop him was that the damage had already been inflicted and there was nothing to do but enjoy this section of the disaster that would surely unfold.

"I'll assume for a minute that you don't know any better, that you were raised by a beast who did the same. That is a travesty; one can only hope that you will fight to change your ways, because either way the cycle will be broken. Our people can't afford another generation of males raised by wolves to drag us down. Don't you see that? We simply can't afford to waste our energy on people who act like you. So I'm going to let you in on a little secret. Can you keep a secret?" Anderson nodded in response.

"That's good, because this is a big one. OK, here it is. It's about accidents. The thing about accidents is that the cops never bother to look further. It's not like on TV – the police simply don't have the time. As long as there's no reason not to, they just take it on face value and go on to more pressing matters. No investigation, no autopsy, nothing. But that's not my secret, here's my secret: You keep

treating your boy the way you been, the next accident's going to happen to you." Baron Anderson was crying now. Not sobbing, just tears. Angry ones, like a pot boiling over. He was shaking as well; the way Lester had his hand around his neck, it was like he was trying to keep him still. "Since we are decent people, we're giving you one more chance, one more opportunity to find salvation and change your ways. If we hear any more crap about you mistreating that angelic little boy, though, see as much as a bloody knee, then we're going to kill you. You having an accident is as easy as – ghost, get me that sing-along thing."

Snowden went over to where the karaoke machine sat on top of the toilet basin. It was as big as the thing it was sitting on, covered in colored knobs that had been lit and flashing when they entered the room. Snowden picked it up. Might as well break it, Snowden agreed. As long as they were here.

"Give it to me."

Snowden walked over. Still sitting on the edge of the tub, Lester kept his gun on their host, had one blind hand out to receive it.

"It's heavy," Snowden warned him.

"I know what I'm doing. Give it to me, I can handle it," Lester told him. Snowden decided to agree with him, just because he wanted to go home and have this be over. One hand armed and occupied, Lester reached down underneath the middle of the machine with the other, balanced it against his arm. Lester turned back to Anderson, unsmiling. "If this monstrosity just happened to crash down into the water and give your life a little poetic justice, no one would think to look for any other cause of death, or want to." Baron Anderson, naked and fetal in the gray water, flinched, but it was because Lester didn't really have a good handle on the karaoke machine, and its falling weight alone was capable of damage. "Put this back now. It is important to respect the property of others." Snowden walked forward, tripped on its industrial cord. It was not enough to send him falling, but was enough to do that to the large electrical appliance in Lester's hand.

To his credit, Lester compensated with his arm as the karaoke machine jolted away from him, but it was his overcompensation that sent the appliance backward, down into the tub in little hops as it bounced off Lester's desperate hands. All he succeeded in doing was knocking the power button back on, giving it a moment to flash frantic and scream wordlessly before going down into the bathwater of Baron Anderson.

The white flashes came from the front of the machine as the water poured in the ventilation holes in the back. The blue flashes came from where its cord met the socket in the wall, streaks that left smoke and brown marks on the surface around it. Snowden, who kept shooting his hand toward the plug only to pull it back when an electric flame shot out again, was in part relieved when Lester held him back from trying. Past him, Snowden could see Baron Anderson sharing his favorite place with his favorite possession. He wasn't shuddering violently as Snowden expected. Instead, Snowden watched as Anderson remained nearly still throughout the ordeal, every muscle clenched in unison until the lights went out.

In the dark, Snowden said: "Oh shit I think we just killed Jifar's dad."

Lester shuffled through his pockets blindly, responded by illuminating the room with a penlight. They walked over to the tub together. The dim yellow glow encircled Baron Anderson's face. It stared intently at the side of the tub from beneath the water.

"Accidents happen. You just tripped on a cord, no reason to suffer for that. Go down the hall, wipe off everything you touched with your hands as we came in."

"I didn't touch anything," Snowden said. This was a plan. Plans were good in times like this one.

"The inside front doorknob, the space in the middle of the wall where you leaned to take your shoes off. I saw you. Start with this door here and that monstrous noisemaker." Lester laid his flashlight down on the sink, aimed up toward the ceiling. It didn't give much light but enough as their eyes swelled out of necessity.

Snowden rubbed hard. Snowden rubbed his way toward freedom, up and down the length of the door, in places he could have possibly glanced standing. Lester took Anderson's pants from where they sat on the toilet seat, unfolded them, picked up the coins that fell to the floor. Finding the wallet, Lester laid it on the sink's rim before putting the pants back. Pulling his own wallet from his jacket pocket, Lester worked carefully trying to open it with his leather gloves on but gave up and took them off. The faux Caucasian skin of latex gloves covered Lester's hands. "Germs," he said when he caught Snowden looking, and began counting his money, whispering the sums as Snowden waited to move past him to rub down the murder weapon in the tub.

"Just give me a second. Five, ten, fifteen, twenty, twenty-five," Lester said as he tallied his bills. Snowden was still, yet still managed to become frozen.

"What are you doing?"

"Well, we don't want this looking like a robbery, do we? Not even a murderer would resist stocking up on spending money on the way out the door. Makes it look more like an accident, and that's good for us. It's what's best for the neighborhood." Lester put the bills together neatly and placed them into Anderson's nearly bankrupt wallet, folded it up, and stuck the contents back into the pants. Snowden took a deep breath after moments of no breathing at all, his lungs as preoccupied as the rest of him.

"But why . . . why did you use all five-dollar bills?" Snowden managed.

Lester, realizing that the other had no intention of passing him and getting on with his job, relaxed back into the middle of the small room once more.

"What? Does that really matter right now? No reason. All right, then, the only ATM I can use Uptown without the dollar-fifty surcharge only carries fives – better to serve the broke, I imagine. Banco Republic, crappy services but the interest rate on checking is way better than Chase." Lester laughed. Snowden didn't. Snowden

was too busy grabbing the toilet plunger, aiming the rubber end like a sword at Lester's head as he backed out into the hall.

"Get the hell away from me man, I don't believe this shit! You did this. You set me up!"

"Snowden please, this is a stressful situation, I know, but this is not really helping. This was just an accident, calm down."

"This wasn't an accident, none of them are accidents, they were you!" Snowden, overwhelmed enough that when the wall hit his back it was a surprise to him, darted the plunger forward to stave off an imagined attack.

Lester looked back, shook his head in disbelief, folded the chinos in his hand to a perfect re-creation of how he found them. Snowden saw himself reflected in the frown, saw that the one obvious madman in the room was the one who seemed poised to defend himself with suction and potty germs. The deluded one. Snowden dropped the plunger on the floor, put that hand to his head, started to apologize when Lester interrupted him jovially.

"Five-dollar bills! You know what, that is just too crazy. All night, ever since you came to me with this, really, I wondered if you already knew. It's so wild how your mind plays tricks on you because part of me thought you were just playing along the whole time." Lester, grinning, rubber-covered hands in the air in surrender, or as if he wanted to reach up and feel the moment. "You got me! You really did. That's so funny because at times I feared I might be leaving behind some sort of unseen connection on all these bits of social gardening, but I never would have caught that. I've got to tell you: You are going to be such a fantastic addition to the Horizon inner fold. Five-dollar bills; you must tell me how you came across that connection. Later, though. For now, finish cleaning up this place. Don't worry, I know you can do it. You've been doing a great job of removing evidence from crime scenes for months."

SITUATION

"**H** E L O O K S A little . . . peaked," Cyrus Marks noted. "Does he always look like that?"

"No, no, not at all. I think it's just the stress of the immediate situation. And I gave him a Valium as well." In response to a look, Lester followed with, "Just a Valium, just one. Just to calm him down."

Snowden was sitting on his usual chair in the lodge's basement classroom, the other two men were in front of him. Cyrus Marks with a brown yarn mane circling his head, whiskers drawn with greasepaint on his cheeks, a plastic cup of fruit punch still gripped in one felt paw as it was when Lester pulled him from the children's party. Snowden was silent. Snowden had nothing to say anymore. He kept thinking he would start talking again, but since they'd left Baron Anderson's it hadn't happened.

"If you're worried about the boy, don't be," Cyrus Marks consoled. "Of course he'll have some sad days ahead, but after that his future will be brighter than it's ever been. Lester already introduced . . ."

"Jifar," a smiling Lester helped.

"Right! Jifar, already introduced him. A lovely, sensitive boy. Intelligent. You can see it in the eyes. He'll come here now, and he'll fit into the Little Leaders League perfectly. Several of our young ones were the offspring of accidents."

"Almost all, actually," Lester clarified. Cyrus Marks nodded in agreement, leaned in closer.

"It really is an amazing program, now that you're moving closer to

the inner circle I can tell you. Some of the best tutors in the city, museum trips weekly – we really take advantage of all New York has to offer. We're even planning a new language component, we'll have them fluent in French in two years. Plus, of course – did you tell him about the scholarship fund?"

"No! Not yet, I didn't want to spoil it. Snowden? Snowden? Can you hear me? You'll like this, listen."

"All of their college tuition will be paid for. Horizon has done better than even I could have planned. I'm selling vacant shells right now I bought at forty thousand dollars for ten times that! If the housing boom continues just a bit longer, we'll even be able to set up graduate school funds as well. Imagine that. Not only are we breaking poverty's cycle of ignorance and violence, we are literally producing the next generation of leaders right here."

"Why?" Snowden muttered. It was a breakthrough. Snowden said it several more times immediately after, each utterance bringing his mind closer to the surface. Cyrus Marks is dressed as a lion, he realized. The congressman is dressed like a lion but still reminds me of a hedgehog, only now he looks like a hedgehog dressed up as a lion.

"Why? I think I just explained a good enough reason to you. In the larger sense? It's time. Harlem, like so many black communities, has just been getting by for years now. We've been treading water, focusing on keeping afloat. Thing is, we've never swum ashore because so much of our energy goes toward overcoming the leaden weights – like your Mr. Anderson – that pull us down. It's simply time to cut them loose, isn't it? Move on."

"There's something wrong with my ears. I hear words, but none of it makes sense. Lester? I think it was that pill you gave me."

"I just gave you one Valium."

"Lester." Snowden turned to him not in search of a sympathetic ear but out of the hope that he was the less mad of the two before him. "What you're talking about, what you're both being all matter-of-fact about, it's crazy. You know that already, right? You're talking

120

about killing people. Shit, you're talking about lynching! You can't commit . . . atrocities and think that good can come out of that."

"Oh but Snowden, it does!" Lester said, looking to greet Cyrus Marks's gaze so they could nod back and forth their mutual agreement. "It's very sad, really, but if you look at history, you'll see that almost all drastic social improvement is the result of moments of inhumanity. It was the staunch disregard for the humanity of blacks and Indians that made America the great nation it is today. The world can be changed. A terrible beauty is born all the time."

Cyrus Marks, hand on Lester's shoulder, interrupted. "This is a new age, Mr. Snowden, we need new ways of doing things. My generation, the last of the civil rights warriors, we've done our part, but our way of thinking and fighting has become as old and weak as our bodies. We were raised to fight white oppression, and guess what? We won! Not every battle, but that war is basically over, as we knew it. Nowadays, black folks' biggest problem isn't white racism, it's *ourselves*. White people aren't breaking into our homes, attacking us on the streets, or selling drugs to our children, it's black people who terrorize us, isn't it? You don't fight drug lords like Parson Boone with marches, sit-ins, or rallies. Harlem doesn't need another mural or community center, another law or bill, we need new blood, new ideas to fight new enemies. That's why you're here. This is your destiny. This is our last stand."

"But I don't want to stand. I don't want to stand for anything," Snowden told Marks, but the congressman wasn't listening.

"Those coons, those liabilities who hold us back, will be eliminated! In their place, we're bringing the best and brightest of our people to make this place thrive again. We do a dark deed, my brother, but when the price is paid Harlem will become the shining jewel of the black world it was meant to be. Harlem is a symbol! Imagine what it would mean to all those other ghettos across the world if we could prove that it is possible for the oppressed to rise

from the ashes, seize their own destiny, and thrive like never before. Don't you want to be a part of that?"

"Wow . . . You're really fucking nuts, aren't you?" Snowden said. It wasn't even meant as an insult. It was an observation. Either way, the older man leaped from his seat and in an instant had both thick hands around Snowden's neck, his momentum knocking the two of them to the floor. Once there, Cyrus Marks continued trying to slam Snowden's head into the linoleum, the smell of his boiled cabbage breath stronger with every word.

"Now you listen to me, you little shit! You're already so deep in this you should be breathing out the top of your head. We could go to our friends in the police department and get them to book you for Anderson or any of the other executions you've been cleaning up after and leaving fingerprints behind for months. Don't think we couldn't use a fall guy: No corporation ever has enough insurance. In light of Lester's recommendation, though, I'm going to forget your attitude. I'm going to chalk it up to nerves, little Cedric, give you a second chance to redeem yourself. You're going to pay me back with two – "

"Fuck you," Snowden managed to get past Marks's choking hands.

" – three more accidents. Lester needs a break anyway. If, at the end of that period you want to quit, I'll let you. I'll have enough leverage on you to last a fucking lifetime. If you shock me and rise to the level of the challenge, learn to believe in the wisdom and importance of our mission, then you will be a welcomed permanent addition to the cause. How's that? You have my word. The choice is yours, then, so enjoy it. It'll be your only bit of free will for a while."

The congressman found his way back to standing, carefully brushed off his fur. Snowden stayed on the cold linoleum until Marks had left. Lester offered his handkerchief, then his hand.

"Well, that certainly could have gone better, but surely it could have gone much, much worse too. Our congressman is a very

122

passionate, driven man, that's what makes him so good at everything he attempts. Does he remind you of your father?"

"What? No. Why would he? My father was a loser. He was vicious and crazy, too, so I guess there's some similarity if that's what you're going to go by." Snowden wanted to cry. He scrunched up his face, tried to cry, but nothing came out so he gave up.

"Come now, it won't be as bad as you think. I'll help you with your assignments, teach you the tricks. No rush, we won't be dealing with any accident business for a while, anyway. You probably didn't see it, but an article slipped into the *New Holland Herald* that touched a little close to home on the topic; we're working to figure out its source. Just in case though, I think all around a break is needed."

Snowden sat at attention. Snowden's mouth forced into its first smile of the evening. "I did see that but I'm sure it's nothing. Nothing to be concerned about. I mean, let's face it, it is the *New Holland Herald*. I mean, nobody actually reads that rag." Snowden tried to smile.

Lester covered his mouth to contain his laughter. "How irreverent, Snowden. You are just so bad," he giggled indulgently.

Snowden took Jifar back from the lodge with him. The boy had made friends, it was the first time Snowden had seen him with children his own age or that happy. Back at their own building, he knocked on Jifar's front door like he actually expected Baron Anderson to open it, thought he heard a noise on the other side and became utterly petrified that the knob would turn. The image stayed with him in sleep, was not evaporated by daylight when he and the boy were back again, banging loud enough to wake the dead if that was possible. Jifar slept on the couch, watched cartoons and three *Planet of the Apes* sequels, and didn't seem to get worried until it got dark once more.

Lester buzzed the cops in. The boy was upstairs eating the ordered pizza; Snowden spent most of the proceedings sitting on the step Jifar used to sleep on. They walked in, they walked out,

Snowden looked shocked when they told him. That wasn't hard, the hard part was not seeming like he was in a state of shock when he called 911 and they showed up in the first place.

Lester went off to intercept Child Welfare, Snowden went back upstairs to tell the boy. Jifar took the news of his father's death fairly well, Snowden knew, because he had no real understanding of what it meant.

Snowden knew what loss meant. Jifar's crying over the next two days, it was just the harbinger of the real pain. Snowden also knew guilt and profound regret, and understood that as agonizing as it was to listen to, it was only the beginning of his own suffering.

None of Jifar's cousins were prepared to take him in, but Horizon of Harlem was, and those relatives who cared in any way about the boy were thankful for it. They toured its halls en masse after the funeral, marveled at the Little Leaders League's fully loaded toy room in the basement, the oak walls of their dining area, the luminescent glow of their computer room. Thank God for these good people, they said to themselves as they signed the papers. Maybe they were right. Maybe some good can out of this, they told each other as they left Jifar behind.

OH TANNENBAUM

PPARENTLY SOMEBODY DID read the *New Holland Herald*, it just took a week. The issue in question almost made it successfully off the stands without incident, was a day away from being replaced by a newer edition destined to go equally unnoticed, when political events brought the eyes of New York to Harlem and then suddenly left them there with nothing to look at.

The source of Snowden's misfortune was an improbably large pimple on the nose of the former president of the United States of America. It was a painful, intrusive ball underneath a red mound of porous skin, and the moment it broke through in a white dot smaller than a period, the leader of the free world attacked, against the advice of his closest advisers. Sadly, the move proved an impertinent one, as the zit became infected, and the following morning returned fire with an expected display of swelling and pus, so that no amount of professional makeup could hide it. Luckily, the president had just recently finished his term and left office, so all public events scheduled for the day could be, and were, canceled. Despite the fact that all the news crews had arrived and were set up there waiting for him.

So apparently, somebody did read the *New Holland Herald*, somebody associated with UPN 9 News, who was spied on by someone who leaked E-mails to WB 11 News, who employed another person, whose idea of corporate sabotage was to call in all proposed exclusive stories to her contact at New York 1, because by eleven-thirty A.M. all three set up live feeds on 125th Street to run with the *New Holland Herald*'s front-page story.

Their broadcast vans double-parked, their field reporters impeccably manicured, they may have arrived to cover an appearance by the ex-president to announce the site of his new office (canceled due to "flulike symptoms"), but now they fought vigorously for positioning on the filler story. UPN 9, the first to arrive, maintained their positioning at the entrance of the Adam Clayton Powell Federal Building, while the crew for New York 1 maintained their position across the street as well, satisfied with the more scenic view of the entire structure in the background and confident they could keep their presenter standing in just the right position that his head would block out the sight of the UPN 9 crew and van behind him. WB 11 chose instead to broadcast a block away and use the Apollo Theater as a backdrop, partly because it was Harlem's most recognizable landmark and partly because the WB network had recently begun airing reruns of *Showtime at the Apollo*. The onsite producer had received a call, soon after the presidential story was delayed and the unusually high accidental death rate filler was pushed in, that this location would be in his best interest.

The three men of the Second Chance Program sat in the lodge's basement classroom, one profoundly miserable, the other two simply happy that this morning was not one of the ones when they were required to move something heavy. It was a beautiful thing, getting up tired and feeling the remnant of every muscular overindulgence, walking into a house and seeing the couch, each chair and dresser, and not having to motivate your body to abuse itself once more in the process of lifting them.

Mr. M. R. Linden brought his typical level of passion to his lecture topic of the day: creating and facilitating a bidding war on a property. M. R. Linden kept using that word for it, *war*, repeating it regularly with visible relish, the tick-sized beads of his sweat re-forming every time he wiped them away. The basic point was simple: Force the buyer to bet not simply on the worth of the property but also against the net worth of the fellow bidders, and the settlement price inflates to a figure all parties would have laughed at the beginning of the

seduction. M. R. Linden's technique, that's where the beauty was. The "missent" faxes and E-mails, assisting the banks in preapproving loans far beyond the interested parties' intended mortgage range "just to be sure," the early "steadfast" bidding due dates that induce high offers to serve as mere starting points when the date magically became malleable again. When Linden concluded, Horus was so moved he provided a one-man standing ovation, one that M. R. Linden took solemnly and with much grace, offering a simple, courteous nod before turning his cell phone back on and departing with the same swiftness he arrived with. Silk that fine made no sound no matter how thick the legs it covered or how fast they walked away.

The Chupacabra was dressed in purple, a melanzana suit lined with golden pinstripes, violet dress shirt, gold socks and tie, his processed hair ever wet and parted to the other side on this day for no given reason. Lester began his portion of the day's lesson as he often did.

"Why are we here? Are we here to make money?" The way Lester said it, the disgust on the final word made even Horus respond in the negative, give his one-word answer with nearly as much conviction as he had just shown at the prospect of ripping people off. Snowden looked over at Horus, looked at the tiny pupils dotting the whites of his eyes, and was convinced you could bring in fifty different insane ideologues in as many hours, each contradicting the last, and Horus would believe every one of them equally. There was a gang lord somewhere in Chicago missing this guy. There was a neighborhood out there were he remained, as myth, a resident.

"Then what are we trying to make here?" By this time, Lester had preached the Horizon message so many times he could come in cold, not having lectured since the week before, and his crowd was still warm for him.

"Community," two said in unison. Snowden remained silent, engrossed with staring at the floor, imagining what hell would be like beneath it.

"I think I heard a whisper. I said, I think somebody forgot and left their radio on because I heard the whisper of a word but I don't know what it was."

"Community!" the three screamed. Snowden felt nauseous but yelled with the others anyway just to move the day on so he could go home and cry again.

This goal asserted, Lester began to diagram the preferred Horizon buyer, a status not achieved by a high bid but based on the other assets this prospective resident brought to the community. At the top of the list were families with children, nuclear and otherwise, in which the adults were heavily invested in those children's education and lives in general. These were given a happy face on the black-board. Four quick strokes done effortlessly, not since Michelangelo had there been a freehand circle as true as this one. Conversely, parents and/or guardians who were involved in their careers and/or social lives at the expense of the children's needs, or adults whose children had an established history of antisocial behavior, were given a thumbs-down, a symbol Lester took the time to draw, knobs for the four folded fingers and the nail on the downturned digit included. Same-sex couples and households where the adults had an ongoing record of community involvement were given a happy face as well. Same-sex couples, particularly male ones, Lester explained like he wanted his class to write this down, on the whole were more likely to invest in their property and its general appearance, those without children having a much greater disposable income and time to invest in the community in general.

Credit ratings, no matter how disparaging, should be considered only if they displayed a clear weakness of character. Credit card debt, in fact, could be erased with the purchase of the house, included in the price of the home and then passed back to the client as a rebate to assist him in lowering his interest payments, getting him on the right track to afford the household maintenance cost he might not be prepared for.

Lester was in the process of telling them how to enable a happy

face buyer with bad credit to circumvent the bank when someone knocked on the door behind them. All turned, all surprised, because while they'd certainly heard a door knocked on in their lifetimes, they had never heard this one. Snowden, closest to it, got up and walked to it when no one else did. It had opaque glass at the top of it, and the light was on brightly in the hall leading to the stairs beyond, and Snowden could see a little brown head at the bottom. Swinging the door open, it wasn't Jifar but an even younger boy who walked in wearing the Little Leader sports coat and went to Lester with a note in his hand. The child was no higher than Snowden's belly button and at no more than six years of age could not have written the message he was offering. After reading it, a blank-faced Lester picked up the child and held him at his side like a monkey as he walked out and closed the door behind him.

"He's coming back, right?" Horus asked no one. "Cuz, yo, I did the homework. Whole time I was in school, I think I did the homework maybe once. Y'all read that stuff? I loved that shit."

Bobby enjoyed the fact that both his and Snowden's seats were just far enough behind Horus's that he could offer mocking glances and not get his face punched in.

"I knew you'd love that one," Bobby offered, the smile he was wearing hidden in his voice.

"*The Art of War*," Horus said, turning around to hold up the title to them as if on their desks were not two identical copies. "I heard about this shit before, but yo, I didn't think I could relate like that. That part about training the harem, that's for real. I seen that before, no joke. Back Chi-Town, there was this pimp down by the old stadium, a Ranger, had a stable just like that. Killer hoes. He trained them, I bet he read that shit. Straight up, cold-blooded killer hoes. Sounds funny but I ain't even joking. I seen them jack a nigger up before, right in front me. That's all a general is too, a pimp getting you to sacrifice yourself for what he wants, just like a ho."

Snowden was actually disappointed when Horus's take on the philosophy of Sun Tzu was interrupted by Lester again at the door,

this time saying class would be canceled for the day and made up the following Thursday, when the only move on the schedule was a studio coming up from ninety-third and Columbus. By the time the three had rebuttoned their jackets, repacked the briefcases they'd appropriated just for this occasion, Lester was nowhere to be found. Upon walking out the door, Snowden could hear the unusual sound of a television coming from upstairs.

It was a lovely day with only a few hours wasted. There was a deep blue above them that stretched all the way across to tenement horizons. There was elation on the part of Bobby and Horus, and they insisted on sharing that with their inexplicably gloomy competitor. The president was supposed to arrive today, they could go now instead of waiting for their lunch hour. Horus, determined not to let Snowden slip home, clamped a hand on Snowden's slumping shoulder as they passed his block, kept it there firmly until they'd walked two streets past it.

With no radio present to inform them otherwise, they walked over toward the Adam Clayton Powell building to see the former leader, but more to participate and witness the spectacle it would create. It guaranteed to be an impressive one because this was a president so beloved by black people that he was referred to with some regularity as "the first black president." Unfortunately, this was not because the white man had shown an emotional commitment to the black community, though he had, but because he grew up on welfare in a broken home, was raised by his mother, couldn't keep his dick in his pants, and had a penchant for big bootie women, but when you'd never had a president to call your own you didn't get particular.

For years, every black bookstore and stand had sold a pamphlet claiming several presidents as secretly black, based on unreliable reports of distant African ancestry. However, most of these presidents hated black people anyway, so what was the point in claiming them? It was refreshing to have a president who publicly embraced his perceived "blackness," who truly loved black people,

because this is what it was all about, anyway. This was the only voting issue in the black community. Education, drugs, crime, affirmative action, all secondary, none of them driving masses to the polls. The only issue black people voted on en masse was whether the candidate hated them. Loved was better, but a rare luxury. This was what they asked, this is what they responded to. This is why some politicians could propose a bill for slavery reparations and still most black folks wouldn't vote for them: because they could look at their lips and see the word *nigger* floating effortlessly between them. They would vote for a crackhead if they knew he had a place in his heart for them.

When Snowden, Bobby, and Horus arrived to find that no crowd had assembled in front at 125th and Adam Clayton Powell other than the one that always surged there, it was Horus who was most disappointed. He had, repeatedly, pointed out the fact to the others that he hadn't been laid since Chicago, a period of time going on five months now, a span of drought he claimed was unheard of. This comment was usually followed by a complaint about New York women, "Them bitches act like they don't want to speak when you call them out on the street" being Horus's primary grievance. Considering the ex-president's well-documented sexual escapades, Horus was expecting a legion of lustful females in attendance, scores of potential "Horus Adorus" to recruit from. It was due to Horus's insistence that instead of turning around, the three instead found themselves in front of the chipping white paint of the once majestic Hotel Theresa, amid the small crowd surrounding the television news crew set up there.

For producer Byron Harding, the objective of field reporting was not simply to announce information, but to capture and convey the energy of the location itself. Anchors could give facts, what field reporters offered was feeling, bringing news to life for the viewers. For this reason, when conducting street interviews, it was always his mission to select people who truly represented their environment.

On Wall Street, whenever the financial news crossed over into the mainstream coverage, it was important to have at least one man in an expensive suit, one floor trader in his signature jacket, and one street vendor, for the everyman color. In Chinatown, older Asian market women were preferable for an emotional, less educated response, and younger Asian student types were pulled for the more intellectual commentary (glasses preferable). On the Upper West Side, white women with strollers and white men in casual clothing, both between the ages of thirty and fifty were essential. On the Upper East Side, older women in expensive outfits were all you were looking for, preferably with small dogs in hand, captured under the awnings of their buildings and with doormen behind them. Of course, there were always other people in all of these neighborhoods, out-of-place ethnicities and classes either passing through or local minorities, but Byron's goal was to get the true voice of a community, the archetype with an opinion.

So Byron was doing a story in Harlem. He had already taped two morbidly obese black women, one of whom had actually reached into her shirt and pulled a Kleenex from her bra to wipe her forehead during the interview, a detail he was particularly pleased with. Byron had also collected tape of several large, sweating dark men, the kind he associated with Harlem, but while all the sound bites had been good enough to edit down to the fifteen-second piece they were being collected for, he was still searching for that one interview he needed to collect before they left for Chelsea and their next story. The interviewee with a bit more color, the easy plug-in for the closing of the segment. One of those salt-of-the-earth characters places like Harlem were associated with in the minds of the viewers, a much less refined and much more flamboyant character who would speak his or her mind with little regard for restraint, propriety, or grammar. Byron Harding wouldn't have used the N-word. It was always a shock, considering his understanding of Harlem, that it took so long to find the right one. When he saw the answer to his problem approaching, a muscular, feral, brown-skinned man in a

green suit covered in luminescent gold buttons and tassels, all Byron could think was, *Jesus Christ a walking Christmas tree*, thanking the heavens that he worked in the age of color television.

When the camera crew charged in their direction, Bobby and Snowden spread with the rest of the crowd. Horus didn't even shift weight from one leg to the other. Whether it was that there was no question in his mind that he was their target or he simply didn't get out of people's way as rule was uncertain. Snowden watched him and he didn't even see Horus glance at the camera, he was so captivated by the woman who came with it, the one with the makeup too heavy for the weather, the primary-color ensemble, and the microphone.

"Sir, are you a Harlem resident?" the woman asked. Luanda something, Snowden recognized the woman from watching her in other neighborhoods talking about their problems. She was usually the one they brought out when it had to do with Negroes. Next to Horus she looked like a mannequin for children's clothes. Why were they all so short in person? Wasn't there one tall person out there insecure enough to sacrifice all for fame too?

"Fine, fine lady, I am not only a Harlem resident, I am the salvation of folks who dream of being a Harlem resident. I am the man who makes that dream come true. Horizon Properties, ask for Horus when you call. Horus, like the black god, not like the thing the Lone Ranger rides on." Horus reached into his uniform and whipped out one of his business cards like the reporter had asked for it, but as soon as she hesitantly reached out to take it, Horus whipped it away, held it up with two hands by its corners against the camera lens. The look of the producer looking back at this fool: like he'd just won something. Smiling, giving the camera and reporter the thumbs-up to continue.

The reporter, behind the press badge and mask of makeup, was Luanda Mullins, once ashy kneed like the rest of them, her own baby-powdered chest the closest she ever got to white skin growing up in Spring Falls, South Carolina: how sick was she of this shit? When am I going to just take this microphone and hit someone, be

133

they coon or coon hunter? How can I make a difference if by the time I'm in a position to do so I've given up so much of my soul? Luanda Mullins, reporting for WKPS News, leaned the microphone forward to the latest amusement, promised herself to make a three-figure donation to the Urban League tomorrow and an equally expensive visit to her massage therapist that night.

"Are you aware that a recent report done by the *New Holland Herald* shows that residents of Harlem have a forty-two percent greater chance of accidental death than any other neighborhood?" Horus took the information, curled his pointer finger over his lips and bowed his brow, but only long enough for the gesture to be registered, snapping back immediately to his previous position.

"Well, as you know, Harlem's own *New Holland Herald* is a very respected paper with a long tradition — I myself am counted among its readers — but I would have to disagree with the article itself, the way you're telling it. I am an extremely graceful individual, and if y'all are saying black folks are particularly clumsy as a people, I got the names of several hundred millionaires in the NBA who might disagree with you." The last comment almost got Luanda Mullins to laugh, an urge exacerbated by desperation not to do so. In exchange for his lucid, if odd, statement, Luanda decided to offer him the benefit of the doubt. Maybe there was a reason he was dressed like that. Maybe the Universoul Circus was in town.

"So you don't think there's anything odd about it? Have you heard people saying it's the Chupacabra running around?"

"What the hell is that? They like the Latin Kings? I'm from Chicago, I don't have no type of association with those dudes."

"No, it's an urban myth, a monster. Just, could you give us a comment on whether you think this might put a damper on its current real estate boom?"

"Harlem is the savior of New York City, the top of the island because that's where cream rises, understand? There ain't no problem up here. Where else in Manhattan you gonna go, you gonna get a beautiful brownstone for under five hundred thousand

dollars? Where you going to rent a fine two-bedroom for less than fifteen hundred? The only monster around here is me, sweet thing, and I'm a monster of love."

The last sentence got edited. So did the bit with the business card. The rest didn't. Horus was shown in mute clips behind the teaser ads in between the cartoons until the four o'clock news finally came around as promised. After that, aside from the begrudging nod between six-thirty and seven P.M. to the entire world that somehow existed outside New York City, the segment played regularly at twenty-six and fifty-six past the hour, sports then weather, then Big Daddy Horus breaking it down.

Every time he saw it, Snowden noticed something new about the moment as well, like Horus giving the reporter a long wink after his "graceful" line, or the look on Snowden's own gray face behind Horus's right shoulder. That Snowden kept mouthing "oh shit" to himself for the length of the interview, a fact that had not Bobby joyously pointed out Snowden would have remained unaware of.

Every single time, at twenty-nine and fifty-nine past the hour, the anchors concluded with commentary on either Horus's personal appearance or his visible interest in their windblown coworker. Every time they found this funny, more so as the evening continued. By the news's final episode, the last representation of the present before reruns promoted the past again, the sports anchor, a white man much too old for his haircut, followed the clip with the sole comment, "Thank you, General," and the entire cast lost it. The weatherman, by breed a particularly jolly fellow to begin with, was literally caught off balance by the comment, falling off his stool and to the floor in laughter, taking several once neat piles of notes with him. Laughter could be heard coming from off camera as well, both before and after this minor accident. As the light dimmed on the set, Snowden could see the outline of the four who remained seated, their heads bowed, their backs bouncing, each to the rhythm of their own hilarity.

For Snowden, it didn't get old either: that sinking feeling it evoked, the way it made his nipples poke firm and the top of his lip sweat though no other part of him did. The growing certainty that he would spend the rest of his days in prison and then in hell if the Christians were right about the afterlife. In Snowden's imagination Lester mouthed "loose lips sink ships" as he "accidentally" pushed Snowden over his own building's banister.

"Look, I don't see what you're getting yourself worked up about. It's not like this is going to ruin the market up here," Bobby offered. "It sure as hell doesn't help, Snowden my man. People already have enough little horrid fantasies about Harlem, but it's not like everything is over. It's just an anomaly, there're tons of old folks and users up here messing up the curve. Look at it this way, with the housing situation as tight as it is, the more of them that knock off, the more places we got to move people in. By 'any means necessary.'"

"You know what? That's a cliché."

"No it's not, it's a quote. I am a literary writer, Snowden. I don't deal in clichés," Bobby dismissed.

Snowden ignored Bobby Finley, kept drinking. He'd started at two in lieu of pizza but threw up after the first telecast so felt he had some making up to do.

"I wish I was Catholic," Snowden confessed. This time it was his turn to be ignored as Bobby desperately surfed channels for something as absurd as Horus to keep his good mood going. Snowden wished he was Catholic because he wanted to do some talking. He gave himself a count of sixty during which he would tell Bobby about his side project, about Jifar's dad and his final song, even how he'd messed around with Piper and told her about it, that she'd blown the whistle and they were all surely doomed now, them, the Little Leaders, even Harlem. Bobby lay on his couch atop a layer of rejected pages of *The Tome*. Their sense of housekeeping — yet another thing Bobby and his soul mate had in common.

"I slept with her," Snowden offered. It was meant as an opening toward much greater revelation, a warmup. *I am a sinner*, he heard

himself saying. The engravings, the monks' self-mutilation and torture, Snowden understood them now. Catholics could drink as much as they wanted too, the religion was made for him, he could only hope he'd remember his conversion tomorrow.

"What the hell are you talking about?" Bobby asked, but there was already pain there. There was already a mental image because, even though he wanted it to be different, at the vague reference "her" it was Piper Goines he thought of.

For Snowden's part, it was simply stunning how quickly his desire for self-flagellation and revelation abandoned him. In the moment between when punishment was instigated and the blows were to come, it had absconded, leaving a flow of dread to fill out the cavern burned by desire. "Oh shit" once again emerged as Snowden's mantra.

"Look, I mean, you were right about the whore thing. Totally. She was just not your 'one.' I think this just proves that more than anything."

"You fucked her." Bobby had picked up his lighter, was practicing opening the lid and lighting it at the same time with just a snap of his fingers. Perfect every time. Snap and then whoosh and then there was this flame as long as an erection, blue and narrow, lighting up Bobby's face and the room beyond it. The sight turned the remaining waste in Snowden's bowels to liquid. Hearing his intestines gurgle like a novelty straw, it was with some awe that Snowden noted, *Wow, I'm so scared I'm about to poop myself.* Lying seemed a better alternative.

"Yo, my man, it was after, after you said you wouldn't have anything to do with her. Days past, you already made it clear you wasn't interested, that she was not the one. I ran into her at a bar, we got drunk, it was awful. An awful, skanky thing. I was immediately ashamed of myself. I just tell you this to, you know, confess my sin to you. I am so, so sorry. And you were right, she's a bad, bad person. And she hurt me, she hurt me too. I got seduced, then she used me, and it hurts, man. It really does. I just wanted you to know that you were right all along. She's evil. I just should have listened."

Bobby said nothing, his face boiled featureless. Snowden hung, waiting to be cut down with a response. After a few more snaps of the lighter, Bobby finally put it away, leaving his arms dead at his sides. Snowden attacked his forty. It was full, but he would empty it, use it as a polite excuse to call an end to the night instead of simply sprinting out the door like he wanted to. Bobby stood staring at him, his arms not even swaying at his sides, as Snowden's bottle went straight up in the air like he was balancing it on his lips.

"She just wasn't the one," Bobby repeated back to him, minus all intonation. "I was clearly mistaken."

Snowden didn't even bother mumbling out a response. Bobby's words seemed the kind of thing someone says aloud just to hear the truth resonate.

The ache in his eyes was the only thing that got Bobby to start blinking again. His body, tired of waiting for its orders, took over. Bobby suddenly became animated and stepped toward him. In response, Snowden took the proactive measure of bracing for the blow. When Bobby merely grabbed Snowden's empty bottle and headed for the kitchen, Snowden didn't abandon his expectation or stance: arms wrapped around his head's top and bottom, both knees pulled up to protect his chest and abs. *I am not a coward, I am Armadillo Man*, Snowden told himself. Waiting for the pitch and the forty bottle to come flying, Snowden watched through the gap between his elbows as Bobby placed the empty in the trash, pulled a full bottle from the refrigerator, opened it with that rubber thing by the sink before walking back to him. Snowden's muscles relaxed and fell to the floor like dead rose petals, his smile of appreciation just that much wider because the gesture was unexpected.

It was that smile that woke up the brain that had for the last minutes been simply floating passively in Bobby's head. Impulse outgunned restraint and Bobby pushed the bottle past Snowden's hand, turned it over, and began pouring the contents into his guest's lap. Then he just held it there, staring into the eyes of the other.

It was not the gesture that scared Snowden, it was that Bobby's

eyes weren't even angry. His mouth was breathing heavily and his chest bounced below it, but his eyes were dead like there wasn't a damn thing their owner could do that would disturb them. They were all mad, the men of Horizon, even the best of them. Snowden remained seated, took the glare and offered his own learned numbness in response to it. The beer soaked Snowden's pants, the couch, and the papers around him. The sound as it left the bottle and made its way to the hard floor died down, and then Snowden listened to Bobby's breathing even clearer until he decided to walk off down the hall.

At the door, Snowden paused, called back, "So I'll see you at work tomorrow?"

"Tomorrow," Bobby offered. "You'll be working for me next year. You know that, right?"

Snowden was so drunk he didn't care that he was walking down the street looking as if he pissed himself. He didn't, but what if he did? To the few people he did catch looking he was like, "Come on, now you mean to say you've never peed yourself before? Never felt the shame and release as the warm spray runs down to your legs, unbound? Who among you can say that?"

At his door he barely managed to locate his keys, get them out and working to keep from peeing himself for real. A struggle through the dark, into the bathroom where he did his business and left his jeans hanging over the shower curtain. It was Snowden's habit not to turn on the lights when he came home on nights like this: The orange glow of the street lamps provided enough to get by, any more would tempt him to toward distractions that would keep him awake until it was time to go to work the following morning.

Tracing his fingers along the walls down the hall toward the kitchen, Snowden adhered to the greatest lesson his father ever taught him: how to avoid hangovers. As he had so many nights, Snowden found the bottle of vitamin B, chased down five pills all at once with the jug of water from the refrigerator. It was after he'd put

the jug back, in the fleeting light of its closing door, that he turned and saw the dead body lying on the couch past the counter.

Snowden stood as still as the jar of grease by the stove, the box of cereal in front of him, and every other inanimate object in the room. The flash of light had left him momentarily blinded and he was absolutely certain that if he turned on a lamp there would be nothing on his couch at all, and not because it had been an optical illusion, either (it hadn't, it had been a man), but because it was the ghost of Baron Anderson, come back to haunt him for tripping on the cord and stealing his son. Snowden was absolutely certain of this and equally so that he didn't want to witness the miracle, that it would scare him even more than he already was and force him to believe in something he'd rather not even if true. Then it farted and Snowden yanked his longest knife out of its drawer before hitting the light and finding Lester passed out on the couch, shoes still on.

The light did what the sound didn't, Lester blinked a bit as Snowden stood in disbelief before him. The man looked startled at first, as if it was his home that had been invaded, his eyes blinking till they were answered with the replacement of his glasses.

"You have beautiful legs," Lester managed. His voice wasn't slurred, but even the drunk Snowden could recognize that the man was floating several miles above his usual plane.

"Sir?" Snowden looked down at his own boxers, made sure his penis wasn't hanging out. I am standing here with no pants, my boss has broken into my apartment, stoned off his ass, and I'm not dreaming. "Sir, what are you doing here?"

"No, no, I ain't the one in trouble. You the one in trouble." Lester's voice sounded like he was talking in his sleep. Snowden kept the knife in front of him, but Lester paid it no mind. His lids kept nodding, his voice trailing out between sentences as his eyes skipped open and closed.

"You told that woman. That paper bitch, the one you're fucking." The most terrifying thing about what Lester was saying was not that he knew it was Snowden who'd leaked the story: Snowden assumed

that eventually he would get busted. It was the lazy way that Lester mentioned it, no hint of taunt or recrimination, casually adjusting the pillow beneath his head as he talked. It was as if Snowden's most private actions were Lester's common knowledge.

"It's all right, though. A couple, a couple TV spots, that won't matter. We're going to take care of that, take care of your indiscretion."

"So I'm fired now. You want me to leave?" Snowden asked. The Peter Pan bus rode to Philly all night, at least that was a way out of all this. Lester laughed at him. "You're cute, I mean that. You ain't fired, you ain't kicked out the program, and you ain't going nowhere. You just screwed up, trusting her. Trusting anyone. Not fired, just back with the pack. You was in front the other two, now just running with the pack again. You still got the potential. Just can't mess up no more." Lester's last words drifted off when he did, were replaced by the much louder sound of his snores, and still they managed to scare Snowden enough that he kept the butcher knife in front of him until his hand cramped from gripping so tightly.

Snowden remained standing in his underwear waiting for more. "It's hot," Lester finally mumbled, eyes still closed. He was right, the radiator had the room so hot the windows were steamed.

"Help me," Lester said, his arms hanging out limply before him; he hadn't even loosened his tie. His forehead had been invaded by an army of sweat beads, they joined into battalion streams to invade his pillow. Snowden opened the window, stuck a fan in it. Accidents happen. They'd both cleared out the slovenly apartment of a senile senior citizen after she'd fallen victim to the last heat wave of the summer. Her windows were painted shut and at the time Lester had said she hadn't called about it. Now Snowden could clearly see him painting her windows immobile in June, then refusing to return her desperate calls to fix the hazard.

Lester stopped his latest round of snores, grumbled, "Undress me."

The knife placed on the coffee table, within reach, Snowden went

over to him cautiously, started untying and pulling off Lester's shoes. Yellow socks, so much foot powder that when Snowden yanked them free the cloud sent him sneezing. Lester responded by cracking the bones in both feet unconsciously before rolling onto his back, arms passively bent up to the sky like a newborn. "Shirt," he said.

The tie was a clip-on. A couple buttons down the front and a closed-eyed Lester responded to the stimuli by assisting Snowden with an effort to pull his own limbs out of the sleeves. Snowden could see the needle marks that lined the veins of Lester's arms even in the dark, like chicken pox on parade. We are all weak, they said to him. Count how many times I gave into temptation. Snowden was considering shoving Lester's arms back in his shirt so he could play it off in the morning, but then he looked down and saw his boss staring at him.

Lester beckoned lightly with his other hand for him to come closer. Before Snowden could pull away, Lester had raised himself close enough to whisper something in his ear. Snowden gave up, leaned into it, but the secret became a kiss when Lester finally reached him. It landed on the side of Snowden's nose, was wet, quickly turned into a tongue licking lower before Snowden could yank away, offer, "Sir, you're wasted," as an excuse for him.

"Just because I suffer from a chemical addiction doesn't mean I'm a bad person." Snowden heard the voice and opened his eyes and there Lester was, sitting on the foot of his bed, fully and impeccably clothed. *No, you're a bad person because you kill people*, Snowden kept thinking later. "Quite the contrary, I hope you've realized that by now. Everything I do I do out of love, for the betterment of our people." Crisp shirt, pants pleated, starched tie, hair greased into its permanent currents, the only evidence that proved to Snowden the reality of the night before was the fact that it was six A.M. and Mr. Lester Baines was sitting there on Snowden's mattress.

"I've had my sorrows, my weakness, like many men. I understand loss, I don't take what we're doing lightly. It eats at the soul, I'll warn you, but we too must pay a price for our goal."

"Yes, sir. I totally understand. You have my word. Really," Snowden said, politely waving him away, but Lester just took a seat beside him on the bed.

"I lost someone. He was very dear to me. It makes things, I find things . . . difficult. At times, difficult."

"Me too."

"No disrespect to you, your home, then," Lester said standing up again.

"None taken."

"I've decided that, outside of work, you can call me Lester. Respect."

"Respect," Snowden repeated back to him. Then Lester was gone. Snowden listened to his boss walk down the hall and lock the front door from the outside with his own set of keys, then spent two unsuccessful hours trying fall asleep again.

CHUPACABRA

T O B E B O B B Y Finley on the following morning was a beautiful
thing. The night before it seemed a dire lot for sure, but the next
day, when Bobby woke up in the fetal position on his bathroom
floor, his spirit traced the sunbeams back out the opaque window,
past the sky and into the starlit heavens far beyond. When he got to
his feet, Bobby realized he wasn't drunk anymore. It was as if in that
last bit of violent vomiting before he passed out he had rid his body
not only of the remaining alcohol but also of the months of romantic
indulgence he had poisoned himself with. Such foolishness, that
Piper Goines thing. It seemed now only one more bitter taste in his
mouth to be spit into the Irving Howe with the rest of his bile.

Bobby was very much a man who believed in lessons. From every
misfortune, no matter how grave, he searched for the golden rule to
be salvaged, that thing to keep the experience from being a complete
loss, to comfort himself that the same situation wouldn't happen
again. On November 7, right there in the bathroom of Apartment
16, 342 East 123rd Street, Bobby Finley declared the End of
Romanticism. No more carelessly using the L-word, misusing his
heart as if it was no more than his liver. From this moment forward,
Bobby swore that he would treat his own affections with the
solemnity and respect they deserved, not throw them about without
care and then become hurt when others treated them in a similar
manner. When the one came, he would take his time in identifying
her, would not be foolish enough to be confused by something as
insignificant as the cut of her clothes, the relative pleasantness of her
face, or her physical conditioning. When looking for a soul these

were all just hindrances. As a popular song of his youth had put it, "Never trust a big butt and a smile." This shall be my motto, Bobby decided.

So much is said about being in love, finding love, losing it, why had no one raised the trumpet for having no love at all? Devoid of the phenomenon, Bobby felt light, buoyant, prone to giggling fits and whistling, both of which he stifled on the job, particularly around Snowden whom he was no longer mad at but was punishing by pretending he was for the remainder of the week. Of course, the woman Piper Goines could clearly not have been the one. The one would be his complement in every way, she would certainly share his passion, his idealism and dedication to uplifting of the race, his artistic fury. There was no way a goddess such as that could be attracted to the likes of Snowden.

Snowden was attractive in the purely physical sense, granted, Bobby could see that, but Snowden was so determined to believe in nothing he'd made that a belief system in itself. The man was dedicated to no more than getting unharmed from one day to the next one, shrugged lazily at this Horizon opportunity when it should have sent his heart soaring. Snowden preferred tuning the radio to the Top 40 station and never got sick of those same songs over and over. Although he claimed to be a book lover, the only thing Bobby'd seen Snowden read consistently was the sports section of the *New York Post*. For the love of God, the guy was a Bo Shareef fan. Snowden provided entertaining company, true, and Bobby did enjoy him as a complement to his own admitted intensity, but that the Goines woman had chosen Snowden as a lover was irrefutable proof that Bobby had been blissfully mistaken. Snowden's betrayal was a blessing, actually. It left no echo of doubt in Bobby's mind that an error had been made.

Snowden, for his part, adopted a demonstratively sullen posture he'd abandoned years before. It started at work as a ritualistic display of submission for Bobby, like a dog rolling onto its back to show its belly, but Snowden noticed his mood remained the same when he

was off the job as well, home alone with no one to perform for. The week that followed was a somber one. Regardless of the time he spent on the dilemma, no alternative course of action that didn't involve himself in jail for the rest of his life and all the Little Leaders being sent off to foster homes presented itself. During his most optimistic moments, Snowden hoped that Lester and Cyrus Marks would decide that enough community pruning had been done and forget the whole thing.

Aside from brief encounters with the clients in the morning, Lester was barely around at all. Snowden appreciated this greatly. Wendell was left behind in the cab of the truck, a patch of mange over his right hip leaving it scabbed and balled and making him particularly irritable. There was to be no slacking under his watch. Wendell demanded vigilance via incessant barking, ensuring that the three worked quickly just to escape from the racket.

Horus was deputized to go over the inventory with the clients at the end of the day and get their signatures, a duty he boasted of daily, throwing in comments like, "Y'all better get used to the way I run my ship. I'll let you come for tea when they give me my brownstone!" Though a big man, Horus provided little company. As soon as he and Snowden ran out of merits to debate between the 1996 Bulls and 1968 76ers and the conversation slowed, it was Horus's habit once again to remove his laminated cutout photo of his dream Mercedes and hijack the discussion to one about the merits of the CL-class coupe versus the SL-class roadster, pointing down at the faded image like he already owned it.

After work on Sunday, a good four days after his conversation with Robert M. Finley, Snowden finally admitted to himself that he'd become a truly unhappy person. He wanted to get drunk but didn't feel like getting drunk alone, and the TV lineup was so bad he couldn't even be bothered to flip through the channels as he was apt to. Left with his thoughts, there were no distractions to keep him from realizing that the majority were not happy ones.

Throughout his life, Snowden was sure he'd seen people on the street and behind cash registers, heard them on the other end of phone lines, who were perennially pleasant. Truly happy people among us. Snowden could barely imagine them even crying, but he was sure they did, short bursts never louder than their normal talking voice, things they wiped away like mucus before returning to their state of happiness once more. These people often seemed bland and stupid as well, but what a small price to pay for true happiness. The ones Snowden envied the most were those who seemed to be happy just because they believed in something, something so big it shrank all their own obstacles down to minutia. It didn't seem to matter what that thing was, either, just as long as it was big and depended more on faith than reality. Nursing his anxiety, Snowden wished he could believe in something big and beautiful, even this Horizon insanity he was being pushed into, that he could rid himself of the certainty that eventually it would engulf him.

The most beautiful thing Snowden could think to believe in at the moment was love, and even though he was pretty sure he wasn't in love with Piper Goines and that it was good sense to avoid her in general, he felt overwhelmed by the need to be near a woman, inside her, and Piper's door was already open for him. The urge to be touched, listened to, overshadowed the fear that Lester would see him near her, so once more he found himself at her door, greeted by her patented lack of surprise, customary silence.

"I'm here for consolation," Snowden said as soon as he'd ducked inside the vestibule, out of sight from the street.

"Good."

"Would you rub my hands for me? They hurt from lifting shit."

"OK. It's a deal, then."

Upstairs, Piper obliged. There were too many bottles for it to take so long to find a little something to rub into his skin, but it did. Snowden sat on the fuzzy lid of the toilet while Piper pulled through the stalactite jars in the cavern under the sink, most of which ended up on the floor in the process. Snowden begged for her to settle with

the petroleum jelly but Piper chose instead some pink paste meant for hair moisturizing that stank like a perm but felt good. They had sex in the bathtub because when they started kissing they were next to it and it was the only bare surface in her apartment.

Snowden woke up paranoid. His dream hallucination that he'd been sleeping in a coffin-sized office drawer turned out to be the product of the manila files underneath the sheets of Piper's bed, ones she hadn't bothered to mention or clear when they'd collapsed there. Snowden was pulling them out from beneath himself when Piper reached out for his hand.

"I didn't expect this, you know. I mean, it wasn't an expectation, do you know what I mean? I realize, at least it's my understanding of this whole thing, that we're just messing around here. But I want to tell you I really appreciate it, you coming over here to console me, taking into account how I must feel."

"Console *you*." Snowden sat with it a moment, admitted there was no way he could hold that statement that it would make him see it clearly. "I'm sorry, did something happen to you?"

"Jesus." When Piper flopped back on the bed like that, Snowden could hear that there were even more files hidden beneath her. "You didn't even see the article, did you? You probably don't even read the *Times*, do you?"

"Oh, I don't just not read the *Times*, I don't read nothing at all. I'm a total moron." Snowden caught the flash of white from Piper's rolling eyes as she jumped out of the bed and past him. He was beginning to wonder if he should follow her when she returned to drop the weight of the Sunday paper on the bed beside him. As she went searching through each section, Snowden became certain that when she was done she would leave the periodical right there where she dropped it for weeks, kicking it piece by piece onto the floor in her sleep.

"You know what? The most annoying thing about all this is now you're going to be all freaking happy about it too, about my travesty."

Piper threw the section at him, bouncing it off his slow hands and down to the floor in front of him. The paper looked as if it had been shared by a bored army for a month, its sides soft and rounded from repeated bending, gray with the ink of smeared words.

"My editor in chief called me last night to tell me about it. The bastard even sounded happy that I'd been scooped. He's supposed to be my advocate and I could almost see the old fool smiling on the other end of the phone. He must have gone through my insurance records to get my home number. It was like his little payback for my piece knocking out his Special Report, as if I had a damn thing to do with that."

Snowden heard none of this, the auditory processor of his brain being infringed upon by the visual overload of seeing Cyrus Marks right there on the cover of the real estate section, his smiling visage centered and in color, Horizon Realty's swinging sign over his shoulder, the number showing clearly. Déjà vu as Snowden found himself reading the paper with his fate caught in the text, but now the anticipation of each additional sentence given the context of joy. The article's title, AMID ACCIDENTAL ASHES, A NEW HARLEM BLOSSOMS.

"See? See? Not only does the bastard not mention that I'm the one who broke this story, he doesn't even bother mentioning the *New Holland Herald* at all. You know, you think sometimes that black people are starting to get respect, then you look at the way the black press gets dissed . . . It's goddamn antebellum. It really is."

"Although much has been made in our local tabloid press about the high number of accidental deaths in the historic Mount Morris section of Harlem, it must be taken into account that these figures apply entirely to the lower-income residents of the area, the elderly, the drug-addicted, and others who are obviously at a much higher risk than the flourishing and unaffected high-income newcomers." After that, Snowden read the sidebar about Mr. Marks, Harlem's favored son. Cyrus Marks was the only real estate agent profiled, his optimism for Harlem quoted and unquestioned, his hope for all

Harlem, rich and poor, beyond reproach. A long, run-on sentence listed his charitable contributions and affiliations.

"The thing that kills me is the morally reprehensible tone this guy gets." When Piper got mad, she had a habit of slamming her fist down. The bed shook. "It's like he's implying it's some bourgeois Manifest Destiny, like Harlem is just weeding itself to make room for the moneyed fucks to come steal it away for themselves. It's disgusting."

Snowden got to the quote from Lester at the end. "A well-groomed, courteous man, Marks's one-time parolee, then chauffeur, and now lead agent. 'Of course white New Yorkers are welcome in Harlem, just as the former president himself. Black Harlem enjoys the diversity they bring to our community.'"

If there were any lingering suspicions about the accidents, this article dispersed them beyond the borders of memory. It was the first moment since he saw Baron Anderson's lifeless body that Snowden could actually believe he would make his way out of his situation. Snowden had never considered sending flowers to a man before, but he promised as he read that Lincoln Jefferson, the reporter, would be his first recipient.

"You know, you could at least give me the respect of not smiling like that until you're dressed and out of here," Piper told him.

The following morning, Monday. The phone rang at seven-ten and it was Lester. Snowden heard the voice and groggily begged to know what was wrong, what did they want of him now, what the hell was wrong with this world.

"Everything's fine," Lester chirped cheerily. "Everything's fine now. Horizon has many friends, in many places. It's all been taken care of."

The day's relocation was originally scheduled for noon, but Lester wanted Snowden to show up at nine instead, back up Nina in reception by clearing the messages off the voice mail. Snowden had performed the duty before and disliked it. Nina was an adherent of

the Ebonic school of customer service, felt rudeness as much her right as her paycheck, got even worse when she was forced to share her small territory behind the reception desk. Her image in Snowden's mind was intertwined with the smell of rotten flowers, provided by a decade of her sweating through her perfume in Horizon's cramped front office. The job was easy though, involved sitting in the small space behind her with a notepad, transcribing the messages from the eight or nine calls that, on busy days, overflowed.

When Snowden arrived, Nina didn't even look up, not even to roll her eyes. There were four calls blinking on hold. The voice mailbox was nearly full. Aside from two magazine reporters, every single one of them wanted to know about available properties, when they could come in for a tour. Snowden handled 114 calls by noon, left the rest for her when he went to change into his banana suit again.

THE GATHERING

A NIGHT OF designed levity, a bit of glamour to add to Harlem's luster, a moment to celebrate the unprecedented success of the last few months. Horizon Realty's black tie celebration was conducted along the entire 400 block of West 119th; the Fruit of Islam security force began clearing cars and sealing off the block after sunset. Dinner and dessert were to be held in the lodge's ballroom, but to highlight what the celebration was all about, Horizon-sold brownstones along the street were selected to host the preliminary courses.

Lester noted to the three that this location would have been impossible just two years before, but the comment was unnecessary. The location would have been impossible only eight months ago when they got there. The single-room-occupancy on the far corner from the lodge where the guy used to bring his TV out on the stoop attached to an extension cord – sold to a "happy face" buyer last April. The one across from that whose residents opted for stereo speakers and stained sheets in their windows instead of curtains – now the home of a vice president at HBO whose parents uprooted from Mount Morris to Mount Vernon in 1958. Those three vacant shells? Sold in the boom of the last three months. The one whose contractor had yet to start made an impressive donation to the Little Leaders Foundation in exchange for its art class painting images of polka-dot-curtained, flower-filled windows over the cinder-blocked ones.

The second Mrs. Bryant began serving hors d'oeuvres before the blockades were even erected, her home the perfect starting point, the

incarnation of the brownstone dream. Bought in 1927 by the late Charles Bryant (1972) and refurbished by the first Mrs. Bryant soon after, enjoyed by her for nearly ten years before she was hit by an errant taxi somewhere in Murray Hill. "She had excellent tastes," said the second Mrs. Bryant, tray in hand, blooming under her guests' collective gaze.

Appetizers were up the steps of the Franklin townhouse. Joshua Franklin, two-year resident, his fiancée Regina Butler, resident for half that time. They had the food catered from three different Harlem restaurants: Bandana (Dominican), Bamboo (Creole), and of course M&G's Soul Food. The decor of the Franklin house could best be described as a mix between old brown wood and old brown cultures, the African carvings blending seamlessly in with the dark Victorian fixtures.

The residence of Daniel Harper and Gil Meehan was of much lighter bent, eggshell walls serving as perfect screens for the colorful mirages projected by outside lights through their many stained-glass windows. "All original," they assured their visitors. Mr. Harper was a set designer, Mr. Meehan a makeup artist. Everyone found Gil a treasure, appreciated that the white man seemed so at ease to be so outnumbered, appreciated the diversity he brought to the crowd.

Charlene and Bill Dougal were scheduled to offer coffee, tea, and cider in their living room, but the contractor had worked late and there was so much dust that they ran his industrial extension cord out to the front stoop and served from there. Originally excited about the idea, Charlene had called Lester Baines just that morning to try to back out, fearing that in comparison to the others, their brownstone, which had only just begun its transformation back to a single-family-home from a single-room-occupancy, would serve as a cautionary tale as well as an embarrassment. By nine P.M., when all participants were called to the serving of the main course in the lodge by Ghanaian talking drums, Charlene was relieved Lester'd never returned her call. The Dougals' home; its shredded floors, its barren caulk-filled walls had indeed seemed stark in comparison, but

the emotion it prompted in the visitors was awe, and not simply for how little they'd paid for it. Strangers openly marveled at her strength in the face of such a momentous undertaking, the undertaking itself and goal at the end of it. The crowd grew in what would one day be the Dougals' dining room, forsaking the more comfortable alternatives to listen to the woman as she stood in front of the tent covered in plaster dust and nailed to the floor between the wood beams that the Dougals' were at this stage sleeping in. Engrossed in the tales of the trials she'd already encountered, the guests eased her fears with their own projections of how beautiful it would be when completed. They listened and believed for a moment that they too could be pioneers up here.

Having one's waitstaff dressed in Harlem Renaissance period clothes was so overdone, it was decided to have them dress up in traditional African garb instead. Ibos served entrées, Ashanti warriors handed out bottles of Star Beer while struggling to keep their kente wraps on with their left hands. Masai stood on one foot, aperitif trays attached to the ends of their staffs. Roles were assigned based on ethnic resemblance. Handing out the costumes, Horus joked that Bobby, by that logic, should be forced to "hold one of them spear trays as well," which was funny the first time, but Horus just kept saying it.

Horus's date was not a stripper. Horus's date was not a stripper. If Horus's date was not a stripper, then why was he smiling like that, repeatedly pulling Snowden to the side to deny something she was never accused of? Why was she wearing shoes with glass heels the size of hot dogs? Why was she handing out his business card? What other possible explanation could there be?

Snowden was dateless. Piper was there but had come on an invitation to the staff of the *New Holland Herald*, and that relationship was dying down anyway. With Snowden extremely careful about what he said to her, they had run out of things to talk about, or rather, after two months of little more than polite banter, they had become embarrassed that they'd found no shared interest to elevate

the dialogue. They'd found a few things to argue about, but since the relationship had yet to develop enough animosity to need an outlet for it, those topics felt pointless as well. Mostly they had sex, and mostly to cover up the silences, and not even that often anymore.

Snowden had never had a relationship that lasted longer than five months. Once one was started, he'd begin immediately asking himself how it would end. When would be the last kiss? Would the relationship explode in a heated exchange over some perceived insult, or would it simply dissipate into nothingness, a phone call never returned or followed up? With Piper, even ignoring the inherent danger of her inquisitive nature, they were so ill matched. Snowden had begun hoping that their end would come quickly and quietly, but was willing to risk a violent confrontation if she took offense at him trying to meet a new, better-suited partner among the night's attendees.

Aside from the minor distraction of Piper, the evening marked the return of the upbeat Snowden (it had been so long). This mental state was due largely to the fact that in all this time no more accidents had even been mentioned by the senior men of Horizon. Snowden had begun to strongly suspect that after the success of the *Times* article the tactic was deemed no longer necessary. This seemed possible, logical even. Cut your losses – made perfect sense. Snowden adored this suspicion, took comfort in the idea that he could just do his best to take care of Jifar and forget the rest.

The lodge was crowded with the beautiful women of New York City, glowing princesses emigrated from smaller towns and uglier cities, drained of aloofness by the humbling proximity of so many others. Bobby Finley, two cocktails in hand as he circled the room, trying once again to identify his romantic counterpart, his one, past failures far behind him. If she was here, Bobby would go to her and raise the extra glass to ask, "Martini?" and that simply his destined love affair would begin. *The Great Work* laid as bait back at an apartment somewhat cleaned for the occasion.

The three in immaculate tuxedos, good shoes, even their socks

matched. The three affording this because of two months of actually showing clients around, the Second Chance stipend being increased, and Metzer's Formal Wear's buy-two-get-one-free sale. The deal was only for wedding parties, so Horus played the groomsman. Temps had been hired to lift boxes into the homes they'd helped sell, taking the job now beneath them. The three looked so respectable even they could believe they were.

Most of the attendees had never spent much time in Harlem before. (Sharing the dining room of Sylvia's with busloads of German tourists didn't count.) Snowden had seen the guest list, typed out the envelopes himself, had gathered enough from Lester's comments to know who many of them were, even the ones whose faces he didn't recognize. The majority were the highest-ranking black employees of New York's most respected industries, male and female. The rest were cops and parole officers.

The parole officers could be easily identified by their cheap shoes, but Snowden didn't need that marker. Even in the context of these festivities, they stood out to him. They looked like people who spent all day being lied to. They were what happened when the secular, unblinded by faith, spent their lives dealing with humanity's worst at their worst. Worn, mundane, bitter – they were like office coffee left to burn on the plate for days. Snowden hugged walls, kept his nose in his drink, assumed they too could identify him at a glance. They were nothing like the congressman who greeted newcomers at the front door, transcending his bestial frame with elegance, success, and by standing at the top of steep steps. It was obvious to Snowden that the homicidal hedgehog was their hero. His rise from their ranks to become the president of the Parole Division Union, to Congress, to wealth back in the place he served as a public servant was legendary. Tens of them, dusty, smiling creatures, walking around the lodge like they owned it as much as he did.

No cameras, aside from private ones. Regardless of the many media folks in attendance, no press reports were to be written about the event at all, as per the invitation's request. A large but private

function. A moment for black America's best and brightest to enjoy Harlem's renewal, take note that its time had returned, sample its possibilities, and maybe take a Horizon card from the discreet stand by the door on the way to their cab back downtown. No party worth attending was publicly reported on.

The upper tenth of the Tenth. Most seemed to at least recognize each other, or pretend not to, or assume they were being recognized themselves, their private motions a dramatic interpretation of ease.

A lack of notable weather patterns raised the prominence of housing as a casual discussion topic, a New York City favorite made that much more appropriate by the occasion. Where do you live, what part, what size, how much? In New York, the questions were not considered rude or intrusive, because there was no way you could answer wrong. If you paid a lot it was a tribute to your wealth, bonding ground for the overpaying majority. If you paid barely anything at all it was a testament to your good fortune and ingenuity. Residence in the best neighborhoods was a source of pride, but residency in the worst even more so. It meant you were a visionary pioneer, braving the urban elements to bet on the next slum to become the next utopia.

Not used to free food or drink, Snowden was both full and drunk by the time he'd arrived at the lodge for his entrée. The rest of the guests weren't far behind him. This was when he noticed the first accident talk. Someone walking up the lodge's front steps slipped, sent a hand shooting for purchase on the wide stone banister. A voice in the crowd behind said, "Careful there, hold on tight! You don't want to be another clumsy Negro at the morgue!" Snowden, who always clenched the railing for that very reason, at first thought the warning was directed at him, then loosened his grip ever so slightly.

Inside and warmed, that incident had already been drained of reality for him, a moment of paranoia, vestiges of guilt he knew he was still susceptible to. Then came a guest's joke announcement warning the crowd to be "extremely careful" with their leftover

appetizer toothpicks. Followed by a yell from across the room to be wary of the electric sockets, followed by another's calm reassurance that with nearly 200 folks in attendance, statistics said at least 190 had absolutely nothing to worry about. Greater laughter greeted everyone. All the fear returned, Snowden moved quickly away from the sound, was the first to find his place card at a table and sit down. From behind him, a man in the crowd claimed to have dressed as the Chupacabra for Halloween as well. Together, he and his companions threw out conjectures about what one might look like. Snowden tried to hum them out, still heard pieces of the man's story, something about sewing on dried pig snouts from the pet store.

"A morbid bunch, aren't they?" The other man had a place card in his hand, picked up two more to read before selecting the seat next to Snowden. He looked boring and the kind of person who enjoys sharing his gift of boredom with others. Snowden nodded, wished there was something at the table he could pretend to be preoccupied with.

"Well, it's nuts, the way everybody's bugging out. I guess they don't really believe it. Because it's not true," Snowden offered, began busying himself with the pockets inside of his coat as if there was something in them.

"They don't believe it can happen to them. They're not poor, uneducated. Plus," the other turned smiling, "who doesn't love an urban legend? Especially black folks."

"Menthol cigarettes were genetically engineered to be especially addictive to blacks."

"Right, I remember that one. Tropical Fantasy soda was produced by the Klan to make us sterile."

"And the Klan makes all those crown air fresheners too, and Snapple, that's why they have little *k*'s on every bottle," Snowden told him.

"The government tracks us by giving us an even fifth digit number on our Social Security numbers, and whites get an odd number," the man said.

"Right, right! And they're the ones who infected us with syphilis just to see the effects."

"Well, no." The guy paused to frown. "No, that actually happened. You know, it was called the Tuskegee Experiment."

"Oh, that's right, that's right. I knew that. It gets confusing."

"The important thing is that they're joking about it. They're not buying into it. They're buying houses instead. I'm just happy for Congressman Marks, he really deserves this. He's had a hard time of it, over the years, it's good to see things finally working out."

"You know the congressman?" Snowden turned to get a better look at him.

"Oh yeah. I've know him for years. He was my parole officer, long ago, if you can believe that. If you can believe I was ever nineteen with no greater aspiration than to tag up subways with a squiggly nom de plume."

Snowden looked to the table, saw "Lincoln Jefferson" on the card in front of the man.

"You're the guy that wrote the article. The article about the accidents."

"You read that? That's the good thing about having a stupid name, people remember. My dad, he sold beauty products to salons, he swore by it. His name was Bill but just for that he had it legally changed to Thomas. Yeah, that piece was the least I could do for the congressman. It's a good thing to see all this happen for him. I don't know how well you know him – you're one of the Second Chance protégés right? Lester pointed you out. Lester deserves this too. Shit, Harlem deserves this."

"You know Lester too?" Snowden's question at first just got dismissive laughter in response. Lincoln swiped his drink off the table, leaned forward into Snowden's ear. The room was getting so crowded that others were searching for their assigned seats as well. Snowden now wanted them gone, back to their callous laughter.

"Shit man, I was working for Mr. Marks writing press releases on his first election bid when I was going to journalism school up at

Columbia, when he lost his wife. I was there when he got the call."
Lincoln Jefferson looked up for a moment before continuing, made
sure no one was hovering unseen behind him before going on.
"Raped and murdered, can you believe that shit? What a way to go.
Riverside Park, in the morning no less, down in the bushes below the
wall. Didn't die quickly, either. Bled to death, throat cut. Something
like that, the only thing you can hope for is that she was unconscious
the whole time."

"That's beyond rough." Snowden could think of no better
comment to make. He wanted to say, "That's no excuse," but that
wasn't appropriate. Lincoln nodded, then shot to the left to pull two
drinks off a passing Wolof's tray.

"I mean, we all got our sob stories, but that's just beyond. Lester
too. He's had his share of low times. His lover passed last year. Jesse
Himes, a sweetheart. Everywhere he went he'd bring this little
dachshund, had sweaters and shit for it. Overdose. I knew he'd
struggled with it for years, but still, the guy couldn't have been more
than forty-five. I thought Lester was going to crack after that, but he
didn't. Both of them are like that, that's why they've always worked
so well together. Most people, you hit them with so much adversity,
they just split in half, lose it. But these guys, they still got the dream
keeping them going. They believe in this place, in making our world
better. Now look what they've imagined!" Lincoln, both glasses still
in his hand, motioned around the room and then at Snowden before
drinking them.

Bobby could admit it: The evening was not going as he'd planned. It
had indeed been planned, over a week of creative and intensive
effort, so at least he could be certain it was not due to lack of
initiative. The reason was as simple as it was unhelpful: In the
meeting of "girls," planning simply didn't work. Attractiveness could
not be learned, nor could the amount of personal wealth and power
it took for some woman to ignore one's physical deficiencies. Bobby
felt that he had just enough physical positives (height and clear skin)

that he could compensate for what he lacked by using confidence, ease, and charm, but he seemed unable to successfully convey those attributes either. So Bobby relied on what he could master, words. So Bobby relied on cue cards.

For each of his three premier opening lines, Bobby had written three realistic responses, then equally impressive ripostes, repeated this until he felt confident that he had mapped his way from casual banter to a full-fledged discussion. By the end of the week, the three sets of possible conversations were represented in triangles of blue cards on his walls, taped to the spines of *The Great Work* on the shelves. Then he memorized them.

The pyramid scheme didn't work. On Bobby's first run-through, at the Butlers' residence, plate of okra and plantain held high to shield his heart, he was faced with the chaotic impossibility of it all. Lovely-seeming woman, hair pulled back in an intelligent knot, dressed in riding boots, jodhpurs, a hunting jacket. She seemed perfect for the "Let me guess, you thought this was supposed to be a costume ball – so you came as the most beautiful woman in the world" tangent. She was not. While she didn't tell him to piss off or reach for her rape whistle, her response hurt Bobby more than the times in his life those other things had happened to him. She did nothing at all. She didn't smile, she didn't frown, she didn't tell him to go away. The only thing that kept Bobby from repeating the line louder was that she did look over at him as he said it, only she looked away just as casually when he was done. Sipped her drink, tapped her feet to the light music. After a few seconds, Bobby turned around and went back outside.

Climbing back in the saddle, telling himself he'd drawn his joker for the night, Bobby's next target was a woman he selected because she was as tall and slight as he was. Wrapped in evangelically natural fibers, hair just as coarse, uncompromising and severe, she seemed someone who would appreciate Bobby's intellectual and radical passion. It turned out she appreciated the company of her existing acquaintances much more. Bobby really felt he was making inroads,

getting five stages down with his "All this evening needs is Van Vechten to save it for prosperity, right?" tract, when another woman walked up to them, said "Sharon?" and struck up a completely different conversation that in no way involved or acknowledged his existence. It wasn't even a particularly driven conversation. There was a lull, an awkward silence into which Bobby tried interjecting commentary, but the second woman just started talking over him once more, about how hard it was to find parking. Again Bobby simply turned and walked away, more defiant in his defeat this time, pretending the women cared enough that the gesture could be taken as an insult.

He would burn the cue cards later. He would take great joy in burning them, slowly, individually, and he wouldn't feel guilty about lighting them on fire, either. He would try harder, smarter. If it was a matter of confidence, there was always hypnotism to strengthen his mental state. If he truly reeked of failure and desperation as he was beginning to fear, he would buy phero-mones to mask the taint. Success could always be attained through detailed orchestration.

By the time the lights flickered and Lester's voice came from within the crowd to urge it to take its seats, Bobby'd managed to save himself from falling into a reactionary depression. It wasn't until he'd sat, placed his napkin in his lap, turned to his right and saw that the large woman seated next to him was Piper Goines, that his self-pity hit free fall.

She started talking before he could get up. "So you're here. I saw your name there, I wondered if that was you, if you were going to show."

"Look, now I'm sorry about that tape. If – "

"No, you look. I finally picked up your book the other night, I figured I'd see you here, and I told you I'd read it. To be honest, I picked it up a couple of times and couldn't get through the first couple of pages. So I finally did. It's . . . it's amazing. Absolutely amazing. I've read it twice already. I got so much more the second

time, it's so rich, I could just keep going back. It's the most beautiful thing I've ever seen. It's genius."

Bobby tried to contain his emotions, his imagination, failed at both miserably and instantly.

Bobby in bliss. He really had found her. Piper Goines was the one, he'd been right all along and she was more than he'd ever been capable of imaging. Piper Goines was his soul mate, but she was so so so much more than that, he could see this now. Piper Goines was what Bobby Finley wanted even more than love itself, what he'd ceased daring to even hope for. Piper Goines was his reader.

The food was good, but the pain in the ass was that people kept standing at the front of the ballroom and talking. It kept Snowden wondering: Was he the only one who found the speeches to be so unbearable? When were they going to shut up so he could really get down to burying his sorrows with what was on his plate? One speaker would finally end but Snowden wouldn't even have worked his way through a mouthful before someone else was talking, again with the thank-yous, again with the congratulations to Horizon Realty and Harlem, again with the history lesson nobody needed about the bright days of the past and the assurances about the equally glowing future, personal anecdotes thrown in. Picking at his chicken with his hands (what? what? we're all folk here!), Snowden was tempted to shove it in his ears instead. If it didn't taste so good, if he wasn't basically on the job at the moment, he would have done it. Swear to God. Everybody else was probably just as lit too. Who would notice?

First that lead cop was up there, the head of the precinct, talking about how safe the neighborhood was, about the drop in crime in the last two years, the last five. "Safe for who?" Snowden wanted to ask him, but the cop went on to clarify, point out that there had not been one incident of violent crime or robbery against any of Horizon's home owners in over a year, well below the city average. The Thirty-second Precinct was very proud, he said. What else

would he say? Ladies and gentlemen, I really don't know what the hell I'm doing. The streets are run by the animals. Drug lords like Parson Boone still have more control up here than I do. Kill the poor. Applause came from the crowd when he finished, relief from Snowden. Barely a biscuit buttered and the next one was up there, this time the rep for the parole officers.

Oh, the round of applause this guy got, just looking at this loser Snowden could tell it had to be a stacked house. Rolling his eyes, Snowden suddenly wishing someone at his table was paying attention to him just so he could register his disgust formally. The PO made the point of saying he held the same union rep position Cyrus Marks had so long ago, then proceeded to clumsily reclaim all of the credit for the falling crime rate from the previous speaker. They were on them, you could be sure. They were diligent, protecting us all from the wolves. They knew "what them bastards are up to, let me tell you." No mention of the fact that his union had failed to stop the city from buying the old nursing home around the corner to use as the site for the Mumia Abu-Jamal Memorial Halfway House in the coming year, as Lester had been complaining privately for weeks now. No attempt by the speaker to hide the fact that his own ambition outdistanced even his host's accomplishments – the impersonator even called the congressman up from his dinner table to force the room into a premature show of appreciation, not letting him sit back down until they'd posed together for a picture.

Next, publisher Olthidius Cole rocked his weight from one hip to the other till he was up at the podium, taking his turn and liberties. Pancake cheeks flapping, pockmarks almost whistling from the amount of hot air pumping through. Snowden didn't find the publisher's rant nearly as amusing in person as it was on the cover of every issue of the *New Holland Herald*. After a few minutes of trying to make sense of Cole's seemingly random images, proclamations and denunciations, Snowden gave up. Around him, the "happy faces" picked at the carcasses on their plates, carrion shreds on their

greasy cheeks. This is who Horizon was clearing the way for, Snowden marveled. The gluttonous cast as saviors.

Snowden needed to feel good again. Snowden needed to find Jifar, get a chance to be alone with the boy for the first time since he dropped him off months ago, tell him he would rescue him. Realizing that this was his chance, Snowden excused himself to the bathroom and headed upstairs to the lodge's second floor instead. That's it, he would adopt the boy, set things right again. He would serve out his year at Horizon, let Bobby win the job and brownstone, and take Jifar with him. Set up shop in Albany. Maybe get a recommendation from Bobby to counteract the prison record. Or tonight, they could go tonight. Snowden could get a job some-where under the table, illegal immigrants did it all the time. They'd get a little apartment, Jifar'd have his own room, they'd be happy.

"But I don't want to go," Jifar told him, his eyelids barely parted. Jifar was as awake as Snowden was sober. Snowden stood next to the boy's top bunk mattress. There were drawings taped to the wall next to it that Snowden could tell were Jifar's without looking at the signature. Behind him, Snowden heard some of the other boys whispering and told them sternly to go back to sleep, waking several more up in the process.

"What do you mean you don't want to go? I'll do it, I'll be your new dad now. You don't want to go with me?" Snowden asked. He was starting to tear up. He felt silly but that just made him more upset.

"All right. If I have to, I'll go. Can all my friends come with me?" Jifar nodded to the other boys around the room, the ones pretending to sleep through this. "Will we have a Dragonball-Z Meglo Jungle Gym set in the backyard like the one here?" Jifar blinked, rolled over, and was quickly back in dream before Snowden could answer.

Defeated, Snowden stopped in the hall bathroom, its septic smell alone bringing back some of his senses. At the sink, he kept splashing water to his face as if on its surface lay all his difficulties, a film enough tries could rinse away. When he turned off the tap, the

sound of an evacuating bowel in the closed stall behind him told him he wasn't alone before the voice did.

"Snowden?" Lester asked. Snowden said yes, covered his eyes with his hands so he could roll them. "I love those shoes you're wearing. Are those Florsheims?" Lester continued. Snowden confirmed this.

"Yes, I thought so. Florsheim makes an excellent shoe, always have. You know, the heat's died down a bit. It's hunting season again. There's going to be a tragic accident tomorrow night, about eleven P.M.. I'll pick you up at nine-thirty. You should probably wear sneakers instead."

The Great Work refuses summarization, defiantly.

The Great Work was never intended to be reduced below its 374-page form.

If one were to be so callous, so impetuous as to strip it of its weight, to disregard its intricate artistry and hack it down to a list of mere events, harpoon those damaged, bleeding chunks together into a lifeless time line, one would probably come up with something much like the following:

A social worker from Galveston takes a job as an employee counselor in an isolated logging camp in central Alaska. The company that hires him is too cheap to hire an actual licensed psychologist for the job. It's also too cheap to hire a competent clerk at their home office in Anchorage, and a careless error by an uncaring temp results in the main character arriving at the camp two days after the end of logging season, as opposed to the beginning of it. The entire site is empty, something the social worker doesn't figure out until his pilot (the camp is accessible only by biplane) has already flown away. It is scheduled to remain vacant until "breakup," when spring comes and the ice melts and work can be done once more, which is seven months after his arrival.

Amazingly – and this is really a tribute to the mastery of craft of one Robert M. Finley – all of this happens on the first page. The rest of the novel is set in a closet.

As the company relies on cell phones, there's no way for him to contact the outside world. All but a misplaced barrel of rice has been removed from the kitchen to discourage the seven-foot-tall, eight-hundred-pound grizzlies that inhabit the region from breaking in again. There is no running water as the pipes are frozen (it's negative ten degrees Fahrenheit outside), but there's plenty of snow. The furnace will not work, but the electricity's on and he finds one plug-in heater powerful enough to keep a closet forty-eight degrees above zero.

Much of the novel is description. Much of the novel follows his battle to get as close as possible to the heater without lighting the fax cover sheets he's stuffed in his clothes for warmth on fire. They say that the Eskimos (who don't like to be called that as it is an Indian derogatory term meaning "raw fish eater") have twenty-seven words for "snow." Perhaps to underscore the uselessness of the English language to capture this environment, Finley uses just that one word, *snow*, so many times that the reader becomes so numb from it, it's as if they'd shoved their eyes into a mountain of the stuff.

He will not starve, but he has only rice to eat for months, and no seasonings of any kind. He will not freeze, but he is never truly warm, either. He is completely free to roam, but he must remain primarily in a closet. He even finds company in a sensitive native he meets by tracing the road out of the camp for six miles, but he quickly offends the other man and is chased off the hermit's property by gunshots (thereby learning the derogatory nature of the "Eskimo" descriptor). There are the man-eating bears the size of fuel-efficient cars, but (not to ruin it) he never sees one, so in the end they are no more than every other monstrous looming fear that haunts everyone, everywhere. Going neither up nor down, unassisted by plot or question, the prose is forced to crawl forward word by word, digging deliberately for purchase. No matter how quickly one reads *The Great Work*, the process never feels a moment less than seven months.

The genius is the balance of it all, in spite of such harsh

surroundings a medium is found. Civilized man stripped forcibly of wants and left only with essentials. What at first appears a horrific circumstance reveals itself not only to be sustaining, but to offer the greatest freedom of all. Nirvana via situation. Stunning. Absolutely.

All this was Piper Goines's interpretation. And she should be qualified to review literature: She wrote for a newspaper.

"That chapter where he learned how to cook the rice by sitting it overnight in the coffee tin with a handful of snow, the whole thing about how many centimeters it should sit in relation to the heater, that was just gorgeous. I loved that," Piper admitted, blushing.

Surprisingly, the new-found intimates spent very little time actually discussing *The Great Work*. Perhaps because it was so precisely written, so thoroughly read, it mooted any questions or possible debate. Bobby certainly had no inquiries into the source or merit of Piper's interpretation. He found absolutely nothing questionable about it. It was exactly like his own.

They spent the evening talking about Piper Goines's life, Piper Goines's passions, Piper Goines's artistic ambitions. Throughout the night's procession they huddled at the back of their table in whispers, mostly hers, both their plates ignored despite the Dogon who acted pissed off every time he came back to reclaim another untouched course.

Enamored. By the time guests were asked to rise, grab their coats, and climb to the top of nearby Mount Morris for a final champagne toast, Piper had had enough to drink and not nearly enough food to absorb it. Bobby felt the same way and hadn't had a sip since sitting down. They lined up with the others for the door, snickered at the group's annoyance at the forced march up a mountain that was only half a block over and only half a block from base to summit. At the stairs, Bobby offered his arm for balance despite the fact that he was far too slight to ever stop her from falling. Piper kept her hand there after they were down.

"Do you remember that Mount Morris Park was where the main character did the eulogy in *Invisible Man*?" Bobby was never more in

his element than he was at the moment. Piper stared forward, squeezed his arm. It hurt a little, but not nearly as much as he enjoyed it.

"The hill itself is an outshoot of bedrock, glacial. The Dutch called it *Slang Berg.* It means 'Snake Hill.' You can imagine why the brownstones' original realtors renamed it." In the park, there were no more snakes, that went without saying. All other predators had been discreetly removed by the Fruit of Islam security force hours earlier, after which the Mount Morris Historical Society lit and laid out handmade earthen oil lamps from Mali along the path.

The view from the top – they might have been only up five or six stories but there were no tall buildings around them and Bobby and Piper stood with a fresh glass of champagne along with the rest of the crowd, admiring the lights of upper Manhattan.

Piper said, "You know what? I have to admit, I never thought this place could be this beautiful. Maybe I hoped, but I never thought."

"That was built to look for fires, since this is one of the highest vantage points in Manhattan," Bobby said pointing to the iron crow's nest that towered fifty feet above them. "Some guy, it was his job to sit up there all day – rain, cold, it didn't matter – and look for smoke to tell the firemen."

Bobby leaned in so she could follow his line of vision perfectly, used this as an excuse to place his cheek against hers. Needing to hold it there, Bobby went on to aim her vision uptown to the building past Sugar Hill where Hughes himself had once lived, along with Du Bois, Locke, Hurston, and many of the others. Piper said, "Cool," and then Bobby tried to kiss her. Piper kissed him back. Then she hugged him tighter than it was cold and said, "This has been so much fun. I'm drunk. Are you drunk?"

Bobby Finley, Robert M. Finley himself, was so high his feet were dangling. Bobby Finley was looking at the night continue as it was planned, a final speech, a final toast, the fireworks rigged to go off above them as a last nod to celebration, and he knew he was floating. One of the rockets shot up, and unlike its exploding mates, it kept

going. That was Bobby. His hand locked into place at the shallow of Piper's back, he felt like he really was flying, and with his hand on her Piper was flying with him. Bobby Finley was so high he'd forgotten what the ground looked like. He stayed that way too until Piper said, "You know what, I'm sorry, I better get going. Snowden's not here and we're supposed to be leaving together."

The crowd was leaving too, going back down again. Piper moved with them, walking the fastest, leaving him to watch until she was a little person far, far on the street below. Bobby suddenly remembered what the ground looked like again. Brown, hard, inescapable. He was filled with its growing image as he came crashing back down.

BOBBY FINLEY, THE FURY

BOBBY WOKE UP and thought, *I got lucky!* Bobby blinked into being and he didn't recognize where he was and he was naked and he could feel the crusted remnants of the party in his skull and in that instant before his lids stopped their flutter Bobby Finley thought, *I got lucky with a girl and now I'm at her strange apartment!* and then realized he had, in fact, passed out on his bathroom floor again, just this time with his head toward the door instead of toward the Irving Howe.

There was a phone ringing. Just to shut it up, Bobby went to it. Her voice said, "Oh my God, did I wake you up? I woke you up."

There was that bliss again. Unadulterated, immeasurable. The moments of the night before feeding him joy, almost worth the moment later when Bobby was gutted once more with the memory that she was Snowden's whore, and all the joy poured painfully out of him.

"I was there, at your place, this morning. I didn't hit the bell, it was like seven. I couldn't sleep last night, I was so charged. Robert, I had such a good time. I left you a package, though, outside your door. I got your name on the directory, someone was walking out so I just, you know, came up. Don't think I'm a freak, OK? I wanted to thank you for the book before I forgot. When I put something off for a minute, it can be months, a year before I get around to it. Right?"

Listening to Piper's voice over the receiver brought visions to Bobby's mind. Although he'd never actually read the *Kama Sutra*, suddenly Bobby could imagine what the poses looked like, imagine

173

them very easily with Snowden and Piper as the sweating, heaving partners. Positions as absurd as a world that would do this to him.

"So did you and your lover Snowden have an exciting evening last night? He's not there now, is he?" There was a halfhearted intention at lightness, at carefree flirtation, it was just that the amount of sugar needed to make his voice not sound bitter was beyond Bobby's means for the moment.

"What? No. I just crashed. I was so tired. I just . . . I had such a good time talking to you, I was pretty much exhausted. From the whole night. I didn't see him; I don't know where he is. He's probably off working on his Special Project, right?" There was derisiveness there. Bobby liked that, in theory, but he didn't know what she meant so asked for clarification.

"You know, that's what he calls the overtime work he does for Horizon, cleaning out the apartments and stuff. It's what they have him doing for extra credit in that little competition you've got going there. It's just grunt work. I'm sure whatever extracurricular assignment they have you doing is far more interesting."

"Oh yes," Bobby said, but *Oh no* was what he was thinking. Snowden had soiled his soul mate, now he was secretly slipping past him in the Horizon game as well. What kind of world was this where genius meant so little, where mediocrity was so often the champion? What was the worth of a species that recoiled from the brilliant and rejoiced in the dull? Another question: Was it the hangover that was hurting his head like that, or the force of the overwhelming dread that had besieged him?

Outside Bobby's door was a cardboard cylinder. Bobby told Piper this on his phone and she sighed back through hers. She told him to wait and open it until after she hung up, which wasn't much of a request since she hung up right after saying that.

Bobby put down the phone. Piper's package sat on the floor leaning against the hall wall, and soon he was as well. He knew what was inside it. It was one of the paintings she had talked about the night before, she wanted him to see one. Bobby wondered if it would

be any good. Bobby began to pray it wouldn't be any good. Bobby began to believe, in those few seconds, that the unseen painting would reveal itself to be very bad, hackish, an arts and crafts reject, hence proving that he'd been right the second time, that Piper really wasn't his destined companion. There was no way his soul mate could be a hack. This painting, Bobby realized, could be the one piece of evidence that would turn this whole series of events from a tragedy into a funny sidebar. It was his emotional out.

The one relationship that Bobby had been able to maintain for more than a year had been with a mentally ill administrative assistant (Borderline Personality Disorder – DSM IV) who had believed with all her crazy little heart that she was put on earth to be a singer. She took classes, she sang in studios, she sang in bands. The thing is, she never sang in key, and there lay the problem. She was so tone deaf she didn't even know she was, and it meant so much to her that nobody had the heart to tell her otherwise. The longer the charade went on, the more impossible it became to end it. She was attractive enough and had a British accent so bands kept asking her to sing with them, and even though each pairing never lasted more than two practices after she first opened her mouth, it encouraged her to keep at it. At times, at those deluded times when Bobby feared she was it, she was the one, he would imagine with great horror that he would spend his whole life this way, contributing to the conspiracy. Lying to her. Lying to himself until he went mad and actually believed that her shrieks were beautiful. When she'd dumped him to go on tour with a ska band who'd only heard her (computer-enhanced) audition tape, Bobby had actually laughed. It still hurt pretty bad, getting dumped, but while she was still midsentence in the dumping he'd burst out laughing.

Praying for ugliness, Bobby yanked the canvas from its container, unrolled it, and looked for liberation. The work was a mess. There were colors everywhere. All primary. A bunch of cartoons traced onto the background. None of them seemed to bleed into each other, yet just by sitting so close together in space they seemed to

blend in the eye and create the illusion of tertiary colors everywhere. The illustrations were originals, not tracings, done in one unlifting pencil stroke, freehand. It was making Bobby's heart race, just looking at the energy of it. It was so vivid you could almost hear it talking to you, almost smell things that weren't there. It was brilliant. It was the greatest work Bobby'd ever held in his hands. Bobby rolled it up, shoved it back in its tube, and then really got down to the wailing portion of his morning.

Bobby got himself to stop by saying, "That's it, I'm done playing. I accept the rules of this world, and I vow to win by them. As I owe this world nothing, I hereby free myself artistically and morally to do whatever I have to. I will use all of my intelligence, my creativity, my passion to capture everything I want. I will reclaim the love that is rightly mine and forge a life for us together. I will write the book that makes the world bow before me. In this Horizon contest I will burn brightly, high above the others."

Bobby was in his suit when he went down to the storefront. Walking by Nina, he went straight into Lester's office, closed the door behind him. Lester was sitting behind his desk eating a corn beef special on rye, the juice from the coleslaw streaming down the man's fingers and into a pool on the wax paper. The sight made Bobby want to vomit, but he stayed focused, began the speech he'd spent the last hour rehearsing.

"My name is Robert M. Finley."

"I know that, Bobby. Good afternoon. Did you have a good time last night? I had a ball. No pun intended."

"Yes, but listen, sir, my name is Robert M. Finley, and I know you have an idea of who I am, but I don't think you understand who I really am, or what I'm fully capable of. That is my fault, because while I feel I've outperformed my contemporaries, I know I haven't really pushed myself to realize my potential. May I continue, sir?"

"Continue."

"I am by far the smartest, most dedicated participant in the Second Chance Program. No one believes as much in the goals of

Horizon Realty, Harlem, or in the African-American community as a whole than me, sir. I, Robert M. Finley, dedicate myself with all my heart and by any means necessary to the uplifting of all three, and I live to prove that to you. Now, I have been made aware that Mr. Snowden has been involved in a special project for the cause, and I am here to ask for an extracurricular opportunity as well."

Lester took another bite, a big one, before licking the juice off his fingers, careful to taste every drop. After wrapping the remains of his lunch back up again, Lester fished in his drawers for napkins, used several. Dried, the man folded his hands before him, gave a sigh with a smile chaser.

"I can't tell you how pleased – strike that – *ecstatic* I am that you've come to me today with such passion, Robert M. Finley. Your talents, your experience, are what make you such an important addition to this community. Particularly during these times, when the Department of Corrections would see fit to build a halfway house in the middle of our historic community, despite our considerable protest." Lester removed a folder from the stack on the side of his desk, slid it over. Bobby picked it up, opened it. There were photocopies of blueprints inside.

"The convicts are expected to pour into the Mumia building this Friday, barring a miracle. These are not hand-picked Horizon men – I don't have to tell you what type of men these are. I'm sure you've seen it: corner lot on 121st, sleeps thirty-eight. Those new buildings have such shoddy construction, just drywall and plywood. Like a four-story box of matches, if you ask me. But of course, they're just not built to last, are they?"

Just two guys sitting at the Lenox Lounge, nothing to see here. One beaming, one bowed. One saying hi to a seemingly endless parade of old friends and acquaintances, one wishing the other would just shut the hell up and get drunk so he would give up on murdering for the evening. This was Snowden's plan A: He would get Lester so drunk that nothing more could be done with the night except put it to bed.

He would do this before every one of Lester's planned exercises, for a lifetime if need be. It would be like one of those fables, and if that didn't work, plan B was that he would get himself so drunk that he would be incapable of complying. Even though one plan was marked A and the other B, those letters in no way represented a hierarchical order of feasibility or allotted effort.

Snowden's wallet was padded with six twenties to make this happen, and he'd insisted repeatedly that the night was on him, but plan A clearly wasn't working. Lester didn't just baby-sit his drink, he'd adopted it. The contrast grew as the night progressed. Snowden's once broad shoulders evaporated, his neck slumping straight to his elbows in defeat. Lester would have been glowing even if he wasn't wearing neon. "Lester, you ain't changed in twenty years," they said as they passed their table. "Black don't crack, baby," they declared loudly at the sight of him. "Life looks good on you, brother. Good to see you out, back on top again." Lester sparkled – literally, the metallic threads sewn throughout his suit. Snowden's dreary presence beside him just added to the shimmer.

Everyone at the bar either seemed to know who Lester was or pretend they did. He even called their waitress by her first name and she wasn't wearing a tag, either. She smiled and said, "Knob Creek, right?" and Lester said, "Thanks, Maisy," and that's it, not a word to the fact that though she couldn't have been much older than thirty she had teeth missing on the top and bottom of her left side. Not one mention that, despite the clear complexion provided by pancake makeup, parts of her face were so swollen it looked as if there were plums in utero under its surface. Lester took the fact that Snowden was looking up at all to once again try to engage him in conversation.

"Not trying to pry or anything, but your file says your father was a Panther in the early days."

"Oh, OK, so I have a file. And that's in it."

"Yes it is. Well, I've been thinking about that the last couple weeks, about your father, your apprehensions. You know, his involvement in the Black Liberation Army after the Panthers crumpled means

your father was one of the few who held on. That's amazing that he was still in the BLA up till his last arrest in the early eighties, hardly anyone was. That's a true believer, you see what I'm getting at? A warrior for the people. That was part of why we selected you: It's in your genes. You really should take pride in that, use it as inspiration. This is your chance for redemption, renewal. You get to make up to the world what it lost when he passed away."

Snowden liked that idea. If the world needed another bitter, drunken Cedric Snowden to sit around and complain about how it and its inhabitants had betrayed him, Snowden felt very capable of taking his father's place.

"To renewal!" Lester toasted, finally lifting his glass and Snowden's hopes, then dropping both back down again, nary the drop of whiskey removed. In disbelief and defiance, Snowden swallowed another double of the same, determined to make himself useless if no alternative presented itself.

"Renewal has to be the most beautiful, the most unexpected thing life has to offer. Things fall into ruin and you think, *That's it, it's over.* But you hold on long enough and you see that even the worst things fall apart, eventually. This joint we're sitting in, it was closed till last summer. Now look at it. See that mirror behind the bar?"

Snowden was very familiar with the mirror behind the bar. Snowden had been waving a twenty at it for nearly five minutes now in the hopes Maisy would recognize the universal symbol and send replacements for the fallen soldiers standing hollow on the table before him.

"It's hung up there sixty years, since when Billie Holiday played here on the regular. Had a nicotine film on it a centimeter thick; you could barely see through it before they renovated. Had to use razor blades to get it off. Now look at it. So clear you can see the future in it if you look hard enough."

Snowden was rescued. More for the battle. He tried to order reinforcements for his ally, but Lester declined, asked for a glass of water instead since the pretzels made him thirsty. Maisy didn't smile

this time and Snowden was immediately awash in regret that he'd been caught registering her condition the visit before. In response, his tip was far, far more than her service merited and still failed to emit more than the rumor of a grin in response. Same drink still full in one hand, Lester pointed toward her receding presence before reaching for his snack.

"Take Maisy. Renewal, that's what she needs. Breaks your heart, doesn't it, seeing decent, polite folk like her walking around like that? It's an affront. Can you believe she's homeless?"

Snowden looked over at the woman making change at the register behind the bar, got excited, "See, that's it! That's where we got to put our energy tonight! We got to hook her up with a place to live. She's decent, you just said, right? She got a job. Right now, couple more drinks, that's what we need to get into tonight."

"Oh no, you misunderstand me. She has a lease. She has a Horizon lease, a lovely fifth-floor two-bedroom with original tile in the bathroom – I cleaned the grout myself. But two weeks ago, I was dropping off some late tenant's clothes at the women's shelter and there she is, Maisy Williams who works at the Lenox Lounge, walking past the lobby to do her laundry in the basement, looking even worse than she does now if you can believe it. See, Maisy has a nigger. He moved in with her this year – so far she's visited the shelter three times since. Three times, and once the year before. Always the same thing. Comes in beat the hell up, heals, goes home, doesn't press charges. At this point, she wants to kick him out but won't because she thinks he'll kill her. He will, of course, if it continues on this tangent."

"She told you all that?" Snowden asked.

"No, no, decent folk like Maisy don't go spreading their pain like that, man. They know it's wrong, see? Not only would they not perpetrate insanity like that, they're ashamed of even being a victim to that mess. The social worker who takes the donations from Horizon told me this info – he wanted to know if I could evict the bastard. See, this nigger, he's got no job, he's just sitting up in her

apartment all day, smoking weed and playing video games on her television. Orders pizzas every night, the exact same time too – during the opening montage of the *Star Trek* reruns on Channel Nine. This bully, he even has whores over after that, calls them out the phone book and screws them right there on her bed, doesn't even change the sheets before he passes out."

Snowden collapsed further with every additional detail offered. He took care to swallow the remainders of every bottle before him before breaking the silence.

"Lester, how the hell do you know all that?"

"The apartment's on the top floor. The windows are tall, nearly all the way to the ceiling. If you go on the roof, lean over the edge carefully, you can look down into the rooms through the space above the curtains. You'll see, we're going there now," Lester said, slapping a hand on one of Snowden's near vertical shoulders. Lester looked at his other hand, shrugged before sheepishly pushing his drink across the table. "You want to finish this? At six bucks a glass, I just hate wasting."

Nine streets south and half an avenue over, it was raining. Sloppy, uneven precipitation that left Snowden with the feeling that the universe was giving up just like he was, that it wasn't even bothering to perform consistent weather anymore. Lester, several steps ahead since they left the bar, finally paused to aim his watch at the light from the street lamp. Walking ahead even faster, Lester stopped farther down the block at the meager shelter of an open pay phone.

"I can't be out in this climate. For real, I get pneumonia easy," Snowden said when he reached him. From his black raincoat, Lester pulled a leather organizer, located a folded piece a paper that he then pressed into the closest of Snowden's limp and swaying hands. By the time Snowden pulled it up the page was already darkening and distorting from the water on his cold, rain-pickled fingers.

"What am I supposed to do with this?"

"What in God's name do you think you're supposed to do with it? Just stop the bitchy moron act, OK, Snowden? It's not cute. Read it back to me," Lester snapped. This was Lester nervous. Spend

enough time with someone, you get to see his interpretation of all the standard emotions. Snowden could think of several common ones he hoped he'd never see Lester demonstrate.

" 'Nine-one-one. Shit, you got to come – ' "

"Oh bullshit, Snowden, that first part's the freaking telephone number. Tell me you did not know that. The sentence, just read the sentence. And act it this time. It has to sound completely real, understand me? They tape emergency calls, they'll review it later, so do it right."

Snowden closed his eyes, put his head down for what he hoped was a demonstratively reverential time before announcing his intention to read again with a long sigh. " 'Shit, you got to come quick. There's someone shooting in this apartment. There's screaming, there's all this shooting and shit you got to send someone quick. It's 425 West 116th Street, off Adam Clayton Powell. It's apartment 5E, that's 5E, I could hear the kids screaming right through the door! Repeat facts as necessary! Hang up!' "

"Jesus, you're not even joking, are you?"

"Look man, what do you want from me? It's cold, OK? It's raining, for chrissakes. I haven't even eaten dinner. And I didn't write this thing, did I? Like, maybe you should have given it to me earlier, huh? Don't blame me for that shit."

In response to Snowden's whines, Lester's arm swung back and Snowden prepared to be slapped, but Lester only pulled something from out his jacket, stepped within inches from him. The silent prayer, *Dear God, don't try and kiss me again,* was answered when instead Lester stuck the barrel of his snub-nose under Snowden's jaw, the rest of the gun hidden in his raincoat's cuff. "Turn around and dial the number." The metal reached Snowden's throat just as the operator's voice reached his ears. Snowden's tongue ran, from one to the other. When he was done, Lester put the gun back in his shoulder holster, hugged him. "That was . . . inspired. You are a natural. I mean that," Lester whispered into his ear as he was pulling away. Then he hugged him again, gripping tighter.

The building was only a hundred yards away and a left turn at the corner. Lester hopped up the steps in perfect peppy rhythm, past the fifth floor where he pointed at an apartment door without breaking stride. The door to the roof was open by the time Snowden caught up to him, his own breath and heartbeat loud, their rhythms clashing against each other. It was raining harder. Water filled abandoned buckets of tar and made the loose shingles slip from under the feet when walked on. Lester went to the ledge at the rear of the building, leaned over like he could break the laws of gravity as easily as he did so many other ones. Seeing something he liked, he turned around and gave two thumbs-ups before walking back again.

"I'm really afraid of heights," Snowden told him when he got closer. Lester grinned, nodded, pulled the gun from his holster and stuck it sideways in Snowden's hand.

"Only natural, nothing to be ashamed of. Biological, I think. Just takes practice," Lester assured him. The gun had felt cold on his neck, but in Snowden's hand it felt hot, heavy. It made him want to shoot it. He could easily shoot Lester. The thought was comforting, that he was in control of his destiny after all because he could shoot Lester. It was just that after that he would have to shoot Marks too, and then things got a lot messier. There were all the children. There was also of course the fact that Snowden didn't think he was capable of shooting anyone, or at least in any place other than a limb or foot.

Lester wrapped his arm around Snowden and with gentle assurances pulled him to the back ledge, pushing him down into a squat once they got there. It felt good to Snowden to sit down. Even in the rain, even with the cold water finding its way quickly to the more intimate regions of his ass, it felt good, or at least better. They both sat leaning against the little brick wall just tall enough to give their lower backs support. Lester slapped his own bent knee, then Snowden's.

"Now the fun part. I'm going to ask you to turn around, kneel, then bend over the roof's ledge and look in the bastard's window. The trick is, once you're about to go over the edge you close your

183

eyes. Otherwise you get nauseous. The apartment window's only a foot below the level we're sitting on. The trick is you got to lean as far forward as you can, OK? And bend your head down as far as it'll go. Once you get into position, then open your eyes, not before. Trust me, you'll feel much better if you do it that way."

"Lester, I get on my knees and lean forward as far as I can, I'll fall off the side of the building," Snowden said and immediately regretted it. Part of it was that he worried he had insulted the Chupacabra, part of it was he didn't want to give him any more ideas. "Why don't we just go to the back fire escape, peek in that way."

"Too risky, we could be seen. Besides, it's raining and you could slip on the wet metal and break your neck. Don't worry, silly, I'll be sitting on your legs. You're lucky, when it was just me I had to tie myself with climbing rope back to that vent. Come on, move it, they're going to be here soon."

"Who'll be here?"

"One thing at a time, I'll tell you in a minute. Hurry."

Snowden got on his knees. This was an appropriate position, because Snowden was praying, and since in moments of normalcy he professed not to believe in God, Snowden was praying really hard to compensate. Lester sat on his legs. The man's ass was sharp and bony and underneath it Snowden's shins were shredded into the gravel lining the roof. As Lester began pushing Snowden's shoulders forward over the edge, the pain was the only thing to hold on to.

"Pretend you're flying." Snowden tried, but it didn't work, so instead, hands gripping the rail so hard flecks of mortar fell five stories down like industrial dandruff, he tried for the less ambitious goal of pretending he couldn't fall.

When Snowden opened his eyes again, he realized he was crying. Despite that, he could clearly see the solidified air bubbles in the bricks only inches away. A glance up (or down) and there was the room and guy in question, Snowden's view was inverted but otherwise lucent and unobstructed. There was a knocking at the base of his spine.

"What's he doing?" Snowden heard lightly behind him. He was sitting and watching the television, as foretold. He was a moron. It was evident to Snowden on first glance, even from looking upside down in the rain twenty feet away through the window. There was a reason for the descriptor *slack jaw*. There were simple etymologies for the words *lumbering* and *blockhead*; staring at this subject's profile, Snowden was struck with the notion that it had been carved from an uprooted stump with a butter knife. There was a Wednesday class, during the history portion months before, when Lester made mention of the days when white would-be scientists would stroll 135th Street trying to measure black people's skulls to prove the race's mental inferiority. Looking at the mug on the guy through the window, Snowden – so much blood rushing to his head he could smell it – wondered if anyone had ever tried to measure intelligence via facial expressions as well. It seemed so obvious an indicator to him, hanging there watching the look on this guy's face as he sat inches away from the television scooping handfuls of cereal from out of the box and shoving what he could fit into his mouth, letting the remainder fall to the floor in front of him.

"Now that it's aimed right at me, I have to say this: You've got a really lovely derrière," Lester told him.

"What?" Snowden started squirming, trying to pull himself up again. Lester laughed, slapped him lightly on the region in question.

"Oh come on, just a joke. Just a bit of humor to lighten the situation."

Maybe he just wants me to hang here, Snowden assured himself. *Maybe it was as simple as making a phone call and whatever the Chupacabra wants to happen was put in motion and nothing more will be asked.* Snowden decided that could be true, chose to ignore the gun that had become a part of his hand. There was an optimist deep inside Snowden. No one could be more surprised than Snowden himself, but there was an optimist deep inside him, hidden in some dark, warm, waterproof crevice. As Lester tugged on his back and Snowden began pulling himself back up, this internal optimist decided to make its voice heard. *I've been in*

worse situations than this one, most definitely. See, it's over, I didn't fall. I haven't done anything really serious. I'm an innocent, it's true. I don't even know what's going on.

"Let me tell you what's going on," Lester whispered as soon as Snowden'd risen all the way back up. "In a minute the cops will be here, coming to this apartment, guns drawn. Mr. Trevor Barber down there goes to open the door thinking it's his pizza fix and as he does the cops get nervous and shoot him. End of story. We go back to the bar. I'll buy this time."

Snowden thought about the scheme for a moment, particularly its lack of demanded action and the fact that it was probably impossible to calculate the improbability of it unfolding successfully without a very large military grade computer, and offered Lester his unbounded enthusiasm and admiration for its construction.

"Aren't you going to ask why they're going to shoot him?" Lester wondered.

"No, no, I like the plan just the way it is, no need to question it. I mean, I'm sure the police officers have their own personal reasons, but why pry?" Snowden told him.

"Because as he goes to the door, you're going to shoot a hole through it. Don't worry, I knocked out the lightbulbs in the hallway and he keeps the light in the living room on, so when the officers hear the shot and see the hole glaring through the door, they'll get the picture."

Snowden got the picture too. The picture was that there was no way he was going to shoot the gun as suggested, so he began immediately setting up his excuse. "Hey man, I've never even shot a gun before. I'm nervous. What if I shoot him by mistake?"

"That's fine, the bullet should pass right through him and still do the job. The way his body should look at the end of this, no coroner will have reason to question it."

"But the cops, man. It ain't right, setting up the people sworn to protect this place. That's not the Horizon way." Snowden was suddenly excited by the discovery of a rational argument by which

186

the irrational might be swayed. "That ain't right! I mean, did you even check this over with Congressman Marks. Congressman Marks has friends in the department."

"And those friends have enemies, and that's who's scheduled to show up tonight. Now be a good boy and bend over."

Snowden hung upside down over the edge of the building for six minutes, his sinuses taut and painful, his back aching and promising great reprisals if he ever tried to straighten out again. He knew six minutes had gone by because at the top of every one Lester complained about police tardiness, that someone should be there by now.

"This is deplorable. Really, what if an innocent really was being shot at? You think he'd have to wait this long on the Upper East Side?"

Lester was so busy complaining he didn't hear it when the downstairs door buzzer was finally rung. The dunce did. Snowden watched Barber rise from the couch holding his wallet, walking slowly backward so his eyes never had to leave the television screen, buzzing them in without even checking the intercom.

"Really, Snowden, do you think? Because I've never lived on the Upper East Side. What was that?" Lester asked. That was a bit of bad luck, because just as Snowden had begun to hope that the moron had his TV so loud that the police would come and go without Lester's knowledge, a moment's pause in the starship action gave the apartment's doorbell silence in which to assert itself.

"This is it, wait till he gets right in front of the door," the voice said from above Snowden. As if he could see the moment the subject stepped into the proposed line of fire, when the guy did Lester continued with, "Shoot it."

Snowden wanted to shoot himself. The guy he was now pointing the gun at, he only had one dirty white sock on. From behind, the brown crack of his ass peeked through his drooping sweatpants belligerently, threatening to go lunar with every step. It was a sad life he was watching, and it made his life seem that much sadder that this

boar was worth risking it for. "The trigger, pull it or I'm dropping you!" Lester punched Snowden in the ass. Trevor Barber paused a yard from the door, stretched his head so far back Snowden became afraid he'd see him, and over top of the sound of screaming Klingon the man produced a fart so momentous even Lester heard it. Vicious abuser of the weak, unrepentant parasite of the downtrodden, now also freakishly flatulent: Snowden suddenly wanted to kill him. Even so, it wasn't until he could feel Lester starting to let go of his legs that Snowden fired the gun, and even then he waited until the moment the bastard got his door open and the cops had a chance to see him clearly.

Snowden aimed at the patch of dried dirt by the trash cans far below on the ground. He saw the cloud of dust when the bullet hit, then heard the echoes as the sound bounced off the backs of so many tenement walls. Then Snowden realized it wasn't echoes, and that was when he looked back in the window and saw Trevor Barber dancing, except that that wasn't dancing. That was getting shot. That was glass breaking on the back windows. That whining was the sound of bullets shooting by. That hot rain pouring onto Snowden's face was him peeing himself.

By the time Lester pulled him back up, Snowden's mind was as much a mess as his clothes. Lester tried to hug him, calm him down, but Snowden pushed the man away. The gun was not his friend, it was not a natural extension of his arm, and Snowden slammed it down in front of himself and as it bounced yelped in fear at what he'd just done. Lester just picked it up, then pulled Snowden by his arm out of there.

Snowden found himself standing atop an entirely different roof at least five buildings over and didn't remember walking there, climbing over the small brick walls that divided each of them. Lester was talking. Lester was saying, "Snowden, listen to me, I'm so sorry that I didn't just trust your judgment, your timing. I don't know what came over me, but I would never have dropped you. You know that, right?"

"I let him get to the door, open it." Snowden finally started talking. Actually, this wasn't strictly true: Snowden had been saying "shit" repeatedly since he reached solid ground, but now he was moving on to complete sentences. "I let him get to the door. He opened it. They saw him standing there with his wallet in his hand and they shot him anyway. They shot him. They shot him so many times."

"Oh my God," was Lester's response. He pulled away, walked hands to his head ten feet on only to say, "I can't believe it," and walk back again. Snowden, who'd taken to hugging himself, pulled his head up to watch the man. There were so many emotions, too many things to be reacting to, moments and things to feel, but Snowden looked at Lester's shock and felt hope. He realizes, he finally gets it, the insanity of all it all. He finally gets it.

"You get it," Snowden said when Lester returned.

Lester smiled back at him. "Are you kidding? I get it! I totally get it. The wallet, letting them get a glimpse so they thought it was a gun when they heard the shot. The Amadou Diallo shooting, right? I'm just . . . I mean . . . awe. You improvised that hanging there? Forget Bobby Finley, you're the artist. All I can say is, 'Wow.' An *homage*."

They went back to the Lenox Lounge. Lester insisted on this, and then he walked so fast Snowden could barely drone stiffly behind him. As soon as they were inside, Lester wrenched off his coat, yanked his watch, and laid it faceup on the table. "We stay till at least one," Lester said as he ripped through his organizer in search of the leather pouch, cursing till he found it then shooting off to the bathroom.

Lester came back a half hour later, sat down at the table, and then nodded for another half. They weren't sitting in the same seats as before. This was a good thing because their new seats where secluded far in the back by the leopard-print wall, and Snowden was just coming back to himself enough, was just starting to worry about less significant things like the fact that he was sitting in a public place absolutely soaked, in part by his own urine.

"Drunks. Make great. Alibis," Lester said. It took him a couple of minutes, eyes floating in their lids, but he got it out. Snowden ignored him. He didn't feel like listening, he felt like drinking, and he wanted to do that and watch her. She was still there, working. She was still there and her face still looked like someone had used it to kick the dirt off his boots, and Snowden was glad she still looked like that. He wanted to remember every detail of the abused face, every pus-bloated curve, every darkened shade her makeup failed to camouflage. Take that as the image you remember from this night, Snowden begged himself. Those fists will never hit that face, Snowden kept forcing himself to acknowledge. It offered little solace, but a little was something so he kept doing it. Slamming it down with six-dollar shots of whiskey until the logic made more sense.

Even by Snowden's standards he was exceptionally drunk by the time the watch admitted it was one o'clock. It was a belligerent, deceitful device, and he was pretty sure it had paused a few times when he wasn't looking (eleven twenty-seven, for instance, went on forever, and it had been twelve forty-nine for generations). Snowden fell asleep watching it, woke up thirty-four minutes past confused about where he was and what reality everybody was using, the one from his dream or the other one he now could recall only vaguely. Trying to stand up, it was pretty clear that by consensus the world had changed its rules of gravity and nobody had bothered to tell him which pissed him off but Lester was saying something about "be careful" so maybe that's what he was talking about. The bladder said bathroom first, then when he was walking back out it was her again at the table collecting her tip and saying "Thank you" and Snowden said "Just be careful who you love next time" but it was loud and she didn't quite hear him.

Outside Snowden remembered more about who he was, the place, the time, all that. And what he was doing. He was walking, each step deliberate – got to land on the foot's ball, lift the knee up high enough, do the right then left or left then right but never the

same legs consecutively. It got easier every time he got it right. Then there was where he was going. Snowden was going back there. Snowden was going to tell them what happened, apologize, all that. Shhh, don't tell the sober mind, just keep walking.

Snowden trudged south on Lenox. The brownstones, they lined both sides of the street, leaning in and bearing witness with so many eyes. This is how it was supposed to happen. The night smelled of burning wood and Snowden knew this could mean only one thing, barbecue, but he stayed course anyway. He was tired, but the weight of his burden propelled him forward. He was lost, but then there came the sirens and they called to him, gave him the sign of flashing red lights and Snowden knew they were waiting for his arrival. Destiny was so amazing, even in this state there was room for awe at this. Just when Snowden feared he'd been led asunder another vehicle would coming running by, its lights and call demanding that he follow, moving so fast it was pretty clear whoever was driving was hungry too.

As Snowden got closer, the smell of smoke-roasted meat grew stronger, so that by the time he turned the corner and saw all the red and blue lights flashing on top of their vehicles, Snowden was starving, pushing toward them despite the fact that the fog made it hard to breathe. There was a whole house on the corner on fire, but that made sense because there were a lot of people there to feed, and it was that new flophouse, which was fine because nobody wanted it here anyway. People were gathered halfway down the block from it. Negroes love some barbecue. Wooden horses had been erected. Snowden, who was finding his ongoing battle simply to keep his eyes open complicated by the gray air, couldn't find the line for the serving area, where to get the paper plates or plasticware. But he did see Bobby in the middle of the street at the very front. Oh friend of friends, so good to see a face of love on a late Harlem night. Bobby would know how to get a meal ticket, where the beer tent was.

"Where's the food, man?" Snowden put his hands on Bobby's neck, shook it. Bobby's head bounced a little, but the skinny man

191

didn't even bother removing his grip from the FDNY barricade, let alone turn and offer a response. This was not good at all. Snowden was tired, and if he didn't get an answer, goddamn it, he was going to turn around go home, eat leftovers.

"Bobby, where's the food?" If Bobby knew he wasn't saying. Snowden felt pissed but powerless. Bobby was black and motionless and shiny from sweat, staring forward and up like he was watching a movie. Snowden wanted to punch him, but Bobby looked too much like a tar baby to risk it.

THEN SHE KEPT COMING BACK

PIPER WAS BEING followed.

From the first time she showed up at the smoking ruins of Mumia Abu-Jamal Memorial Halfway House he identified her, noted her presence. Then she kept coming back. On her third visit, as she walked around the site taking yet another set of photos, he walked with her, unnoticed, staying directly behind her the whole time. On her sixth recorded visit back to the scene of the fire, when Piper ignored the police tape's yellow order not to cross its line, he was there waiting for her. He watched intently as she forced herself through the space where the temporary fencing almost met the wall. He was disgusted by the soft, rounded gut that revealed itself when her shirt became stuck on an odd barb, but he crossed the street to get a closer look anyway. To see exactly what she was looking at. As Piper moved through the blackened remains of windows and walls, he kept careful pace with her on the sidewalk beyond. Wondering what she was thinking. Fuchsia fedora pulled down low, raincoat collar up, pretending to walk his little wiener dog.

What Piper was thinking, in order of least to most importance: If I don't eat that lo mein today it's going to go bad; look for something suspicious; how the hell am I supposed to know what looks suspicious; thank God I finally got assigned a real story; the only reason they gave me this story is Gil Manly is covering the police shooting of Trevor Barber; I bust my ass every day for this paper and now they're cutting me out of Harlem's most newsworthy event.

The last thought was the one that resonated the most, whose hum had endured since she'd listen to Cole Jr. dole out the stories four

days before. The Trevor Barber shooting was *the* big story; the NYPD shoot an innocent, unarmed black man every year or two and it's always *the* big story. Piper's big story was she was being denied it. The ripples of that fact grew as they moved farther away from the source, leaving questions in their wake. These questions varied greatly in their complexity, creativity, and merit but were uniform in their destructiveness as well as their subject matter: the worth and prospects of one Piper Goines. To drown them out, Piper began creating new ones of her own. They were good ones. They included such enticing distractions as: Why would a building that's just been built burn down as fast as a nineteenth-century log cabin? Isn't it a little convenient that the bane of this community was thwarted before it could even fully open its doors? Who will champion justice for the three parolees who died if I don't?

"Oh snap, it's Sherlock Homegirl!" was Dumbass's response as he clanked away at the pipes under Piper's bathroom sink with his immaculate tools. He'd been eavesdropping on her and his wife's conversation, his rare visit to the third floor sparked by a brown water stain that had appeared on his office ceiling directly below. "Sister of my love, just because you didn't get the story you wanted doesn't mean your fire is going to magically become more than just that. The dryer in the basement had a bad cord, they already said so on TV. That police shooting is already dying down anyway. I mean, the mayor himself reported the guy had a bunch of sexual assault convictions. Who cares about a hood like that?"

"Jesus Brian, those were supposed to be sealed juvenile records, the mayor broke the law just by leaking them, and they were almost a decade old. Are you going to tell me you're as gullible as those cynics think?" Piper rolled her eyes for emphasis. Dumbass didn't know what he was talking about. Piper would consider that a general assessment of her brother-in-law's worldview, but in this instance it applied more specifically. Brian hadn't spent the afternoon shifting through files at City Hall, pulling evidence on past building code violations of 437 West 121st Street's contractor. Brian

194

had no idea who Maverick Construction was, let alone that it had been cited on four different occasions in five years for using subgrade insulation, including Propex, a highly flammable form now banned. Brian hadn't spent the week learning what burn points or burn patterns were, or had a connection from his alumni association who worked in the arson division whisper that there'd been only one of the former, and the latter was defined by the ignition of the insulation in the interior basement walls. The fire had shot up a crawl space that went – against several building codes – uninterrupted from the foundation to the roof. No one else knew these things, either, or, she hoped, would until the *New Holland Herald*'s next edition.

Brian also didn't hug Greg Tanen's mother every time she broke down describing her son's life, see the photo from Quinn Jefferson's prom where he smiled as big as the date his arms could barely wrap around, or listen on the phone as Dio Demilo's sister kept repeating, "He was just turning around his life, you know?" so Piper tried to forgive him for saying the following:

"An armed burglar, a telephone con artist, and a habitual car thief, and a center that was going to bring more of the same if it stayed open the rest of the week, I mean, come on. It's messed up, sure, but you can hardly be surprised the Red Cross isn't handing out Kleenex on 125th Street."

"I don't know if you know this, but not everybody got to have both parents around growing up, OK? Not everybody got to belong to Jack and Jill. There are actually some people out there who don't have private school educations, who didn't get to go to college, or have their frat brothers hook them up with high-paying jobs for the rest of their lives."

"No! Really?" Brian jumped up, leaned out the bathroom door to see Piper sitting on the couch in the living room, his shirt wet and monkey wrench in hand. "Are you sure about this? Oh my God! Honey, quick, get me Cornel West on the phone. Underprivileged black people – why, who knew of such nonsense? I tell you, once my

man Cornel hears about this, there's going to be some changes around here!"

"Leave me out of this. Do you want onions in this?" Dee asked her sister. Dee was in the kitchen cooking omelets. They weren't for her. They were for Robert M. Finley, author of *The Great Work*, and for her sister who would leave them on the skillet and pretend to reheat them when he got there.

"Yeah, but could you caramelize them separately before adding the eggs to the pan?"

"Oh right. Isn't that funny how someone who claims not to cook knows how to properly prepare caramelized onions?"

"I can't cook," Piper told her, "but if I could cook, that's how I'd do it. I hate it when they throw in pieces of raw, crunchy onions. It's tacky. Who wants to seem tacky?"

"I thought you weren't interested in this guy," Dumbass chimed in. "This is the mover, the guy you wanted me to punch in the mouth if he kept calling the house a couple months ago, right? See honey, I told you it was that guy. So what, he broke down your defenses?"

"This is not someone I'm interested in, OK?" Piper protested. "This is a talented published author, someone whose work I admire. We had a very long, very enjoyable conversation at the Horizon Ball, and he turns out to be a very sweet guy. He enjoys my work as well. We have an artistic connection."

Brian came back out from under the sink again for this one. "Wait a minute, he told you he likes your paintings? Those paintings in there, the ones I've seen? Fascinating," he said, hand on chin. "This guy must really be in love."

"Stop," Dee ordered, distracted by her attempt to wrap both ends of the egg evenly underneath it as instructed. "You guys want to talk about art, look at this, this is art. You sure you don't want these on a plate? I'm feeling very homemakerish at the moment. I could make a garnish with toothpicks and turnip shavings."

When Piper's phone rang, Dee picked up because she was the closest and it was her habit if not her privilege. By the time Piper had

196

risen to take it out of her hand, the person had hung up. Dee handed the dead phone to Piper anyway, along with the message that Robert M. Finley, author of *The Great Work*, had canceled.

"Forget him. That's rude, that's not how a man handles things. If he was considerate, he would have called hours ago," Brian offered. "If you want I can still go and beat him up. Uh, he was that real skinny one, not that big, mean-looking bastard, right?"

"No, it's not like that," Piper responded. "The guy like had this huge crush on me. I mean, why would he just blow me off after I've gone to the trouble of preparing a meal and everything? Did he say he was sick?"

"No, he didn't say anything. Just, 'I am Robert M. Finley and I will not be leaving my apartment.' Then he hung up."

Piper ate both omelets. Then she went back to work, more determined than before. It was difficult reaching contacts on a Sunday, but she searched the Internet for home numbers. On her next job interview, if they asked her what her weakness was, Piper would say, "I work too hard. I'm too thorough. News is the compilation, synthesis, and disbursement of information. I can't stop looking until I know everything, and there is always something more to know, another facet to uncover, which changes the view of the whole. I live for deadlines," Piper would tell them. "It's the only way I can stop myself from looking."

The doorbell rang and Piper's first thought was, *It's him*. Jumping down the steps, surprised at her elation, the nature of it, trying not slip or produce a rhythm that betrayed excitement. At the door, it wasn't him. It wasn't Snowden either. It was just odd.

The reason Piper unlocked the door wasn't that she recognized the man. She did, but he wasn't the type with whom familiarity bred comfort. He looked like someone who would hurt someone. He didn't look particularly mean, not like he brought pain out of any sadistic enjoyment or malice. It looked like his nature, as if soft things bruised and hard things just broke in his hands. No, the

reason Piper opened her door was that not even the most criminally insane would come to do someone harm dressed like that. Like an admiral in the Martian army.

"You're Horus, aren't you? The underwear freak. Did Robert send you over with those?" Those were flowers. Birds of paradise, Piper assumed a dozen, their screaming red beaks just adding to the messenger's otherworldly presence.

"You mean Bobby? Hell no. I was sent here by the man. The man!" Horus pushed the flowers forward. When Piper didn't react by actually taking the massive vase, Horus just pushed it toward her farther till she did, then removed a letter from inside his jacket.

" 'Former Congressman Marks of New York City's Fifteenth District and current high chairman of the board and COO of the Horizon Foundation, hereby formally invites you to join him in a moment of fine conversation at the company office this very evening. On behalf of Congressman Marks, I, Horus Manley, his humble servant, have been empowered to both invite and escort you. Let me add that the congressman would be greatly honored by your presence, and that he apologizes in advance for such short notice, as it in no way was intended as a slight against your person.' "

Finished, Horus stood frozen, eyes skyward, arms behind his back.

"What? You mean now?"

"Yeah, that's right, now. Look – I want you to look at it, it's all there. It's all true, see? Except for that servant part, I'm more a junior partner if you want to get real about it."

Piper spent most of the walk marveling at her judgment's complete inability to overpower her curiosity, even for long enough to say the word no. Horus spent most of their walk talking. A bunch of teenagers passed, at least ten of them, goose-down jackets puffing them up like blowfish, and one yelled out to him, "Who's your tailor? Marcus Garvey?" but Horus was not to be interrupted. Horus was

from Chicago. Horus was a legend in that town. As a baby, Horus took Old English with his Enfamil. Finally noticing the lack of response, Horus turned his sentences into the form of questions.

"So what's that Bobby shit? I thought you were kicking it with my man the Snowball."

"Robert's a kindred artistic spirit. I'm enamored with his literary skill, that's all." In a wave of practicality, Piper thought to ask if Horus was also going to walk her home but stopped when she couldn't decide if he was really that less scary than anything else she might run into.

"I like the way you talk, you talk real educational. So you into brothers that write. I write too, you know that? I got me a book, it's going to be printed and everything." Horus snapped his fingers, pointed at her. They were long digits, each joint its own distinct ball. Horus's knuckles looked like he used them to walk on.

"That's great. What's it about, who's publishing it?" There were moments in conversations that Piper found for whatever reason to be particularly strained or laborious, when she thought, *How am I ever going to get through this? How am I ever going to string enough words to get through to the other side?*

"Well, OK, you see it's not really one of those get published kind of books. I'm thinking of getting it photocopied and spiral-bound at Kinko's, though, that's what I'm thinking of. It's called *People I'm Gonna Kill When I Get My Gun*. It's not actually a story in the traditional sense. More of a list, I guess you could call it. Yeah, it's a list. People who pissed me off, people who tried to fuck me over, play me for a sucker – you get the idea. I started it when I had to take this . . . class-type thing. It felt so good, I just kept working on it after I got out again. See, I do a name, then a strategy, you know, break it down line by line. Don't get the wrong idea, it's more a fantasy thing. I mean, I been had my gun since I started it, I just kept the title 'cause it sound so good. Man, I get in a zone, you'd be scared how I pump out them pages!"

"I bet I would," Piper said through clenched and smiling teeth.

Don't run, she kept telling herself. Nuts are like rabid dogs, trying to run away from them only makes things worse.

It was only a conversation like this that could inspire joy at the sight of one Olthidius Cole Sr., as it did when Piper saw him waddling out of the Horizon storefront, pulled forward by his dented aluminum cane. Piper used him as an excuse to break away, yelling, "Hi, boss! Did you get a chance to read my draft?" to drown out everything else that was being said. Cole looked so startled to see her that Piper thought for a moment he might try and whack her with the stick, but instead he rolled his eyes, flapped his cheeks, wagged his head at her impudence, and kept moving.

"So now you know all three of us, who you think is going to make it all the way? Who you think is going to win?" Horus asked as he unlocked the front door.

"I'm sorry, I don't know what you're talking about." Piper wasn't sorry, she wanted to be inside, beyond him.

"Oh, you know what I'm talking about. Yes, you do," Horus insisted.

"First let me confess, I'm already a fan. I've been following your byline since your revealing article on the accidental death rate." Cyrus Marks wore a smoking jacket, silk, Asian markings. He seemed to think this jacket made him charming, or at least added to his charm, this Piper gathered from the dramatic ritual he made of repeatedly tying and untying its belt, a gesture she found both absent and vain.

"The one I got scooped on. Well, I'm glad somebody saw the original piece. The *Times* ran a very flattering likeness of you, I remember."

"Yes, well, I have been reading your work with great interest ever since. Olthidius Cole was just in that very seat telling me how thorough your research into the fire at 121st is, I look forward to seeing the final draft. I love your movie reviews as well. Even when they forget to print your initials I know if it's you because you're the

only one at the *Herald* who ever dislikes anything made by another black person."

"I'm just honest, but I also try to be fair. There's usually some good even in the worst, when there is I mention that too." It was a small black world. Piper wondered which mediocrity's creator Marks was related to, and why it had taken this long for her call to task. Her last printed review was a dissection of Bo Shareef's new hit, *Don't Go There*, where she traced the book's three central clichés back to their origins in *Uncle Tom's Cabin*, *Birth of a Nation*, and *Nigger Heaven*, going on to list the book's uncanny plot similarities with episode twenty-three of *Malcolm & Eddie*.

"Of course you do. I find your reviews very fair. And honest. Blunt, but all true honesty arrives bluntly. I appreciate that. There seems to be a general consensus to avoid self-criticism in our community, doesn't there? Not simply in the arts, but in general. I agree with you. It's a new age, I'm all for calling a spade a spade, if you will. Without addressing our deficiencies, how can we ever hope to improve?"

"I guess. So why am I here?"

Marks took the question like a child had slapped him with it, laughed at it, and pushed it away. "You studied at Columbia. They have an excellent journalism program. So you had Akers, Pavez, Wharton."

"Pavez was my adviser."

"I imagine he'd be an excellent one. He's got a good head on his shoulders, albeit a fat one. He had many good things to say about you as well."

This comment, this was the official alarm. This was the thing that Piper knew made ordinary people pull back yet compelled her to plunge forward. "OK, now this is getting a little bizarre. Why are you calling and asking people about me and why did you invite me here?" Piper made like she was trying to gather her coat from the back of her chair, but Marks must have known she was bluffing. He didn't even attempt to talk until Piper had stopped moving and was looking at him in the face again.

"I have a job for you. That's the short of it. Let me assure you, though, that I was not trying to pry. It's just, well, you know the black middle class is only but so big, you run into people, topics arise. This whole community, it functions on the network of friends, the currency favors. I'm really not trying to be obtuse, it's just that I feel this is a large proposition, so it takes a bit of buildup."

"All right, you got me. Talk." Piper felt herself getting very excited and felt equally foolish about that.

"Right. Well, I just have three questions. Indulge me in those and I'll tell you whatever you like. You went to one of the top journalism schools in the country, you're obviously very intelligent, talented, it's not like you're over the hill in any way. Why are you working at a shameful rag like the *New Holland Herald*?"

"That's easy, because it wouldn't be the 'shameful rag' you seem to think it is if more qualified black folks didn't run away to the bigger papers and leave it behind," Piper defended.

"Exactly. That's what we are trying to do here at Horizon — stop the brain drain in our community, stop the financial drain as well, build something we can all be proud of. I know I don't look it, but I'm old enough to remember what the *Herald* was like before the white papers would hire our best and brightest. It resounded. It was important. It covered issues the way no other source could."

"So there's your answer. I want to help bring it back to that point. My goal is to make it something to be proud of again."

"And how would you do that? That's actually the second question, so feel free to elaborate." Marks leaned back in his chair to provide room for her answer.

Piper felt very free to elaborate. There was her plan to dump the tabloid's front-page articles in favor of a full-page illustration cover with teaser lines like the *Village Voice*, there was her plan to switch from underpaid hacks to clip-hungry interns from New York's top journalism schools who would work for the same peanuts but actually be good, there was her plan to publish short stories and novel excerpts, in exchange offering mere exposure as payment.

Piper kept going. There was a wall of self-restraint within her, it was great and wide and as tall as her mind's imagination, but unfortunately it was made of paper and already shredded from all the times she'd plowed right through it. Still, there was a pause for air when she noticed Cyrus Marks's look of amazement and thought that might not be a reaction to the ideas but the fact that she'd just mentioned at least two dozen of them in less than three minutes.

"Well, the *Herald* could reach its potential again," Piper tried to conclude. "I mean, I guess with these things you just have to have patience."

"Oh, no I don't. I don't need patience," was Marks's response. Piper wasn't surprised at the statement because Cyrus Marks looked to her like a man who believed he didn't need patience. "We, as a people, have had too much patience too long for our own silliness. No, what I need is you. In charge of the *Herald*, raising the standard, doing all those ideas you just said. So I might as well continue on to my third question. If Olthidius Cole chose to retire in the next year – which he has – if he didn't want his son to assume full control of the mantle – which he doesn't, apparently – and if it was within my power, would you consider becoming the new editor in chief of the *New Holland Herald*?"

"You know, that's a lot of ifs." *If* this was a joke and Snowden was behind it, if this was some sort of passive-aggressive revenge for any past grievance Piper might have cost him, Piper would hurt him. Physically and with great vigor.

"There are no ifs. I've been an investor in the *Herald* for years now. As of an hour ago, I just upped the percentage a bit. Called in a favor from a friend, you could say."

"I . . . I really don't believe this. But say I did, say I did believe this. Say I believe you're going to call me out of the blue, someone you don't even know, and give me a job that I might on paper seem barely qualified for. Say I don't think this is a sick, sick prank, then what's the price? What do you want from me in return?" Piper wouldn't sleep with him, Piper wouldn't put one cell of his body near

her own. When you want something so bad sometimes you ask yourself what you'd do for it, but it turned out that no, she wouldn't do that. But where was the line? Piper asked herself, because there was one and it probably wasn't that far away from there.

"You are qualified. Pavez said you did a lovely job editing the *Columbia Spectator*, and this really isn't that different, is it? Everyone I spoke with attested to your character. So to the 'price.' Just a little project I'd like you to get off the ground. Of course it will involve dropping what you're working on and cutting back on your *Herald* hours in general, but I assure you you'll find this worth the sacrifice. It deals directly with creating the next generation of black journalists, a talent pool that ten years down the road the *Herald* can pull from. So, Ms. Goines, I actually have one extra question for you: How good are you with children?"

SLIPPERY

S NOWDEN WAS A new man. Unfortunately, that man was a paranoid, guilt-ridden wreck of one. Don't kill people and think you can remain the same. This new guy, he was completely sober, had stayed so since the morning he'd awoken in clothes that reeked of smoke and it had taken till late afternoon to remember why. The new one didn't watch television, either, not out of any social purist motivation, it was just that even the most escapist of shows ran ads for the news he was trying so hard to avoid in the first place. Snowden was a new man. He didn't like the one he'd become, but the more Snowden thought about it the more he realized he didn't care for the one he'd been before, either.

As a reward for his loyal service, Lester was assigning Snowden the best properties, throwing him the best clients at the day job, happy-face customers with seven years of clean credit, 30 percent down, and low consumer debt. Snowden spent every encounter with these fine happy-face buyers petrified they would spin around with badges and cuffs instead of checkbooks and pens. Be a good realtor and just keep walking through the empty rooms smiling, Snowden kept telling himself. Say stuff like, "The thing that's really wonderful about this," and point at something.

Solace was sought from Bobby Finley but not found. This was because Bobby Finley was not found, either. Eventually Snowden remembered clips of a conversation they'd had when they ran into each other outside the Mumia Abu-Jamal fire, but his state during the encounter had left the images and audio distorted. Since Bobby refused to answer his door when Snowden came around, or even

return his calls, it was a safe assumption that his behavior was in response to some forgotten slight Snowden may or may not have intended. It was only when Bobby didn't show up for work for days that Snowden decided not to take the silence personally.

Further concern was somewhat banished when Lester said he'd seen Bobby Finley, that Bobby was just adjusting to the strain of the job and would be out of the office during regular hours indefinitely. Snowden just didn't like the way Lester said it. The mounting fear that Bobby was in fact dead, however, was shown to be groundless, irrational even, as Bobby Finley was seen exiting a property only doors away from the one Snowden was showing. Very much alive, with his own set of prospective buyers in tow, shaking his own set of hands.

"Yo nig, where you been?" Snowden asked. Bobby walked down the townhouse steps, put his clients back into their taxi-hack downtown. Snowden's own were deciding on whether to see the three-bedroom condo two blocks south or take this Uptown opportunity to walk over to the Studio Museum instead. Snowden ceased pretending to care either way and ran from them toward his coworker.

Bobby Finley didn't run from him, he just didn't acknowledge Snowden's calls or cease walking in the opposite direction, Snowden's hand on his arm the only thing that stopped him. He'd lost weight. Snowden would have never guessed that Bobby had any weight he could misplace, but now saw that both the padding under Bobby's eyes that kept him from looking haunted and the thin layer of flesh that kept every single vein in Bobby's throat from showing had both gone missing.

In response to the earnest concern of, "Yo man, where you been?" Bobby Finley had only a shrug and a drained smile to give. When more was demanded, Bobby gave the weak excuse, "I'm sorry, I've been busy. I'm writing."

"I thought that shit was supposed to make you happy. You don't look happy. You look like a burnt scarecrow."

Giving up on trying to smile, Bobby Finley started walking away instead. Snowden yelled his apologies behind him, but they were like wind in Bobby's sail.

In the absence of fraternal comfort, there were new vices to be had, sober ones that didn't lead to memory lapse, the will to perform self-sacrificial acts, or any form of confession in general. For instance, the new Snowden was an ardent smoker. At least a pack a day, never the same brand twice, as life was short and he wanted to keep the entire nicotine world available to him. The packs he didn't like Snowden smoked even faster, eager to get to the next one. They made him feel calm. Their death-bringing gifts gave him a new, rather ordinary mortal fear to occupy his mind and replace more flamboyant ones.

The other vice, Snowden found even more addictive, was pretending that what he and Lester were doing was morally right.

Dangerous, yes, Snowden knew that, could feel its seduction, that it was just the easy way to deal with what was happening. Yet there it was. Going away but never for too long. The only thing that made all the chaos grow fat and heavy and fall stilled to the ground was to imagine it. Lester was right. Therefore those deaths were no tragedy. Therefore Snowden had done nothing wrong. Minutes could go by when Snowden could sustain this reasoning. Snowden went back to the Lenox Lounge and saw that woman Maisy still waiting tables and her face had healed and Snowden'd felt that reasoning take over him, sipped his soda, and had his delusion reaffirmed every time he saw Maisy smile so easily. Felt the same thing in ecstatic pangs as he stood at the lodge's third-floor window and watched Jifar run screaming with child joy in the backyard along with so many other uniformed kids. No matter the free fall Snowden felt when guilt finally crushed the pillars of this logic, those moments before were his most peaceful. Ever. The fantasy was not just that he'd done nothing wrong, but that that he'd done something right, daring, and bold. That the universe had a discernible order of negative and

positive and that he'd been blessed with the purpose of contributing to the good of it.

The strategy necessary for successful urban renewal was rather simple, or at least appeared so, having been repeated with nearly every Wednesday class of the Horizon Second Chance Program.

First, urban renewal must happen as a mass movement, entire ghetto blocks must be seized simultaneously by decent people, taken over and converted to outposts of hardworking, taxpaying folk. The problem with attempts to reintegrate the middle class back into Harlem in the past was that they came as lone pioneers and were invariably mugged and otherwise discouraged into moving by the lumpen without making a dent in the local culture of poverty. Take heed from Roanoke, colonization works only when settlers arrive in droves.

Second, decent residents must have pedestrian access to the subway system that is the city's lifeline without having to pass through ghetto staging areas (otherwise known as "bad blocks"). They must be able to commute to work and New York City's amenities without risk of personal safety. Otherwise they were virtually trapped in their homes, small islands surrounded by a hostile ocean.

Third, designated areas should be dead-ended. A basic strategic consideration, this not only ensured there was only a finite territory to convert but also took care of the larger issue of "walkthroughs." There was no point converting an entire block to decency if random thugs roamed up and down it, if burglars could pass unnoticed, staring up through residence windows to glean the contents inside. This is what made Mount Morris such a prime location to begin the terraforming of Harlem: It was back-ended by the park, behind that was just the hospital and then nothing but industrial ruins and raised lots till Park Avenue's train tracks.

Once "good blocks" had been solidly established, they would slowly spread beyond their original perimeters. As one block filled,

the next would be occupied, continuing the link beyond. When that pattern was established, new satellites would be started, maybe toward the north around Strivers Row and Hamilton Heights, maybe south closer to Central Park. The Horizon position was that this revolution wouldn't even need that many people, as Harlem was already populated by a vast majority of decent, hardworking folk. The monied newcomers would just be replacing the Terrible Tenth. Eventually, all the links would meet. Then the struggle would be over.

All of this, which in class Snowden had found compelling in its own right, became even more engrossing when he was forced to sit in Lester's office and watch the man tape his map of Mount Morris to the wall, each property marked individually with either a green smiley face or circled repeatedly with red lines. Lester in lemon, the white shirt like the pith just below the peel, saying things like, "If we could just get rid of the bastards squatting at 671 West 117th, we could link the 3200 block of Lenox to Adam Clayton Powell Boulevard!"

The files covering Lester's desk were numbered with addresses corresponding to the map's angrily circled residences and were attached with photos of the actual subjects – mug shots and surveillance shots.

"So, come on, the suspense is killing me." Lester tittered. "Who do you want to hunt first?"

Like a high diver preparing for the jump, Snowden was so far in his mind that all that noise, all the sounds of large objects banging the walls in the hall outside, all the screeches of children that accompanied them couldn't reach him. Lester loved this. Lester saw the concentration of his protégé and thought this was impressive, this was the sign that great things were about to be done, said so out loud too, though that was ignored along with the rest of the clatter.

Snowden had a plan, that much was clear. Snowden would do his absolute best to execute it as well, that was also evident. What was

probably less clear, at least to Lester in his banana peel shoes, was that Snowden had no intention of killing anyone. Snowden had figured it out. Snowden had the answer. He would just tell the targeted bastard this time. I have been sent to kill you, he would say. Get out of town or be dead.

"This is exciting, isn't it? Gives you a sense of power, right? There are some real scumbags in there to pick from, rapists, there's even a guy who served for kidnapping at 209 West 118th and that's a really important block so that could work great."

First, Snowden's pick had to be somebody who wouldn't try to kill him just for breaking into his apartment, preferably somebody small with no violent history.

"You know, don't feel you have to limit yourself to felons. There are a lot of petty menaces in the pile as well. If you want, I can find you good a one."

A true criminal, but a puny, cowardly one, and just in case Lester decided to take a more proactive role than his assigned one as lookout, the chosen target had to be a complete and utter scumbag as well. Just in case – it was a dangerous mission.

"They don't even have to have a prison record. I mean, you yourself are proof that's not a defining factor in moral character. I've got a ton of 'quality of life' crimes in here. I've got a guy on this very block who gets in his car at six-thirty every morning and turns his radio on full blast – it wakes the children, it's just criminal. We've tried calling nine one one, stealing his radio, his car, he just pays the fines, replaces them, so trust me there's no other way. Not trying to push you in any direction, but you'd be doing us a real service. Otherwise I won't be able to fit him in till next Thursday."

There he was. Ryan Waters. Even among all those pictures of all those little weaselly bastards, this guy stood out like the refugee of another, elfin species. Ryan Waters. He looked like a jockey's runt son.

"Ryan Waters? OK. All right. I mean, I guess he's a good starter project, it being your first time going solo. He's not really much for

sport, though, is he? The man can't weigh more than a buck twenty-five Thanksgiving night. He is a real lowlife, if that's what you're going by. Ryan Waters, then. Well, there's going to be a bunch of old ladies who're going to have to find a new way to get their groceries home from the Pathmark." That was because Ryan Waters would no longer be waiting for them in his car, volunteering to carry their bags up to their apartments and taking anything he could shove in his coat on his way out again. The less alert ones would no longer have him to thank for his repeated visits. The more alert ones, the ones who went to the police only to recant their accusations later, would no longer have to worry that Ryan Waters knew where they lived.

Outside, more banging, more uncharacteristic childish yelps. That was the first time it struck Snowden: For a building filled with children, he almost never heard them. It was like a school perpetually in class.

"So you saw her already, didn't you?" Lester asked the question like his teeth couldn't hold his tongue back anymore. "You saw her on the way in."

"Who?"

"Oh come now, no secrets here. You must have at least heard her thumping around out there. Let's call her." Lester picked up his phone, hit the line for Nina, and asked her to send in "Horizon's newest employee." There was a pause, orchestrated by Lester sitting there, smiling, hands entwined over the top of his folded legs. "To be honest, we took her primarily to keep a closer eye – she seems to make a habit of staring too long at things best ignored – but she's already proven herself to be a hard worker. You have good taste in women, Snowden. I can admit that."

When he heard the knock on the door, Lester rose to let her in, made introductions with the aside that they were not needed, then left the two of them. Snowden was the one who jumped up and shut the door, quietly locking it.

Piper Goines. She seemed to Snowden so out of place standing there, an image clipped from one reality by dull scissors and pasted

211

into another with too much glue. An image anxiety attacks were made of, specifically the one Snowden was having at the sight of her. Snowden didn't know the specifics of how she'd arrived at Horizon, but he was pretty confident he could guess the general reason. Piper had poked her nose into this world so deep that now she was in it, and that type of behavior is exactly why Snowden knew she shouldn't be there. So don't be. Don't be happy either. Don't offer answers to questions I specifically didn't ask.

"We're going to have our first issue up by next week, can you believe that? I'm teaching all the kids how to write articles, they're coming up with the story ideas, it'll be great. I'm talking a three-thousand-copy print run, that goon Horus is putting thirty-five-cent news boxes all over Harlem as we speak!"

"Piper, you shouldn't be here," Snowden begged.

"Are you kidding? This company's amazing! It's going to be called *Harlem Outcry*, you like that? It was my idea. This is nothing, this is just a favor I'm doing in exchange for things to come. You wouldn't believe the offer they made me." Piper winked at him like maybe he did know.

"This is going to end badly," Snowden thought aloud.

"No, don't be pessimistic. In a couple of weeks I'll have these little runts writing great."

Lester refused to talk to Snowden about Piper. They passed the Channel 9 News crew on 116th doing an editorial on the police shooting of Trevor Barber, but aside from shutting up until out of earshot, Lester was undistracted. Snowden was saying things, disparaging things, about Piper Goines, the obvious hazards of her inquisitive nature, her lack of moral character, her unsuitability to be left alone with children, slandering her as viciously as he dared without making her a potential hunting accident. Most of it was lies and Lester didn't pretend to take them as anything but, yet Snowden kept talking till they were almost at the building and it was time to kill someone.

Wrapped in trash bags and duct tape, Snowden had brought something big to hit Ryan Waters in the head with. It was heavy too, after a couple of blocks walking, Snowden was getting tired in both arms. The weapon of the evening was that lid that sits on the back of the toilet. The constructors of the building they were about to go up in had used the same manufacturer for the sink basins, toilets, and bathtubs. All three were made from the exact same East Rutherford, New Jersey, porcelain, so that even the closest forensic study could confuse a blow to the head from this toilet lid with a simple slip in the shower.

Lester was unimpressed.

"The blood splatter marks would be different," Snowden confessed. "But I thought I'd just leave the shower on to get rid of them."

"No, bad idea. It's not that it's not a good plan. It's just . . . he's a puny thing, isn't he? Do you really think he deserves the A material? It's freezing, and it rained till two last night. That fire escape up there is going to be covered in ice; that's all the alibi you need. Just go up and throw his little ass out the window and then we'll go get lunch."

Snowden was not impressed, either, pulling his potty lid close to him like Lester might try to take it away.

At Waters's door the lock stubbornly resisted several turns before finally admitting that Snowden's key was the right one, and even still it barely opened for him. It was getting easier. It was getting mundane, Snowden heard the faint music inside and didn't once worry that Waters would hear the door opening. If black people just lowered their radios they really would be a lot safer. Lester motioned to his eyes to emphasize that he would use them, then went over to where Wendell was balled near the stairs, his cell phone out and dialing before Snowden could even close the door quietly behind him.

The apartment was hot, damp, smelled like sweaty socks were preheating in the oven. The place was obviously a hermit's, just like all the other hermitages Snowden had bagged up in the months

before. The way people lived, the way people really lived when they were alone, when they didn't think anyone would ever be coming by and shame had no hold on them, was like this. The smell, the curtains pulled to hide from satellites and God, the dishes kept in a dirty sink jam and cleaned one at a time as need arose, the total absence of a bare surface of any kind. We resent rats for their similarities to humans, not their differences.

The clothes lining the narrow hallway made it easier for Snowden to walk down it without being heard, but not much. The toilet top wanted badly to swing out and bang into the wall, and Snowden's left hand threatened to drop the thing altogether if it didn't start cooperating. Snowden's right hand held the gun and it was pretty comfortable with that. A string of slow steps to avoid creaking on the hardwood floors. Snowden was doing well until about eight feet in when his foot went down and made a sound like a giant eating wooden cereal without milk, echoing down the hall to the room of the man he was supposed to be surprising. The only thing Snowden could think was, Oh poop.

It couldn't have been as loud as he'd heard it, that was silly, no mere footstep could thunder like that. I'm not Paul Bunyan, I'm Cedric Snowden, the second (the first one didn't turn out quite right). Snowden calmed himself and he felt, in a way not familiar with rational thought, that if he could focus hard enough he could calm his entire surroundings as well. As he concentrated, it seemed to be working. No shadows started moving toward him, no new sounds, creaks responded, just that sound of the radio and the constant call of sirens outside. I have nothing to fear, Snowden reminded himself. Then, without warning, the music stopped and a man Snowden immediately recognized as Ryan Waters (smaller in person) came screaming down the hall, an ax held above him.

Irving Howe's hairpiece served as a pretty good shield, composed as it was of good old-fashion porcelain almost an inch thick. It was heavy and hard to lift up to meet the repeated blows, but Snowden found just enough strength in his arm to do it. Snowden's lid was at

almost no risk of even chipping, because even though Waters's weapon was a blur as it rained down, up close Snowden could see that it was not actually a metal ax head at the end of the wooden stick but instead the question mark crook of a cane. Emboldened by the revelation, Snowden pushed Waters back with each pounding, yelling several fragments such as, "I mean you no – ," "I come in – ," "I'm trying to – ," "Oh for the love of God – ," all of which went unnoticed as Ryan Waters kept screaming, "Die! Die! Die! Die! Die!" at the top of his lungs.

A block stronger than a blow and Ryan Waters went down the short distance to his feet. It was a hard fall, a leg caught completely off guard shot out from beneath him and Waters went straight down on his tailbone. That crunching sound, it wasn't just a product of loose floorboards. Snowden almost leaned his toilet top against the wall and offered a hand, but instead offered, "Ryan Waters, I'm here to help you."

Maybe Ryan didn't want help, at least from Cedric Snowden. Maybe the look on Waters's face was just because Snowden pushed his own face to mere inches away and was talking in the lightest audible whisper to keep Lester from overhearing. Maybe it was simply the fact that this intruder knew his name that sent Ryan Waters running down the hall, but it didn't matter because, like that, Waters had scrambled away and was gone.

Snowden stood, gun in one hand, oversized potty protection in the other, stunned at the spurning of his offer. It took a good three seconds of Waters not coming charging back for Snowden to remember himself and chase after him.

It was the décor of the bedroom that caught Snowden off guard. It was a mess, more so than the rest of the apartment, but it wasn't the clothes that lined the floor that were so startling, it was the clothes affixed to nearly every inch of the walls. The man had taken women's panties and nailed them up as trophies. Huge panties, most of them, Snowden saw the big thick and dull fabrics and was imagining the big thick and dull women who'd been in them when

Waters popped up from behind and slammed his cane full force into the back of Snowden's skull.

The reason Snowden didn't pass out was pure physics, and the luck that he'd looked up to see the drawers hanging saggy from the ceiling so that the cane hit where his head was the hardest. Snowden's legs did buckle, a hand did reach out to find this world again, but when Snowden righted himself, even Ryan Waters seemed a bit impressed as Snowden managed to lift the gun and point it at him.

They went into the bathroom because Snowden found the bedroom disgusting and he was the one with the gun in his hand. It was a good choice – it was the least cluttered room in the apartment and the slight smell of urine actually canceled out some of the more aggressive odors of the place. Snowden told Waters to sit down, nodded the gun barrel at the lip of the tub, and Waters did it. *Now we're getting somewhere.*

"Look, I am sorry for this little unannounced entry, but you have got to believe me, it could be worse. I've been hired to kill you. If you listen to me, I can help you save your life." Snowden used Lester's gun as part of his hand gestures and Ryan Waters stared at it like it was a ventriloquist's dummy. Sweat dripped down Snowden's face in a long stream, he could feel it. Only when he followed Ryan Waters's growing eyes to the floor did Snowden see that it was blood instead.

"Hey man," Snowden touched his scalp with his gun hand; his hair was like a wet sponge. "You almost freaking killed me."

"What are you bitching about? You're the one that just broke in my place, ain't you?" Waters asked. "Oh man, that's disgusting!" The last thing Snowden wanted to see, as his vision began to blur, was the face of revulsion on this man, curator of the bloomer museum. "Goddamn, brother," Waters cringed. "You're bleeding all over my floor. Why don't you put some toilet paper on that shit or something?"

Snowden the Snowman felt as pale and cold as his nom de guerre. Looking down at the blood referencing Pollock on his shoes,

Snowden felt pathetic too, powerless to stop the flow, one hand refusing to drop the gun that kept his captive at bay, the other refusing to drop its heavy shield in case the first hand failed its objective.

"You want me to get a tissue for you?" Waters asked, grimacing.

"I came here to help you. There's someone out there who wants to kill you. You have to get out of town."

"Sure there is. I really appreciate you coming out here and sharing that with me. Could've just looked me up in the phone book, I'm listed, but you know, that's your thing, I can dig that. Come on, let me get that tissue for you. Maybe you should put that shirt in cold water so it don't stain."

It was a really nice shirt. A nod, more defeated than permissive, and Ryan Waters was wrapping toilet tissue around his fist, nearly two inches worth when he was done, which in no way buffered the blow when instead of wiping off the blood from the floor the little weasel chose to punch Snowden as hard as he could in his groin.

Males spent lifetimes watching other men simulate taking direct, deliberate, forceful blows to the testicles. Sit-coms, women's self-defense shows, children's movies, it didn't matter how inane or stupid the presentation, men would cringe every time they saw it because they knew somewhere out there this most painful, incapacitating of attacks was waiting for them. It turned out that Cedric Snowden's was biding its time in the bathroom of Apartment 24 of 433 West 128th Street, sitting patiently on the toilet like his balls were Godot.

There was the dropping of the toilet bowl lid onto the top of his own foot, but really, what were a few skinny little bones at a time like this one? There was the screaming, but that was later, that didn't even start till after Snowden'd collapsed to the floor, whispered dryly out of a wide-open mouth until his lungs regained their air and gave voice to him. Ryan Waters had already pushed past and closed the bathroom door by then, Snowden could hear the man placing furniture on the other side to keep it from opening again. By the

time Snowden reasserted his status as biped, he could hear the desperate jiggles of Waters down the hall trying to open that tricky front door lock and abandon him.

The wood of the door was old, not very thick at all. Snowden flung open the cabinet under the sink in search of a monkey wrench to hammer through it, found only stacks of brown plastic pill bottles, noticed even in his frenzy that they were all nearly full, all prescribed to different women's names. *I should have hit him*, Snowden thought, *not just to assert dominance but because this bastard deserves a pop in the mouth.* Bottles spilled to the floor followed by a sweeping hand, but there was nothing useful behind them. Desperation growing, Snowden yanked open the mirrored medicine cabinet above, was taken completely off guard by the dozens of disembodied human teeth inside grinning back at him, plastic grimaces bobbing and swaying in excitement.

Snowden stared in disbelief at the collection of stolen dentures lining the glass shelves, each set floating in its own dirty glass, each set with its own typed name tag pasted proudly at the base, and whispered, "Oh this motherfucker needs to die," before turning to kick the door in.

The rage had come back and it was like, *Welcome! Akwaaba! So good to see you!* With his full weight behind it, Snowden's foot made a big enough hole in the door's wood to reach his arm through. The dressers on the other side fell to the floor like they owed gravity money. Bursting into the hall, Snowden could see Ryan Waters still at the front door, both hands on the knob. On first sighting, Waters gave up his efforts, let go, and ran deeper into the living room. The knob kept turning wildly without him. Snowden wondered how many seconds he had before Lester would get the lock to work from the other side.

The sound of a window creaking open was the answer to Snowden's unformed prayer. Go, Ryan Waters, do all of us a favor. When Snowden reached the living room, Ryan Waters was already halfway out onto the fire escape. Escape me. Incompetence was

Snowden's plan B, as always. Oh Lester, I'm sorry, but that wascally wabbit was just too much for me. Snowden for the first time in so long felt the muscles below his cheeks contract and realized he was really smiling. In growing glee, Snowden ran toward Ryan Waters to help him out, to make sure he made it down to the ground safely before Lester could see. It was just that Ryan Waters didn't know that.

Ryan Waters saw that the paranoid schizophrenic who'd broken into his home was now running toward him grinning like a maniac, and Ryan Waters got nervous. Ryan Waters ran too. Ryan Waters, on the iced metal landing, just didn't stop. Waters had so much momentum as he slid out and over the railing that for a moment it seemed to Snowden like the man might fly across the street instead of plummet down to it.

The sound that came from Ryan Waters's mouth as he fell was like nothing Snowden had ever heard before. Nor the thud when his body hit the ground, the first time. People bounce, apparently.

Staring down out the open window, Snowden's own screams were interrupted by the shock of seeing Lester on his cell phone at the opposite end of the block, standing by a mailbox as Wendell pissed on it. Lester looked down, then looked up, then gave the thumbs-up before calling Wendell and walking off toward Lenox. Once the sight registered, Snowden spun around to see Waters's doorknob still jiggling. The sound of the tumblers on its lock finally giving was the loudest thing he'd heard all day.

Horus walked in, closed the door behind him.

"Where is he? What was all that yelling? Why the window open? It's freezing out there." Horus pushed past him to get a good look out the window. "Oh hell no, you didn't. See, that ain't no way for a black man to die. I thought you were gonna to hit him in the head with a toilet lid?"

"What are you doing here?" Snowden stepped cautiously backward away from Horus and the open window.

"Why you looking at me that way? Oh let me guess, so you

thought you was the only one had some special projects. I get it, you thought it was over, that you'd already won, didn't you? See, I'm here in case they needed a real man to get the job done. Hey, don't think this means I'm like your backup or something. More like quality control. Yeah, 'quality control,' I like that. You better act like you know. Skills like mine gets recognized."

TESTIFY

CEDRIC SNOWDEN, IN the closet, in the dark, on the floor, behind the coats, armed with only one lighter, a portable phone on which he kept hitting Redial, and the remains of four different packs of cigarettes. By the time she picked up her phone his battery was giving its death beep and the tobacco smoke was so thick Snowden realized he couldn't stop crying even if he wanted to.

"I don't care what the hell they're offering you, I don't care what you think you're going to get out of this, you got to get out of there now! Why the hell has the phone been busy for six hours!"

"I was on the Internet. Who is this?" Piper knew who it was, but she felt the question was still her prerogative.

"You don't even understand, oh yeah you think you do but you don't know what they have planned. I don't know what they have planned, but I do know you don't need to be there. You don't even like children." The phone battery was beeping faster, Snowden heard it as the desperate rhythm pushing his pleas forward.

"Fuck you, I have a maternal instinct. Look," Piper sighed, "sex is a funny thing, we both know that. The intimacy, it's inherent, even when you'd like it not to be. It creates social discomfort later. I know Horizon is sort of your pissing territory, and I can imagine you'd find my arrival very threatening."

"Piper, listen – "

"Snowden. I'm a big girl."

"Marks is the devil," Snowden said, but it was a parting shot, he'd already remembered she wouldn't listen to him. He couldn't imagine

Piper listening to anyone who had something to say she didn't want to hear.

"The congressman is not the devil. The devil makes you sign a contract – I got a handshake deal. I never make my soul part of the negotiations, anyhow."

"Fine. Look, there's actually one more thing." It took Snowden the entire ritual of illuminating his hiding space with his lighter, igniting one more cigarette from the pack with a long dry gasp strong enough to turn two centimeters to ash before daring himself to ask it. "You think, I don't know, that maybe I could swing by? I could really use a hug right now."

"I'd like to say yes, but . . . no. That wouldn't really be for the best, don't you agree? That reminds me, have you seen or heard from Robert lately? He doesn't answer his phone no matter when I call."

"Bobby? I don't know what the hell's going on with him. Look, I'm not trying to get into your pants. I mean, honestly that'd be nice, but what I really need – " Snowden caught his tongue, held it down while his thoughts caught up with it. "Hold up. Why the hell are you calling Bobby, anyway?" Snowden demanded, only to spend the rest of the night trying to figure out if his phone had died or if she'd hung up on him.

Two days later, hours into the afternoon, the doorbell rang. Snowden wasn't surprised at all; the phone had been ringing for hours the day before and even that morning, and when you considered the four appointments yesterday and three this morning that Snowden had simply not shown up for, you would assume that someone would eventually come calling. At first Snowden's inaction was out of shock and hysteria, but after a couple of naps his motivation for immobility had evolved into resistance and passive aggression. He just sat, watched the same cartoons Jifar used to. The door buzzer went off, Snowden heard it and realized that had to happen eventually. He just never expected it would be Bobby Finley's voice coming back through the intercom.

"Where you been? And why the hell is Piper trying to get in touch with you?" Snowden asked, hoping the sound of his suspicion would be relayed along the crackling system.

"Don't be a jackass. Lester sent me, he wants you to come back to work now."

"Lester can go to hell." Snowden had pushed the Talk button so hard he'd jammed his finger.

"Don't worry, if there's a hell I'm pretty sure Lester is already going there. Screw work, I'm here to take you to church with me. Get dressed and meet me on the steps of Mt. Zion around the corner."

Snowden was very excited about getting saved. In his lifetime, Snowden had met many saved people and even the ones in prison seemed fairly happy and Snowden was definitely not a happy man right now. Plus, Snowden found he was finally ready to believe in something, something bigger than himself, something huge to hang his load on, and he no longer feared it would crush him because his burdens were doing a pretty good job of that already.

Bobby Finley was standing at the base of the gray steps, nodding politely at the men going inside and helping the older women with a balancing hand between car doors and the entrance even though they didn't look as frail as he did. When Bobby saw Snowden coming, he turned around and started walking inside, pausing in the lobby for Snowden to follow, then heading up to the balcony.

"I think you'd better call in," Bobby whispered on the stairs. "At least tell them you're sick or something. You don't want to get on their bad side." Through a glass door and onto the balcony, the only other person was the organist. She waved, winked. Bobby did the same.

"Cuz, I barely seen you around the office for over a month, so who are you talking to? Trust me, I know how crazy they can be," Snowden snorted his incredulity.

"No you don't. Listen, you might not have seen me hanging around lately, but I call in, I make all my appointments, pick and drop off my keys at night. I've been busy."

"You been busy," Snowden said, recognizing Bobby's self-involvement as much as his face.

"Yes. I've been doing a lot of thinking and a whole lot of writing. I started a new book, actually."

"Piper Goines asked me about you, she was trying to find you too. What you got going on with her? Just tell me, does it have anything to do with Horizon?"

"Sorry, my relationship with the lady is private." Bobby held out his palm like a cop stopping traffic.

"Oh, it's a relationship now, look at that. With a lady, no less," Snowden chuckled as he took his seat. It was a bitter sound; it made his nose itch when he made it. Snowden had other sarcastic, ill-humored comments to make, but when he looked out below and saw the coffin laid lengthwise before the altar he forgot them. "This ain't regular services."

"Snowden, it's two-thirty Friday afternoon. I doubt there's a religious institution in Manhattan having regular services at this moment."

"Man, I cannot believe this. I hate funerals, I don't even plan on having one of my own. How the hell you expect to convert me to the One True Faith if you don't bring me to a proper sermon?" Snowden kicked up his feet on the chair in front of his own, sighed loudly enough for one attendee down below to stare up at the two of them. In response, Bobby reached his arm around his coworker sympathetically until the man below nodded his empathy and returned to his own mourning. Snowden was as shocked by the gesture as much as he was by how soothing it felt. *See, that's all I really need*, he told himself. *A good hug.*

"I'm not trying to convert you to Christianity, Snowden. I'm not even Christian myself."

"Then what the hell do you want? I don't see your black ass for

weeks on end and then you decide to reappear. Why? What do you want from me?"

Bobby looked back, waited for Snowden to stop breathing so hard so he would listen.

"I want you to hear my confession."

One sound Snowden doubted would be tolerated at a funeral: hysterical laughter. Bobby's elbow to Snowden's stomach was the only thing that kept both from finding out exactly what that reaction would be.

"I'm not listening to your confession," Snowden said as he rose. "Don't dump your crap on me, I got my own problems."

"Snowden, I've committed murder."

Snowden sat back down again. This wasn't because he wanted to listen to more, because he really really didn't, not one word, not one tiny little fact, not even the sentence he'd just heard, it's just that Bobby said it so loudly that more heads from below were looking up and now Snowden was the one worried about attracting attention.

"Jesus man, what the hell is wrong with you? Do you have to confess right here, with the guy's family right below?" Snowden whispered.

"Not him," Bobby said, pointing till Snowden knocked his hand down. "I don't know anything at all about that guy, he's a complete stranger."

"If he's a complete stranger, then why the hell are we here?"

"Well, I killed complete strangers. So for the last month I've been coming here every day to complete strangers' funerals. I mean, existentially speaking, one complete stranger's as good as the next. Snowden, I'm the one that burned down the Mumia Abu-Jamal House."

"No you didn't," Snowden assured him.

"Yes I did. It was arson. It was me. Three people died, people I didn't know, had no grudge against. It's OK, I know you believe me, you saw me there. I know you weren't that drunk."

"I saw nothing, I don't know nothing," Snowden had said this to

himself so many times in so many ways lately that there was actually a part of him that believed it.

"Lester told me to. He didn't say it in that many words, but basically he told me to. He had the whole place cased out, its weaknesses, everything. He told me nobody'd be there. You know what? Not that it makes me any less culpable, but I don't think he really cared that those men who died in my fire were there at all. I'd turn us all in if I wasn't absolutely sure those poor kids in the league would get totally lost in the shuffle. And to be honest, I'd sooner kill myself than go back to jail again. I mean, what purpose would that serve, anyway?" Bobby asked, shifting in his seat with his discomfort from the thought of it.

"It's nothing," Snowden offered him.

"What?"

"What you did, don't worry about it, it's nothing. Nothing at all. That's how you have to look at it," Snowden told him.

"Snowden, I'm not out here messing with you. This isn't some kind of joke, I'm being serious." Bobby managed to lean even closer. "I broke in and lit a basement fire below a wall of subgrade insulation and now three people who cried and laughed and loved are dead. Just because a couple of ex-cons cared more about a dream for a community than the people who actually lived in it. Snowden, I killed three human beings."

"I know who you killed, I read the paper. You killed a guy who used to call up people and claim they had outstanding balances on their credit reports to get their MasterCard numbers."

"Dio Demilo. He had a nine-year-old daughter Tio in foster care he wanted to win back when he got on his feet. I guilted Lester into letting the poor girl into the Little Leaders League. She cries in the middle of tutorials – your little friend Jifar told me that."

"The other guy, the bastard who used to work at the post office, he would go break into homes that submitted hold-mail requests, he was a scumbag."

"Greg Tanen, he was first arrested for drug possession at the age of – "

226

"Nigger shut up. Just shut up. Stop doing this to yourself, it's stupid. You don't think they would have caused more misery on their own if they'd stayed around? You can't bring them back, so just stick with your dream. Accept it as the worthwhile cost. It's the only way."

Head wagging with pity, Bobby Finley bent forward, reached under his seat, and yanked out a plastic cooler. Snowden made the oath watching him that if there some kind of burnt body part inside that he was going to start screaming, regardless of the consequence. "Peanut butter and jelly?" Bobby held out to him.

"Bobby, why in God's name do you have peanut butter and jelly sandwiches sitting under this church bench?"

"Peanut butter and jelly just sits better. I tried using balogna, figured it has a lot of preservatives so it would stay good under there for a couple of days, right? Gave me the shits something fierce."

"You know what pisses me off the most about all this?" Snowden demanded.

"I'm sorry, I don't understand. Why would you be annoyed at all?"

"Because here I am basically agreeing with you about all the stuff you yourself are always going on about. I'm seeing you in pain and I'm telling you what you need to hear. I'm giving you an out, I'm repeating your schtick back to you and somehow you're still managing to sit there with that smug look on your face like I'm the idiot."

"I'm sorry that's how you feel." The way that peanut butter looked sticking to Bobby's mouth, the smacking noise it made as he talked, it wasn't helping Snowden's mood in any way.

"Those guys died and that sucks, but Harlem just got that much closer to being the promised land. 'Any means necessary,' right, like Malcolm X used to say."

"Yeah, thanks for bringing that up. Turns out that's bullshit. Turns out the means just might be the most important part. You were right all along, Snowden. Belief isn't safe. Look man, that's really why I asked you here," Bobby said, swallowing the rest of his mouthful,

wishing he'd brought some milk to go with it. "I've watched you almost a year now, and you don't believe in anything! Not in God, not in humanity! You have no higher cause than your own and yet you still manage to get out of bed every morning without losing it. You want to help me? Then tell me, Snowden, tell me how do you do it. How do you keep from being blinded by ideals?"

"Are you nuts? I want to be blinded! You're supposed to be guiding me, inspiring me with your faith! You were always the one who had the answers," Snowden tried to remind him.

"Yeah, and now my answer is you. Tell me, Snowden. I want to believe nothing, but I'm just not a natural so you're going to have to help me. Give me your secret," Bobby pleaded, but it was useless. His best chance at nihilism was already gaining momentum, moving physically and ideologically away from him.

CEDRIC SNOWDEN,
WARRIOR IN BLACK

L ESTER IN TWEED. Tweed jacket, tweed pants, tweed socks. Snowden couldn't believe that last bit existed, but there they were covering Lester's ankles with their jagged woolen lines. Far behind his desk, Lester sat with his legs crossed. The folders laid out as before, each glossy face staring up, pleading to be overlooked.

"Pick your poison. No, that's not right, should be, 'Pick their poison,' that'd be a bit more accurate, wouldn't it? This is your last mandatory extinction, so make it a good one!" Wendell, in the corner, seemed to appreciate his own tweed ensemble much less, wiggling his long body around in his vest in an attempt to break free from it. "OK, fine," Lester said to him, rising to help the dog remove it. "No accounting for taste."

Snowden was going to pick very carefully indeed. Snowden was going to make it a very good one. A lot of thinking, a lot of thinking had gone into this, and he told himself he would think his way out this time, that it was possible he could actually save a life besides his own and get through this. The problem with his last effort was obvious: Don't think small, don't think weak and scared. Think confident. Think secure. Don't think nonthreatening, think nonthreatenable, somebody capable of hearing out a warning and not acting like a cornered animal. Someone who felt in charge, assured that the world moved forward solely because he willed it.

"Him," Snowden said, putting down the file.

"Him?" Lester saw who it was. He picked up the picture, looked at it again anyway. "You're joking, right? I mean, I just put him out

229

there for contrast, to let you know the other guys were nothing. To be honest, I was thinking more along the line of Horus on that one. It's not an apartment, it's a townhouse – don't have keys for his place, and believe me it's a fortress. The guy's got more thugs coming in and out of there than you can count. I'd do it but I've had run-ins with him in the past, so that gives me motive. To be honest, I figured it would even take Horus a couple months to work the nerve up."

"I'm not joking. Him. I can do it," Snowden told Lester, pumping his chest with simulated confidence. "I'm a cold-blooded killer, aren't I? I'm the bastard responsible for the death of three mothers' sons. I'm going to do him and that's it."

Parson Boone knew someone was trying to kill him, he just didn't know who, how many, or for what reasons. He was pretty sure whatever those reasons were they were valid ones, he just didn't know which of the shit he'd sown in the world was coming back to haunt him. Parson Boone was sure someone was trying to kill him, or had been in the past, or would be in the future. It was just the kind of life he lived, so he took actions in accordance.

Parson Boone rarely went outside his 137th Street brownstone and even inside it never below his top-floor apartment. Boone allowed the people with a propensity for violence in his employ to live on the floors below, so anyone who wanted to get to him would first have to go through them. The top-floor apartment was completely soundproof and fortified with security cameras covering nearly every room in the house below. There were more locks on the door to the fourth floor than there were on the front one. Good locks, a quality job. Lester knew this because he knew the contractor who did it.

The most obvious way to break into the brownstone of Parson Boone was to come in through the abandoned shell it was connected to. Even Parson Boone knew that, that's why he'd personally seen to the cinder-blocking of all its doors and windows. To Snowden it looked like a tomb. *Here is a Bunch of Crackheads Who Smoked Their*

Very Souls, the hieroglyphic graffiti seemed to say, *Only a Damned Fool Would Enter.* At this point in his life, Snowden was pretty sure he was a damn fool, and he had the key to the overlooked back basement grate so that's exactly what he set about doing. Horus was sent to the block in a van on the night determined, armed not just with a gun but a cell phone and a pair of binoculars to aim at Boone's windows. On first sighting he called Lester and it was time for Snowden to go in.

Lester wasn't stupid. He was homicidal, delusional, addicted, but Snowden couldn't really call him stupid. As they made their way through the ravaged remains of the abandoned building, flashlights the only thing saving them from being swallowed by the profound darkness, Snowden listened to him explain all of his research into the blueprints to come up with his strategy and recognized for the first time that Lester was actually very clever. That that's what had kept the Chupacabra from being caught all this time.

The only thing easy about doing this job was that it didn't have to look like an accident; in the case of Parson Boone, no one would have believed that anyway. Lester's was a finesse plan. Snowden was not surprised to learn that Cyrus Marks, being the belligerent, homicidal hedgehog he knew him to be, had imagined a much more violent, blunt assault to get rid of Parson Boone: Shove a pound of C4 explosives against the adjoining living room wall, walk through the burning hole, and shoot everything living. Apparently, Marks had envisioned this job as the men of the Second Chance Program's graduating project.

"You and Horus leading in the assault, Bobby burning the whole thing to the ground before the police get there. That's how our congressman thinks. Big," Lester said, only the slightest slur. Snowden could tell when the man was stoned now, his nods in the wake of the first hit, the dilatory calm after, the frantic energy when his system was running out again. If Lester hadn't expressed his reservation about dynamiting a load-bearing wall in a condemned building, Snowden knew Marks would have actually forced them to

go through with that. Snowden wished Bobby knew that too. That he would stop whining about a little shit on his shoes when people like Snowden were swimming in it.

When they made it to the fourth floor of the ruin, a long process in which no step assured purchase, Snowden could actually hear the echoes of talking Boone on the other side. Lester pointed his flashlight to the adjoining wall, illuminating its torn wallpaper of pink and blue lilies. Seeing the pattern, the optimism and life of the colors depressed Snowden more than the walk through the entire rotting house did. It reminded him that somebody had actually lived here once. Lester's spotlight found the fake fireplace from his Polariods. Its grate was of ornate iron, as Snowden walked closer to it he realized it was totally solid, it only looked like it had holes in it.

"There's the old oil heating unit," Lester said lightly. There was yelling coming from the other building. Even without being able to make out the words, Snowden could recognize the sound of a man defending himself.

"It was never meant for burning wood," Lester continued. "The mantel, the way the wall comes out, real popular around the turn of the century. The look of traditional elegance with the latest in modern convenience." A hand on each side, Lester bent and strained to lift the lid away. The mechanics of the oil heater were attached to the back of it, leaving a brown, shiny stain along the wall as Lester attempted to lean it. Behind it were just two thin tubes and a lot of empty space.

"Like I said, right? Perfect little tunnel, big enough for a 1920s heating specialist to squeeze his immigrant butt up the faux flume and across the crawl space between the ceiling and the roof to check for leaks. Just go up and over and you'll find yourself in the residence of a Mr. Parson Boone. That easy."

"Up and over. That easy," Snowden mumbled back. Even that seemed too loud in the empty room.

"Just up and over and down again, and you'll find yourself staring

at the back end of an identical grate. Unscrew it with the pliers and you're in. Use the gun first thing," Lester instructed him again. "The silencer's attached. Don't let him talk, don't let him do anything, just use the gun then come back through here, and Horus will be waiting in the green van on Frederick Douglass end."

"Horus in the van, waiting for me," Snowden repeated a final time.

"Horus in the van. Worse comes to it, use the cell to call him and he'll come in blazing. I'm off to the lounge to meet the congressman for a drink and an alibi. One more thing, then." Lester held up one finger, made sure Snowden committed to the digit before going to his bag and opening it. From within it, flat from being pressed between folders, Lester pulled a package covered in silver wrapping paper, pulling at its matching bow to get it to fluff before handing it to him.

"In honor of this being your last mandatory job and everything. I was going to get you a card too but I couldn't find anything appropriate. I hope it fits," Lester said, and before Snowden could even get it out, followed with, "It's a ninja outfit."

Snowden held it up to himself. He didn't know what else to do with it.

"Put it on, it'll save your clothes from getting ruined. I'll look this way. I promise, no peeking," Lester said, turning to face the cinder-blocked windows. Arms wriggling for freedom in the top half of the costume, when Snowden finally got it on he could barely pull it down to cover his belly button. The outfit was so small, Snowden's pants' waistline was only halfway up his calves when he felt the bottom of the pants revealing his ankles. "I had to fight myself to keep from getting you the white version. Of course it wasn't practical, but it just seemed to be more appropriate to me, us being the good guys and everything. Can I turn around yet?" Lester asked and started to. Snowden flew up the chimney just to get away from him.

In the days before, thinking of this night, it was the small space that most frightened Snowden, not just the cramped situation but

the actual fear of it itself, that halfway through, trapped, he would succumb to it. Yet inside, crawling along the lines of oil, water, and waste tubing, ceiling so close the exposed plaster scraped along the top of his head, Snowden found that claustrophobia in no way threatened to consume him. There were too many other fears vying for dominance. Leading the pack was the one that the small flashlight in his mouth would go out and leave him stuck in the eternal darkness unable to find his way back again, but not far behind that fear was the one that the pipes he gripped so fiercely would break, sending him flying through the ceiling, as well as the one that the people he could hear so clearly below could hear him. The last bit was actually the least rational, as the men below were screaming so loudly he could barely hear himself. Somebody had done something wrong, was found somewhere he didn't belong. Somebody had been caught. Somebody refused to explain himself. There was more than one person yelling at him, aggressively listing the man in question's personal deficiencies. Things were pounded and slammed to punctuate declarations and Snowden kept thinking, *And that's how he treats his own people*, touching the gun strapped under his arm for reassurance.

The hole seemed narrower on the other end, seemed steeper, too, as Snowden inched his way down headfirst, using the fact that he could barely fit through the space to his advantage. Hands gripped to the metal poles, body wedged in the space directly above, Snowden timed his movement to coincide with the yelling in the next room, fighting the urge to cough as the dust fell directly into his nose.

The back end of the grille was identical to its counterpart, no holes to see through but thin lines of light from where it just barely failed to meet the wall. Staring through, Snowden saw a bedroom just like he was supposed to and got hopeful, laying its image onto what he remembered of Lester's blueprint's grid. That was the hall right there, the kitchen and exit door would be on the left, the living room was where the voices were coming from, on the right. The same yelling he so appreciated as he sneaked above it became an

immediate annoyance as Snowden waited upside down below, body weight resting on his skull and arms and shoulders, all of which were numb by the time he heard the men who populated the next room evacuating it.

From his vantage, light aligned along his iris, Snowden could only see as far as their knees as they passed by the doorway, but it was enough to understand the earlier commotion. Somebody had shown up for work stone drunk, it was obvious, as two sets of sneakers walked stiff and steady and a third set dragged limp between them, toes pointed straight to the ground they scraped across. "Wake up, nigger. I ain't trying to carry you neither," one said. If there was a response, it was nothing more than a facial gesture. Snowden could hear the others making their way down the stairs when a pair of plaid slippers drifted casually into his line of vision, closed the entrance door softly on the way to the kitchen. Parson Boone had ashy ankles. Snowden got out his pliers and started unscrewing the bolts from the inside, tried to ignore his full bladder and keep the metal handle from slipping out his sweating hands.

Even if you didn't want to kill a drug lord, even if you didn't really want to break into his home at all, you had to admit there was a rush to standing in his bedroom with a gun in your hand. Knowing that if you wanted to do it, you could, ending his reign was at your personal discretion. That as powerful as he was, his life was still in your loaded hands. You needed to recognize that as a normal reaction and not confuse it with something more, Snowden told himself, or you just might pull the trigger when you had the chance.

Snowden caught a look at himself in the hall mirror as he walked lightly past. The sleek ninja of his mind was replaced with the image of an asbestos-covered freak in black, wrists and belly exposed in a top so tight his arms looked locked into position. Reaching into his pocket, Snowden pulled out the mask, reminded to hide his face by his own embarrassment.

Following his gun down the hall, Snowden inched closer to the kitchen. He saw Parson Boone's back. It was definitely the man from

the mug shot, yet he was an altogether different person from the one Snowden imagined. Maybe it was the locks that hung in the space between his shoulder blades – Snowden gave the hairstyle a connotation of spirituality, so the fact that Boone's hair was gray just reinforced that prejudice. It could have been just that the man was there doing his own dishes, an act Snowden assumed Boone, from Lester's description, would consider beneath him. Parson Boone was simply a man in his home, serene in his mundanity. Snowden kept the gun pointed directly at his head, anyway, politely clearing his own throat.

Parson Boone wiped off the dish in his hand, placed it on the shelf, and closed the cabinet door before turning around. The expression of surprise or primal fear that Snowden expected to see flood the man's face when he got a good look at his guest never came, only a tired acceptance. Only a sigh, like dying was just another task he had to do at the end of a long day.

"Who sent you?" Parson Boone asked him, leaning back against his sink as if to brace himself for the name.

"That's not important. I'm not here to harm you, I'm here to warn you. Someone is trying to kill you. These people, they got me over a barrel so here I am, but this is as far as I go in this thing. Don't think they won't just send someone else, because that's exactly the way these people operate. You don't get out of Harlem tonight, your life will be over. That's the message." Snowden reviewed his own words, the voice that delivered them: perfect.

"You sneak in my home. You hold a gun on me, you can at least tell me who sent you. I don't have the energy to go running anywhere, so if you want to help, just tell me what direction to look in." It was a reasonable request. Even in this state, so nervous he was forced to hold the gun with two hands to keep it from shaking, Snowden could see that. It just wasn't a reasonable situation. *I need a bigger gun*, Snowden thought. *That's why nobody ever listens to me.*

Parson Boone crossed his arms and kept staring, and Snowden

was about to rephrase his earlier statement when the other man said, "It's Cyrus Marks, isn't it?"

Snowden had attempted to play poker once, failed miserably. It was his eyes, he realized, because that's the only thing Parson Boone could see clearly and already it was like he knew everything. "No, no, you're wrong," Snowden started to protest, but the older man just ignored him, continued as if the fact had been admitted.

"The 'over a barrel' thing, I know that cat well so that's a bit of a giveaway, but don't worry, I would have said his name first anyway. Why do you think I'm hiding from life, trapped on this floor like this?" Leaning forward, Parson Boone pulled out a seat from the kitchen table in front of him, sat down, and pointed like he expected Snowden to join him.

"Don't move again, stay there," Snowden told him, poking each word forward with the silencer's muzzle to get the point across to him. "Look man, I don't give a damn why you live like this. You don't like it, that's even more reason to skip town. Move to the islands or some shit."

"Marks's got you in a tight situation? I can get you out again. Sit down. Let's talk about this. I know how the dude works, I know exactly what you're going through on this. *Exactly.*" Snowden turned to the sound of someone coughing behind him, but it died and he realized it was on the floor below them. Turning quickly back, Snowden half expected to see Parson Boone lunging at him, but the man was seated in the exact same position, hand still to his chin earnestly. He's not afraid, Snowden realized. A masked man stands before him with a loaded gun pointing at his head and he's not even slightly nervous. *Kill him.* There was part of Snowden that was saying this and he didn't expect it, but it was there and it said, *Kill him, he's not going anywhere, he's going to fight this, he's going to end up getting you killed and still won't save himself in the end. Kill him, save your ass, get it over with.*

"Don't be fooled by his self-righteousness, son. All his race talk don't mean nothing. Hey, I'm not saying he don't believe in it now, but the man ain't half as clean as he'd like to pretend. Let me ask you

237

something: How do you think a so-called civil servant got enough money to buy up half the prime real estate in Harlem? Better yet, how you think a two-bit parole officer gets enough money to run for Congress in the first place?"

"How?" Snowden wanted to know. Snowden wanted him to shut up, too, but wanted to know what he knew before this.

"It's a rhetorical question." Boone frowned, removed a cigarette from the breast pocket of his T-shirt, reached across the table for a pair of matches to light it. "Drugs, obviously. By forcing a hump like me to go out there and risk my neck for years. I look like the big bad drug dealer he probably represented me as? I was a pawn, his pawn. Now I'm retired, so I'm no longer that. Now I'm his loose end. Why do you think he sent you to kill me?" If what Boone kept saying was as interesting, Snowden would take a seat. He would take a cigarette, too, to help him think. He wouldn't take off his mask, but he would lift it up just far enough to stick it in.

"You think that's so far-fetched, look at yourself. Who's pulling your strings? I heard he had some young bucks under his wing. I know exactly who you are, kid. You know who I am? I'm your way out," Parson Boone said standing up again, coming towards Snowden with only a nod to caution.

"Sit down," Snowden ordered, but it came out with only slightly more force than a question. The gun was up, but it felt like a starter pistol in his hand. The only reason Parson Boone stopped coming closer was that it would have forced him to push it out the way and that would have been rude.

"I'm not some violent beast, you can see that. I'm not the criminal type in the slightest. There was nothing I did I wasn't forced to. I'm just another victim, like you. Put my trust in him, look where it got me. You really want your freedom? I do too. I need a man on the inside of his operation, you need a man on the outside who can make things happen. Put that gun down and let's talk. Together, we're going to make this happen. You and me, we're the same man."

Snowden was about to say yes yes yes when the door in the hall

opened behind him and in came, connected by their shoulders, the three other men. Snowden didn't know he had stopped pointing the gun till the disturbance shot it back up again. His fear convinced him he would see guns pointed directly back at his own, but not even their eyes were on him. The two men on the sides were too busy trying to carry the unconscious one in between them. The man's head hung limply on his own shoulder. There was blood splattered across all three of them, but the most was on the one in the middle, increasing in density the higher Snowden looked on him. The bloody man's face looked like someone had tried, rather successfully, to open it with a rusty can opener. An animal, was all Snowden could think. The only thing that could mutilate a man's face like that was an animal. Even if it was *Homo sapiens* it was nothing more than an animal. What was not ripped was so swollen that it took Snowden a moment to recognize that it was Horus he was looking at.

"OK boss, you win. This nigger ain't saying shit so we'll kill him," the beast to the left of Horus said.

When Snowden looked back to the kitchen, Parson Boone had scurried across to the far counter, gotten his paws on a gun from the cutlery drawer, and was about to turn around with it. Snowden caught him first in his shoulder and then directly in the middle of his throat when the force of the first shot snapped him back again. Spinning around, Snowden saw that Boone's brutes had finally deemed to notice him. Horus flopped hard to the floor. *Hostages, you can just tie and leave them here*, Snowden's mind was already bargaining, but both reached behind their backs for their weapons simultaneously and Snowden was back to shooting, his will to live directing him. Aiming the thing as it bounced in his hand turned out to be harder than he'd imagined, but Snowden kept pulling the trigger, anyway. That Horus was already on the ground was the only thing that saved him from the fate of his captors.

Horus was so damn heavy that Snowden kept checking his pulse, half hoping the he was dead so he could drop him. If there was

239

anybody downstairs when the shooting started, they were gone now, but Snowden didn't put the gun down until they were at the front door and, despite Snowden's screaming, Horus refused to wake up and open it. The green van was down the block just like Lester said it would be, but the tires were slashed and the back window was broken. His spine feeling like it could snap like a pencil, Snowden ran with the weight of Horus folded over him, dropping him against a bodega grate before running out onto the street and praying for headlights. A hack, a hack, my kingdom for a hack, yet when one finally appeared it only slowed down long enough to see Horus's blood and Snowden's hooded face before peeling off again. From the sidewalk came moans from the fallen brute, so Snowden yelled, "Shut the hell up, you're not helping."

The situation had started to gain comic momentum when the #3 bus came down the street towards them. Who am I to choose? Snowden asked himself, and then ran back to get his compatriot. It actually stopped. The driver actually waited for Snowden to drag Horus on board, he even dropped the hydraulic lift a bit to help them climb up. As they started moving, Snowden dug through Horus's pockets for the change that would save them. That's what it took to wake Horus up. "Cheap bastard," Snowden cursed at him.

Snowden had always heard that New Yorkers never pay attention to anything, that no one will look up to stare at even the most extreme irregularity. This rumor was entirely untrue, spread by someone with a fairly rigid idea of normalcy. You take a guy in an extremely dirty ninja outfit two sizes too small for him, add a barely conscious man whose face is bleeding so much you can't differentiate the skin from the meat, stick them both on a downtown bus at half past three in the morning, you'll see people staring. Staring shamelessly. Snowden stared back at them, refusing to take off his mask till after they got off at 125th Street. What the hell were they looking at in the first place? Had they no concept of the creatures these men had just rid the world of? Who were they, to look at these men like that? What kind of people rode a bus through

Harlem at three-thirty in the morning, anyway? Snowden wanted to know. He and Horus were not the problem elements on the bus, most certainly. Snowden looked around from under his black hood, and he could identify the people who needed to go immediately. "Her, him, and him," he said out loud to no one. It was so obvious. All you had to do was knock them off and then their little mobile community would be heaven.

FICTION OR NON

T HE SAD TRUTH was that the little runts couldn't write worth a
dime, let alone the thirty-five cents an issue they were charging.
Sitting behind the fortress of her large wooden desk, face to face
with them at their little plastic ones, Piper looked out and silently
resented them for their illegible prose, their erroneous grammar, the
fact that they seemed to find it impossible to sit still for more than
two minutes or keep from yawning at least long enough for her to
turn to the blackboard. Piper kept saying to herself, *Give them a break,
they're so young*, and as guilty penance even made a rare call to Abigail
Goines, put up with several reminders of why she rarely called to get
her box of childhood writing samples sent down express to her. A
bad idea, it turned out. For one thing, asking her mother to go into
the attic for one box started the discussion about all of the others
Piper had quietly decide to leave there, but more disturbing was the
quality of her own adolescent clippings. When Piper was eleven years
old she was writing comparative essays on the difference among
private, public, and home school education, pondering the larger
sociological significance of the Emmanuel Lewis–Gary Coleman
miniaturized Negro craze, and experimenting with present-tense
second-person-singular in her review of the double-loop roller
coaster at Great Adventure ("You feel the bar press down upon
your lap cold and hard. As your car goes into free fall your grip on
that metal is colder and harder because you know no matter how
loud you yell no parent nor teacher can save you."). Now, as a teacher
herself these decades later, the most impressive submission Piper
Goines had received from her class was "That X-Men Cartoon Isn't

Real," which distinguished itself not by its prose, or even by managing to spell the majority of its words correctly (it didn't), but for the utterly original proof on which it based its thesis: the fact that there were discrepancies in character age, team composition, and story line between the cartoon and the comic book version, which the author took as the definitive, factual text.

At first, Piper was convinced she'd been stuck with the "special" class, that the hidden clause in Marks's offer was that she spend the year baby-sitting the runts of the Little Leader litter. After a while, though, their editor realized they were too well behaved for that group, and the ones who did act a fool were quickly removed. An advocate of not naming names, Piper hadn't even reported the boy who'd decided it was appropriate to use the class tape recorder to preserve a repetitive, derivative string of expletives for posterity, yet the boy, like all the other discipline problems Piper had encountered over the weeks, never appeared for class again. When asked where their housemates had disappeared to, her remaining students explained that the bad kids had to go out on the street and sell candy bars to raise money. Having read their work, Piper thought that was probably a better career path for them, anyway. Regardless of how many disappeared, the class continued to grow. Piper was sure there'd only been a little more than a dozen when she started.

They were good kids, for kids, Piper came to realize. They were just poorly educated and talentless, even for nine- to twelve-year-olds. Though, to be fair, the last bit was hard to say, for most lacked the basic skills necessary for style, although Piper still had her suspicions. After reading their papers, after all her self-pity that her lot had been linked by fate to their own had subsided, Piper cursed the New York City public school system for failing them. It was a large, slow-moving target and therefore should have been perfect for assault, but Piper found it lacking in its ability to carry the full burden for her writers' inadequacies. There were parents to be blamed. It was inevitable. Regardless of whatever tragedy had created these orphans, those parents dead or missing could not avoid responsi-

bility for much of it. Even destitute, Abigail Goines would never have let her daughters wallow in ignorance. Of course, Abigail Goines was the product of middle-class education and values and wasn't faced with the challenge of breaking free from poverty and ignorance in the first place.

In Abigail Goines's place, these kids had Horizon Property Management, and they didn't even know how lucky they were. Scholarships, private tutoring, one of the wanna-be Eliza Doolittles even wrote a somewhat legible piece mentioning a proper speech and manners course. Their misfortune was their greatest asset. That's how Piper's book would start, the one she sat in class and imagined herself writing on the Horizon Little Leaders League after she seized control of the *New Holland Herald*. Piper would donate her advance back into the program, use the publicity tour to cross promote the *Herald*, so everyone's interest would be served. Young, innocent, harmless black orphans saved from the ghetto during their darkest hour, led by a young, attractive, affluent person from the suburbs who believed in them so that they could believe in themselves. Hollywood put a movie out like this every four years, so this would be the next one. A descendant of Lassie would be bred to fill the role of that mutt that insisted on lying in a long smelly pile by the front door every class. Of course, they would insist on putting a Caucasian savior in the "Piper" role, so Piper'd put a racial bonus clause in the contract as a trap for them.

Piper was planning a speaking tour in her head when one of the boys in the back raised his little suited arm, tie hanging out like a lascivious tongue on the desk before him, and yelled, "Yo! It been time to go!" All the other children turned to look at him, shaking their heads. Piper took a good long look at him too, figuring she'd never see him again, then looked around the room to try and guess which snitch would rat him out first.

Bag packed, the anticipated Chinese take-out entrée already haunting her mouth, Piper turned back to the room to see that one seat had not been emptied. The dog, awakened by the commotion, sat proudly

before this little boy. The *Harlem Outcry*'s star political cartoonist, who didn't know a thing about politics but whom Piper had to admit was really good at drawing monsters and superheroes, for his age group. He was a true artist, effete and everything.

"Look, you want to do an illustration for the X-Men story, that's fine. Copyrightwise, I'm still saying it's not legal, but I doubt those corporate bastards would have the heart to sue you, so what the hell, go for it."

"Cool!" the boy said, but that's all he did. He wasn't moving.

"Good-bye," Piper hinted.

"Good-bye," the boy mimicked, hand running down the dog's head as they both stared intently back at her.

Piper flopped her bag back on the desk, located her seating chart. One thing she'd already learned about the little urchins is that they didn't respond well to "Hey kid."

"It's Jifar, right?" Piper asked. The boy smiled politely back at her. "So what do you want? Why are you just sitting there looking at me like that?"

"We're supposed to. We're supposed to watch out for you, make sure you're OK," Jifar said. He seemed very proud of his duty.

"We?" Piper began asking, but Jifar nodded and looked conspiratorially to the dog and Piper lost all motivation to pursue that line of questioning. "Why don't you just go now, OK? I'm doing just fine, thanks for your concern, but I got my real job to get back to."

"I'm sorry, I can't. I promised. I told Mr. Snowden I'd watch out for you, so please let me, OK?"

"Oh, here we go. That's just great. Look, you tell Snowden from me that I can watch my own back, OK? You tell him that, and then you kick him, right in the shins."

"What are shins?"

"Nothing, I was just joking. Don't worry about him, I'll take care of it. You just work on the art. You play your cards right and I'll have you syndicated before puberty."

*   *   *

When Piper returned to her block that night she saw a man trying to shove a package under her front door. Piper wasn't prepared for the sight but didn't need to be. It was who it was that caught her so off guard, and more than that how excited and nervous she felt just seeing him there. Robert M. Finley didn't even notice her coming. Piper was already at the bottom of the stoop when he saw her between his legs, stood upright, then pulled his pants from were they were lagging.

"You're late. More than two months late, actually," Piper managed. She wished she was darker. She wished that she had enough melanin to inure her from obvious blushing forever. Piper was fairly sure certain she wasn't blushing just at the sight of him, but simply by questioning if she was blushing or not was enough to increase the chances she was exponentially.

"Hey, hi, I'm here to . . . I mean I wanted to ask you if I could get the master key to the *Harlem Outcry* news boxes because I have a bunch of *Great Works* I need to give away." He wasn't expecting her or he was even more awkward than she'd remembered. "It's just, you know, I did call that morning to cancel," Bobby said. "I had a lot going on in my life at that moment. I'm here now, so can I get that key?"

"Pick it up in the office. What's that?" Piper poked the air toward the large envelope jammed a third of the way under her front door.

"Nothing."

"Not nothing. Something. What is it?"

"I brought you a gift." Robert M. Finley turned again to the package, spent an equal amount of energy trying to pull it back out again. "Please, take this, read this. My number's on the last page. When you get to it, call me."

The envelope pushed into her hand had to weigh five pounds. Before Piper could even manage a firm grip, Bobby was past her, pausing only to give her cheek the quickest peck it had ever received before moving on.

"Wait! What is this? This is the book you were telling me about, isn't it? *The Tome*, right?"

"No, this is an entirely new one. This book I wrote for you." The last sentence Robert M. Finley delivered more to the steps than the woman standing on them.

"Oh my God, I think that is about the sweetest thing anybody's done for me in I don't know how long. Wow. I've never been in a book's acknowledgments, let alone dedication."

"No, you don't understand. Not the dedication, the whole book. Read it, call me so we can talk. Please, if you still want to," he said, nodding at the manuscript in her hand.

"I don't understand. Come on, you're coming inside. You're already here, we can talk now. We'll order food. I'm paying." Piper reached in her pocket and pulled out a rumpled twenty as proof of this statement.

"No," Bobby said to her, but he wasn't walking away, either.

"Well, why the hell not?" Piper wanted to know.

"Really, I got a lot to do. If I'm going to get rid of these extra copies of *The Great Work*, it's going to take me all night, even if I can get Lester to let me use the moving truck and Snowden to help." Piper just stared at him, lips sucked up into a disdainful ball on the side of her face, so Bobby kept talking. "I mean, I own 2,871 copies of it," Bobby confessed. He couldn't figure out if Piper's look of incredulity was because of the amount or his entire excuse in the first place, so he started up yet again. "OK, fine, I have to go because I know I'm a socially awkward person, and I had one of the best, most fulfilling conversations of my life at the Horizon Ball and based on past experience I'm pretty sure if I stay here much longer I'm going to ruin any chance with you I might have. Because you make me even more nervous than usual. Because I find your beauty, in every sense of that word, literally stunning. If I could but beseech fate to be so generous as to offer me the opportunity to build a love with you, then that amour would resound with the – "

"Jesus Christ, are you reading off a cue card?" Piper uttered in disbelief. Bobby looked even more shocked to see it in his hand than

she did, despite the fact that he'd been staring down at it during his entire monologue.

"Let me see that!" Piper demanded, started stepping down after him. Bobby backed up, ripping it into desperate little pieces as he went.

"Look, I'm sorry, I was supposed to memorize that. That's what I'm saying, I'm nervous talking to you. When I write something out, I can reread it, edit it, make sure it's exactly what I want to say. Look, just read the book, OK? It's about us. I mean, it's about what we could be. It starts right now, with me sticking this novel under your door, and follows our relationship over the next six decades. It's called *The Orphean Daze*. It's a love story . . . See, I told you I shouldn't be talking before you read it! I can see you getting creeped out already!"

"Oh my God, that's so not true, I'm not creeped out at all! I'm just . . . looking forward to reading it," Piper said. She was lying about the first sentence, underplaying the second. Front door locked carefully behind her, Piper wasn't even done climbing the stairs before she was on to the second page.

Snowden was very happy in his closet. Happier than he'd been in years. The closet was great because there was only one door and no windows so nobody could sneak up on you, and it was too small for anyone to be hiding in there with you as well. The closet was great if somebody did break in your apartment in the middle of the night because they'd just think the place was empty, and even if they did open the closet door, if you went to sleep underneath a pile of dirty clothes like Snowden did they would never find you. In the closet, when you turned out the lights, you were invisible.

Snowden had his phone in there, a couple of bags of flavored tortillas, and boxes of snack cakes; it was great. He had eleven different brands of cigarettes and eleven different cigarette lighters he'd assigned to them with careful consideration. He had a couple of books he'd been meaning to read for years and was at around page

11 in all of them, he had an AM radio with only one earphone so he could find out the time and weather and never drop his guard. He had caller ID so he knew who was calling before he picked up, before the voice said, "Cedric Snowden, this is Congressman Marks."

"I am on top of all my appointments, sir. I know I missed half a day last week but I had a really rough time hunting the night before and I called the Armstrong family and apologized profusely and they said they understood and I'm showing them a new property tomorrow and I think it's an offer they can't refuse, I really do."

"Mr. Snowden, I'm sure you're doing fine with your daytime duties. I'm not calling to bother you about that. I'm calling to compliment you on your handling of your nighttime ones."

"Sir, we shouldn't be talking on the phone." Snowden wondered if cordless phones could be traced. Apparently mobile ones could be very easily, a guy in the joint who'd been busted for selling stolen ones told him that, but as far as cordless ones he didn't know.

"No one's listening. No one cares enough to. What you did, that was a big deal. The problem you solved was a major one. The man was a menace. Strategically, this greatly reduces the amount of resistance our efforts will encounter in the year ahead. It puts us far ahead of schedule. I want to thank you. I'd like to apologize to you as well. To be honest, I didn't think you had it in you. I was wrong."

"No, no, no, no apologies. I don't want your apologies. Keep them to yourself," Snowden told the congressman.

"Look, I'm trying to be contrite here. I'm being a very big man by admitting I was wrong, and you're going to be gracious and accept that from me," Marks insisted.

"No, no. I owe *you* the apology. I owe you, sir, because I been thinking a lot about this lately, trying to not let my emotions or preconceived notions get in the way and now I know what the problem was: I was wrong. You see I been thinking that we are people, right, and the reason we're not just animals is that we have

civilization, decency, morality, consideration, right? We have society, that's what makes us people and not just bald apes. But then you think about it, some people are human, but they don't have decency, they aren't civilized, because that's learned behavior and they never got educated. So then I was thinking about the folks. I think – and don't tell any white people I said this because you know they already think we're all this way – that during slavery, when they were trying to turn us into animals, that on a tiny bit of us they succeeded, and these beast folks been running around for a hundred and fifty years breeding like crazy because that's what beasts do. The responsible people, they have little families, do you see where I'm going? So with every generation the ratio gets more out of whack. So I get it, the whole Little Leaders thing, now. I really do. You're saving them and their descendants from a life of inhumanity, right? And really by killing the parents we set the offspring free, which in a way is a blessing to the victim since . . ."

Snowden kept talking. The thing about sitting in the closet all the time, about just going to work and wearing a face that you took on and off like a blazer, was that you never had someone to really talk to. Snowden felt very lucky he had someone. Even if he got to the point when he'd been talking so long he couldn't remember who that someone was. Pausing to focus on the receiver, Snowden listened for a change. As seconds passed Snowden became sure no one was even there, until a voice said back to him, "Exactly."

The new novel started with a character named Robert M. Finley slipping a package under a woman named Piper Goines's Harlem door. Even the weather conditions were the same: clouds in "white streaks, softly smeared on a lazy sky" and "the boastful warmth of an immature spring." The day of the week, the date, the time of day – all were identical. What he was wearing, what she was, it was maddening. The only thing that kept Piper from getting completely freaked out and throwing the pages away was the same thing that stopped her fictional self from doing so: the artistry of the prose and

the innate curiosity on the part of the reader, pages that kept turning fast enough for her to be captivated.

There were several assumptions within *The Orphean Daze* that Piper took critical exception to, if this speculative story was going to be as true to known fact as it purported. First of all, Robert Finley could not be accurately described, Piper felt, as "an upright assemblage of bones, charred and dusky, grinding dryly forward." Regardless of how skinny he seemed there was some muscle to him, and the whole burnt theme applied to him throughout the work just didn't fit, didn't acknowledge the fiery passion Piper felt was the character and man's most prominent feature. Second, when you compared this description of the Robert Finley character with that of the Piper Goines one, "lush lines curved from the pressure of her bounty," the narrative played into the whole Beauty and the Beast myth, which besides being an extremely overused cliché was a pretty pathetic male fantasy to begin with. "Ugly guy wins beautiful girl," the fraternal twin to the equally vapid "poor girl wins rich guy" Cinderella idiocy.

Piper read, looking for more faults to distance herself from the work, but didn't find many. On the page were two people struggling to make a life together. Not a perfect one, just a life, compiled as it was from the building blocks of minutia. Piper recognized the sorrow at the core of all living, the unexpected blessings that resonated because of it. Bargaining with eyes that managed to feel dry and watery at the same time, Piper's mind kept making the promise that after the next chapter she would close her lids and go to bed, but she never did. It was as if Fate had dropped its notebook and Piper had to finish as much as possible before he noticed it was missing and came looking for it. Piper kept reading because she couldn't bring herself not to, out of control and hell yes resenting that, but her only defensive action was to read faster.

In the last chapter, decades in the fictional future, after one widowed lover has buried the other and had months of mourning, *The Orphean Daze* follows them moment by moment as they visit

their safety-deposit box. The way it proceeds, it gives the impression it's for some official papers, possibly insurance documents. Inside the box, however, its papers oxidized yellow by time, is the fictional version of the book Piper couldn't stop herself from reading. The character takes it home, and the last paragraph is about them reading it. How none of the facts are true but everything else is. It wasn't until she finished the last sentence, at four fifty-four in the morning, that Piper realized she didn't even know which of the couple was dead and which was the survivor. That the point was they'd come so far that even to the reader it didn't matter anymore.

Bobby Finley, ladies and gentlemen! Bobby Finley, Creator of Worlds!

Piper had fallen in love with writers just by reading their work before. Ugly ones. Dead ones. There'd been times when she'd read the beauty of their work and felt like their souls must be the same, looked to the back jacket picture, and pined for someone she felt was no longer a stranger. Piper was a lover of books, writers wrote to entice readers, it was an understandable weakness. So how the hell was she supposed to defend her heart against a book intentionally written to seduce her?

Demanding to know just that, Piper found Bobby's number and started calling. I will not be manipulated, she was going to say as soon as he groggily said hello, but he didn't. After two rings, the voice mail service did instead, and Piper had not prepared a statement for recording so slammed the phone down again, only to keep hitting Redial for the next half hour in an effort to get him to answer, which he didn't.

Not a damn thing you can do if you stay up until four fifty-four in the morning. If you have to be somewhere three hours later, as Piper had to be at the *Herald*, it was best to stay awake, not torture yourself by nodding off and then having to rise from the deepest valley of your sleep cycle, Piper told herself. There was only one rational thing to do. So Piper put on her coat and shoes and set out into the cold morning darkness to go wake Bobby's black ass up.

Coat lapels gripped around her neck to hide it from the nocturnal breeze, baseball hat pulled down over her head to obscure her gender to any sexual predator, Piper stomped down Lenox and saw the Horizon office across the street, light on inside and its security grate still up. The company truck Bobby said he'd be using was parked right there in front of it and Piper was surprised at her wave of disappointment at having found him away from home and awake. The element of surprised will be diminished, was how she explained her reaction to herself, but that rational voice was drowned out by another, shriller one that sounded eerily similar as the one belonging to Mrs. Abigail Goines. *You were going over there to screw that young man, weren't you?* it said. *All that righteousness, and this was just a booty call. You're just disappointed that his body won't be hot from sleep, that you won't be able to throw your own on top of it.*

Piper rang the bell, but the Horizon door was open. She called out his name, several times, walked inside reluctantly when no voice answered it. See, this is how people get shot, Piper told herself. They show up unannounced in the middle of the night, just start walking around private property, and then bang, that's it. Piper kept walking, anyway. The only light on besides the lobby's was in Lester's office. Piper, unable to locate another wall switch among the tiles of framed photos of Congressman Marks standing next to major and minor celebrities, moved toward it.

Lester's office was big enough to fit a full couch, several rows of file drawers, and a desk that seem bigger than most kitchen tables. Regardless of how much space the desk offered, every inch of it was still completely covered in paperwork, specifically file folders. It was the photos attached to them that attracted Piper. Some were actual police mug shots, originals it looked like. Others were random streets shots, always taken from a distance, always with the subject staring off in another direction as if they didn't even know they were being photographed. How can I be expected not to open these up and read them? Piper asked no one. How could someone like me manage not to do that?

*   *   *

Horus wasn't following her. He lied, he wasn't following her. He just happened to be there when she came in. "Boss, I said to myself, something suspicious. From the get-go I was like, there's something ain't right about that one. Better keep an eye on her." This was bullshit. The only thing Horus had been following at the time was the swollen nose on his face. Horus had been in the office trying to pick his next special project, something to top Snowden's coup de grâce, something to regain his lead. It was because Horus had been so excited he'd come down there in the middle of the night and laid those files out that Piper saw what she did in the first place. "Boss, I said to myself, better watch that bitch." Horus wasn't watching Piper as she went through the files in the office, not for most of that time. Horus was too busy sitting on the crapper, reading auto magazines, the fan too loud to even notice her arrival. He came out the bathroom without flushing or washing his hands, heard the sounds coming from Lester's office and thought it was a ghost in there. He sure did. "I'm on top of things, boss. I'm your man, I think that's pretty clear after these eleven months, ain't it?"

GOING DOWN

CONSIDERING HE'D MISSED the chance to get the truck's keys from Lester and was instead reduced to delivering them on his bicycle, Bobby Finley was fairly impressed with the amount of *Great Work*s he'd been able to disperse in one night's shift. One milk crate load each run, fifty copies a milk crate, three newspaper boxes a run on a total of eight trips. By nine A.M. every *Harlem Outcry* box was filled to the brim. Bobby's legs were sore about the abuse, but in a couple of days they would forgive him. The exhaustion became evident as the adrenaline ebbed, but Bobby knew that even if he'd stayed in bed he wouldn't have slept in it. With her out there reading it. It was best to keep focusing on releasing *The Great Work* back to the world again and be thankful for a monumental task at a time like this.

What was obvious already was that in order to find a home for every copy, more direct measures would be in order. It would have been nice to stick with newspaper boxes, guaranteeing that *The Great Work* went to homes that at least made a habit of reading, but the feasibility of this plan was questionable, as well as the exclusivity of it. Pedaling around in the morning hours of Harlem, sticking to the center of the street to avoid the muggers and rats that populated the sidewalk, Bobby had decided that to truly make restitution for his artistic arrogance, *The Great Work* should be dispensed indiscriminately for all, with no care to whether they appreciated, despised, or were utterly indifferent to this most sacred of texts. *I am repenting,* Bobby kept reminding himself. Just hand them out at the 125th Street A train. Do it right: Reserve the truck in advance, get

Snowden and some of the Little Leaders to pack it up the night before, then go down by the turnstiles during rush hour and hand them out like loaves of bread. At least that way, if someone didn't like it, he or she could leave it on the seat for a commuter with better taste.

This was the plan Bobby was prepared to pitch when he found Lester in his office after ten. "I need to ask a favor" was the sentence Bobby never got to utter after Lester motioned him urgently through his office door, closing it behind them.

"A very serious problem has arisen," Lester said, but he didn't have to. The nervousness he exhibited, the uncharacteristic bulging of the eyes, the thumbnail getting chewed off like there was a bomb attached to it.

"It's about the fire, isn't it?" That was Bobby's fear talking. It was his mouth, but it was his fear that was using it because the real Bobby didn't even want to say the F-word aloud anymore, and least of all with this man with whom he intended on seeing out these last weeks before the end of the program in joint denial, as if their shared crime was nothing more than an episode of regrettable sex.

"Well, in part, yes. It does deal with the fire, actually. You see, someone broke into my office. Somebody read my files and knows all about it. Worse, it's a reporter. That's how deep we're in the shit, if you'll pardon me."

Bobby thought, *If only I'd given away all my books sooner, if only I'd sat in the bottom row of the funerals and offered more direct solace, maybe I just might have karmicly avoided this.*

"It gets messier, unfortunately. The good news is we know who the person is and it's doubtful she's had a chance to move on the situation, so this can still be handled neatly. The bad news is, this person touches a little too close to Horizon than is comfortable, even worse is that she's also connected personally to one of our own. Have you had the chance to meet Snowden's lover, Piper Goines, since she's been working with the kids?" Lester asked him.

"Yes," Bobby whispered, the rest of him screaming firmly in the

negative. Lester could clearly read his intern's pained reluctance and wagged his head in solemn sympathy as he opened his desk drawer, pulled out a gun, and handed it handle first to him.

"I know this is a very difficult thing to ask of you. I'd prefer it to look like an accident, but I understand we're under a time limitation. I know this is not your style, Robert M. Finley, so let me add that at review time this act will not be taken for granted."

Bobby had never held a gun before. Even pointing away from him, it scared him. *I was wrong.* Bobby realized now that he had one in his hand. *I'm not a killer,* it dawned on him. *If I was a killer I would just point this forward and shoot Lester in the head.*

"It's for the best, coming from you," Lester kept talking. "I'm sure Snowden would appreciate that if it had to be done, it was done by a friend."

Bobby started running as soon as he was out of sight of the lodge's windows. The first pay phone he found he seized, Piper's number still imprinted from all those calls so long ago. When she refused to pick up, Bobby settled for a frantic message and immediately after disconnecting checked his own machine.

That Bobby had seventeen messages was a complete shock to him. The first fifteen were the repetitive the sound of a phone hanging up again. Number sixteen was her blessed voice accusing him of creating "a damn Trojan horse for my heart" and declaring defiantly that she was on her way over to break in. Number seventeen was Piper's voice too. The words were almost identical to the ones Bobby had just left on her machine. Slightly different phrases, but the same basic warning of danger. The same person to avoid. The same promise of relentless search, the same rushed parting, "I love you, be careful."

Snowden was pretty damn sure it was Piper even before he opened his door. He'd met other people in his life relentless and stubborn enough to ring someone's bell for twelve straight minutes, but none of them lived in New York.

"Where is Bobby? Did you help him with his books? I need to talk

to him. If he's at work, I need you to find him and get him."
Snowden's apartment was so dirty that he decided it would seem
insincere to offer an excuse for this. Instead, Snowden offered Piper a
drink, which she declined with such annoyance that he got offended.

"Oh so you laying up with him now? That's fine, I'm cool with
that. You're a good person, showing pity on that cat. Don't go
breaking his heart when you get bored, though, all right?" Snowden
requested. The light was still hurting his eyes and he was tempted to
invite her back into the closet.

"Snowden, this is some serious shit. I need to talk to him. I need
to talk to you too, you're both in it. I'm not joking, I'm talking real
danger."

"Oh fuck," Snowden managed. He had begun to recognize mortal
fear, and this wasn't an act. Snowden seated himself in shock, left her
standing. "Jesus Christ, you're about to tell me you're HIV positive,
aren't you?"

"No! Could you at least pretend not to be an idiot for one
second?" Piper asked. Snowden shrugged a maybe, went looking
through his pockets for cigarettes. "Look, there's something going
on at Horizon. I was in Lester's office and I found folders – "

"What the hell were you doing snooping around Lester's office?"
Snowden asked her. "Damn, woman! I told you about that shit, I
told you not to enter that world! What's wrong with you?"

"I . . . found," Piper continued louder, rolled her eyes, and
punched out the words to knock his own back once more, "I
found folders on the people who died, Snowden. The accident
victims. All of them, right there in Lester's drawers, every name I
could remember."

"So? Maybe the man's got a crime fetish. Yo, people are into that
death stuff. Perfectly normal, don't worry about it. Or they were
applications. Most of those people lived in Horizon-owned housing," Snowden offered, involving himself in the ritual of tobacco
lighting so he didn't have to look at her as he said it.

"These weren't applications, Snowden. I'm not a moron. I know

the difference between prison records and credit reports. You're not listening to me. Some of these folders even had notes on the subject's lifestyle habits – it was like whoever wrote it was stalking them. I'm going to check, but I'm almost certain some of the dates on the fax receipts for the documents predate their deaths."

Snowden kept shrugging, putting more emphasis into his shoulders. He tried, and failed, to laugh. "Piper, Piper, Piper," he started, half relieved when she interrupted him, as he had no idea what to say next.

"Snowden, look up at me. Do me this favor: listen. Don't tell me I'm being hysterical. Don't just come up with uninformed explanations, OK? Snowden, some of these people listed, I didn't recognize. Some of these people aren't dead yet. I know it sounds nuts and, if it is, I would be the happiest one if you can give me a rational explanation for this, but I think your boss Lester is somehow connected to all this. It makes sense, right? I mean, who else would have the keys to all these apartments in the first place?"

"I don't know, how about a locksmith?" Snowden attempted.

"All right, so I'll say it, I'll put it out there and if it sounds ridiculous, that's fine, I can deal with that." Piper paused before continuing, taking a deep breath as if she needed a lot of air to push the statement out. "Based on the evidence I just read, I'm eighty-five percent positive Lester Baines is some kind of mass-murdering, vigilante maniac."

Piper waited for the laughter, for Snowden's patented derision. Piper waited to be exposed as the pathetic snoop with an overactive imagination she knew herself to be. There would be a rational explanation coming, and it would undoubtedly make her look like a fool, but Piper was prepared to face that. What Piper was not prepared for was Snowden smiling calmly back at her, shrugging yet one more time and saying, "Ah, come on, I don't think you're being fair. Think about it, is what Lester's doing really all that bad?"

"Excuse me?" Piper asked, and she really did want to be excused, because even though he was sitting down, the look on Snowden's

face made her start stepping back. Her imagination, in a backlash against its earlier forced restraint, really took off as Snowden got up and started following after her.

"Piper, be honest with yourself. You read their folders. These people were scum, they were parasites. I know it sounds harsh, but just be real for a second. Armed robbers, burglars, drug dealers, pedophiles, they were all people who specifically lived by creating misery for the rest of us. In lots of countries people are executed for living like that. Come on, if you read the files, then you really saw them. Imagine what this neighborhood would be like if all those animals were still around?"

Snowden could tell that Piper wasn't even trying to imagine. She was too busy walking away toward the door. He jumped forward after her, regretted that the action just made her turn and start running. "Piper, it's me, relax, just stay, we have to talk about this," Snowden said, but Piper just started screaming, "No!" back at him, yanking her arm away violently every time he tried to hold it.

When Piper got to the door, Snowden couldn't bring himself to slam it. He couldn't bring himself to do anything more, either. As Piper flew out into the hall, Snowden remembered her naked, on top of him, what her hair looked like as she leaned forward to kiss his mouth, what it tasted like when she did. It was a shame that it would all end like this, Snowden was thinking as he watched her literally run away from him.

Snowden wasn't expecting Horus to pop out from the shadows of the hall any more than Piper was. But there Horus appeared in all his destructive brilliance, ready and eager to change everything.

As Piper got to the stairs, Horus came from behind her, in motion. He must have been hiding in one of the other doorways the whole time, Snowden figured that out later, when there was time. His shoulder forward, his head down, Horus slammed into Piper Goines's unprepared spine, her body folding backward like a fortune cookie from the force. Standing in his doorway, Snowden watched Piper hit the metal railing from the momentum, saw how in that

instant she tried to lean her torso away from the void. Horus took his two thick hands to her two soft ankles and lifted her up and over like he was dumping a wheelbarrow. Piper cleared the railing as smoothly as if she wanted to. Snowden never even got to see her face again, just a blur of limbs and clothing as she grabbed at the air. Then she was gone. That quickly. Horus leaned over the ledge to watch her land.

If Piper made a sound falling down to the lobby five stories below, Snowden didn't hear it. He was too busy lunging forward to the last place she was standing, firmly grabbing the railing that she'd failed to. Piper was already lying still on the ground so far below by the time Snowden arrived to help her.

It wasn't that bad, is what Snowden said to himself to contradict the horror he was feeling. She didn't suffer the terror of the whole drop, surely she hit her head in the narrow stairway before she got that far. It's a shame that had to happen. Dear God it's a shame, that it had to, that it had to happen. An unspeakable tragedy, that this was a necessity. To ensure that Horus, who appeared beside him with a hand firmly on Snowden's shoulder, didn't attempt a repeat performance, Snowden repeated those thoughts aloud for him.

"It's a damn shame," Horus agreed, looking down, a direction Snowden looked purposefully away from. "A fine-looking woman like that one."

"They already know, don't they? You were sent to back me up, in case I didn't do it, weren't you?" Snowden asked him. Horus kept looking down at the body but started squeezing Snowden's shoulder so hard that it hurt.

"First of all, I'm not no one's 'backup,' OK? I done told you about that shit before. Think of my role in this venture as more 'quality control' if you want a name for it. Second of all, it ain't always about you, is it? See, that right there is the man I'm supposed to be overseeing." Horus pointed below.

Snowden forced himself to look down in the direction of the

corpse once more and this time saw Bobby standing over it. The faintest of hopes fluttered through him and he thought Bobby would reach down for a pulse and find one and just as suddenly as things turned morbid they would spring back to being merely bleak again, but looking down at the body's anatomically impossible position, Snowden wasn't surprised Bobby didn't bother with the formality. Nor that Bobby should look straight up with the anger and pain distorting his face as they did. So many exhaustive trials Snowden had undergone since arriving in Harlem this last year, so many elaborate tests of moral fortitude and determination, but none more demanding than just meeting Bobby's stare without flinching.

Even after Bobby ran off, Snowden kept looking down because there was no turning away or back anymore. All the fear, the revulsion, the guilt, and disgust bubbling within him at the distant sight of Piper's broken body, Snowden identified, named as the price for utopia. Doors on other apartments started opening, other heads poked out into the stairway just as his did, but Snowden forced himself to keep looking, to acknowledge the price before continuing.

OF SHRIMP AND
OTHER SMALL BAIT

A YEAR CAN go by rather quickly when you're busy. Exactly 365 days after their first Horizon meeting, the winner of the Second Chance Program's leadership challenge was announced, and Cedric Snowden Jr. accepted gracefully. No balloons, no cake or streamers, just a firm handshake from a former congressman and a date for the press conference when, on site, the keys to the prized brownstone would be handed over. "If it doesn't happen in front of cameras," Marks chuckled away Snowden's reservations, "then it doesn't exist." In the end, the competition was far from stiff. Bobby hadn't shown up for work or answered his phone in the two weeks since the incident, and Horus was Horus, so the choice was rather obvious. Snowden felt proud anyway, took it as an honor because he felt he'd earned the right to.

Cedric Snowden tried to think about this honor as much as he could, about the responsibility of watching over the new recruits in the year to come, of overseeing their evolution into the men of Horizon. Cedric Snowden like to think about this because he found that when he wasn't, he was thinking about Piper Goines instead, a subject he drifted to even more despite a concerted effort not to. In Snowden's waking moments in the days before Piper's funeral, it was the image of her disappearing so easily over the railing that had captivated him. Snowden thought *bloop* every time he remembered it, as if attaching a cartoon sound effect would minimize the impact for both of them. *Bloop.*

At night, asleep, the image Snowden was haunted by was

altogether different, though equally singular. It was Piper Goines falling down the stairway wearing a long flowing white dress, endless folds flapping. It was the type of dress Snowden doubted the real Piper would wear even if you gave it to her. In the dream, Snowden's view was centered on her as she fell down, the dirty tenement stairs a blur for both of them. Eventually his own vantage would halt and Piper's body would go flying below it, upon which point Snowden would kick himself awake as quickly as possible. The dream tended to come to him in those transitory moments at the beginning and end of sleep, leaving Snowden unsure if he was just imagining it, an uncertainty that led to Snowden rejecting his closet hideout for his well-lit bedroom instead.

The vision continued until the funeral, a bleak, silent affair even for its kind. The event created new images of Piper to replace all the others, surprisingly pleasant ones fueled mostly by the childhood pictures arranged as a collage before Piper's closed casket. Snowden had feared meeting the famed Abigail Goines of Piper's tales, but the woman up at the front pew was so drugged that Snowden doubted she knew that he or most of the other guests were there, even as she nodded and smiled at them.

People pointed at him, the last one to see her alive, the fateful friend with the fourth-floor walkup, yet nothing more came of it. But why should it, Snowden kept reminding himself. It was an accident.

Snowden kept looking over his shoulder, up into the rafters of the Episcopalian church, for Bobby Finley to arrive and declare differently, but the skinny man never appeared.

The congressman arranged for the ride to and from Connecticut to be provided by Piper Goines's former editors Olthidius Cole Jr. and Sr. The younger of the two drove. The older of the two yelled at him to pass any car within fifty yards, once going so far as to shove his battered cane onto the gas pedal in response to the disobeying of a direct order. For a while, Snowden amused himself by watching the large man cursing at his son and every single driver he managed to overtake on I-95, pausing only to go off on tangental tirades about

the Jews, the honkies, those bastards at City Hall, "those goddamn Dominican Puerto Ricans," and the niggers. Excluding the mention of the last two groups, Mr. Cole's private rants sounded much like his front-page editorials, evoking in Snowden the same exhaustion from their tediousness, only this time he couldn't just shut it off by putting the page down, so Snowden closed his eyes and pretended to fall asleep instead.

It was dark, late, and they were approaching a toll booth when Snowden had the dream he'd been waiting for. One minute his legs were numb and Olthidius Cole was leaning over his son to curse out the collector, the next Snowden closed his eyes and it began. In his mind, Piper came to his house just like before, dressed like her too, the same bags under eyes, the lack of makeup – it was very realistic. The biggest difference was that this time she knew everything. Everything. Like how important it was, what they were doing. Like how a piece of their soul was part of the deal, but that it was worth it. It wasn't just Piper who understood now, they all did – and by that Snowden took to mean all the unintentional martyrs even though she spared him the pain of listing them. "I understand," she said again to him, and then Piper looked right at Snowden and said, "*Bloop*," and was gone again. Snowden opened his eyes and they were in front of Horizon's storefront grate. Olthidius Cole turned around in his seat screaming, "Get out my car you freeloading prick," out his flapjack face.

Walking back home with that night-city elation, Snowden went to bed and slept well, got up the next day feeling even better. For the week that followed, the same thing kept happening. When Snowden finally recalled the dream, he couldn't remember if it really was one or just his groggy mind imagining, but it didn't matter. Either way it paused his anxiety long enough for his life to get going again.

Snowden found it was a glorious thing to have a purpose, to have one was to know what he'd always been missing. When each day began Snowden knew what he had to do and why he had to do it. When each day ended Snowden found himself running out of hours

267

instead of having to drink the last few away. There was bliss in certainty. The Horizon man found being one intoxicating.

It takes a while to build a home out of a Harlem shell. You start with the abused structure, long the victim of poverty and neglect, and you salvage what little you can from it: a façade, some original wood-work, a porcelain fixture nobody in fifty years could figure out how to rip out for profit. Put a new roof on top to keep the elements from causing further damage, then under its protection you can begin to develop what's inside of it. The first thing to do is get the electrical work and plumbing up to date, followed by the windows and walls, winterizing and painting. Unless you're doing major structural construction, the last thing you deal with is the floor beneath your feet. To look at his prize in the beginning, Snowden's brownstone seemed a hopeless cause, a place that would never be inhabitable let alone one he'd enjoy living in. But it was, like all things in Harlem, a matter of small steps and patience, dedication to a vision, the determination to see it to fruition no matter what the cost.

They got as far as the wiring by the day of the Second Chance Program press event. It was enough that there would be power for lights, video, and sound equipment. Snowden was allowed to come inside his new home for the first time that morning. It was a prime location on 120th Street, directly across from Mount Morris Park, you could even see the fire tower from the street. Walking up the front steps Snowden thought, *This is my stoop.* Moving through so many empty, dark rooms Snowden thought, *These are mine and I have a lifetime to fill them.*

The townhouse was full of surprising details. The removal of the mirrored wall off the sitting room had revealed a chipped but salvageable mural that Lester hoped would prove to be an Aaron Douglas when authenticated. Between the stairs was a full-sized manual elevator, installed for a wheelchair-bound resident in the thirties and still fully functional. Lester took great pleasure in

showing Snowden how to pull on the looped rope to make it go up and down as they stood inside it. On the third floor, Snowden found the remnants of a building-length bookshelf built into the eastern wall, a beautiful if battered piece of oak cabinetry that caused Snowden to wonder out loud if he'd ever own enough books to fill it.

Lester let the comment hang out there for a moment, echoing in the empty space, before saying anything. "Look, I made an awful, unfortunate mistake in going to him about the Piper situation. I didn't realize they had any sort of relationship, let alone what I now know of it. That was a horrible position I put him in, inadvertently of course, but it was my mistake. That said, you're the one in charge of the program now. He has to be dealt with."

"Bobby will be just fine," Snowden told him. "He'll get over it. You want to worry about something, worry about your dog, you know what it means when he starts sniffing the floor like that."

Wendell's butt rocked back in forth as it wandered out of the room. Lester called the dog, but Wendell just looked over his shoulder at him in annoyance before turning around again.

"Snowden, you don't get over losing someone you consider that important easily. I know, I was a mess after Jesse passed. Don't tell anyone, but I missed that man so much I used to spray Wendell with his cologne at night just so I could pretend it was him sleeping next to me," Lester confessed.

"I will deal with Bobby. Reasonably. I sent him an invite so you never know, he might show up today. You put me in charge, so you'll just have to trust me with it. I tell you who is in mortal danger, though: your dog. I don't care if the floors aren't done, if he shits on my new home he's dead."

"Wendell would never do that," Lester said, but he hurried down the hall in search of him anyway.

There was a joke told by white supremacists that all you had to do to round up black people was get a big bucket of fried chicken. This

was not only racist and offensive, it was also entirely untrue. It wasn't fried chicken, it was shrimp. If you sent out flyers advertising free all-you-can-eat jumbo shrimp, you could attract more Negroes than a Red Lobster on Sunday. Another little-known fact: The same rule applied to a subset of journalists as well, the lazy kind who actually liked press events, liked having their stories prepackaged and lobbed underhand to them. Tertiary news stories were chosen or ignored based on the quality of the buffets at their press events, and a good seafood teaser could make the difference between peripheral public awareness and complete obscurity. Combine these two categories and you could create the kind of mob that began to form in Cedric Snowden's future living room early that evening, struggling to push past each other without spilling their plastic plates and champagne flutes.

Congressman Marks stepped up on the stool he'd placed discreetly behind the podium and began clearing what little throat he had to get their attention. When that didn't work, Marks pulled from inside his lapel what Snowden hoped was a starter pistol and shot it straight up above him. "Ah, an ode to the bad old days of Harlem," he joked to the stunned and silent crowd, but it actually garnered a few laughs after a second.

"Ladies and gentlemen, thank you for joining me in bearing witness to this great day for Harlem. In a time when more black men go to jail than college, it is more important now than ever that we create a second chance for our men, our community, and ourselves . . ."

Snowden closed the door to the kitchen. He'd listened to the congressman's speech twice in practice, and while he agreed with it, he didn't feel the need to spend ten more minutes of his life listening to it again. There were so many of them in there, looking up at him, chewing his food and words. Snowden wondered if Piper had known any of the reporters in attendance and what she would have said about them.

"This is it, the big moment, the culmination of so much work,"

Lester said from behind. Snowden turned to him. Lester in white. Patent-leather shoes so shiny they seemed made of melting vanilla ice cream, a matching fedora whose black band was his outfit's only dissent.

"Horus – I don't see him out there. Did you even tell him I won yet?"

"Of course I told him. Yesterday. Took him down to Chelsea Piers, stuck a suitcase and a ticket for a ten-day Caribbean singles cruise in his hands, then I told him. Went fine, nothing to worry about," Lester said. He was missing a molar about halfway back his mouth, you could only see it when he smiled real big.

"Good. So he wasn't mad."

"Oh he was absolutely furious. A real murderous rage, I'll tell you. But I managed to get him on the boat," Lester said. "Then I sat there watching the little bridge for four hours to make sure he didn't sneak off again. He should be cooled down by the time he sails back. The man's too great an asset to lose. You wouldn't believe how hard it is to find a sociopath with a sense of loyalty."

Lester turned to look once more at his charge, noticed the strain in Snowden's face as he stared off toward the room ahead.

"Mr. Snowman, you better get used to this kind of thing. When the congressman retires – and now that things are going well I really don't think that will be long now – you'll be in charge, most likely." Snowden looked up, saw Lester smiling a confirmation of what he'd just said.

"Why not you? Lester, if the congressman retires, why wouldn't you take over the whole thing? You're the most qualified."

"Oh, no," Lester waved the silly thought away from him, thought about it another moment before shaking his head. "I could never do that, all the planning and everything. That takes a gift. Besides, all that paperwork, all that time behind a desk. I'm more a man of the field," Lester told him. "I like to get my hands dirty."

There was applause. Responding to his cue, Snowden pushed open the door and walked out. All eyes on him as he shuffled his

speech on the podium, Snowden forced himself to look up at the room as he was trained to before he began.

"I was once was lost," Snowden began, pausing to the count of two-Mississippi, "but now I'm found. I was blind, but now I see."

It was that easy. That African bass thrown into his voice for resonance, his pointer finger raised for emphasis, thumb resisting halfway up it as a nod to Martin Luther King, and all of a sudden he was a leader. The words kept coming, falling after each other easily, even the intonation came naturally. A couple of minutes in and he wasn't even listening to what he was saying, but that was OK because he was busy reading the crowd instead. "Yes, searching for tomorrow's leaders among yesterday's failures is dramatic and extreme, but what Horizon's Second Chance Program recognizes is that facilitating dramatic change in the ghetto is going to take the extreme." When the front door opened across the room, Snowden was in such a flow he instinctively raised his voice to keep the spell from unwinding. When Snowden saw the top of the black hat, then the uniform below it, he didn't stutter, he didn't lose one bit of his passion or speed. He just thought, *Well, that's it. They've finally come for me.*

Starting to lose the attention of the room as the cop pushed his way to the front of the crowd, Snowden slammed his fist down on the podium for emphasis. Lester was the one who went to the officer, cut him off before he could get any closer. Snowden watched as the two clasped like family and asked himself, *How could I ever question that this was meant to be?* As Lester guided the officer back to the kitchen, Snowden nodded and smiled but didn't stop speaking for a moment.

By the time Snowden heard the door behind him open again he was firmly into the stride of his conclusion and had forgotten his moment of panic. It came back to him, though, the feeling if not the specifics, when midsentence a tapped shoulder was followed by the ear-whispered, "We have a serious problem." When Snowden turned to look at Lester's face he almost didn't recognize it, having never seen it shaped by fear before.

*   *   *

272

Bobby Finley sat on the top of the Mount Morris watchtower with a bullhorn, a child hostage, and at least a thousand hardback copies of the same book soaked in gasoline. This last number was an estimate and varied considerably depending on whether you asked the crowd of firemen, the crowd of EMS workers, or one of the many representatives of the police. It was a clear and sunny day and Bobby was really buoyed by this, because after all the exhaustive work preparing for this moment, rain would have really put a damper on things.

Jifar, kicking his legs as they hung over the railing and pointing, was the one who saw Snowden coming, just another exciting addition in the growing spectacle of the day. The boy deserved a good show, Bobby felt, after being such a good sport about the heavy lifting and the fumes and everything. The two of them watched in great amusement as Snowden broke from the crowd and started climbing up to them, leather-soled shoes loosing their purchase on the metal beams wet from the dripping *Great Works*, tie flapping desperately over his shoulder in the wind.

"Let him go," was the first thing Snowden said when his head poked over the edge. Jifar looked at Snowden's huffing sweaty face and stuck his tongue out. As nervous as Bobby was, it was actually good to see the man.

"Yeah, I need your help with that." Bobby pointed at the mountain-climbing harness already tied around Jifar's waist. "I didn't want him slipping climbing down so I need your help lowering him."

Snowden looked at the rigging on the boy like it was some sort of pedophiliac bondage gear, asked Jifar if he was hurt in such a tender voice that the kid just laughed at him. Jifar was sitting on white paper Snowden recognized to be the loose pages of *The Tome*, strewn everywhere like kindling.

"He's fine, and don't worry, it'll more than carry his weight. It's on a rather ingenious pulley system," Bobby said pointing up. Snowden saw the dark color of the other man's jeans and realized they were

soaking. It was also then that Snowden noticed that Bobby had his favorite lighter in his hand. "The two of us have been hoisting up boxes and gas cans twice that weight all afternoon without the slightest problem."

"That shit was dope," Jifar confirmed. "You should have been here!"

Snowden reached down and patted Jifar on the head, in part to see if the boy was as wet as *The Great Works* that were piled everywhere around them. Satisfied to his dryness, Snowden walked closer to Bobby, motioned for them to both move farther along the perch for privacy.

"This is sick, Bobby. You got me, just like you demanded, now let him go." Snowden didn't even have to whisper for privacy, another batch of approaching sirens covered his voice for him. Looking down, even at this distance, Snowden could recognize some of the press people he'd been sermonizing only minutes before, some with their little hors d'oeuvres plates still in their hands. Marks had barked at Lester immediately for interrupting Snowden's speech, but their guests would have noticed the sounds and lights of the emergency vehicles climbing up the little hill right outside the window anyway. Forget shrimp, everybody knew a lazy journalist's first love was a newsworthy spectacle.

"Oh, you can go too, just help me get the kid down safe and do me a little favor once you get on the ground again. I don't blame you for what happened, Snowden. I don't. I blame myself for creating the situation. I sure as hell blame you for the part you played, but you're going to have to deal with your conscience in your own way. This is just my way of offering repentance, making the best out of the situation," Bobby said, holding up the lighter, knocking off the lid with a snap, and just as fast closing it again. "Tell me something though, does that look like pretty much all the media whores from your little coronation down there, or should I wait another minute before I get started?"

Snowden looked down. There seemed to be even more of them.

Two news vans had appeared, both racing to raise the masts of their broadcasting antennas. "Don't do this, man," Snowden told him. "You have a cause that really needs you, your intelligence, your passion."

"I don't have a cause, not like that anymore. What cause could be worth it if it ends up with people like Piper Goines dead?" Bobby asked, then smiled and waved to the crowd below, clearly enjoying himself. He finally has an audience, Snowden realized.

"So that's it. You're just going to light yourself on fire as some medieval self-punishment. You're just going to give up on life like that, Bobby." Snowden frowned his distaste. "That is so stupid."

Bobby stopped waving, stopped smiling too, just turned and stared at him for few seconds before gaining a slight grin again. "Don't you see? This isn't about giving up. This is about love. This is about sacrificing myself for the one thing in the universe that actually is worth believing in."

"Bobby, you idiot, you're about to kill yourself for the biggest cliché there is."

"Yes, Snowden, but then considering my life, that's an *irony*, which makes it all better."

Bobby was right about one thing, Snowden concurred, getting Jifar to the ground was effortless. The boy floated below them screaming in glee the whole way, his blood replaced long ago by adrenaline. When Jifar got to the ground a female cop ran forward from the barricade to get him, and as soon as he was detached Jifar ran away from her as fast as he could, through the crowd and down the hill back toward the lodge because he was a good kid and followed his instructions. Once he was out of sight, Bobby pulled a box cutter from his pocket and handed it to Snowden, then pointed to a tarp hiding something the size of a car at the far wall of the plateau, behind the crowd.

"You're a goddamn fool," Snowden told Bobby before starting to climb down again.

"Just go open those boxes, first thing," the fool said, dripping.

When Snowden reached the ground safely, the crowd couldn't help but show its disappointment. This was supposed to be a news event. Without a hostage, the man on the fire tower was just another crazy nigger in Harlem. It was five fifty-five P.M., there were cameras here ready to go live, if the nut was going to call in this whole thing to 911 and drag an audience out here, the least he could do was keep the show going another five minutes for the six o'clock lead-in. As Snowden was ushered through the mob, reporters pushed their mikes past his police guardians. "Who is he?" and "What does he want?" they were all asking. As if on cue, and possibly so since the lunatic was looking at his watch right before he said it, the man above announced that he had something to say, and that at 6:01 he would deliver it, which all the telecasters greatly appreciated.

Snowden was led away to the open ambulance before the cops returned to the front. He could still smell the gas all the way back there, even with the wind blowing in the other direction.

"People of Harlem, people of New York, people of the world. My name is Robert M. Finley," Bobby began, yelling into his megaphone. Yelling even louder at Snowden at that exact same moment was the congressman, with Lester and Wendell beside him looking equally grave. "He obviously orchestrated this entire scenario!" Marks was saying. "Tell me what the hell he's planning on saying!" Over his balding head, Snowden saw the tarp only a few yards away. It was green, heavy canvas, probably military surplus. Looking at it, Snowden thought *Bomb!* and jumped off the gurney past his employers in its direction.

"I'm here to tell you about a woman, the love of my life, even though we got to share so little of it together," Bobby's amplified voice said. A crowd of reporters thought at the exact same time, *Everybody loves a love story.* Snowden reached the mass, yanked off the tarp to reveal at least twenty boxes.

"Her name was Piper and she was beautiful and fate stole her from me. Piper Goines was robbed of a life of promise, a life of love, a life of accomplishment," Bobby continued. His overexuberance

with the gasoline had left his cue cards blurred, but this speech he felt etched inside of him. Far below him, Bobby Finley could see Cedric Snowden opening the first box. "She deserved more, she deserved the chance to live a full life, the kind I, a humble novelist, once imagined for her. I am here today to bestow that imagined existence unto you, the blessed readers, so that through your hearts and minds Piper Goines might in some way continue living. Please take a copy of my manuscript, *The Orphean Daze*, with you on the way out, they're available from that gentleman there in the back," Bobby said, pointing at Snowden. It was like his finger had reached out and turned every member of the crowd's head simultaneously. Even the television cameras turned, and they were broadcasting live.

"Thank you for giving Piper Goines, and our love, a chance to live eternally. I couldn't afford to print that many, so you might have to share. If there are any pages missing, contact the Kinko's on 111th Street. Thanks again for coming," Bobby concluded, putting the bullhorn down politely before snapping on his lighter and holding it to his chest, igniting everything.

Snowden stood looking at the blaze, knowing that it was coming having failed to prepare him. The tower was like one massive match, the inferno a thick ball at the top of it. There was so much movement on the surface of the flame it was impossible to see what was happening inside of it. Fire was so beautiful even as it was horrific, Snowden could see why Bobby had always liked it. Snowden was so captivated by the sight, the way it swayed, the black smoke trailing above as a beacon to millions, that he failed to notice the mob stampeding toward him until it was too late to avoid being knocked to the ground. Stomping across Snowden's screaming body, it clawed and it tugged, it yanked and it pulled, all in its ravenous frenzy to get its hands on the hot new novel by one Robert M. Finley.

NEW BEGINNINGS
(ENDING)

W HEN OLTHIDIUS COLE Sr. finally announced to Olthidius Cole Jr. that he was retiring and leaving the *New Holland Herald* in his son's complete control, Olthidius Cole Jr. thought that was a really good thing, because if that had not happened soon there was a good chance he would have come into work one day, taken off all his clothes, and started screaming. Still, neither he nor any of his employees truly believed the old man would let the mantle be pried from anything but his dead, cold hands until that last box was packed and Olthidius Cole Sr. was walking down the staircase with it, weeping and wheezing in equal measure.

The celebration began immediately. Tears continued for the rest of the evening, mostly of joy this time. The ones that weren't were confessional, cathartic, were tinged by the context of victory. Raises were announced, the Web site revealed, the new computers finally carted up from their hiding place in shipping. A real design team would be hired immediately. Freelancers would be paid the living wage of a dollar a word instead of forty bucks an article. The paper would go double-size biweekly to provide the opportunity for work to be properly matured and edited. Predictions of future victory were declared by all in attendance, a dawn of new quality was heralded, Harlem was entering a new era and its favorite periodical was going with it! The keg was tapped at about nine-thirty, but it was midnight before the headquarters of the *New Holland Herald* was emptied.

By eleven-fifteen the following morning, it was officially the same

shit all over again. Only half the workers showed back up at their desks; the rest were late. Olthidius Cole, the sole one by that name in the office anymore, had to listen to three people he'd personally seen stumble into a cab and tell the driver, "Sugar Shack!" call in and claim "flulike symptoms" with utter earnestness. The first submissions on his desk that day consisted of three film reviews from the *New Holland Herald*'s senior entertainment editor, all of which began, "This movie is really good. It shows a lot of positive images of black people. You should go see it." The next piece the new editor in chief braced himself to read was an article by a regular freelancer on an altercation outside the Harlem Heat nightclub. The first sentence was, "Renton Johnson got shot, in front of the tittie bar at night." Olthidius Cole read no further. He was too stunned to continue. His head hurt too much, and it was his turn for crying. All these years he'd assumed that the poor grammar, bad writing, and spelling errors the staff of the *New Holland Herald* produced so consistently were because of the low pay, deplorable working conditions and, of course, the fact that they hated his father as much as he did, and all this time they really were as incompetent as the old man said.

The new boss sat in his father's former office with his head down and wrapped in his arms on the desk, his own things still on the floor in front by the door where he'd first dropped them. There came a point, a couple hours in, when he'd accepted his situation, when it didn't even seem so unbearable anymore, but he couldn't bring himself to stand up and go face his staff knowing what he knew, so he just kept his position and took a nap instead, hoping to wait them out till the end of the workday.

When the last person had left for the night, fluorescent lights silenced behind them, Olthidius Cole crept out of his hiding place, grabbed the day's submissions from his secretary's in-box, and shot back in his office. The last of them read from beginning to end, the younger Cole began to calm down again. It wasn't that bad, really. It was bad, but not so bad that it made him question his calling. The *New Holland Herald* was just like any other floundering entity, no

worse. There were a couple of writers who were really good, there were a bunch who were OK, and then there was a minority who needed to be eliminated immediately. It wasn't like doing that would be easy, some of these hacks were staff, had been at the paper for decades, people who'd given him gifts of candy on childhood visits, kisses on the cheek up until the day he too came to work here. It wasn't like these people had voice mails from headhunters at Knight-Ridder to fall back on. Unfortunately, none of that mattered. Revolution meant disregarding individuals for the sake of the whole. The *New Holland Herald* simply couldn't afford them anymore.

Laying out his articles upon his desk, Olthidius Cole organized the submissions the same way: the ones to be cut, the ones that had potential or were just satisfactory, and those pieces that were exemplary. In the most esteemed pile was, of course, the consistently impressive sports writing of Charlie Awuyah and classical news reporting of Gil Manly, one set for the front page and one for the back automatically, but there were also two other articles of interest that gave Olthidius Cole hope for the future. Both were longer, three-thousand-word-plus pieces he himself had personally solicited the moment he caught his father starting to pack his things, both were written by graduate students from the New York area whom Cole hoped to recruit directly out of their respective schools of journalism.

The first story, written by the Columbia grad student Althea Woods, coincidentally dealt with the last Columbia J-school alumni the *New Holland Herald* employed. It was a look back at the Mount Morris burning books fiasco from over a year ago. Hands down, it gave the most insightful critique Cole had seen of the continually blurring line between news and morbid entertainment that was further obscured when New York City local news chose to run live images of a man lighting himself on fire, reshowing them repeatedly in the days that followed, their clips becoming increasingly graphic to compete with the national and cable news outlets that had jumped on the story's bandwagon. It was also the first critique Cole had read

that questioned author Robert M. Finley's motivation for the suicide at all, which was surprising considering the book's numerous reprints since it was first rushed to press. Woods had even obtained an internal document from his publisher citing the abysmal sales of the original release of Finley's *The Great Work*. The article also examined what actual percentage of the book's gross was going to the family of Piper Goines as requested, as well as the issue about the book's title, if Robert M. Finley would have actually agreed to changing it to *Burnin' Luv in Harlem*, but so many articles had been written about both of those subjects already that Cole planned to edit out those bits. If the actual book was half as interesting as this article about it, Cole mused, maybe he would have read more than twenty pages before giving up. Dry, dry stuff. Just dreadful. Still, some people were just fanatical about it, a good-size group, apparently. Dry, dreadful folks, Cole imagined. The man was no Bo Shareef, Cole snorted. Now that's a writer.

The second story was from the student at NYU, Lucretia Yates — a lot of potential in that one, very astute, knowledgeable, she was white, but the rest of the staff would just have to get over that. Her submission was a collection of profiles of the new pioneers of black New York, the next generation of leaders taking control as the baby boomers were forced into retirement along with their old ways. Olthidius Cole saw himself as being a prominent member of this movement and — if he did manage to keep from calling up Yates and requesting a profile of himself be added — wanted the foreword to put it in the context of his own recent ascension. Besides that context shift, Cole loved her whole thesis: that this was a less sentimental group, secure enough for the harshest of self-criticism. They were the first generation of black leaders not formed by the struggle against a hostile white world, Yates argued, so were more likely to be focused on their own world's internal dilemmas.

One thing Olthidius Cole would alter about Yates's piece was the order of the subjects, particularly which profile would come first. If this was to be a cover story, the most compelling profile should be

the first thing the reader sees. The person Cole chose for that honor was the new president of Horizon Realty. In the wake of the announced retirement of flamboyant former congressman Cyrus Marks, Horizon was continuing its tradition of high-profile front-men with the appointment of Cedric Snowden Jr., a product of Horizon's own Second Chance Program. A swashbuckling figure in his public relations photo, a rags to riches story, it had all the ingredients that *New Holland Herald* readers demanded. The man even answered questions in the form of sound bites. When asked what was the key to Horizon's success, particularly in light of their planned expansion into Brooklyn, Newark, Pittsburgh's Hill District, and Washington, D.C., in the year to follow, Cedric Snowden smoothly replied, "When you believe in what you do, what you can do you won't believe."

A NOTE ON THE AUTHOR

Mat Johnson, a former resident of Harlem, has returned to his native city, Philadelphia. He is also the author of *Drop*.